November 13th 1997

Dear Dr Simmonds

I write regarding ___ ___ Mr Philip Drummond. After assessing Mr Drummond, I am in agreement with you that he is exhibiting signs associated with dysfunctional emotional behaviours. I have reached the conclusion that he is suffering from post-traumatic stress disorder (PTSD).

He suffers classic symptoms of persistent re-experience (eg, nightmares and flashbacks) and has had prolonged sleep disturbance, combined with feelings of anger and hopelessness.

Mr Drummond was reluctant to engage in discussions about his experiences in Bosnia and appears detached and isolated when the subject is raised.

I have discussed treatment options with Mr Drummond and have prescribed a month's course of paroxetine 50mg. I have also referred him to our outpatients' department for trauma- focused cognitive-behavioural therapy (CBT). Mr Drummond's blood test showed no evidence of drug or alcohol dependence.

I have recommended to Mr Drummond that he make a follow-up appointment with you for a month's time for you to review his progress.

Yours sincerely

Dr Alec Newman FRCPsych

One

I do not have a stitch. I feel no pain. I am Tirunesh Dibaba. No – I think Tirunesh's the Ethiopian women's 1000m winner. I am Liu Xiang; did he win or was he the one the Chinese were crying over? The guy who went out with the Achilles tendon injury. Phil didn't want to imagine he was someone who was injured; the idea was to think himself out of pain. He wished he'd paid more attention to the athletics.

He couldn't understand it; he'd done his usual warm up. He hadn't eaten; he'd not even stopped for a wake-up cup of tea. Maybe it was his body protesting about the early start. Normally, he'd run between eight and nine, pick up the papers and some bread as he looped back through the village and then head home. He'd fix some well-deserved brekkie: thick, toasted doorsteps oozing butter, topped with a generous dollop of marmalade, washed down with a scalding mug of builder's tea - perfect.

Not today though. Today he was off to his publishers in London to meet Mal, his agent, and rather than skip his run, he'd hauled his body out of bed an hour and a half earlier than usual. The sun had beaten him out of bed, but only just; it had yet to burn off the dewy mist hanging around the roots of the trees in the little copse at the bottom of his lane. The only sounds of life were his battered trainers on the Tarmac, the unruly twittering orchestra of the recently returned birds and the throaty chug of a tractor up on the top field.

I've got it, I'm Usain Bolt. I bet Usain Bolt doesn't get stitch while he's out for a gentle jog in the Dorset countryside. Well, of course he doesn't, but that's because he's probably never been to Dorset. Still, I bet he doesn't get stitch ten minutes after he's set out for a run along the sandy white shores of Jamaica. And he doesn't look a complete knob in Lycra - bad choice of words.

According to his sister, even Usain's golden shoes couldn't distract Becca and her friends from his lunchbox... it was all they could focus on. That's girls for you. Usain might have Becca and her girlfriends swooning, but Phil consoled himself with the thought that Usain probably didn't look as good as him in uniform.

It might be a cliché, but in his experience it was a universal truth - women like a man in uniform and not just any uniform. He was sure postmen and parking wardens had their admirers, but the more dangerous the job associated with the uniform, the more attention you got. Girls would know which pubs the regiment went to and they'd go along to bag themselves a real live action man.

It was all the other baggage that came with the uniform that his girlfriends weren't so keen on. All the moving around, the uncertainty and the long, lonely months while he was away on tour. It was the kiss of death to most relationships, that and... what had Gillian his last girlfriend called it – oh yes, his 'commitment phobia'.

She'd said their relationship wasn't going anywhere; buses, trains and cars were all supposed to go places, but relationships, did they really need some destination emblazoned on the front of them...what was the matter with stasis? What was wrong with just going with the flow? Why did everything need to be a part of some grand plan?

In the early days, they were never happier than when they were hanging on his arm at some regimental do. It was at the moment of realisation that he wasn't Richard Gere and that life as his girlfriend was not going to be like An Officer and a Gentleman that things took a nosedive.

Phil slowed his pace and caught sight of himself reflected in the newsagent's window; he ran his fingers over his angular, stubbly jaw line - not bad, he thought. In the first flush of their relationship Gillian had told him he had a bit of a look of Gerard Butler about him. He couldn't see it himself, but maybe from a distance - if you squinted - there was a likeness. An older, more rough-around-the-edges version perhaps.

Gerard or not, he thought he looked pretty good for a man of 42. Despite now spending hours in front of his laptop, nothing wobbled that shouldn't. He'd kept his six pack, even though over recent years he'd become more heavily acquainted with a six pack from the offie.

None of it was helping. Phil was usually good at thinking himself out of pain; it was mind over matter, except that this morning he really minded about the throbbing pain and nothing else seemed to matter.

He jumped the stile into the top field; he checked his new toy, a Nike+ ipod. Dave, an old SAS mate, had got him into it and now they were competing against each other online; each trying to slice a few seconds off the other's personal best.

Dave was running uphill and down dale in Yorkshire; Phil through woods and farmland of Dorset - the occasional wayward pig acting as his unexpected pacemaker. Dave was giving Phil a complete pasting; consistently completing a 10k run in under forty minutes.

The annual meet up at his publishers was the perfect excuse for a weekend away in London; in truth, it was a bit of a jolly. Most of what they talked about could be done over the phone, but writing could be a pretty solitary job at times and to use an expression he loathed, he was glad to have some 'face time'. While the focus of the meeting was all about his future - for Phil it was often a time when he reflected on his past and how things had turned out the way they had. He'd not taken the most conventional route to becoming a best selling author – but then he wasn't all that big on convention.

Bizarrely it had all started with his CBT thirteen years ago. Phil had railed against his sister Becca's every mention of counselling. He'd only gone to the first session because she'd practically frog-marched him there. He smiled as he recalled setting off that first morning: his mind was set, he'd go to the first appointment to get her off his back and then not bother again. But counselling wasn't at all like he'd expected; no couch, no 'Tell me about your childhood'. He thought it would be all airy-fairy and touchy feely – all the things he hated most; he couldn't have been more wrong.

Mark, his counsellor, therapist or whatever you want to call him was in his mid thirties: tall, slim, with chunky funky glasses and a trendy mini goatee kind of thing going on – not the older, lentil-eating do-gooder type that Phil had expected. Okay, so the tree-hugging lentil eater was a stereotype, but he'd never had cause to visit a head doctor before and hammy hospital dramas were his only reference point. The reality was quite different, and Phil instantly warmed to Mark.

The mainstay of his therapy was writing a journal. To his immense surprise Phil found it a lot easier to write things down than to talk about them. It was like the journal was an intermediary, a sort of go-between. It sounded a bit mad because then they would talk about what he'd written, but somehow it was different. Putting it down on paper disarmed his demons – it distanced him from them and them from him. They were no longer lurking in the shadows of his mind, instead they were out in the open on the page in front of him. They were less threatening there and he felt more able to confront them.

As he neared the end of his 6 months of therapy, Mark had given him a copy of a new magazine aimed at ex-servicemen. It was full of stuff to help people who'd left the forces deal with the issues they faced settling back into civilian life. Phil had had a flick through; it was quite good, if a little sparse. It had job listings, career advice and a few interesting articles.

The magazine was started by Pete Jeffries. Known to all as Jeffers, he was ex paras and a mate of Mark's brother. Mark had said rather pointedly looking at Phil's journal that they were always on the look out for quality editorial content.

Phil had been reluctant at first; talking about things in the confines of Mark's office was one thing, but putting it out there for everyone to read made him feel too vulnerable – it would be like streaking down the high street. Mark was always banging on about the techniques not being a quick fix. And that to really work long term they needed to become a seamless part of Phil's everyday life. Mark had suggested that the magazine could be a perfect way of extending the positive effect of Phil's journal.

Writing things down and sharing his experiences had certainly helped him come to terms with them. It was hard to argue with Mark's logic, but at the time even harder to apply logic to Phil's own irrational reservations. He'd frequently found Mark's medicine hard to swallow, but with the benefit of hindsight he had to admit, it worked.

That was always Mark's way, forever pushing him forward. Phil would just get comfortable and confident with an idea and Mark would introduce the next one; leading, cajoling and sometimes dragging Phil towards Mark's ultimate goal of self-reliant, independent living.

It seemed like a lifetime ago now that he'd had his farewell session with Mark, not at the clinic; instead, at the appropriately named pub 'The Man O'War'. They'd put the world to rights over a couple of beers and ribbed one another about their respective teams' performances in the Premier League.

Writing for the magazine had saved Phil. It had been the lifeline along which he'd pulled himself back into everyday life. As Mark had suggested, to start with he submitted a few edited entries from his journal – the less sensitive stuff, nothing too personal. The magazine had received such a massive postbag of positive feedback that he was offered the opportunity to become a regular contributor. The money wasn't great, but writing for Phil was about sanity not salary.

He'd loved his time at the magazine; the high point had come after he'd been there eighteen months. Unbeknownst to him, Jeffers had entered a piece of Phil's work into the Headline Journalism Awards. Phil felt like a fraud - he wasn't a journalist, just a guy who'd written a few bits for a magazine.

All suited and booted, the team made the trip to London for the awards at The Dorchester. The chandeliers twinkled and cutlery tinkled; many gold envelopes and bottles of wine were opened before they reached the specialist journalist of the year award – Phil's category.

There were four nominations and, in Phil's opinion, they were written by what he considered to be proper journalists; all of them seemed far more worthy to him than his own piece about the assassination of a brutal Serbian warlord. It turned out the judges thought so too. Phil was relieved not to have to go up on stage, but later proudly posed for a photo with the other nominees, clutching his bottle of Champagne and his certificate of merit.

He was chuffed and felt every bit a winner as he stood at the crowded bar with Jeffers, sharing a scandalously overpriced beer. Jeffers bigged it up and wrote a hilarious, wildly exaggerated piece that, with photos, filled several column inches in the following issue of the magazine.

Phil's recollections of the rest of the evening were a little hazy and the following morning he awoke slouched across the sofa in his hotel room, fully clothed and more than a little dishevelled. Amongst the tatty invite, empty mini bar bottles, bar bills and small change on the desk was Mal Jameson's business card. Phil couldn't recall meeting him, any of their conversation or exchanging phone numbers, but a few days later Mal called to discuss the idea of turning Phil's regular column, 'soldiering on', into a book - and the rest, as they say, is history.

For a while, Phil carried on contributing to the magazine, but eventually he stood aside; new wars needed new voices to tell their stories and Phil had other fish to fry or books to cook or whatever the right phrase was. The magazine would often ring Phil to get a quote on that day's hot topic and he was always happy to oblige.

Phil crossed the top field and was on the home straight. Despite his best efforts his pain wasn't easing, maybe it wasn't stitch after all maybe it was a dodgy prawn from his takeaway last night. A long train journey with food poisoning was not going to be any fun. Maybe he should cancel the meeting, that would be a pain too, a different pain from the one he was experiencing now, but a pain none the less. It had been more difficult than usual and taken such a long time to find a date they could all make, it might be a couple of months before they could all get together again.

Perhaps a change of music would help take his mind off the pain. Phil flicked through his library; Springsteen's Born to Run – no, Lindisfarne's Run for home – no - Eye of the Tiger, perfect - a classic power run tune. He was Rocky Balboa pounding the streets of Philadelphia. Rocky would definitely not be hindered by a dodgy tummy. Phil danced some ducking and diving fancy boxing footwork along the footpath and threw a few power punches into the damp April air.

Slumped against the work surface in his kitchen, Phil swigged some J Collis Browne's mixture out of the bottle (his Granddad swore by it – in fact he was always swearing about something). He felt the minty liquid's warming effect as he swallowed it down. He wiped his mouth with his sleeve and hoped it would do the trick. Just to be on the safe side he rummaged in the medicine cupboard and under the jumble of support bandages, blister plasters, assorted tubes of Deep Heat and antihistamine cream he found a strip of Imodium with a couple of unused tablets, he tucked it in his back pocket.

After a long hot, steamy shower he felt a little better and turned his attention to what he needed to pack; as usual, he was combining his meeting with a weekend with his sister, Becca. Everything was meticulously laid out on his bed in neat, regimented piles; it looked like kit inspection. Two of crisply folded clothes, another with his wash bag, shoes and the soft, almost threadbare tee shirt he liked to sleep in. Lastly, was a pile of things he'd need on the train: iPhone, wallet, a printout of his train booking confirmation and his latest manuscript.

He ticked them off his mental list as he packed each pile into his small holdall. Phil was an expert packer; in the regiment, he'd prided himself on how much he could pack into his escape and evasion kit. There was a long history of the E and E kit in the SAS and usually it was nothing more sophisticated than an old tobacco tin. Having the right items could mean the difference between life and death if you found yourself alone and behind enemy lines.

Phil could get over forty items in the battered Golden Virginia tin: a hacksaw blade, tweezers, water purification tablets, Imodium, an animal snare, stock cubes, chocolate and a stubby candle. It wasn't a particularly useful skill in everyday life, although he did help his nephew win first prize in the 'How many things can you fit in a match box?' competition at his school fête.

Phil hitched up his trousers. He could hear the spectre of Gillian as if she was there with him: 'nice as your Calvin's are you're too old to have your pants on display'. She would say that, she'd purged his underwear drawer of all his comfy, baggy grey and elastically challenged trollies.

He opened his bedside cabinet and felt around in the basket on the bottom shelf. As he pulled out his belt an A4 Moleskine notebook fell out on to the carpet. His journal. The book where everything had begun and yet, now he thought about it, it was a book that had no ending. He supposed he was living the ending now; his writing, his books, his house in France that was his happy ending – wasn't it? At least he hoped it was and not just another cruel twist in the plot. He had no time for these distractions... he stuffed the book back on the shelf and closed the cupboard.

This was such a well-rehearsed ritual; he'd been doing this trip for the last eight years. Every year the same: he and his agent Mal met with Simon his publisher and after a short discussion about his new book they went for a leisurely lunch. There was a particular restaurant on Long Acre they favoured. They liked to sit at a table in the window and watch the world go by while they quaffed a carafe of something ice cold and French and caught up on what had been happening since they last met.

Around 3.30, full of bonhomie and wine, they'd tumble out into the street, bid each other farewell and head off in different directions. Phil usually couldn't face the crush of the Tube so instead he'd hail a cab to take him across the river to Becca's. Even though he'd travelled to many far-flung places, he still got a buzz from seeing the sights of London: Trafalgar Square, Admiralty Arch, The Mall, Buckingham Palace, Chelsea Bridge and Battersea Power station. Then, finally, the cab would sweep up the hill and around Clapham

Common; a lush expanse of open green space edged by chunky-trunked horse chestnut trees.

He glanced at the clock by his bedside. It changed that second from 8.29 to 8.30 - his taxi was due. He zipped up his bag and carried it downstairs. Mr Fish was busy with cat personal hygiene matters and looked distinctly unimpressed as he was unseated from his favourite spot on the hall chair.

Phil hadn't really wanted a pet. He thought it would tie him down too much. Becca had persuaded him on a trip to a rescue centre. It was part of her 'phix Phil's life programme' that she'd embarked on after his return from Bosnia. He knew her intentions were well meaning, but her constant interfering and assumption that she knew what was best for him made it a phase of his life he'd never want to live through again.

Becca thought that the mad furry ball of neuroses would distract Phil from his own and give him something to get up for. On the whole, Mr Fish was quite good company, although he did have a nasty habit of leaving things in Phil's shoes. One morning, as Phil hurried into the garden to bring the washing in during a shower, his bare foot discovered a mouse's head in the toe of his boot. Becca said it meant Mr Fish loved him. Phil thought he could live without that particular brand of rodent-decapitating love.

He herded Mr Fish into the kitchen with his foot, then took an old envelope out of the recycling bin and wrote a hurried note to his neighbour Mrs Emerson. He dropped his spare set of keys into the envelope and folded it to a size that would fit through her 'Madame la Guillotine' letterbox. As well as looking after Mr Fish, Mrs Emerson would have a good nose around. He knew she had a good snoop because after she'd been in, a whole string of tradesmen would call offering their services. Services he needed, but just hadn't got around to organising.

Like the damp man ringing up to enquire if he'd like the mouldy patch in his laundry room treating, or the plumber asking if he'd like the strange clunking noise the boiler was making looked at. He didn't mind. She didn't do it in a busybody kind of way; she was looking after him and he was grateful to her. The tradesmen she chose were very professional and reasonably priced. Neither of them ever spoke of the tradesmen's psychic ability to know that Phil had jobs that needed doing.

Phil showed his gratitude by filling his fridge with the finest fare from the farm shop: tasty, cured meats, creamy goats' cheeses and chocolaty desserts. He'd written in his note to Mrs Emerson that she'd be doing him a real favour by taking the food or else it was all going to go to waste while he was away. They were both very happy with their mutual deception.

With his griping pains fading, Phil was in buoyant mood; he was happy to be making the trip – people say don't mix business and pleasure, but this had always been a perfect blend as far as he was concerned. He recalled the words of his bushy-bearded old granddad – 'Find a job you love and you'll never work a day in your whole life.' On reflection, he wondered if his granddad had learned that lesson the hard way – he had been a bank clerk.

As Phil closed the kitchen door, he heard the staccato toot of the cab waiting at the end of the drive. He tapped his old regiment number into the keypad and left the house. The beep of the alarm faded behind the solid oak door as he turned the key in the lock.

While the cab was making a 28-point turn in the narrow lane, Phil nipped through the gap in the adjoining hedge and dropped the keys through Mrs Emerson's highly sprung vertical letterbox. To check that all his fingers were intact Phil gave the cab driver a wiggly-fingered wave as he walked down the gravel drive. The driver opened the boot and Phil placed his bag amongst a collection of battered cardboard boxes containing brochures for agricultural machinery.

'Station, is it?' Asked the cabbie in a soft rural lilt.

'Yes, please,' Phil replied.

'I used to sell 'em,' said the driver, seeing Phil eyeing the boxes. 'Combines and the like - I'm taking them to the tip after I've dropped you.'

'Oh – right,' muttered Phil as he climbed into the back of the car, keen to get moving and to keep conversation to a minimum.

'Farmers can't afford new Masseys and my boss said he couldn't afford me, so here I am at yer service. Where you goin' to… Exeter or London?'

'London,' answered Phil as the car pulled out of the lane and on to the main road towards the town.

'Popular model that one,' the driver gestured towards the mud-caked tractor hogging two thirds of the road up ahead. 'A real honest machine, they built them with proper axle seals...'

Two tractors, one seed drill, a baler and a rotavator later, they arrived at the station. Phil paid the cab driver, thanked him for his detailed advice on what to look for when buying a second-hand combine harvester and assured him, that should he ever be in the market for one, he'd give him a call.

'Ask for Mike,' said the driver with a gappy, crooked smile and handed Phil his change.

The commuters had long gone and the platform was busy with students and shoppers. The lights on the front of the train flashed in the sun some way down the track; Phil walked along the platform towards where the front of the train would eventually stop. Towards the peace and quiet of first class, towards hushed conversations and wide comfy seats, towards a cooked breakfast and a quiet nap and a world away from the merits of different farm machinery.

With a clunk and a swish, the carriage doors slid back to reveal a cool, clean, empty carriage. Phil took a seat in the middle of the carriage facing forwards. He took a few things from his bag, arranged them neatly on the table in front of him then stowed his bag in the overhead luggage rack.

Occupying most of the space on the table was the thick padded envelope containing his manuscript. He knew he didn't need it for the meeting today, but it was just part of the ritual. He always reread the first chapter on the journey to refresh his memory. One chapter was enough for him to reconnect with the other thirty-four chapters. Characters, plot and story were then firmly embedded in his brain.

This was Phil's eighth book and even he sometimes found the storylines blurred a bit. Maybe that was good; slightly blurry recollections were better than the sharp graphic reality of some of the images that still visited him in his dreams. His stories were fictional, but to Phil they were just a little too real.

Phil's drifting thoughts were suddenly anchored back to the train and he realised he hadn't heard a word the smiley-face, first-class carriage attendant had said. Phil placed his breakfast order then kicked off his shoes, put his feet up and settled back in his seat. Green fields and the red bricks of small, long-closed stations flashed past as he removed the weighty manuscript from the envelope and flipped back the front cover.

RICOCHET

By Phil Drummond

Two

Phil drifted along with the current of other passengers and followed signs towards the Underground. He checked his watch; the train had delivered him in good time, no need to hurry. No need to canter down the escalator. No need to wait for a bus. It was a beautiful morning for a stroll and walking would mean he could stop and enjoy the view from Waterloo Bridge.

Halfway across, he paused; resting his head in his arms on the cool metal railing, he leant over the edge of the bridge and watched the river traffic. A large flat barge slowly emerged from one of the arches, taking London's rubbish further down the river to dump at a landfill near the estuary.

He counted 8 cranes on the skyline; the long-armed mechanics of London's ever-shifting shape. He loved the mixture of old and new, glass and steel, bricks and mortar all jostling together like kids with their hands up in class shouting 'Look at me... look at me'.

On the move again, Phil noticed the trees along the embankment were ahead of those at home. They had the early, fresh, zingy, lime-coloured optimism of Spring. He wouldn't tell anyone for fear of sounding like a tree hugger, but on a day like today it was a feeling he shared.

He dodged the traffic on The Strand and turned into an unpromising narrow gap between a theatre and a pub. It looked like a dead end and smelt like a urinal, but opened into a narrow, lopsided alley leading to the road that was home to the offices of Stellar & Matthews.

At the door, Phil ran a puzzled finger up and down the entry phone. All the illuminated rectangles next to the buttons were empty. He racked his brains, but he couldn't remember from his previous visits if reception was the top bell or the bottom. He tried his agent Mal's mobile, but instantly got his voice mail. 'Hi, this is Mal…' Plan B was to push every button in turn.

Thankfully, before he had to resort to that plan, he spotted an elderly gentleman tucked away behind one of the clipped bay trees by the entrance. The man was busily unscrewing the Stellar & Matthews brass nameplate from the wall.

'Excuse me, I wonder if you can help,' Phil called, trying to make eye contact with the gent behind the tree. 'I'm here to see Simon Drayton and I'm meeting my agent Mal Jameson here too.'

'It's a bit chaotic here this morning,' replied the elderly gent, not taking his eyes off the job in hand. 'I'll just get this last tricky little blighter out and I'll let you in.' With the stubborn screw removed, the gent stretched through the railing, swiped his pass and the door buzzed and clicked open. 'I don't know if Mr Drayton is still here, but if you go up to the first floor, someone will point you in the right direction.'

The door slammed shut and the sound bounced back at him in the dark and echoey entrance hall. A whole stack of yellow packing crates lined the left-hand wall, stretching back along the corridor to the rear of the building. Grimy ghosts remained on the wall where once gilt frames had hung. Phil stuck his head around the doorway of one of the ground floor offices. The room was empty, apart from two men pulling multi-coloured cables out of the trunking, like magicians with silk hankies from a top hat.

Normally, this area was buzzing with life. But today there was no grand floral display on the front desk, nor immaculate receptionist behind it. There were no bike couriers dropping off proofs, nor taxi drivers waiting to whisk passengers off to the airport. There were no staff toing and froing up and down the main staircase. Today, it was eerily silent.

Where was everyone? Where were all the people with notepads under their arms striding purposefully to meetings? Acquisition meetings to decide whether to give the go ahead on new titles. Update meetings to hear about titles in production and marketing meetings to plan forthcoming publicity campaigns. It seemed that there were no meetings today except, of course, for his.

Following the advice from the elderly gent outside, Phil took the stairs to the first floor. As he climbed, he noticed just a steel cable hung in the stairwell where the majestic chandelier usually had pride of place. Its absence made the landing on the first floor dark and unwelcoming.

'Something's not right here.' Before he realised what he was doing, and to his surprise, Phil heard himself say his thought out loud.

'It's the first sign of madness, you know?' came a voice from above.

Phil stepped further into the shadows and looked up to where the voice had come from to see the mischievous grin on the face of a young woman leaning over the banister. He wasn't good at guessing ages; he'd say late twenties. After frequently finding himself in hot water for estimating a little too high he'd come to the conclusion that referring to all women as young was a safe bet.

'Still, there's pretty much nobody else to talk to here at the moment and I find when I talk to myself I always get an honest answer. Something that's been in short supply around here of late.' The one-sided conversation carried on as she made her way down the stairs. 'And you're absolutely right. Something is definitely not right here - hasn't been for a while...'

Phil was surprised by her candour, particularly as she didn't know him from Adam. As the young woman rounded the final turn on the staircase she stopped dead in her tracks as if seeing Phil properly for the first time.

'I'm so sorry...' she stammered, colour rising in her cheeks. 'I... I thought you were someone else... I was expecting Darren... err... a man from the letting agents...'

'I'm sorry to disappoint you,' Phil teased.

'I'm not in the least disappointed,' the blush faded and the cheeky smile returned. 'It's just I'd have been a bit more business-like if I'd known who I was talking to.'

'And do you... know who you're talking to?'

'Yes of course – my Dad's read all your books. Besides, your photo's on the wall outside the ladies loo on the third floor. I see your face smiling back at me every day- oops, sorry there I go again - being over-familiar my boss calls it.'

'Being friendly's what I call it,' Phil smiled, trying to put her at her ease.

On his previous visits, it was all 'yes Mr Drummond – no Mr Drummond – 3 bags full Mr Drummond' it wasn't really his style and he found this new meet-and-greet approach a refreshing change.

'Sorry, I jabber when I get nervous, I don't usually get to meet the authors – a bit less of the chit-chat my boss would say.'

'No need to be nervous, give me friendly honest chit-chat over kowtowing any day.'

The young woman reached the bottom step and paused, leaning against the ornate newel-post. And then as if remembering her manners, she held out her hand. 'I'm Ellie, by the way.'

'Nice to meet you, Ellie.' He replied shaking her hand. 'Fortunately there's no one here to overhear my indiscretions,' she glanced up towards the loftier levels of the stairwell. 'The firing squad left last week. It's a bit of a ghost town on this floor. A couple of weeks back a whole load of people were made redundant, told to clear their desks and go, just like that.'

To make her point, she opened a door behind Phil, revealing a room with around twenty empty desks.

'Almost everyone else has gone to the new offices. There are only a handful of us here tying up loose ends - we're the last lot to move across.'

Phil stared at her blankly and as if reading his blank mind she continued. 'Stellar & Matthews was bought a few months back by Lysistra, this place is being closed and we're all moving to their offices in Soho.'

It did ring a bell vaguely. Mal had spoken to him about it and he had received a letter welcoming him to Lysistra, but he hadn't thought too much of it. When Stellar had merged with Matthews back in 2004 to become S&M it hadn't had any impact on him. Other than he couldn't think of Simon without picturing him brandishing a whip in a leather cap and lederhosen. He banished the all-too-vivid image from his mind.

'I'm meeting Simon Drayton. Is he here?'

'Like the rest of us - only just. He's up on the fifth floor; it's probably easiest if I show you the way. We'll have to take the stairs, I'm afraid. The lift is out of order. The removal men loaded it up with too much stuff and it's stuck between floors two and three. It happens all the time. That's one thing I won't miss about this place; one of the cleaners was stuck for five hours the other weekend.'

'So, your Dad, he likes the sort of thing I write, does he?' Phil asked, unashamedly fishing for compliments. Ellie was uncharacteristically quiet.

'Tell him I've got a new book out next year.'

'I would, but he's dead, unfortunately.'

'Oh, I'm sorry to hear that.' Phil replied awkwardly; he never really knew what the right thing to say was in these situations.

'No - I'm sorry. It's a bit of a conversation killer, isn't it? It's just that… it's been a year now and I'm still not used to him not being around. So I'm trying to say it in a matter-of-fact way in the hope that it'll sink in and maybe help me face the fact he's gone. It feels like he's away… on holiday or something. I still keep expecting him to breeze through the front door with his wheezy laughter, which was usually followed by a ferocious coughing fit. It was the fags that got him in the end.'

Ellie paused on the half landing and turned to face him. 'It's tough, when someone or something that's always been such an important part of your life is no longer part of your life…'

'Yeah, Ellie. Believe me, I know…'

As they passed offices on the third floor, Phil could hear more signs of life, a phone ringing and the percussive tapping of a keyboard. Ellie chatted away as they made their way up the rest of the stairs, often not requiring any input from Phil. He admired her familiarity and openness; after four flights of life story, Phil felt like he'd known her for years.

At the top of the fifth flight of stairs, it opened out into a large, bright room with colourful, funky sofas set against three of the walls, one of which was occupied by Mal, who sat chatting on his mobile. He rolled his eyes, showing that his interest in the call had long passed.

Mal was sporting his country gent look, in a green tailored Harris tweed jacket, khaki trousers and brogue boots. A brace of pheasants and a flat cap would have completed the outfit.

Mal slid his mobile into his pocket and stood up, extending his hand.

'Great to see you. How are you? Journey okay?'

'I'll leave you here if that's okay,' Ellie interrupted. 'I would offer you drinks, but it could take me a week and a pot-holing team to find something to put them in.'

'Don't worry, we're going to get some lunch in a bit. Thanks for being my Sherpa and good luck with the move. I'll see you in Soho next time.'

'I bet you say that to all the girls.' Ellie called with a giggle as she disappeared back down the stairs.

With a smirk of amusement still on his face, Phil turned back to Mal, but before he could answer any of his questions the double doors at the end of the room sprung open.

'Sorry to keep you.' Simon Drayton was in his late fifties but had always seemed much younger, full of Tigger-like energy and enthusiasm. 'Since the merger, I spend my whole life in meetings. And then update meetings about earlier meetings, with no time between the meetings to actually do any of the things we've agreed to in the meetings.'

Today, Simon's step was slightly less springy, dark shadows framed his eyes and the lines on his forehead seemed more pronounced - more Eeyore than Tigger, Phil thought.

'Come in guys. Great to see you.' Simon led the way and gestured to two leather armchairs opposite his large and cluttered desk.

Over the years, the building had been refurbed a few times, but Simon's office always seemed to escape whatever the latest workplace needs analysis recommended. And, like Simon himself, the room remained pretty much the same as Phil remembered from their first meeting many years previous.

'Sorry to hear you're all meetinged out,' Mal said, silencing his mobile and tucking it away in his bag. 'Much as I love our lunch and catch up, we could have rescheduled and done it later.'

'That's very good of you, Mal, but sadly the meeting marathon is my lot in life at the moment.'

Mal stretched the marathon analogy further. 'Sounds like you've hit the wall. Hopefully our meeting will be the motivation you need to keep going. A little light relief.'

Simon didn't seem convinced and uttered a noncommittal 'Mmmm' by way of reply.

As they switched topics, Simon visibly relaxed and became more like his usual self. He seemed to feel more comfortable on the safer ground of small talk. They talked about Simon's sons, his upcoming trip to New Zealand and the latest instalment of the restoration of his beloved boat. After about twenty minutes, Mal skilfully steered the conversation back to work matters.

Simon shifted uncomfortably, staring down at his desk, not knowing what to say or where to start. He began to speak a few times and then stopped. He looked tired and sad. He bit his lip to try and stop it from twitching.

'This is difficult... I really have been dreading this,' he said finally. 'I don't know how to tell you.' He paused and took a long deep breath. 'So I'm just going to come out and say it. There are some big, bad changes here, changes that affect you both. Changes that affect us all.'

'What do you mean?' Mal asked. 'When we talked last week everything was fine.'

'Last week seems like an age ago; Last week everything was fine, today, Mal, it's a very different story. All those meetings. All those endless telecoms with the US mean I have to sit here with the two of you and have this very difficult conversation. I'm sorry to say, this won't be like our usual meetings. I have some very bad news for you.'

'How bad is bad?' Phil asked. He was keen to get some sense of perspective. This couldn't possibly be as bad as some of the bad things he'd seen.

'Bad as in Lysistra will not be re-signing you. They will not be publishing your next book. You will not be a part of Lysistra's grand plan.' Simon looked relieved to have finally said it. Clearly this had been eating away at him for some time. 'They'll continue to publish a selection of your back list titles but that's all.'

Mal looked shocked; as if this was not what he had been expecting. He didn't like surprises at the best of times and especially not ones like this. It was a rare moment when Mal was lost for words, but he obviously felt he needed to say something to fill the silence.

'I remember reading their press release,' he paused as if trying to recall the exact phrases. 'It was the usual corporate waffle. It said something about Lysistra looking to the future and building upon the strong heritage of Stellar and Matthews. Continuing their commitment to encourage new talent while reaching out to the growing female readership - blah, blah blah.'

'No mention of redundancies and ditching existing talent then?' Simon muttered as he walked to the mini fridge and took out three bottles of water. 'We all fell for that one.'

'Why drop Phil?' Mal asked incredulously. 'It doesn't make any sense. His books sell. He's got an established readership base – they're mad.'

'No not mad, just American,' Simon passed a bottle of mineral water to Mal and Phil. 'I don't really get it either. It's not the publishing world I'm used to. It's completely alien to me. But let me try and explain it to you as it's been explained to me in my numerous meetings of late. It all comes down to computers. Computerised inventory tracking to be more precise. It charts the exact sales of every book and it's sealed the fate of many a writer. The major players, the online stores, supermarkets and chain stores order new titles according to the way previous titles sold. So, if your next book doesn't sell as well as your last - your card's marked or should I say your book's marked. Three strikes and you're out. Sadly that's today's publishing world and it's the main reason that publishers are dropping authors.'

'But as I said,' Mal blustered, 'Phil's books sell...'

'I know that, you know that, but the bottom line is the last three books haven't reached their projected sales target. To the uninitiated it looks like Phil's popularity is falling. But, if you look at the wider picture – and, believe me, I have been trying to draw everyone's attention to this - if you look at Phil's readership against the national stats for the decline in male reading, Phil's holding his own very well. I've said it again and again and it's fallen on deaf ears. They don't want to know. If anything it's had the opposite effect and has only added fuel to their argument for dropping male titles and continuing their obsession with chasing female readership. To be fair Lysistra are bucking the trend, they've had a very good year.'

Simon slowly rubbed his temples; gathering his thoughts before continuing. 'For me publishing has always been about novelists being allowed to gain a foothold and build an audience. Some of our greatest books would never have made it to the shelves if we'd cut the authors off because a couple of titles didn't reach the projected sales figures dreamt up on a flip chart by some bean counter.'

Simon's frustration was clear. He slumped back in his chair and took a long swig from his bottle.'

Thanks for fighting my corner, Simon,' Phil said, filling the vacuum Simon's revelations had left in the office. 'I can tell you haven't taken this lying down. Whatever else happens I want you to know that I'm grateful for all you've done for me over the years.'

Simon smiled a weak, sad smile. 'The saddest thing for me, Phil, is that the people making these decisions aren't remotely interested in books – their only interest is in bookkeeping and that's something quite different. When I get passionate and emotional about books they look at me like I'm mad. It's just figures on a balance sheet to them.'

Simon shrugged and held out the palms of his hands in a gesture of defeat. 'For me it's the end of an era. I've loved it here. It's been such fun working with people like you guys. I hate the over-use of the word "journey" but it's the only way to describe what we've been through.'

Simon's face lit up as he time-travelled back to revisit happier days. 'I can remember it so clearly Mal, that day you showed me those magazine articles. You knew you'd found something special and after reading them I did too. I just knew Phil had it in him. Even though he took some convincing fully to realise his talent.'

'I'm not sure I do even now.' Phil joked, despite finding no humour in the situation he now found himself. 'I always imagine I'm going to get found out and someone's going to come along and say, "Who are you trying to kid, you can't write." Well maybe I have been found out… maybe this is it.'

'Don't judge yourself on Lysistra's peculiar business development priorities.' Simon mustered some of his old spirit. 'You are a hugely talented storyteller. You write original, emotional and compelling novels. They can take away your deal, but they'll never take that away from you.'

'That's kind of you Simon, but my sales don't seem to have borne that out… do they?'

'I'm not being kind. I'm being straight with you Phil. It's true your recent sales figures don't match those of some of your previous novels. But overall book sales are down and most career novelists will see some peaks and troughs throughout their writing years. You have a strong following. Think about it. You do a book tour and sell… what? Three, if you're lucky four thousand copies tops. So where are the rest of your sales coming from?'

Phil had never really stopped to think about how, where and when his books sold. He was just glad they did.

'Word of mouth, that's where,' Simon continued. 'And what drives word of mouth? Fantastic storytelling. You, Phil Drummond, tell fantastic stories. You're a master of that.'

Simon might be speaking the truth, but it felt to Phil like he was being told he was the perfect candidate for a job; possessing all the required qualifications and qualities while knowing full well there were no vacancies.

'So, Lysistra's loss will be someone else's gain. I'm confident things will work out for you Phil.' Simon looked across to Mal who was busily checking his email, 'you're in very good hands.'

Simon went on to tell them about the streamlining, which translated from American meant redundancies and early retirement for him.

'When I spoke to you last week Mal there was a deal on the table whereby S and M would trade as an imprint of Lysistra; I'd keep Phil and a handful of my other authors and stay on as a consultant working three days a week, but that deal was pulled yesterday.' Simon shook his head and Phil could see all the fight had been knocked out of him. 'I'm too set in my ways to start again. I think it's time I was captain of my own ship; after New Zealand I'll finish my boat and take Mrs D on a proper trip – I fancy going down through France and out into the Med.'

Phil felt very sorry for Simon. He'd always had a real knack for anticipating readership trends, putting new and unusual titles on the shelves just as people developed an appetite for reading them. Simon was old school publishing, a dying breed. Again and again Stellar had been there first with the books that people wanted to read, when they wanted to read them.

Simon had been responsible for signing up great new talent, including Phil. He'd seen a small ember of talent in Phil's early writing and he'd blown on it. Carefully teasing out all that highly flammable, bottled up disappointment, betrayal and fury. He then stood well back and watched his stories explode on to the page. Stories that took over people's lives. Stories that kept them up late at night. Stories that made them sneak off to the loo at work to read a few more chapters. Stories that silenced any bedtime conversation.

Simon's unique approach had transformed the company from a small niche market publishing house into an internationally renowned literary powerhouse. He rose through the ranks of the rapidly expanding business taking on bigger titles and bigger salaries. Whatever else he took on he never allowed this success to be rewarded by the removal of the things he was good at.

Phil and Mal sat passively and listened in stunned silence as Simon told them more about his meetings with S and M's new owners and what they called Simon's 'managed exit'.

'So, no lunch?'

That was so typical of Mal. Simon was a crushed man, telling them that he was being forced to dismantle, book by book, all he'd spent the last thirty years building, and all Mal could think about was missing out on his grilled sea bass and several bottles of crisp dry Sauvignon.

'I'd love to, Mal... old time's sake and all that, but I've got another two of these delightful tête à tête's today. And I don't feel as positive about the other two's futures as I do about yours Phil. You'll find a new publisher and in the meantime still earn a decent living from your royalties.'

'It's not about...' But before Phil could finish, Simon interrupted.

'I know Phil and that's why you mustn't take this too seriously. Just carry on as normal. Mal will sort this mess out - you'll see. And when you've got your new book out there I hope you'll send me an invitation to the launch.' Simon stood up indicating that their time was up.

As he walked them out, Simon chatted optimistically about all the various options open to Phil. On the third floor Phil caught a glimpse of Ellie at the far end of the corridor with a sharp-suited raffish young man, brandishing his laser tape measure like a Jedi Master – Darren, he guessed.

At the front door Simon stood on the cobbles, shook them both firmly by the hand and then without a backward glance, disappeared into the dimly lit and atmospheric gloom of his offices.

'I'm sorry Phil,' Mal patted his stomach. 'I can't think on an empty stomach. Let's go to that Spanish place around the corner and make a plan.'

'Look, so Lysistra want to focus on female titles, good for them. 70% of books now bought by women, supermarkets outselling bookshops, yeah, yeah, I've seen the charts. But that still leaves a big chunk of the market for you. Simon's right, there are other houses who'd bite both my arms and one of my legs off to have you. Look at that bidding war we had at the end of your last deal. We should have done it then while we had the chance. I know you felt a sense of loyalty to Simon – don't beat yourself up over that. Don't worry, this is going be great. We'll re-launch you with your new book, it'll be a fresh start. Leave it with me, this is a fantastic opportunity.' Mal paused for breath and took a large swig of wine before continuing his monologue.

Phil was looking at Mal, seeing his lips moving but the volume was turned down. He couldn't hear the buzz of the piazza, he couldn't hear the chinking of glassware nor the scrape of cutlery on china. All he could hear were reruns of Simon's conversation.

Had 'Handbags at dawn' really outsold him last year? Was it true that games consoles had replaced the book as man's favourite travelling companion? He knew literacy levels in boys had been falling for years. He'd seen it first hand through a government initiative he'd been involved in. He went into a few schools to try and reignite a burning passion for books.

The boys suffered from diminished imagination. They didn't want to work to get the excitement of a story. They didn't want to work to create the images in their heads. Why would they? All they needed to do was flick a switch on their games console, limber up their thumbs and there it was all laid on - no effort required. How could a book compete with that?

They didn't need to read it, they could live it. Virtual guns and virtual blood; razor-sharp 3D graphics with enhanced pixel display and video recording functionality so they could relive their gameplay in slow motion from every angle. They thought they were living it – they had no idea.

To be fair, in the early days Phil had no idea either. No amount of training could prepare him for what combat was really like. He'd tried to fight it. He didn't want it to happen to him, but it was inevitable, a losing battle. After he'd seen about a dozen casualties it became normal - but what kind of normality was that? What kind of life was it where death was just another day at the office?

He'd count the seats on the plane at the end of a tour and there'd be four, maybe five, empty and in the end that's how he began to feel too - an unfillable emptiness. He'd locked it all away; he'd thought he was dealing with it, but he wasn't, he'd been kidding himself.

One similarity between the games and real warfare was the playback feature. Less so now, but when he returned from Bosnia he'd endlessly see Campbell taking his last steps back along the embankment towards the Landie. In his dreams he'd see every detail. Campbell kicking up the dust as he walked and calling out over his shoulder as he went. Maybe that was what attracted the sniper's attention.

He could see him now - Campbell laughing and taking the piss out of Phil's driving; he said Phil drove like an old lady, he said they should get some cushions and a tartan blanket to go in the back of the Landie. His banter was swept away on the warm dusty breeze, but Phil watched him from a distance acting out theatrical doddery gear changes and hand signals. In playback mode Phil laughed and shook his head and that's when he heard the first crack of gunfire.

It came from the blown-out office blocks across the river. Campbell turned quickly – he was on open ground about a hundred metres from the Land Rover, making him easy prey for the sniper. There was more gunfire, this time much closer to Campbell, who ran for cover. He scrambled up a pile of rubble and into a tumbledown warehouse. And that's the last time he saw him.

If Phil had stuck to his guns, if he'd insisted on driving and he'd gone back to get the Land Rover instead of Campbell, it would have been him who ducked into the booby-trapped building. It would have been him who tripped the wire attached to the grenade pin. It would have been him scattered across no man's land and Campbell would still be here.

He'd still be a husband to Jane, a dad to Lottie, Jack and Tom and a mate to Phil - except of course Phil would be dead - he'd be free. And who'd have missed Phil? His Mum, Dad and his sis' Becca maybe. But it wasn't the same as kids losing their dad. Campbell's kids needed him; Phil's family didn't need him - not really. At Campbell's funeral he couldn't keep his eyes off the flag-draped coffin. All he could think was, 'I should be in that box.' At the time, he wished he was.

He still blamed himself. His casual agreement to let Campbell drive back to HQ had robbed them of the most important man in their lives. Who'd pick Lottie up from parties and park around the corner so as not to embarrass her in front of her mates? Who'd interrogate any boy brave enough to call for her?

Who'd explain quadratic equations, girls and how the central heating worked to Jack, and all before breakfast? Who'd have endless light sabre duels with Tom? Who'd glue the heads and legs back on his action figures and read him an extra chapter when he ought to be going to sleep? Nobody, that's who. Campbell had everything to live for and what Phil wouldn't give to rewind that day and walk in his boots one last time.

In Phil's dreams there was another cruel twist – sometimes he was cast as the leading man. It was him he'd see scrabbling up the rubble and disappearing into the warehouse. But then, when he could almost smell the sulphur of the grenade, he'd wake up dripping with sweat, confused and shivering.

For a millisecond he was relieved; then, creeping like a dark shadow, the guilt, icy cold, slowly seeped through his veins. From the tips of his fingers to his brain, ripping at his stomach as it flowed. The guilt turned to anger and then disappointment as he realised that he was alive with another tortuous empty day stretching ahead of him.

Despite much cajoling by his nephews, he never played warfare computer games with them, he didn't need to – unlike them, he really had lived it; Northern Ireland, the Gulf, Bosnia – he'd been there, done that, got the Kevlar underpants.

Not surprisingly the government's school's reading initiative hadn't worked, they'd well and truly 'Wiied' on Phil's bonfire. Boys weren't interested in books and, as he was now discovering, didn't grow into men who would read his books – it was as simple as that.

Mal was still talking, gesticulating wildly and laughing at his own jokes. Finally he paused for breath and stopped talking to check his phone.

'Do you know what day it is today?'

'…Thursday…?' Mal replied distractedly; he was a man who couldn't send a text and hold a conversation at the same time. He quickly signed off his message and then returned to Phil, giving him his full attention. Beaming across the table at him as if the meeting with Simon couldn't possibly have had a better outcome.

'It's April Fool's Day Mal – and that's what we are…We had our chance to jump ship and we missed it.'

'Listen, I know this is a bit of a blow, but a new publisher with new ideas could be just what you need. Maybe we've become a little set in our ways. Sometimes you need something like this to shake you up. It's completely understandable that you might feel unsettled now, but I'm certain in six months from now you'll look back and wonder what all the fuss was about.'

'Yeah maybe.' Phil uttered in glass half-empty mode.

'Do I look worried? Rebound's going to be a turning point for you, you'll see.'

Mal didn't look worried, at least not outwardly. But then if a meteorite was about to strike earth Mal wouldn't worry; he'd just see a publishing opportunity in it. Phil admired Mal's ever-present optimism and enormous self-belief.

Mal finished the last of the calamari; in truth, he'd finished the king prawns, the baked aubergine, the spicy potatoes, the whitebait and the tortilla. Phil didn't mind as he didn't feel like eating; unlike Mal, a crisis didn't give him an appetite. Besides he could feel the grumbling pain from earlier rearing its ugly head again.

'It's Ricochet… my book, it's called Ricochet.' Phil interrupted.

'Yes of course it is, Ricochet – Rebound they sound similar don't they?'

'Have you read it?' Phil asked suspiciously.

'Not all of it, no, but what I have read fills me with every confidence.'

'So you haven't read it.'

'Phil, we go back a long way, I know your style. We're a great team you and I. I know you'll do your bit and you know I'll do mine…'

Mal returned to waving his arms around whilst scoping out his grand plan for Phil's re-launch. Phil tuned him out and returned to rerunning the conversation with Simon.

Message received Wednesday 12th May at 17:05

Hi Phil it's Becca here again, just calling to check that you're okay. It's weeks now since you were here and I've not heard a peep from you. I'm guessing that you and Mal are busy sorting out your new book deal, but if you could find a minute to give me a call, it would set my mind at rest. Love you Bruv.

Message deleted, next new message

Message received Sunday 16th May at 11:26

Hello Philip it's Mum, just calling to say we're back from Lanzarote. We've had a fabulous three weeks, your Dad played golf most days and I stayed by the pool and caught up on the latest goings on at the No. 1 Ladies' Detective Agency – just my cup of redbush, not all your death and destruction stuff. I'll lend them to you if you like. What else did we do?…oh yes, I did few of José's aqua fit classes – he was a bit of a one for the ladies if you get my drift. Dishy the others called him– but at my age the only dishy I'm interested in comes with a generous slice of gateau in it. Even with the aqua fit I've put on a few pounds, still, it's back to line dancing next week so that'll work off all those extra puddings. Sad news while we were away: Mrs Davies has passed away – you know, she moved into number 12, the rector's old house – she's got the one-eyed Corgi that kept stealing the sausage rolls at my garden party last year. Now, your sister says she's worried about you and when she's worried I worry. Why don't you come and stay with us for a few days, it's ages since we saw you last and your Dad could do with some help in the garden. The pond needs emptying and the hedge is due for its annual hair cut. You know what your Dad's like with that bloomin' trimmer, he'll lose an arm one of these days… Any road, give me a call love when you have a mo'. Take care son.

Message deleted, next new message

Message received Wednesday 19th May at 09:56

Hello, if you've been injured in an accident at work you could be entitled to compensation. Call our accident helpline to hear about our no win no fee…

Message deleted, next new message

Message received Thursday 27th May at 07:43

Phil it's Becca , I'm on the train on my way to yours. I called Mal last night and he told me he hadn't heard hide nor hair of you since your meeting with Simon and that you weren't returning any of his calls either. It made me feel a little better that it wasn't just me you were ignoring. But then of course I felt worse, imagining all the reasons why you might be shutting the world out. I'll be there as soon as I can. Love you!

Message deleted, end of messages

Three

Thursday May 27th 2010

Becca's cab pulled in behind the delivery van parked across Phil's driveway.

'Keep the change and thanks, I'd never really understood the difference between silage and manure.'

She pushed open the gate, and saw the courier, crouched down, calling through the letterbox. Hearing the scrunch of gravel, he turned to face her.

'Ah, brilliant love, I thought I was going to have to put this monster back in the van. I nearly gave meself a hernia getting it out. Can you sign and print there.'

Becca scrawled a squiggle bearing little resemblance to her actual signature on the handset screen; then, leaving the large box where it stood, she went around the back of the house. All the curtains were drawn and the garden was neglected and overgrown. Mr Fish emerged through the weeds like a tiger through the jungle.

All that was needed to complete the scene was a man in a loincloth swinging from the wisteria. She was quite enjoying this fantasy, when she was rudely interrupted by the back door creaking open. What greeted her would not have looked out of place in a jungle. Her brother's hair was both long in length and long overdue for a wash. His usual stubble was a full-grown beard and he was modelling a stained tee shirt and torn trackie bottoms. In short, he was a complete mess.

'Hi Sis - if I'd known you were coming I'd have baked a cake.' Typical Phil, she thought, always trying to hide behind that boyish smile and a joke.

'Looking at the state of your kitchen I'm glad you didn't – I'm no stranger to botulism, but I prefer the forehead-smoothing variety.'

'Come in. I was just going to put the kettle on,' he mumbled, avoiding eye contact.

The house was in a similar state to Phil. Every surface in the kitchen was covered with empty takeaway cartons and pizza boxes. Empty cans of lager were stacked sideshow style around the room. He'd used every piece of china in the house.

He had even used some of the souvenir plates showing Spanish pastoral scenes that their Mum and Dad had brought back from Alicante - he really was a desperate man. Flies buzzed around the numerous unwashed cat bowls; the bins were spilling out on to the floor and the smell was rancid.

She was heartbroken to see him like this again; she'd worked so hard to get him back on the rails after Bosnia and yet here they were again back at square one. She gave him a hug and, despite the full-on exfoliation of Phil's spiky Velcro face grazing her cheek, she hugged him more tightly than a much-prized handbag she'd pounced on in Selfridges' sale.

Not only did Phil not look good, he didn't smell good either. A meaty, stale sweaty armpit smell was holding all the fresh air in the room to ransom. Still holding him in her grip, Becca sniffed his breath.

'Have you been drinking?

Phil struggled to escape her grasp, but Becca held him tight under her scrutinising eye.

'Yeah maybe - one or two…'

'Phil, it's eleven o'clock in the morning…'

'Yeah, but I'm not sleeping so good at the moment…'

'And drinking in the morning is helping?'

'Yeah… no. You're twisting things. It's not as bad as it looks.'

'It looks and smells pretty bad to me.'

'My body clock's all up the creek. I've been getting up at 3.00am every morning, so it might be 11.00 o'clock for you but for me the sun's very nearly over the yard arm.'

'Well, you're going to have to knock that on the head if we're going to get you straightened out. Comprende?'

Phil shrugged noncommittally.

'Did you get my messages? You knew I was coming, right?' Becca asked, scanning the devastation and mentally prioritising which jobs to do first, assessing how long it would take to get everything straight.

'Yeah, sorry,' came Phil's muffled reply, still held in Becca's bear-hugging grip. 'I got your voicemail, texts and emails; sorry for not getting back to you - I just haven't felt like talking to anyone. I've just been chilling out and getting my head together.'

Phil finally broke free. 'Tea or coffee?' he asked, swiftly changing the subject; rinsing two filthy mugs he'd skilfully extracted from the precarious Jenga tower of crockery in the sink.

'And have you… got your head together?' Becca called, reopening the back door to let the acrid smell escape and bring her suitcase in. Phil's silence spoke volumes. 'I'm here to help, you can get over this, we've done it before, we can do it again.'

Again, Phil was silent. Becca took the mugs from him.' Why don't I make the drinks while you get cleaned up?' she asked with uncharacteristic diplomacy.

After cleaning the bathroom to such a level that a forensic team would have had trouble finding evidence that any human had ever set foot in it, Becca ran a deep hot bath. She added a splash of disinfectant and placed a freshly laundered towel, still warm from the tumble dryer, on the small, round gate-leg table. She laid out some clean clothes, and then left her brother to it.

Becca continued her whirlwind, one-woman emergency clean-up of the disaster zone that was Phil's house. The dishwasher was on its fourth load and the house was beginning to look like Kim and Aggie had been in and worked their magic. The floor had stopped feeling like the sticky boards used to catch mice and was smooth and cool under her feet. And the newly scrubbed fridge no longer resembled an experiment that Pasteur would have been proud of.

Becca glanced up towards the ceiling; Phil had been up there for hours. She knew herself how long serious deforestation could take, but it seemed a bit too quiet. She turned down the pan of water bubbling on the now-gleaming range. Looking for the salt, she opened the nearest cupboard and a couple of packs of paracetamol fell out on to the work top.

The cupboard was full of boxes of medicine. She counted 8 boxes of paracetamol – that was some headache he was anticipating - why would he want so many packs? Suddenly the penny dropped; realising she'd severely under-estimated Phil's mental state, she flew upstairs.

Becca knocked urgently on the bathroom door.

'Are you okay in there?' No answer, just the rhythmic drip, dripping of the tap. She knocked a bit louder. 'Lunch will be ten minutes.'

Still no reply. Suddenly, feeling slightly panicky, she put her shoulder to the door and put all her weight behind it - it flew open - it wasn't locked and Becca stumbled into the bathroom.

'Oh my God! Oh my God!' Becca squealed in panic.

Phil lay almost completely submerged in the crimson bath water. Becca's heart felt like it was about to explode, she was trembling and she could feel a tsunami of adrenaline surging through her veins. How could she flit about downstairs playing Anthea Turner while it was her brother who desperately needed her attention, not the house? Stupid, stupid Becca. Why could she not rid herself of her Mum's ingrained bizarre set of priorities?

While she struggled to remove her mobile imprisoned in her skinny jeans pocket, Phil's head twitched and, like something out of a Stephen King novel, he slowly sat up.

'Do you mind? I may be a bit off the rails, but a man still likes his privacy.'

'Thank God! Thank God!' Becca wrung her hands as if in prayer.

'What do you mean thank God? You're an atheist.' Phil replied, irritated by Becca's bathroom invasion; to cover his modesty he neatly arranged a flannel over his groin.

'I am not,' she replied, a bit thrown by the timing of Phil's ecclesiastical grilling

'Eating Easter eggs does not make you a Christian.'

Becca couldn't believe she was having this conversation and tried desperately to order her thoughts as best she could.

'Are you okay? Are you hurt?' She asked in first aider mode.

'Well, I am a bit upset you put loo cleaner in my bath.'

'I mean - have you cut yourself, nicked yourself shaving by accident?' Phil's beard was as bushy as ever. He looked down at the water that was more reminiscent of a scene from Psycho than a slight scratch from a disposable razor.

Suddenly, realising how Becca had added two and two and made five, he laughed, sending ripples of water splashing over the edge of the bath.

'I don't think it's funny Phil. I was seconds from calling an ambulance…'

'I'm fine… no cuts.' Phil splashed the surface of the water gently. 'It's not a blood bath, it's a beetroot bath bomb – well three actually. They were a birthday present from Danuta. I don't know what you'd put in the bath water, but it smelt like a gents' loo.'

Phil held up and read from the damp paper packaging on the side of the bath.

'I felt I needed a bit of the old beta vulgaris, you know invigorating essential oils and stuff… I thought it would pep me up. It didn't work; I must have dozed off.'

Becca collapsed back into the Lloyd Loom chair, suddenly exhausted by her two-minute emotional white-knuckle ride.

'Now if you don't mind, I'd like to get out - without an audience.'

Feeling she needed something stronger than tea, Becca poured herself a large glass of wine and placed two large bowls of pasta on the table. Phil, who looked like he hadn't had a home-cooked meal in a long time, wasted no time digging in.

'I still can't believe you thought I'd do something like that,' he said, idly twiddling spaghetti around his fork.

'Well things aren't that great for you at the moment; I didn't know what to think.'

'And you don't even know the half of it…'

'So tell me…' Becca pleaded, 'what's going on Phil?' She swirled the wine in her glass before taking a sip.

Phil sighed a long and despairing sigh; he sat low in his chair visibly deflated, staring down at his plate. It was hard keeping up the 'everything's fine' act, the 'I'll be all right tomorrow' act, the 'I'm just a bit tired' act. He could pull it off with some people, but not Becca – she'd been here before. She wasn't falling for any of his act.

'Dave's dead,' he whispered flatly.

'Oh god no!' Becca cried, coughing a little as the wine went down the wrong way.

She stood up and walked around behind Phil. Taking his head in her hands, she cradled him to her.

'Now I get it - now I understand.' she said softly

'I've lost my book deal. I've lost another mate. And now that's how I feel – lost - again.'

'I guess it must have opened old wounds...'

'Campbell you mean?' Phil asked, feeling the need to say his friend's name out loud, even though uttering it when he was feeling low still gave him a sharp pain in the pit of his stomach.

Becca nodded, gently wiping a tear from his cheek. 'Yeah...' Phil sat up and tried to compose himself. Becca hunted in her pockets for a tissue. Phil just used his sleeve.

'Yeah, it's opened that box again although it's not quite the same. All my demons are because I feel responsible for Campbell's death. I don't feel Dave dying is my fault. I know I have some kind of Midas touch at the moment whereby everything I so much as brush against turns to shit, but even my twisted brain can't find a way of pinning Dave's death on me.'

Dave, like Phil, had made a mess of his early civilian life. Dead-end jobs, divorce and drink had all taken their toll and then he found running. Dave had taken up coaching kids at a local athletics club – it had turned his life around. Running was, to Dave, as writing was to Phil – or as writing had been to Phil. Running had returned a sense of purpose, routine and structure; all the things he'd taken for granted in his old life.

Dave didn't have kids, but the kids he coached became his kids; he believed in them and, more importantly, he taught them to believe in themselves. He showed them their true potential, both on and off the track, and inspired them to reach it.

'How did you find out? You know...' Becca asked, not sure whether talking about Dave and Campbell was making things better or worse for Phil.

'That Dave was dead? Through the runners' message board – well, kind of.'

Phil rewound his fork, but spotting Becca still looking none the wiser he stopped short of eating and paused to tell the story from the beginning.

'Well, it's over a month ago now. The Sunday evening I got back from yours after the fateful meeting with Simon I went out for a run. I was tired and cross and I thought a run would help to burn off my mood. I was angry with Mal for taking it all in his stride; for being so preoccupied with making plans he didn't stop to ask how it was affecting me. I was angry with myself too; Mal had suggested a change of publisher last year and it was me who put the kybosh on those plans. If I'd listened and followed his advice everything would have been kushti.

I used to be able to trust my judgement, but it's all gone to pot now. Anyhow, I went for my run and maybe it was my anger I don't know, but I smashed Dave's last run time; when I got home I gleefully posted a suitably rude note on his message board. Monday morning I went for my run as usual; there was no reply from Dave. Tuesday came and went - it wasn't like him - usually our banter pinged back and forth on a regular basis.

On Wednesday Julie, his ex, called to say he'd had a heart attack and died. Hearing the news knocked me sideways. It seemed like one by one all my mates were leaving me. Julie said he'd been coaching at the track when he collapsed. He wasn't much older than me; he was certainly fitter than me. Dave was me practising what I'd preached at the magazine; Dave and I were a "civvy street team" looking out for each other.'

Phil finally stopped waving his fork around and put it in his mouth before continuing his story with his mouth full.

'I know it's selfish, but I needed to tell him what had happened at the meeting with Simon. I needed his no-nonsense views. I needed him to be there for me like I was there for him when Julie left, but he's not going to be...'

'You don't have to do this on your own... I'm here for you.' Becca leant across the table and put her hand on Phil's.

'I know you are...' Phil said with a tight half smile.

'I'm not Dave, but I'll always try and do the right thing by you even if I don't really understand what you're going through.'

Becca squeezed his hand and held his gaze

'I've been thinking a lot about Campbell...' Phil confided, quietly wiping his nose on his sleeve again. 'All those old feelings have been bubbling to the surface again. I recognise all the signs this time - the joyless, suffocating, claustrophobic feeling. I know what I should be doing, Mark gave me all those ideas to sort my head out last time, but it feels like all those handles to help me get a grip on reality are just beyond my reach at the moment. Things might not be going my way right now, but don't worry I wouldn't ... I couldn't... I'm not brave enough...' Phil tailed off.

'When I saw all those packs of paracetamol in your cupboard...'

'You jumped to the wrong conclusion.'

'Yes, I'm sorry, I didn't know what to think.'

'Well, just so you know they're Mrs Emerson's – for her hip. She gets through stacks and they'll only sell her a few packs at a time.'

'Can't she get them on prescription?'

'I've suggested it to her, but she's funny about things like that. Anyway, whenever I go to the chemist I pick up a pack for her.'

'I should think they're doing her hip the world of good in your cupboard.'

'I know... I kept meaning to drop them round, but I got a bit sidetracked by the demise of my career.'

Phil was glad to have straightened that out. He'd clocked Becca's suitcase in the hall; if she thought she had to be on suicide watch, she'd be digging in for the duration and he'd never get rid of her.

'You'll be glad to hear, I'm not going to use the beet bombs again,' Phil said, trying hard to lighten the mood. 'They've stained all my bits red, I look like I've got a bad case of scurvy in my nether regions.'

'In that case, eat your dinner, you need all the vitamins you can get.'

'I forgot to ask. Where's Danuta?' Becca called from the kitchen as she tided the pots and pans into the cupboard.

'She's away,' Phil replied from the sitting room.

'Yes, I could tell that from the state of the house. Is she coming back? She's the best cleaner you've ever had.'

'She's my housekeeper, and yes, maybe next month; I'm not sure, she's gone back to Lithuania - her sister's about to have a baby.'

Becca came and sat on the sofa next to Phil

'I'd feel OK leaving you here knowing that Danuta was coming in each day, but I can't let you stay here on your own... not like this.'

'I'll be OK, I just need some time – a bit of space. Don't do the big sis' thing on me.'

He knew she hated it when he played that card; she was, in fact, six years his junior. True to form it pushed all her buttons.

'You're not okay. You're up all hours of the night, you're drinking in the day. You're shutting everyone out, you're not looking after yourself…'

'Well yes, but apart from that I'm fine.'

'What are you doing with your days? What's that huge box on the doorstep and all those others in the study?'

'Just stuff.'

'What kind of stuff?'

Phil became the most animated she'd seen him since she'd arrived.

'Have you seen Price Plunge?'

'No.'

'It's great, a real buzz, like gambling but without losing loads of money. I'll show you.'

Becca frowned, folding her arms. In fact, she could have been a case study for the embodiment of negative body language. Phil turned on the TV and flicked through the channels. They went past soaps about people with damaged relationships, reality shows about fixing damaged relationships, programmes about training your dog, programmes about training your kids. Boot camps for kids, boot camps for dogs.

'Is there a programme for retraining wayward brothers? The brothers could swap families; it could, of course, have the obligatory canine element and a 'big reveal makeover' moment at the end.'

Ignoring her, Phil carried on channel surfing

'Here we go… oh this is a good one - it's the garden show. I got a great thing on here for spraying wood preservative on to fences. It's like the high-pressure patio cleaner I bought, but with liquid borax - no splashing and no more messy brushes.' Phil parroted the sales patter in a perfect parody of shopping channel spiel.

'But Phil, you haven't got any fences; you've got an eighteenth century walled garden.'

'It does sheds, too.'

'You haven't got a shed either.'

'I haven't at the moment, but I'm thinking of getting one. I can't keep all that stuff in the study for ever.'

Becca picked up the remote and flicked the TV off.

'What's happening with Mal?'

'I don't know, he's left a few messages.'

'And?'

'And he said he had a few irons in the fire, but reading between the lines he pissed so many people off during negotiations at the end of my last deal that a lot of people don't want to know. He's suggested meeting up to talk through the options, but I'm not really feeling up to it.'

Phil reached for the remote, but Becca moved it out of his reach.

'When you're flavour of the month,' Phil explained. 'Everyone wants to sign you. What's happened at Lysistra is common knowledge; it puts us in a weaker position - I'm tarnished by what's happened. I'm not such a hot property – not even a lukewarm property - even Phil and Kirstie would have a job selling me.'

'Maybe you need to start looking at some different avenues other than writing,' Becca trod carefully. 'I'll help you, we'll make some plans, think about all the things you like doing, all the things you're good at...'

'I'm good at fighting…, I'm good at writing…, I'm good at writing about fighting.' Phil grumbled, irritated by Becca's misplaced do-gooding interference.

'Well let's try and fight this; fight whatever it is you're going through at the moment. And as for the writing - you're not writing. Writers write, they don't sit around the house with the curtains drawn, drinking and buying crap from shopping channels.'

It was a bit harsh, but he was in denial and only by seeing and recognising how bad things really were could he start to move on.

'Everyone's worried about you. It was all I could do to stop Mum and Dad driving over here today. It was only when I told them you were coming to stay with me that they relented…'

'Oh no. No way. I'm fine here.'

Now it was his turn for negative body language - Phil folded his arms defiantly.

'You can't fix this Becca, not this time. I've got to do it myself - I'll be fine… I'm just taking a break to sort myself out. I know what I need to do, I know how to sort this…'

'Well the bottom line is this, you can either come and stay with me until Danuta returns or Mum and Dad are coming to stay here with you.'

'Then I really will slit my wrists,' Phil muttered under his breath.

'Well that's that settled,' Becca said, getting up from the sofa. 'Let's go and get your stuff together, there's a train to London just after four.'

Phil hated playing mind chess with Becca; she was so much better at it than him. Maybe a few days in London wouldn't be so bad. It would be better than having Becca here with him, once she had her claws into him he'd never manage to shake her off. At least this way, after a few days he could slip away and go back to doing as he pleased.

He could hear Becca opening cupboards and drawers in his bedroom and he hurried up the stairs to try and wrestle back control of his packing. Having your sister rummaging through your undies drawer was against the natural order of life.

To get Becca out of his hair he sent her on an errand. He asked if she'd drop off the paracetamol at Mrs Emerson's and ask if she'd look after Mr Fish while he was away for a few days. With Becca out of the way Phil set to work putting stuff away that Becca had got out and doing his packing properly – the way he liked it done.

As he was zipping up his holdall, a thought occurred to him. He walked around the far side of the bed and opened the bedside cabinet. He felt around at the back and, finding what he was after, he pulled out the black Moleskine book and tucked it in his bag down underneath his clothes.

Four

Becca kicked off her heels and added them to an already untidy pile of shoes in the hall; she hung her keys on the hook in the little cupboard and then switched the kettle on.

'You can have the top room, it's all made up; you'll have your own bathroom, your own space up there,' Becca called from the kitchen. 'The boys are in Ireland with their Dad, so we'll have the place to ourselves.'

Phil felt a pang of guilt to add to the collection of other negative emotions he was stockpiling. He hadn't given them a second thought or even asked how they were. Normally he took great pride in his nephews; bought them generous presents, enjoyed talking to them and taking them on days out.

He arranged trips to theme parks; he loved all the stratospheric propulsion rides and all the bonding camaraderie that followed them. Phil let them eat all sorts of things that Becca wouldn't. He was a good uncle or at least he had been in the past.

It suddenly dawned on Phil that despite all his bluster and denials, he was actually in quite a bad way; there was barely room in his life for him, let alone concern for, empathy with or interest in anyone else. He knew the mechanics of getting straightened out; he just didn't have the energy or the motivation starting handle to get it going.

Becca poured the tea and spoke to Phil over her shoulder.

'Now tomorrow, we're meeting Sam and Fi for coffee at eleven, we're having lunch with Kitti and then I'm having my hair done at 3.00. I texted Nigel from the train and asked him to squeeze you in after me – okay?'

'I know you're trying to help… including me and that, but I'd rather stay here… You go. I'll be fine.'

'No way, mister. Welcome to Rebecca's rehab. If you're just going to mope around my house you may as well be in your own. No, you'll be joining in and coming with me.'

Phil did not have the strength to argue with his sister: he'd learnt that when she had one of those heads on, it was best not to.

'Now look I've started to draw up a few rules.'

Becca laid the sheet of notepaper on the counter

'I'm not one of your boys… you can't enforce discipline or behaviour change or whatever it is you're after through your own crappy ten commandments.'

'I've only got three so far, but I'm sure we could easily get to ten.'

Phil remembered her telling him about a parenting course she'd been on. Admittedly it had worked wonders on James when he'd been a bit… a bit… spirited was probably the word Phil would use to describe his nephew's early behaviour. James would have been highly prized in tribes of old, but in the new tribes of SW11 he needed some of his native Anglo Saxon tendencies tamed a little.

'Maybe rules isn't the right word. I just think it would help if we set a few boundaries – for me as much as for you and then we'd both know where we are.'

Becca rotated the page so Phil could read what she'd written so far.

'I need your input too…'

'It looks like you've done a pretty good job on your own.'

'If you don't agree we'll talk about them – scrub them if necessary. It's no good writing them down if we don't both agree to them. That won't work at all. So what do you think?'

Phil shrugged in a way that could be taken either way. Becca chose to take it as a sign of acceptance.

'Okay then, here's my first three for starters. Point one: No drinking alcohol in the day.'

'What is this a Friends Meeting House? I like a drink, I find it relaxes me – maybe I might want to talk a bit more about what's happened when I've got a drink or two on board, besides how are you going to manage not drinking for the whole time I'm here?'

'This is good, this is what it's all about.' Becca added an addendum to point one. 'Right how about - No drinking alcohol in the day except at mealtimes and in moderation?' Becca finished writing and turned, smiling at Phil. 'Doable?' she asked.

'Doable,' Phil smirked, already seeing ways to stretch the rules. Becca added a last bit to point one 'So that's - No drinking alcohol in the day except at mealtimes and in moderation excluding breakfast.'

That was that idea scuppered.

'I'm not having you putting Guinness on your Weetabix.' Becca quipped, before returning to her list. 'Point two: Exercise every day.'

'Yeah, I'm okay with that.'

'Point three: Sleep hygiene.'

'I've brought clean pyjamas if that's what you mean?'

'No – it means going to bed at a sensible time and getting up at a sensible time. Getting back into a regular sleep pattern.'

'Well yes – I'd like to, it's just that I wake early. I can't control when I wake up.'

'If you're getting enough exercise you should be tired enough to sleep through until six thirty at least.'

'Okay that sounds fine. Is that it? Just those three?' Phil started to wander off to the lounge with his tea

'No you have to say some for me.'

'Like what?'

'I don't know, I'd have thought you'd have a list as long as your arm: you've been pretty resistant so far to any suggestions I've made.'

'Right, okay. Here's one for you. No bullying.'

'I don't bully you Phil... I make suggestions... I strongly recommend, yes, bullying no.'

'You can write it how you like, but you know what I mean.' Becca paused with the pen to her lips while she found the right phrase. 'A discussive collaborative approach to all matters.' she said aloud as she wrote. 'Any more?'

'I think that's enough for now...'

'Oh I've got one more and that makes five. No buying any more crap from the shopping channel. Agreed?'

'Agreed,' Phil muttered, already halfway down the hallway.

They sat in silence and drank their tea on opposite sofas in Becca's lounge; a large teak spice chest acted as no man's land, dividing the two warring factions. Becca's attempt at a truce was to try a few open-ended questions to get him talking, but her amateur psychiatrist routine just served to irritate him, it was all too contrived and he'd instantly cut off each of her attempts. He'd said all he had to say on the subject on the train; he folded his arms slowly and deliberately while slouching back on the mountain of cushions.

Why so many bloody cushions? There was barely room for him, he felt like he was being swallowed alive. Forget UFOs - it was cushions that were taking over the world, or his world at least; they'd orchestrated a silent coup and his sister was part of the plot. It was the same with beds. His last girlfriend, Gillian - a cushion sympathiser - had brought the enemy into his house under cover of John Lewis carrier bags.

Large square cushions at the back by the headboard then two rectangular pillows with fancy stitched edges, then two more simpler designed rectangular pillows then a long bolster running the width of the bed and then three smaller, mismatched, square scatter cushions with tassels and embroidery. These were what Gillian called the accent colours - she used to work in Laura Ashley and apparently this made her an expert - on everything.

Anyhow, the end result was that almost half the bed was a cushion stronghold with very little room for sleeping or anything else for that matter. Maybe that was part of the great cushion master plan, occupying male territories and slowing down population growth through an upholstered barrier method of contraception - 'Don't, Phil, you'll spoil the cushions'.

There were no custodial arguments over the cushions when Gillian left. He had gladly packed them into the boot of her hatchback and quickly adjusted to a life free of plumping.

They'd reached stalemate and he was glad when Becca retreated to the kitchen to regroup. She'd led her horse to water but with the exception of his tea he was stubbornly refusing to drink. He could hear her annoyance expressed in the opening and slamming of the cupboards. She'd said she'd run all the food down as she couldn't decide until she'd seen Phil whether to bring him back to hers or if staying in Dorset for a few days would be enough to straighten him out.

She told him on the train that the minute he'd opened the door her mind was made up. In her view she needed to get him away, she said it would be hard for him to make a change, to break out of his spiral of decline while he was surrounded by constant reminders; framed covers from first editions, photos from book launches and one of Phil and Dave at some reunion or other. Most telling of all to Freud's apprentice was his computer; it sat untouched - she said she could have written a good opening chapter in the dust on the screen.

The banging and crashing had ceased in the kitchen, so Phil tiptoed into the hall on a reconnaissance mission. Becca was wearing her smug smile, she took a couple of soft tomatoes, half an onion and the remaining quarter of a slightly shrivelled red pepper out of Old Mother Hubbard's fridge. She wizzed them up in her blender with a bit of chilli powder and voila! - they were transformed into a spicy fresh salsa.

She rummaged through the snack basket - she was in luck, under the Hula Hoops and Quavers was a bag of tortilla chips. She spread them out on a baking sheet, heaped on the salsa and, having cut off the dried edges, grated over a hunk of nutty hard cheese - perhaps a little harder than the Italian producers had intended. She bunged the whole lot under the grill.

He knew all her tricks; she thought a Mexican inquisition would loosen his tongue. Phil returned to the sofa, he chucked some of the cushions over the back and made himself comfortable. He picked up a magazine from no man's land and flicked through it.

He recognised the covergirl as a news presenter from a satellite station, but he wasn't really interested in why Suzie Lucas loved living loft style. This should have told him all he needed to know - the magazine was an estate agent in paper form disguised as a metropolitan glossy. At least in paper form there were some plusses; no smug shiny suits, floppy fringes or annoying fleet of liveried cars cutting you up at every opportunity.

Phil persevered, flipping through page after page of house specs, if only so he could join in the inevitable forthcoming dinner party conversations about property prices. Becca had bought the house after her split from Dermot; it was a wreck and Dermot had put a few of his best guys on it to turn the peculiarly converted flats and bedsit back into a family house. Which was good of him considering he was no longer part of the family that would live in it.

Guilt graft Becca called it; working flat out to put the wrongs right. She didn't blame him, they'd both become so busy with their own businesses that they had little or no time for each other. It wasn't just her small shop between the launderette and the vacuum cleaner repair shop Becca had outgrown - it was Dermot too. Dermot had his hands full with his expanding property business and, by all accounts, Nancy his new office manager.

Becca was the first to admit they'd been living separate lives under the same roof for years and the natural progression was living different lives under different rooves. Piotr and his band of merry men took five months stripping out the plasterboard-partitioned rooms and chipped, barely enamelled baths.

The greasy, hessian-effect Formica cabinets in what the estate agents would have doubtless described as a compact, galley-style kitchenette were no more. The kitchen was now just a part of Becca's walk-in wardrobe and shoe closet.

Becca returned with her plated peace offering and Phil decided to cut her a bit of slack. He still wasn't in the mood for chatting and to fill the silence he flicked the TV on. He paused briefly over the shopping channel, but Becca shot him one of her well-practised looks and he continued trawling through the channels, finally settling for an American legal drama that they'd missed the beginning of.

Becca talked the whole way through, but he didn't mind; at least the spotlight was off him. She told him what her boys had been up to, about her shop and her planned trip to France. As the closing titles rolled, Phil gathered the plates and picked at the crunchy bits of melted cheese on the baking sheet. He yawned, setting Becca off.

'Me, too,' she said through the tail end of her yawn.

Phil was tired, not just of life, but proper sleepy tired - the guy delivering his 'Abs-a-glute home gym' had woken him from his mid morning nap and then Becca turning up had put the kybosh on his usual alcohol-induced siesta. His attempt at a crafty snooze in the bath she'd managed to turn into a drama; an early night was just what he needed. As he climbed the stairs, he glanced back through the banisters to see Becca beginning her online shop.

Once Becca heard him open the door to the top room she quickly logged into her email.

Hi Mum,

Phil's here with me. You were right. Danuta's away and as you suspected Phil's place was a complete tip - I did all the jobs you suggested including the fridge - so hopefully not too horrible a welcome for Danuta when she returns.

Thanks for your kind offer to come and help me out, but let's see how it goes - let's not call on the cavalry until we need them! Besides I'm sure you have your hands full with the WI flower show just days away. I think your arrangement in the ballet shoes sounds lovely.

Get Dad to send me a pic on his phone - tell him not to be so stingy - I'll give him the pound next time I see him! I'll call you to find out how it all went.

Sorry to hear about old Mr Clements, still as you say he'd had a good innings at 85. I'll pop a card in the post to Audrey.

Send my love to Dad

Love

Rebecca xx

PS Phil will be fine, don't worry - I am my mother's daughter!

The last line made her cringe, but there was no denying it. Besides, having her mum here telling her what to do and then Becca telling Phil what to do was not a successful line of command. No, she was in charge and was confident she could sort this out. Becca pressed send and returned to her shopping. She started methodically planning menus for the week ahead and then gave up and clicked repeat last shop before heading off to bed.

The top room looked like a shot from an interiors magazine. It was decorated in 101 shades - all of them cream. Room 101 he mused, how appropriate. Phil turned round and round trying to find somewhere to unpack his bag without disturbing the consciously styled and carefully arranged still lifes dotted around the room. A cluster of old family photos in silver frames here, a stack of travel photography books there.

He was amazed at how many versions of the same colour it was possible to have in one room, but it worked; it was calm and peaceful, just what he needed. The chunky antique cream, wooden lamp bases with cream shades, on either side of the ivory cream French sleigh bed looked like the kind of things Becca sold in her shop.

The en suite was also a cream fest, tiled floor to ceiling in chalky cream limestone. He put his wash bag on the shelf, took out his toothbrush and gave his teeth a thorough scrub, causing his gums to bleed. Like one brush could make up for all those weeks of neglect. It had been a long tiring day and tomorrow sounded even more exhausting. He took off his clothes and threw them across the room. His shirt caught on the brocade chair and a sock dangled from the table lamp. Now it looked more like home.

Sleep, lovely sleep – it was so underrated he thought - a great escape: an escape from all those expectations, an escape from disappointment, an escape from being him.

He was wide-awake as usual at 3.00am. He went to the loo and then snuggled back under the covers. He lay on his left side for a bit, but couldn't drift off. He plumped up his pillows and turned them over so they were nice and cool against his head and tried lying on his right side. He lay still but his mind was racing, going back over the events of the previous day and working out how and when he could escape from Becca. He rolled on to his back and after what seemed like another hour he finally went back to sleep.

It felt as if barely five minutes had passed; Becca placed a cup of tea on the chest next to the bed and slid back the blinds to the piercing white light of early morning.

'Rise and shine, it's quarter to seven.'

Phil groaned and pulled the covers up over his head, blocking out the light and trying hard to deny the existence of the real world.

'Here's your tracksuit and tee shirt. They're clean, washed and tumbled overnight. Get them on, we're leaving in ten. We'll cycle to the gym. You can borrow James' bike.'

'And why would I want to do that?' mumbled Phil from under the duvet mound.

'Sorry, I forgot to mention it. You and I are doing a class.' Becca called, cheerily opening the blinds on the other side of the room.

'Do I have to?' Phil grumbled with teenager-like defiance.

'No, you don't have to. But if you don't, I'll give Mum and Dad a call and they can come and pick you up,' Becca checked her watch and screwed up her eyes like she was actually trying to work out the timings. 'If they leave now they should have you home in time for lunch.'

Phil groaned again and sat up, grumpily beating his pillows into shape, imagining they were his annoying younger sibling.

'You can't keep using that... What about rule four - no bullying, collaborative discussion thingy.'

'Ah yes, but may I draw your attention to points two and three.' Becca pulled the folded piece of paper from her pocket with a flourish and shook it open. 'Exercise every day and sleep hygiene.'

Becca always knew which pressure points to push to persuade Phil to do exactly what she wanted. She ignored his protest and carried on.

'I haven't booked, but if we're there early enough we should get into the spinning class.'

'Spinning?' Phil asked vacantly.

'Have you ever done spinning?' Becca asked, picking up and folding Phil's strewn clothes.

'No, but I once made a nice macramé hanging plant holder.'

'It's a cycling class Phil. You do it on exercise bikes to music.'

'Oh deep joy. No chance of me pricking my finger and going back to sleep then?'

'No chance. Now, drink your tea and I'll see you downstairs.

Becca handed Phil a Mickey Mouse keyring and he unlocked the boys' bikes from the railings at the front of the house. Phil stood sizing up the bike, looking for any excuse to avoid the gym.

'If you put the saddle up it should be fine, or if you prefer you could use mine.' Becca said with a smile as she wheeled her bike out the bin cupboard.

'My god what have you done to it. It looks like it's been pimped by Barbie.'

Becca's mountain bike had always been a retina-burning shade of pink, but in addition to that it had a few other customised extras that Phil felt sure had not come from Halfords. The central frame was wrapped in mini fairy lights and from the ends of the handlebars fluttered pink metallic streamers like the kind his mum draped from the branches of her Christmas tree.

To finish there was a Union flag in shades of pink on a pole attached to the pannier rack. Phil couldn't help thinking that the bin cupboard was a perfect home for it.

'I'll take that as a no then, shall I?'

'What were you thinking? I can't believe that a woman so obsessed with how everything looks is harbouring a bike that looks like it's got a bad case of tinselitis.'

'It was for the night ride that Fi and I did last month. I sent you my 'Just Giving' link which you ignored. Another black mark in the big book of bothersome brothers, Phil thought.

'You know it's the 'bike to beat breast cancer' thing. Everyone jazzes up their bike, it's a bit of fun. If you think mine's bad you should have seen Fi's. She had a pink flamingo with demonic flashing eyes on the back of hers. It seemed a bit of a shame to take it all apart, especially after James spent such a long time getting the fairy lights to work on the dynamo.'

'I shall be cycling at a polite distance behind you if that's okay?' Phil muttered, making a show of checking the tension of the chain.

'Don't you know pink is the new dayglo yellow.'

'All I know is I wouldn't be seen dead on that heap.'

'Try any more delaying tactics and I might arrange it. Come on, let's get going.' And with that, Becca pushed off with the banner of blushing patriotism waving gently behind her.

Result. Fortunately the spinning class was full. The leisurely cycle to the gym had been quite enough for Phil. The thought of pedalling like mad and getting nowhere was a bit too close an analogy to his own life for his liking.

'And where do you think you're going?' Becca put a firm restraining hand on his shoulder.

'It's full so…'

'So – we'll do another class.'

Phil slumped down on a sofa and tried to lip-read the silent Sky News anchorman; it was all about Cameron and Clegg – the Westminster Morecambe and Wise show. Becca, having booked them in, went to pick up towels and locker keys.

Gyms had a very distinctive smell; they were up there with hospitals, schools and vets. The studio had a unique rubbery, sweaty smell and, despite being somewhere where people obviously got very hot, it was goose-pimply cold. Phil was happy lurking at the back of the room, but Becca, blaming her small stature, said she couldn't see and steered him to the front row.

In one seamless movement, Becca had transformed her shoulder-length curls into a tidy pleat and secured it with a clip. Phil was surprised at how something so simple could make her look so different. He always looked the same whatever he was doing – he'd never thought about adapting his appearance for different situations except maybe in the case of camouflage, but that wasn't really appropriate for everyday life.

Becca wouldn't dream of crossing her threshold without her skilfully applied trusty mascara and lipstick. She said she didn't feel herself until she was wearing it and that Phil was one of a select few people to have seen her without her make-up. He sort of got it - it was a major thing for Becca to show herself without any barriers up; for Phil to see the unenhanced Becca, to see her as herself and not to judge her or reject her was a big deal or it was a big deal to Becca at least.

Without his running partner, Phil had lost interest in his regular 10k cross-country jaunts. It just wasn't the same without Dave, it felt wrong. He was a bit out of shape at the moment, but Phil was no stranger to exercise; swimming fully clothed across rivers in the Malaysian jungle, night hikes with full kit on in the Brecon Beacons and more press-ups than he cared to think about. This would be a doddle.

The tall blonde instructor took her place on the raised stage, switched on her mic and the class began. Warm up – fine. It was pretty basic; he'd done similar kinds of stuff before. But just as he was starting to feel confident, Kylie kicked in and he was exiled from his comfort zone: mambo, speed skater, monkey arms and speedbag.

The svelte Nordic instructor called the moves, but she may as well have been speaking Swahili. Phil had no idea what he was supposed to be doing; for the other yummy mummies, it appeared that Swahili was their mother tongue and they performed the moves with balletic grace.

In synchronised fashion, the whole class went left. Phil went right. The whole class went forward. Phil went back. When they were stretching high, he was bending low. When they were rotating to the back, he was facing the front. Phil had to endure seeing the whole sorry fifty minutes of uncoordinated humiliation reflected back off every wall of the studio.

During the cool down, Phil took the opportunity to apologise to every foot he'd trodden on and every arm and leg he'd collided with. By the end he'd spoken to everyone in the class. No one seemed to mind, they were a friendly bunch; they smiled encouragingly and said how brave they thought he was for having a go.

At the end of the class Becca sat on the floor and took a swig of water and watched with bemusement while the other girls buzzed around Phil. Liv, the instructor, eagerly showed Phil some of the moves he was confused about; a demonstration which, Becca felt, involved a lot of excessive body contact. Others confided they wished they could persuade their boyfriends or husbands to do a class.

Just when Becca thought she might have to throw the remainder of her water over them to break up Phil's fan club, the girls waved goodbye and made a buoyant exit from the studio.

'What…?' Phil asked seeing the look of amused accusation on his sister's face.

'I've been coming to this class for six months and the most I get is a faint smile or a quiet hello. You arrive… you behave like a bull in a china shop and suddenly you're top dog. At one point I thought I was going to have to beat them off with a Theraband.'

Phil smiled and briefly Becca saw a flash of her carefree brother, the one she knew was still in there somewhere, lurking beneath the surface buried beneath his woes, worries and wrinkles. He's still in there, she thought - don't worry I'm coming for you.

Five

Becca introduced Phil to Sam and Fi; he misread their body language and there was an awkward moment when he opted for a clumsy handshake while cheeks were proffered instead. Fi laughed it off by making a remark about never wanting to miss an opportunity for a kiss with a real action man and that she'd always fancied herself as a forces sweetheart. After placing their order they took their seats at a table in the corner.

Phil had never seen a linen teabag before; it really was a different world round here. It looked more like the kind of thing he remembered his mum having in her smalls drawer to keep the moths at bay and the contents were more like the kind of thing his dad put in his pipe. Fi had spotted him surreptitiously sniffing it; he popped it into the pot quickly without any more fuss and zoned out while he sipped his Lapsang Souchong.

He hadn't had it before, but was seduced by its exotic name. Its smoky taste reminded him of his training and the very distinct flavour that infused everything cooked on an open fire. It was a world away from the one he now found himself inhabiting. The tea was not unpleasant, but not what he wanted from a cuppa either. If he fancied smoky he'd plump for a bacon sandwich every time, washed down by a mug of good honest PG Tips.

Becca had given him a quick debrief on their way to the café; she knew Sam as their boys were in the same class at school and she'd met Fi through her book group where they'd hit it off instantly. Both Sam and Fi worked; Sam four days a week as a sales rep and Fi as a freelance journalist, so they understood the pressures of the working mum. They helped each other out when one or others' plates stopped spinning: drop offs, pick ups and sleepovers – the kind of things that their boys thought were fun, yet also managed to assuage a mother's guilt for not being around when she thought she should be.

The whole support network thing was instinctive with Becca's friends; helping each other out, anticipating a need and offering support came naturally. For Phil it had taken him six months of counselling to realise that asking for help wasn't a sign of weakness. Being honest, dropping his bravado had allowed his mates to open up. It made him feel less isolated knowing that all his mates were in the same boat – even if the boat in question was the Titanic.

It had changed his and Dave's friendship; it had made it stronger, less superficial. Dave had still taken the piss out of him and called him a 'softy southerner' but when they needed to, they could talk. No more burying his feelings, no more keeping it all inside. But for all that, when Phil had fallen there was no safety net; now Becca was lending him hers - he was just glad no sequined leotard was required.

Fi was a great laugh; ten minutes in her company was a real tonic. Becca hoped the 'Fi factor' might help lift Phil's spirits. Her larger-than-life personality was matched only by her waistline. Her humour was often at her own expense and she was never short of a sharp one-liner.

Becca, Sam and Fi chatted about their kids, their husbands and some new eye cream that even Phil thought sounded pretty impressive. They were very at home in each other's company; they could talk openly and easily about things that he and his mates would take several hours and many beers to skate around the edges of.

In the past, when he'd returned home from a boy's night out, he'd face a barrage of questions from his girlfriend at the time. How was so-and-so coping with: their mum's death? Their wife's breast cancer scare? Their teen daughter's pregnancy? His answer to all these questions was – "we didn't talk about that". He now understood why his girlfriends were so incredulous and he began to wonder what he'd spent all those wasted (in every sense) evenings talking about.

He felt like an eavesdropper, but the girls didn't seem to mind him being there in the least. They only referred to him as 'present company excluded' when they were complaining about men: their bosses, their sons, their husbands and dads. When it came to who was to blame for the various ills of the world it was spread pretty evenly spread between them.

Fi talked about how difficult it was to have a proper conversation with her eldest teenage son and that the more she tried to connect with him the more distant he became. At last here was a topic Phil thought he could contribute to.

'It might be psychobabble, but when I was having counselling we talked about relationships and in particular why mine always seemed to follow a similar, self-destructive pattern. Mark, my counsellor, seemed to think a lot of it stemmed from miscommunication. I didn't really pay too much attention to his theory, but listening to you chatting makes me think that there may be something to it.'

Becca, Sam and Fi were staring at Phil like they'd forgotten he was there. Phil wasn't sure if he'd overstepped the mark by joining in; maybe his role was passive bystander. Fi finally broke the silence.

'Okay then Freud, spill the beans. I'm all ears... well actually I'm all hips and arse, but what can a girl do...'

'I'm trying to remember exactly… but it was something like women trade their troubles with their girlfriends and it brings them closer through sharing problems. But if they try and do this with their men, instead of making a connection and bringing them closer men just see it as complaining and distance themselves and tune out.'

'D'you know that's exactly what happens,' Fi said, nibbling on a shortbread finger. 'I tell Jon about my day in the hope that he'll trade something and tell me something that happened at school, but he doesn't and so I keep talking and talking and eventually he just glazes over.'

'It's not just Jon that does that Fi,' Becca smiled and did a slow exaggerated yawn.

Fi ignored her and continued. 'So did this Mark guy make any useful suggestions of what to do?'

'I don't know how useful they are, but at least I understood that when a girlfriend was telling me all her worries that she was just reaching out, trying to get closer to me. So instead of trying to find solutions for her like I used to, and getting cross when she didn't try any of them, I would just listen – listen properly. You know, real listening like you girls do, eye contact, nodding, complete attention and all that.'

'He's lovely your brother, isn't he – can I take him home?'

'No Fi put him down.'

'Yeah that makes sense, but what should I do about Jon?'

'Well, I have no idea whether this works, but according to Mark men talk best when they're in the parallel position.'

'Sounds like something out of the Kama Sutra.'

Phil paid no attention to Fi's aside, but the girls all fell about.

'What it means is not face to face, no eye contact. It's too challenging, too confrontational. And I guess if you think about places where men like to talk; standing at the bar; on football terraces and strolling side by side on golf courses it seems to bear out Mark's thinking.'

'Well I'm definitely going to give that a go - thanks Phil.'

'It doesn't work in all situations, but I don't imagine you spend much time at the gents' urinal.'

'The stories I could tell…' Fi winked '…another time Phil.'

The conversation moved on and Phil slipped back into passive observer role. There was a little school gate gossip about goings-on that according to Becca and her friends didn't ought to be going on; it seemed to Phil that the marriages of the betwixt the commons couples would be much improved without the special attentions of tennis coaches and Pilates instructors; briefly he wondered if retraining to teach Pilates or tennis might be an option he should consider.

When the last of the foam from the cappuccinos had congealed around the rims of the cups, it was time to go. After the others had gone their separate ways, Becca left Phil sitting in the sun outside the café and popped along to her shop to see if a delivery of china she was expecting had arrived.

Anything that distracted his sister's attention away from him, he was all for. She'd told the girls of her irritation with her stock deliveries over coffee. The china was probably held up in customs. All the uncertainty was driving her mad and it seemed to be getting worse and worse. She'd decided that rather than just putting in an order and hoping it hit the scheduled delivery date that she would go on a buying trip to France.

She'd said it would be good to meet her suppliers face to face; she might even be able to get a better deal. Becca's plan was to hire a van, load it up with as much stock as she could, bring it back herself and cut out the constant shipping nightmare.

She walked back to the café where Phil was staring trance-like at the window display in the lingerie shop opposite. He jumped when she spoke, rousing him from his hypnotic state.

'Remind me - I need to go in there on the way back. The place we're going to at the weekend is really smart; I need to get a new bikini. You can help me choose if you like.'

'I can't wait.' Phil grumbled, dragging his heels after Becca.

Becca chatted as they strolled down the hill; Phil wasn't listening; he was puzzling over something. He knew a transvestite was a man who liked to dress as a woman and a transsexual is a woman trapped in a man's body or vice versa. He, however, was a man in a man's body trapped in the life of his sister. Did that make him a trans-sister he wondered? This strange line of thought was curtailed by their arrival at the restaurant.

Kitti was already there and was sitting at a table outside under the shade of the canopy. He liked Kitti. She was pretty and fun; a very striking blend of her British Mum and her Indian Dad. Kitti was one of Becca's oldest friends, he'd met her quite a few times and they'd had many a drunken encounter over the years. He'd even snogged her at midnight on millennium night - standing on the Embankment opposite the Houses of Parliament. As the spectacle of fireworks exploded in the sky above Westminster, some were also going off in his trousers.

The following day Kitti went home and Phil went back to Dorset. It was nothing... just everyone getting caught up in the emotion of the moment. It was natural wanting someone to share and remember that moment with - that was all it was.

When the much-hyped millennium bug didn't bite he was gutted. He'd been banking on it. If the computer systems went down, it meant no trains. And no trains meant no travelling back with a hangover that was so massive, it spanned happy hour in one century and last orders in another.

Unlike coffee, where he was pretty much ignored, Kitti was interested; she wanted to talk to him and listen to his story. He hadn't really talked to anyone about it; just a few things to Becca, but not in a joined-up conversation sort of way. Saying it out loud made it real. If it was real, then he'd feel he had to do something and then he'd have to decide what that something was and then he'd have to do it. That scared him.

But this didn't feel scary: he felt relaxed, no pressure, no judgements. He told her the whole story; after all he was good at telling stories and they in turn were good listeners. He even did some of the voices as he relived the conversations - Simon's clipped BBC World Service accent and Mal's afternoon DJ chummy over-familiar patter.

She made all the right noises, she didn't tell him what to do or what she'd do if she were him - she just listened and he was grateful. In return, she tried to make him laugh by telling a few anecdotes about Jachim. How he'd drunk her Mum's G&T down in one, thinking it was lemonade and then slept right through to 9.30 the next morning.

And how one of the nursery teachers had taken her to one side for a private word and told her that at their show-and-tell session Jachim had announced very matter-of-factly 'There was a man with a very big willy in my Mummy's shower this morning.'

'It sounds scandalous,' Kitty chuckled. 'But the disappointing truth of the matter is, I'd called a plumber out to try and sort the water pressure in my shower. Jachim walked in on him while he was using the loo.'

Kitti was clearly enjoying her new reputation.

'I've seen the girls at the nursery giggling when they think I'm not looking and I've had knowing looks from some of the other mums; I certainly seem to have moved up in their estimation.'

A waiter took their order and returned shortly with a bottle of ice-cold Soave. They chinked glasses and with great enthusiasm, Kitti did her usual toast. 'Tulleeho!' She'd explained it to Phil on several occasions, but usually after he was a little the worse for wear. From what he could remember it was a kind of hybrid of the old hunting cry Tally Ho! and tullee, the Hindi word for drinking.

Over lunch, they moved on to practical matters. Becca checked with Kitti on her childcare arrangements for their girlie weekend and they swapped notes on what clothes they were taking and what treatments they'd booked.

'Are you coming Phil?' Kitty asked. Phil had his mouthful so Becca answered for him.

'No, I've said he can have a quiet weekend house sitting. Fi booked the hotel ages ago and it was quite full then so I doubt we'd get another room at this late stage.'

Even with his mouth full, he managed to smirk. He had other plans. He'd be as good as his word and have a quiet time on Saturday; he'd get a curry and a few beers in and watch the rugby. And then on Sunday before Becca returned he'd pack up his things and slip away. If she was lucky he might even do the washing up. He'd return home and go back to doing just as he pleased without his bossy boots sister on his case the whole time. It was his great escape and the best part of it was, no digging or tunnelling was required.

After living on takeaways for the last few weeks, Phil was rediscovering real food again and savouring every mouthful. Reliving the last couple of months had made him hungry. He made light work of his warm chicken salad, mopping up the yolk from the poached egg with the rosemary focaccia, leaving a sparklingly clean plate.

As they were finishing their coffee, a petite lady in a tailored shift dress, with large dark shades pushed up and resting on top of her razor-sharp bob, interrupted their conversation. She leaned through the box hedging that enclosed the outside dining area and tapped Kitti pointedly on the shoulder.

'Oh... hi Aurore, how are you?' Kitti stammered in surprise as if she'd been caught doing something she oughtn't to be.

Ignoring any pleasantries, Aurore abruptly ploughed on, blanking both Phil and Becca.

'Do you know where we are meeting for ze book group? Fi said she'd let me know, but she azn't...' Her irritation with Fi's relaxed approach to arrangements was clear in Aurore's pinched, pained expression. The truth was more likely that Fi was trying to avoid telling Aurore.

'Er... Sam's I think... at eight. Shall I check the date and let you know?' Kitti asked placatingly, obviously hoping that she too could somehow prevent Aurore from coming.

'No, I'll call Sam myself,' Aurore said tersely. 'I wouldn't want to put you to any trouble. I'll see you zere.'

Without another word, Aurore turned on her kitten heels and clicked off along the road.

'Oh no! Who invited her?' moaned Becca when Aurore was safely out of earshot.

'She invited herself,' Kitti said resignedly. 'She said a book group would be good for her English.'

'There's nothing wrong with her English; it's her social skills she needs to work on,' replied Becca, scribbling in the air to one of the waiters.

'I know she comes across as a bit rude, but I don't think she means anything by it, it's just the Parisienne way.'

Kitti's natural inclination was always to look for the best in everyone. Phil could see Becca thought she'd need to look very hard in Aurore's case.

'You know, the mums in Fi's class call her Horror,' Becca said warming to her theme. 'I have to stop and think now when I'm talking to her; I know it's going to slip out one of these days.'

'I'm sure she wouldn't even notice.' Kitti said, amused by Becca's animated indignation.

'You're right, she's always so focussed on whatever it is she wants, she doesn't really listen,' Becca griped.

'She seemed all right to me – a bit uptight maybe…' said Phil trying to be even-handed and add some balance to the one- sided slating.

Phil could recall numerous occasions when Becca had taken an instant dislike to someone, only for them to become the best of friends some time later.

'Oh Phil… you don't know the half of it,' Becca bristled. 'She's so rude… she's manipulative and competitive; look how she just ignored us while barging in on our lunch.'

'Okay… I'm all ears,' Phil sat back with his arms folded. 'Tell me what makes her such a bad person; we're all different you know. Not everyone is like you…'

'Thank God I'm nothing like her, that's all I can say,'

Becca paused while she chose some examples that best illustrated the horror of Aurore.

'Okay… here's one for starters – last term she complained continuously until her daughter got a main part in the school play. Little Amity's teacher tried to explain that they like to share the parts around and that Amity did have a main role in an earlier show; Aurore just bulldozes them, I think they're scared of her,' Becca laid out her evidence as if presenting the case for the prosecution. 'And she knobbled the photographer taking pictures for the school prospectus to make sure photos of Amity were in it.'

'If I recall correctly didn't she enter a cake into the school fête competition that she'd bought from the bakery?' Kitti added.

'Oh yes that was classic Aurore,' Becca exclaimed, grateful for a little back up. 'The woman has no shame. The year before she stole the winning entry into the 'how many things can you fit in a match box' – actually Phil, it was the one you helped Dan with. Anyhow, the following year she added a couple more things then entered it in Amity's name…'

'These are hardly crimes of the century Becca, I think you need to keep things in perspective. I thought you'd moved to London to escape the… now what did you call it? Ah yes, the petty small town small-mindedness.'

Phil didn't really care two hoots about Aurore or what she'd done, but he did care about Becca's bossy, controlling behaviour and he couldn't resist the opportunity to try and put her in her place, but as was often the case with Becca he was fighting a losing battle.

'You're right, Phil.' Becca had her self-righteous pointy finger out and was jabbing it in the air for added emphasis. 'All these things are stupid, petty and pointless, but they're not stupid, petty and pointless to Aurore – they matter and they matter a lot and that's what gets me.'

'Let it go sis' let it go…'

Becca ignored Phil and continued. 'I couldn't believe this, but apparently it's true; she wore running spikes in the parents' race at sports day – I could go on…'

'No no, I get the picture.' Phil raised his hands in defeat. She'd beaten him into submission.

Becca, like a dog with a bone, wasn't ready to let go yet.

'These are all small things, but put them all together and you get a sense of what she's like – she has a completely different set of morals from most people, she doesn't care who she steps on, all she cares about is getting what she wants. The only time she talks to me is when she wants a discount on something from the shop. She comes in all chitty-chatty, smiles and charm, "Zis is such a beautiful shop, you have exquisite taste, what a lovely vase" and then, without the blink of an eye – "can you do a special price for a friend?" The rest of the time I don't exist; I'm of no use to her.'

Becca finally ran out of steam, but the thought of Aurore gate-crashing their book group clearly continued to irk her.

'Have you read the book?' Kitti asked, hoping to change the subject and lighten the mood.

'I haven't even started it, but I thought there would be lots of time for reading while we're away.' Becca replied, punching her pin number into the handset.

'That's a good idea; I must remember to pack it.' Kitti said gathering her handbag and cardigan from the back of the chair.

Roll on Sunday, Phil thought.

Six

Becca returned home looking amazing.

'Nigel's ready for you now, I've paid so you don't need your wallet. And to tell you the truth, it's probably safer if you leave it here. Don't let him give you any of his blarney. I've told him you're feeling a bit down and it would be just like him to take advantage and try and sell you their entire haircare range. Nigel thinks hairdressers are therapists and that a new haircut is better than any antidepressant.'

Nigel's salon was all wall-to-ceiling mirrors, curvy sleek white gloss furniture and etched-glass partitions. Ella Fitzgerald was singing her heart out competing for air time over the hair dryers and the spluttering espresso machine as refreshments for pre-coiffed customers were whipped up in a trice.

Phil sat on a white leather sofa opposite a massive glass tank that acted as a partition between the waiting area and the rest of the salon. A small plaque read "Our chameleons Bert and Ernie live here". Phil looked hard but thought they must be pretty damn good at the whole camouflage thing as he couldn't spot them.

All he could make out between the lush foliage of hibiscus and fig were the ladies of SW11 emptying the contents of their purses into Nigel's coffers.

Phil envied the chameleon's gift for blending in; everywhere he'd been since he'd arrived at Becca's made him feel as if he stood out like a sore thumb. Phil gave up on the chameleon safari and turned his attention to the glass shelving next to him; suspended from the ceiling by tension wires. The shelves were packed with brightly coloured bottles and tubes with wacky names and typography.

In his local barbers, the most exotic things were a box of styptic pencils and the cracked woodgrain-look Lino, its edges curled with age revealing a coarse underlay of old hair clippings. For a man who'd had a lifetime of army haircuts; this was not his world.

Phil picked up a magazine and flicked through it. It was full of tips for luxe living and glammed-up readers who'd been given a WAG-over. Celebrities he'd never heard of were given a complete slating for committing unforgivable fashion faux pas: wearing canary yellow when it was yolky yellow that was clearly on-trend or wearing heels when any fashionista worth their salt knew that flats were the new heels. Phil found it exhausting and he wasn't even attempting to keep up.

It did explain why his previous girlfriends were on some kind of fashion treadmill; buying more and more clothes when he thought they had wardrobes packed with stuff they looked beautiful in. He told them, but they didn't listen to him and now he could see why. Their paranoia of falling behind and becoming out of touch was fuelled by this kind of tat.

There has always been a pressure on women to try and compete with the ludicrously unobtainable images portrayed in women's magazines. Yet this new breed of magazine juxtaposed the usual fake, Photoshopped flawless shots alongside what they presented as a freak show of real-life images, such as a celeb snapped on a beach revelling in her crepey tummy not yet returned to its washboard-flat previous condition after the recent birth of baby Idaho.

What was on-trend and what was not seemed to change at an alarming speed. A spread on "hot bikini buys" was preceded by "what's in, what's not" stating that "all-in-one cossies" were in and bikinis were out. You had to read this magazine quickly as what was on-trend at the beginning of the magazine could well be out, in the turn of a page.

It was mad; stupidly expensive dresses were justified by bizarre financial arguments breaking the cost down by each opportunity to wear, making a £550 dress a real investment. Did anyone believe this crap? Sadly, he knew they did.

That said, he liked the trick of breaking down a big financial outlay into small user amounts. It would definitely be worth a try if he ever needed to justify his spending to a girlfriend in the future. And if Becca really was going to make him help her choose swimwear, this info would be very useful.

He was halfway through an article about a soap star's eating disorder when a commotion broke out in the salon. A petite woman with her back to Phil was berating a stylist and shouting and the young girl whose hair she was just finishing cutting was sitting staring passively ahead into the mirror. 'What 'ave you done? I said a trim…'

Even Bert and Ernie had come out of hiding to see what was going on. Phil slid along the sofa so he had a clearer view of the action. It was slightly surreal watching it all kick off set to the soundtrack of Ella's 's wonderful, which for the woman and her daughter it clearly wasn't.

'It's a pixie cut, it's very fashionable...' Explained the stylist defensively reaching for a picture torn from a magazine. 'Amity gave me this picture and said that's what she wanted.'

The woman swung around to look at her daughter and Phil recognized her instantly as the woman he'd met at lunch –Aurore.

'When she's paying she can choose whatever style she wants, but when I'm paying she 'az what I say… You'd take the word of a child over mine. I shan't pay -

I'm not paying for zis. I'm not paying for somesing zat's not what I asked for. I said quite clearly a trim…'

All the customers were pretending not to look but were discreetly following all the action in Panavision courtesy of the 360^0 salon mirrors.

A tall, tanned, bald man dressed in black left his customer semi-rollered and came to smooth things out. Phil assumed he was Nigel.

'I can see there's been a terrible misunderstanding here. We pride ourselves on exceeding customer expectations and I can see quite clearly that on this occasion we have failed. Of course you must have this one on the house…'

Nigel gestured for the stylist to take over where he'd left off with his customer. Phil couldn't swear to it, but he thought he saw Aurore wink at Amity.

'But, as I say to all my ladies, the great thing about hair is, it always grows back, which is good news for me or I'd be out of business.' Nigel laughed, but Aurore just looked at him deadpan. 'Now as a gesture of goodwill and because we value your custom, why not take a couple of our salon products with our compliments?' Nigel gestured towards the glass shelving - Phil slid back along the sofa out of view.

'It's not going to make it grow back any quicker, but zat would be good wouldn't it Amity?' The girl nodded silently.

'Help yourselves to a couple of bottles – a shampoo and conditioner or a sculpting putty and an anti frizz oil.'

Aurore gave Nigel one of her well-practised hard stares for the impertinence of suggesting she had need of such a product. Nigel was relieved when he was called away to deal with a burning smell coming from the hairdryer of his now fully rollered customer.

Aurore ushered her daughter out of the salon and told her to wait outside while she made her selection of freebies. As she sorted through all the bottles, tubes and pots she trod on Phil's foot without any recognition or apology. As she slid all the products around on the shelf, a large tub of something called 'Luscious Locks' rolled off and hit Phil on the shoulder.

'Ow!' Phil looked at Aurore but she carried on oblivious. He picked the tub up off the floor. 'Is this yours?'

Aurore took the tub from him without a word, she turned it over in her hands, studying the label, before dropping it into her copious Hermes handbag. Aurore carried on picking through the products before casting a furtive glance around the salon. Spotting that everyone was busy she picked another five bottles and tubes off the shelf and dropped them casually into her bag before calmly walking away.

One of the young girls in high, strappy shoes and a canary yellow blouse with a big bow arrived. She held a gown up for him to slip into. Canary yellow? Oh dear, she was already on the slippery slope. She really was losing it. Her boyfriend would dump her, her friends disown her and she'd live the rest of her life in frumpy purgatory. If only she'd read "Fascino", she'd know that yolky was the new canary.

She showed him to a seat, offered him a drink and told him that Nigel would be with him shortly. Nigel appeared completely unfazed by the earlier fracas. Instead of the traditional handshake greeting, Nigel went straight for his hair, grabbing a handful, holding it up and then gently letting it fall through his fingers.

'I've got some ideas of what we could do with this; lose some of this weight on top, cut in some layers here and I love the beard. It looks good on you, but we'll tidy it up, make it a bit less Bill Oddie - more Jude Law. Sound good?' Nigel trilled in his soft southern Irish brogue.

Phil nodded. He had no idea what he'd just agreed to, but it needed cutting and if he really hated it, in a couple of zooms of the clippers he could revert to his trusty soldier style.

'Right, let's get this washed then we can crack on with the new you.'

Phil laid back and studied the large map of the world on the ceiling above the basins. Most of Nigel's customers would be looking at it and mentally putting little flags in the territories they'd conquered, while also searching for new and more exotic holiday destinations. For him, he was studying it and counting the places where he'd been engaged in close-quarters battle. He'd got into double figures when the towel drying his hair fell over his eyes and blocked his view.

He was guided back to the chair where he sat while Nigel scooted backwards and forwards on a stool on wheels.

'So, Becca says you're not writing at the moment?' snip-snipped Nigel. 'If you've run out of material, I could help you there. You wouldn't believe some of the things I hear in here. Some of them treat it like confessional where you can get a nice French manicure. I think the Pope's missing a trick…'

Nigel went on indiscreetly telling Phil about the goings-on he'd heard about.

'Now, I can't name names but one lady who comes in here, her husband's a cameraman for porn films. You'd never guess it to look at her – she's got lovely auburn hair – I didn't like to ask how they'd met...'

The person staring back at Phil in the mirror did not look like him at all. Well it did and it didn't. It looked like a younger, more confident and fashionable version of him. The hairdryer was on, which although an irritating drone, wasn't half as irritating as the drone emitting from Nigel.

The dryer completely drowned him out but still he continued chatting away while he teased, wound and smoothed Phil's hair into place. He clicked the dryer off and fitted it back into the holder behind the mirror.

'… and that's why she left him. Now he's gone to Thailand to have the op.'

Nigel flipped open the lid of a tube and squeezed some pale green gunk on to his palm. He rubbed them together and then roughly ran his fingers through Phil's hair, before doing his final smooth and groom finishing touches.

Phil wondered if he should mention Aurore's light-fingered antics. His general rule was to keep schtum, not to get involved, besides Nigel hadn't stopped to draw breath and was still talking nineteen to the dozen.

One thing was for sure he wouldn't mention it to Becca; he couldn't face another of her rants. His plan was to stay for as few days as possible with as little confrontation as possible – he'd go along with Becca's scheme for a few days, he understood she needed to feel she'd done her thing and then he was out of there.

When she heard the key in the lock, Becca hurried along the landing and came to stand at the top of the stairs.

'Wow! Look at you. He's good Nigel; he's very good. If you weren't my brother, I'd give you one.'

'It feels strange… I don't feel like me.' Phil ran his fingers through the sides of his hair.

'You haven't felt like you for ages. How you feel now, this is the new you,' Becca said encouragingly.

'I like it, I'm just not sure I can live up to it,' Phil said, gazing at the stranger in the hall mirror.

'Of course you can, you're my brother,' she said, dismissing his doubts once and for all. 'Now look… serious question - I've spared you the bikini shopping, but which one do you think?'

Becca was modelling a small halter neck in blue and green and holding up a one-piece in rusty browns and oranges.

'The one you're wearing looks great, but that other one is much more on-trend…'

'Sorted, I'll slip this off and take it back.'

Phil could not believe he'd just had that conversation, what was happening to him? He was a man. He talked about men's things: football, beer, electronic gadgets and motorway routes. Now suddenly he'd turned into Gok Wan.

'After that big lunch I don't feel that hungry,' Becca called from the bathroom. 'I'm going to do dinner a bit later if that's okay? Sit in the garden for a bit and read the paper if you like - help yourself to a beer.'

'I feel a bit twitchy,' Phil replied, still coming to terms with the face reflected back at him. 'I don't think I can sit still and relax. I thought I might go for a run; a couple of laps round the common… work up an appetite.'

Phil untangled his headphones and slipped his iPod into his pocket. He turned right out of the house and hop-scotched his way along the pavement; like a man in a minefield, dodging dog poo and even worse the dog poo incendiary devices. These were innocent-looking plastic bags that owners, having cleaned up after their mutts, left for the street cleaners. Step on one and the pressure would cause an explosion of devastating proportions.

He'd made it - he'd reached the common with his trainers unfettered by canine crap. He jogged across the road and ran along the path under the large conker trees parallel to the stationary traffic on The Avenue. He took a left past the snack van and the fishermen packing up for the night and swung a left around the perimeter path.

A small group who had been playing football were gathering their stuff and heading towards the pub. The lights along the footpaths twinkled into life, Phil looked right and saw the city skyline silhouetted against the dusk sky.

Fifteen minutes later he was back under the horse chestnut trees. He didn't want to overdo it; one more lap and he'd head for home. The traffic was clearing on The Avenue, the fishermen were buying burgers from the snack van and the football lads stood outside the pub having a well-earned smoke after their exertions on the pitch.

As Phil turned on to the perimeter path he realised he needed a pee. He'd needed to go before he left but couldn't be bothered to take his trainers off and go up the two flights to his room. He thought he'd be fine, he could usually hold on for ever. He could nip back to the pub - no best to keep going, he'd be fine. Don't think about it...don't think about it. As he rounded the corner back by The Avenue he realised he couldn't wait and nipped into the bushes.

He pulled down his trackies. Ah, the release, that's what too many cups of Lapsang Souchong do for you, he thought. He was in full flow when he realised he was not alone; a man in a tight white vest and jeans had sidled up next to him.

'That looks well nasty, looks like it's been chewed by a dog; where've you been sticking it?'

Unable to hear, Phil removed his headphones. 'If you think I'm touching that you're sooo wrong,' said white vest man.

Phil was just tucking himself back in and about to explain the whole beetroot thing, when he was caught in the beam of a torch and heard shouting and dogs barking as they broke through the bushes.

'All right... hold it right there.'

'I'm not holding nothing. Have you seen it? I wouldn't touch it with yours,' replied white vest man.

Three policemen stepped on to the path leading to the clearing where Phil and white vest man were standing.

'Trying a spot of bush craft are we?' said the officer with the torch. The torch flashed in Phil's eyes, making it difficult for him to make out any more than the shapes of the men approaching.

The one with the torch who was doing all the talking was older, short and stocky. The other two silent accomplices were slightly taller and hung back, trying to control the dogs.

'What is it with you lot: wouldn't you prefer the privacy and comfort of your own home?' They were now standing face to face.

The officer continued, he clearly liked the sound of his own voice. 'Now, I enjoy the al fresco life as much as the next man - unless of course the next man, happens to be one of you two…'

'There's been some kind of mistake, it's not how it looks,' Phil tried to explain. 'I was jogging and I needed...' The officer cut him short.

'That's what they all say - save it for your statement. Stick 'em in the van.'

Phil had been gone over an hour. Becca was worried but after her over-reaction with the beetroot incident she was trying to play it cool. If Phil was in the zone and wanted to run for a bit longer, then that would do him the world of good. He'd stopped running completely after Dave had died so it was great that he felt he could face it again; she needed to step back and give him some space. After all, exercise was part of her rehab plan.

Becca fussed around the house for a bit longer. She'd eaten her dinner and tidied up. Called her boys in Ireland for a chat – although she did most of the chatting – they were boys and not big on conversation. Not knowing what else to do with herself she was just sitting down to watch the TV when she got the phone call.

Head down and shoulders hunched, Phil shuffled dejectedly down the steps of the police station. Becca flashed her lights briefly; maybe there'd been quite enough flashing for one night she thought. She wanted to laugh but tried hard to keep a lid on it and ordered her face into an expression of deep concern.

Phil opened the passenger door of Becca's Mini and slumped down in the seat next to her.

'Indecent exposure, can you believe it. Me? I've never even had a parking ticket and now suddenly I'm some kind of deviant sexual predator. A man can't have a quick pee in the bushes without being pounced upon and arrested. But dogs? No problem. They can piss and shit all over the place…'

Becca pulled out into the traffic and across the lights.

'Of course you know what this means, don't you?' she asked, changing lane.

'Yeah, I'll have a criminal record…'

'Well yes, but that's not what I meant. There's no way I can leave you on your own this weekend now – you're a liability who knows what you'll do next.'

'Thanks…'

'No, there's no arguments, I called Radleigh Hall while I was waiting for you and they've said they'll squeeze you in somewhere – you'll have to share with me if need be.'

Becca filtered left into the one-way system and as they passed the crime scene, she bit the inside of her cheek hard. This was not funny. Phil was now resigned to the fact that any resistance was futile, maybe he would have to tunnel out after all.

Seven

Phil was worried Radleigh Hall was going to be one of those carrot juice and calorie-counted places; he'd got up early and Googled the hotel and was relieved to find it had two bars, a couple of pools and grounds that he could run in. If he wasn't going with his sister he'd actually be looking forward to it.

The more he got to know Becca's friends the more he realised they were vodka shot not wheatgrass shot kind of girls. Since he was up, he thought he might as well get his gym gear on. If he didn't show willing, Becca in Jack Russell mode, would be yapping at his heels and chasing him out of the house.

Becca unlocked the bikes and leant them against the railings. They freewheeled down the hill in the cool morning breeze. It was Saturday, the streets were quiet and deserted, market stallholders were up and about, pushing their barrows to their pitches and unloading them for the day's trade ahead.

They cycled slowly past the shuttered shops, past a weary dad pushing his early riser round the block; hoping she'd nod- off and hoping he could go home - home to bed. They went past the station and then followed the route of the railway line for a while. Where it forked and continued over a road bridge, they ducked down an alley underneath; the bikes jolted as they bumped along the narrow cobbled tunnel that led through the arches bringing them out on to the main road by the gym.

The class was better. Phil knew the faces, the music and some of the moves. He still felt like an ape in a ballet class, but he had worked up a sweat and felt like he'd really pushed himself. The owners of the squashed toes and bruised arms from yesterday patted him on his sweaty back and offered encouraging words as they filed out of the dance studio towards the ladies' changing room.

One of the girls, Gemma, hung back to thank Phil for recommending an army-style exercise website. 'Eddie, my boyfriend loves it, it's right up his street. I'd never get him down here, but we're going to do some of it together… anyway I'd better get going. I just wanted to say thanks.'

Becca smirked, eyeing Phil carefully. 'You're full of surprises, aren't you?'

Fi had suggested going on the train; a Champagne breakfast of M&S croissants and plastic picnic flutes had sounded like a relaxing start to the weekend. Becca reminded them about the prospect of having all their tranquil relaxation undone as they battled their way home through Sunday engineering works and replacement bus services.

In the end they agreed on taking two cars and sharing lifts; the traffic was slow, but once she was out of London Becca put the roof and her foot down. She turned up the heating and the CD player and they sang at the top of their voices as they zipped along the motorway. It was a CD called "Girl Power" and Phil was surprised and a little embarrassed to discover that he knew a lot of the lyrics.

Radleigh Hall was not visible from the road and they'd missed the sign the first time and had to double back. They drove along an avenue of mature plane trees whose branches leant across the drive and embraced those of the trees on the other side. It created a lush tunnel of green at the end of which stood Radleigh Hall.

It was a large Victorian country house built in weathered, warm red bricks. Jutting proudly from the roof were two chunky chimneys with elaborate decorative brickwork. Twisting its way around the mullioned windows of the ground floor was an intoxicatingly scented jasmine.

The interior was a combination of ancient and modern. The hotel reception desk was in the centre of a wood-panelled, galleried entrance hall. It had a vaulted ceiling of exposed oak beams and around the hall at first floor level was an enclosed glass balcony which the bedrooms led off.

To his relief the hotel had found him a room; he was in a different part of the hotel from the girls. He could imagine them all nipping in and out of each other's rooms and he'd just feel in the way. He was glad to be away from them; to give them some space and have some himself. After all, he was a gatecrasher on this trip. In fact he'd gatecrashed Becca's life, but she only had herself to blame for that. He'd been quite happy at home – well, not happy exactly – but he was surviving, getting through each day.

His room was very much from Becca's school of interior design: simple natural shades, bold artwork and, on the bed, expensive-looking scatter cushions that he was too afraid to sit on. Phil did a quick scoot around his room to check where everything was: hair dryer, ironing board, spare bedding, kettle, mini bar and Gideon's bible. Yep - everything seemed to be in place.

He dumped his bag on the bed and didn't stop to unpack. He pulled on his trunks, put on the white robe hanging in the bathroom and headed for the pool. After the artificial burning heat and the buffeting wind of Becca's car, it felt good to be out in the warm sunshine; a gentle breeze rustled the plants that edged the pool.

He chose a lounger in the sun, put his towel and robe on it then dived into the pool. He felt an exhilarating rush as his body forced a path though the water before surfacing near the other end of the pool. He powered up and down for a bit before returning to his lounger to dry off in the sun.

'Mind if I join you?' asked Kitti. 'I've got fifteen minutes before my treatment.'

'Be my guest.'

Kitti sat on the lounger next to Phil, put her things on the table between them and chatted about the journey. About Fi's driving and how Fi had spent the whole journey swearing and arguing with the man on the sat-nav like he was some kind of virtual husband. It was an amusing habit she had, endowing all her household appliances with a male gender. And then berating them as they conspired against her to make her life as difficult as possible.

Kitti went off for her hot stones massage and left her things with Phil. He dozed for a while, but then felt a bit restless, wishing he'd brought the newspaper down from his room. He noticed Kitti's book on the table under her towel and leant across to pick it up. "Handbags at Dawn" by Lucy Stevens, published by Lysistra. It caught him so by surprise that he dropped the book and it fell under the lounger on to the damp paving stones. Wiping away the water splashes, slightly in awe, he ran his fingers over the embossed type on the front cover.

This was the book that had outsold him last year. This was the kind of book Lysistra were putting all their money behind. This was the kind of book responsible for what had happened to him. Phil flicked through the pages. He read the dedication and the acknowledgements. And then he started reading the first chapter.

As he was a last-minute booking, there wasn't much choice of treatments but Becca had put him down for something called a ritual body treatment. It sounded like something from the occult. Would it involve chalk circles and dead chickens he wondered, or a massage with warm goat's blood? Phil went to the spa treatment rooms, took a seat in the reception area and carried on reading while he waited.

'Hi Philip, I'm Julie,' said a fresh-faced young woman in a white coat. 'Oh I've read that,' she continued, spotting Phil's book. 'It's really good. Where are you up to?'

'It's not mine… I'm just looking after it for a friend,' Phil said defensively, bending the cover back; a little embarrassed to be seen reading such a girls' book.

Recognising his self-consciousness, Julie told him her boyfriend often read books she'd bought, saying it gave him an insight into her world and how her mind worked.

'To be honest I've just started,' he said. 'It seems a bit slow to me.'

'Just wait. It really picks up. I couldn't put it down: my mum's reading it at the moment. It's a real feel-good book. And talking of feel-good let's get you settled in. Come this way, follow me.'

Julie led the way to a dimly lit room where regularly spaced tea lights flickered in votives on a narrow shelf; soothing music played from speakers set in the ceiling. From every corner of the room emanated an all-pervading sense of calm.

'First I need to ask you about your medical history.'

Phil told her about his verruca, but she didn't seem very interested. She went through a list and with crosses in all the boxes she was happy to begin.

'I'm going to pop out for a minute, take your robe off, hop up on the bed lie under the towel and make yourself comfy.'

Phil followed her instructions. He wasn't sure if he should lie face up or face down. Face up seemed a bit full frontal and face down a bit rude, turning his back on her. He wished he'd checked ritualistic etiquette with Becca earlier. As a compromise he decided to lie in the recovery position.

A couple of minutes later Julie returned. As she got everything she needed ready she ran through her well-practised patter. She explained that the spa ritual was inspired by an ancient Arabic bathing custom and that to achieve the authentic hammam experience she would be using black soap to detoxify and revitalise his skin.

He was a bit disappointed. It sounded like the only thing likely to be sacrificed was his pride. Julie folded the towel back revealing the unsightly red blotches on lower half of his body. Phil's skin looked like it was in serious need of revitalising.

'Is that eczema?' Julie asked, poised to add it to Phil's medical history.

'No it's beetroot.'

Julie raised a quizzical eyebrow. 'Was that one of our treatments?'

'No, it was a misguided one of my own.'

Phil told her about the beet bombs but decided to leave out the bit about the blood bath. There'd been quite enough confusion; he didn't want her to worry about being in a confined space with a man who was unhinged.

Julie put on some mittens that looked like the kind of thing he'd seen Danuta use to scour his dirty pans.

'I think a full body exfoliation will clear that up - no problem.'

Glowing and feeling fully buffed and polished, Phil lay on his bed. It hadn't been unpleasant, but it just felt peculiar having a complete stranger rubbing and scrubbing at him in the way he felt sure would be alien to most men. It was more likely that this was the kind of treatment they reserved for their cars.

Julie had told him, for girls it was perfectly normal. They weren't fazed at all, they'd happily chat away about their plans for that evening, while having the most intimate pubic topiary performed without anyone feeling remotely embarrassed or uncomfortable. To him it felt weird.

They'd all arranged to meet in the bar at eight and with half an hour to spare, he settled back on his bed and read a few more chapters. He could see what Julie meant; the heroine was a well-drawn character she was someone even he found himself rooting for as she battled her way through the onslaught of everyday life. He surprised himself at one point by laughing out loud.

The incident where her housebound Gran with Tourette's wins a supermarket sweep competition in her 'Have a Break' magazine. She does it on her Gran's behalf and as she arrives red-faced and sweaty at the checkout, she has her picture taken by the local paper. He had to admit it was writing of pure comic genius.

The book had made Phil late and he was the last to arrive in the bar. The girls were in high spirits, or maybe full of neat spirits. They were talking animatedly about their various treatments, comparing notes and making plans for the following day. Phil got a round of applause as he approached their table and Becca stood up and gave him a big hug.

They had already made good progress through several large jugs of cocktails and as Kitti poured and passed him one she announced.

'I think we should have a little toast. Phil you're a man who's good with words, say something deep and meaningful.'

'Well, I'd like to propose a toast to Fi for letting me barge my way uninvited into her birthday weekend and to all of you for welcoming me with open arms and treating me like one of the girls... so here's to the girls.'

'The girls,' they all chorused.

There was much laughter and clinking of glasses as Phil pulled a chair round and squeezed in next to Kitti.

'Sorry I didn't make it back down for a swim,' Kitti said. 'I felt a bit light-headed after my massage and went back to my room for a lie down.'

'Don't worry. I left not long after you,' Phil said as Fi topped up their glasses. 'And after I'd had my mud bed bath scour – I mean hammam bath I went back to my room to chill out.'

'How was it? Have you done anything like that before?' Kitti asked, curious to hear his thoughts.

'Not exactly,' Phil laughed, recalling the only vaguely similar experience he'd had. 'I had a couple of deep muscle massages when I was in the regiment, but it was nothing like that - there were no candles, no relaxing music and the physio was a big hairy-arsed Glaswegian.'

'Did you like it?' Kitti asked hoovering up the last of her cocktail with a splutter.

'Once I'd relaxed I did, but I did find it a bit strange being touched by a complete stranger; I'm just not used to that.'

'Did you pick up my things from the pool?'

'They're in my room,' Phil said leaning in close to be heard over the rest of the chatter. 'I meant to bring them down… sorry. When we've eaten, come back with me and get them.'

'Is that some unashamed ploy to lure me to your room Mr Drummond?' Kitti laughed.

'Yes.' Phil replied, holding her gaze.

'You may have a new suave haircut but you're still the same man underneath, aren't you?'

'I sincerely hope so.' Phil said raising his glass.

'So do I.' Kitti replied, clinking her glass against Phil's.

Eight

Their table was set in a deep alcove, making Phil wonder if they'd been singled out as a rowdy party and been annexed. But actually it was the perfect spot, their own private dining room. The French windows were open wide, through which a welcome jasmine-scented breeze wafted.

Fi and Sam popped out for a smoke at regular intervals, but rather than there being two parties - smokers and non - the conversation and wine kept flowing as they carried on chatting through the open doors.

While coffee, herbal teas and a plate of petit fours were being passed round, Sam suggested playing a game.

'Let's do the one where everyone writes a secret on a piece of paper. We put them in the middle of the table, each take one and read it out in turn. Then we have to guess whose secret it is.'

One of the waiters went and found a hotel pad and pencils and briefly the table fell silent as they sat thinking and scribbling.

'Everyone done?' Sam asked, emptying the crumbs out of the bread basket before passing it round. Everyone dropped their folded piece of paper in.

'OK, shall I start?' Sam picked a note, unfolded it and read it aloud. 'I have had my nipples painted.' Sam laughed as she continued. 'Could be anyone of us, with the exception of Phil maybe.'

'Don't you believe it; I've had camouflage paint in some very strange places.'

Sam scanned her friends to see if there were any tell-tale give away signs. They all remained pokerfaced.

'Right, I'm going to say Fi, because she's the person I think is least likely to do something like that and in this game, as a rule, it usually turns out to be the one you'd least expect.'

'No, not me I'm afraid. Although I'm sure you'll agree I do have a figure that would feel quite at home adorning any Rubens' canvas.'

'Own up then, who's the artist's muse?' Sam asked. Becca raised her hand to squeals of delight and the sound of Phil choking on a truffle.

Becca went on to explain that when she was in her third year at university she shared a house with a guy studying fine art. His final major exhibition piece was a reclining nude. But he was very unhappy with the nipples on the painting; one night after a few bottles of wine she'd agreed to model so he could finish his painting.

'There was nothing sexual about it… when my bike got a puncture, he'd fix it for me. This was just me returning a favour.' Becca explained, defending her honour.

'Well if only more women returned a favour like you,' laughed Sam. 'AA men would be racing each other across the country to where women had broken down, all too eager to change a wheel or pump up a flat.'

Keen to move the spotlight off her, Becca passed the basket to Phil. He pulled out two and then dropped one back, unfolding it and reading it to himself before sharing it with the others.

'I don't know who the father of my son is.'

The party atmosphere evaporated in an instant. Everyone fell silent. The only noise was a dragging sound as Kitti pushed her chair back and made a quick exit through the French windows. Silent tears streamed down her cheeks.

'Stay here for a minute, I'll go and make sure she's okay.'

Becca couldn't see Kitti to start with and then she heard a sniffle. She was sitting, head in her hands, on the steps leading from the terrace to the gardens. Becca, heels and wine had never been a great combination; carefully stepping sideways down the narrow stone steps she made her way to where Kitti was sitting.

'If you'd rather be on your own, I'll understand.' Becca said quietly resting a hand on Kitti's shoulder.

'No, it's okay – stay,' Kitti sniffled. 'I feel stupid making such a fuss and spoiling everyone's night.'

Becca passed her napkin and Kitti dabbed her eyes leaving an abstract charcoal sketch on the damask.

'I really wanted to tell you at the time…'

'I wish you had.'

'It was around the time you were going through your break up with Dermot… I thought you had enough on your plate.'

'You know me, there's always room on my plate for a bit more; that's why I'm a slave to that bloody gym.'

Kitti smiled and for an instant the worry and anxiety drained away from her blotchy, mascara-streaked face.

'Well I guess the important thing is, you know now.'

'Yes now I know… and just so you know for the future, you can tell me anything… anytime - regardless of what other crap I'm wading through at that moment in my life – okay?'

'Okay… I thought I might get a chance to tell you when we met for lunch. But Phil was there and it's such a hard thing to bring up casually. By the way, Becca, did I ever tell you about the time I had my drink spiked and woke up alone at three am in Victoria Park? Things like that don't happen to me. I couldn't remember a thing, I thought I'd just overdone it, but a few weeks later I discovered I was pregnant.'

'Did you go to the police?'

'No. I didn't. What could I tell them? That I'd had too much to drink and woken up freezing cold alone in the park. No, I didn't think they'd take me seriously. They see that kind of thing on every high street every Friday night. You read about it all the time in the papers; the attitude is, girls who are dressed up for a night out and have had a few too many to drink are asking for it. I couldn't put myself through that… I felt ashamed – I felt I was to blame. I didn't need everyone pointing the finger and confirming it.'

'Hey… none of it was your fault… none of it – do you understand?'

'Why did it happen to me? What was it about me?'

Becca put her arm around her friend.

'I'm so sorry Kitti… sorry for not being there…'

'I didn't want everyone to know, to be looking at me and talking about me.'

Despite the warm evening Kitti shivered, and Becca draped her wrap over her shoulders.

'Here this'll warm you up – as my dad would say "it's a nice bit of schmutter" - cashmere, a gift from my brother… it's Laura Ashley, so more likely chosen by one of his slightly bonkers girlfriends.' Another smile from Kitti.

'Even if I had gone to the police, I wasn't going to be much use as a witness, I couldn't remember anything and by the time I discovered I was pregnant I thought it was too late to do anything about it.'

'That was five years ago. What's raked this all up now?'

'Jachim's started asking why he hasn't got a Daddy and it's just brought it all back.'

'I wish I'd known.'

'What could you have done?'

'I'm not sure - I'd have been there for you.'

'You've always been there for me.' Kitti sniffed.

'I certainly wouldn't have prattled on to you about all my petty insecurities… I'm glad you've told me now, at least you don't have to go through this on your own.'

Becca took hold of Kitti's hand and squeezed it.

'You know I've always wanted a family but this wasn't how it was supposed to be. I guess some people would have got rid of it. But it wasn't an "IT" to me it was a little someone. I couldn't help thinking, what if this is my only chance? What if, when I am ready and settled it just doesn't happen?

My Mum and Dad tried for years for a little brother or sister for me – it just wasn't meant to be. What if the same happened to me? How would I feel, having thrown away my only chance?'

'I can't answer that. I can't imagine how tough it must have been for you. But what I would say is that Jachim is such a lovely boy, everyone adores him and you're a fantastic Mum. He may not have a Dad but not all Dads are worth having.'

The napkin was smearing more of the mascara, snot and tears than it was soaking up. Becca rummaged in her bag for a pack of tissues and passed one to Kitti.

'It's your future you need to think about, you can't change the past.'

'I know but I can't help thinking that what happened always gets in the way of things… you know, of my relationships.'

'Maybe having it out in the open will help you put it behind you.'

'It's been hard keeping a secret from you all. I feel better for talking about it, but I'm not ready for the whole world to know.'

The others stood at the top of the terrace steps, Phil was carrying the wine bucket and Sam and Fi had the wine and glasses.

'Room service,' called Fi, clinking her way down the steps.

They sat there for the next hour finishing off the wine while Kitti retold her story. She was composed and told it calmly as the others sniffed, passed tissues and blinked away tears.

'I'm sorry, I really need to sit in a comfortable chair now. Having a colonic tomorrow with piles really will be no fun.' Fi teetered back up the steps followed shortly by the others.

Phil hung back with Kitti and when the others had disappeared inside he put his arm around her waist and steered her along the path towards the rear of the hotel.

'Come and get your things. My room's this way.'

Phil's room was in what would have originally been the coach house. Although great care had been taken to landscape the area it was still, essentially, in the car park. They walked through the wide stone arch and up the steps to his door. He removed the card key from the slot and held the door open for her.

'Can I get you a drink?'

'I think I've had enough, what I really fancy is a cup of tea. I got a bit cold sitting outside for so long.'

'Here, have this.' Phil took the silk blanket folded across the foot of the bed and wrapped it around her shoulders. 'Better?'

'Yes, thank you.'

'Now, what have we got? Peppermint, green tea, Darjeeling, redbush tea, Earl Grey, decaf or English Breakfast?'

'No PG? I'll have English Breakfast.'

While Phil was making the drinks, Kitti asked him if he'd made any plans.

'I don't know what to do, I'm adrift at the moment, well not adrift, more tethered to the good ship Becca.'

'God bless her and all who sail in her.' Kitti raised her hand in mock salute. 'But seriously, what will you do when you go home?'

'If Becca has her way I might never go home. And actually I'm quite enjoying myself. I used to read in the newspapers all the time about metrosexuals. I didn't really know what one was, now I think I am one.'

104

'There are worse things to be.'

'Like…?'

'An estate agent.'

'You're the nicest estate agent I know.'

'And how many do you know?'

'Only you and the ones I bought my last house from. They were complete sharks. If they ever wanted to do a remake of Jaws, the guys at Giles Peterson would be perfect.'

Kitti finished her tea and put her cup on the side.

'I'm guessing you don't have to work? I mean, financially you're okay?'

'Yeah, I can pay the bills. But writing was never about that for me. Writing is what kept me sane. What stopped me from ending up like this.'

'Then why not write something else? Write stories for the local paper. Write the letters you'd like to have written to famous people in history. Go back to writing for you. You said the whole publishing thing was a happy coincidence, not essential to your wellbeing. It's the writing that keeps you sane, not the publishing. Forget about the publishing, move on. This is a new phase, a new chapter. Be brave and turn the page.'

Kitti looked at her watch. 'I should go. I'm talking too much. I'm telling you what to do, when I promised myself I wouldn't. I'm good at dishing out advice but hopeless at acting on any I'm given.'

'Here's some advice I'd like you to act on.' Phil leant across and put his hand on Kitti's. 'Don't go back to your room… stay here.'

Phil had planned this from the moment Becca had insisted he joined her on this trip. He didn't know quite how he'd get Kitti back to his room, but he was looking for every opportunity and when she left all her stuff by the pool - he heard the knocking.

But now Kitti was here it didn't feel quite right. He wondered if in the past he'd have noticed or cared – somehow since living Becca's life, he felt more tuned in to other people's feelings – no not other people –

women's feelings. It wasn't that he didn't want to; he did – but it felt wrong, it felt like he was taking advantage of Kitti while she was vulnerable.

He felt sure old Phil wouldn't have noticed or if he did he'd have convinced himself that an hour of bedroom gymnastics was just what she needed. It may have been what he needed, but there was no evidence that it would have any impact on Kitti's years of worry about the circumstances surrounding her pregnancy and her concern for Jachim's future.

Old Phil would have said it would be a moment of escape, but new Phil now knew there was no escape: you just had to face it and deal with it. And no amount of under the duvet night manoeuvres would change that.

'I'll make up the other bed. Honest!' reassured Phil as Kitti looked doubtful of his intentions. 'I just don't think you should be on your own tonight.'

'Don't take this the wrong way – but since you've been at Becca's I've seen a different side to you...'

'Jekyll or Hyde?'

'I can't quite put my finger on it, it's like in the last few days I've got to know you more than I ever have in the last twelve... thirteen years that Becca and I have been friends.'

'That's because you've seen more of me – well actually you've seen a lot less of me...' Phil smirked and undid another button on his shirt.

'All I'm saying is, something's changed and it's good; you're more open – you're easier to talk to... you listen.'

'Does that mean you're staying?'

'Yeah, you're right if I go back to my room I'll be awake half the night going over and over the same old things and not getting anywhere except exhausting myself. Besides, after my nap this afternoon I don't feel remotely tired.'

'Neither do I. Before I was at Becca's, I was awake in the small hours every night. I'd lie awake for hours, going over and over things in my head. I'd eventually fall asleep, just as everyone else was getting up. Days and days went past and the only person I'd speak to was the courier or the pizza deliveryman. And he was Polish, so not big on conversation. Our mutual appreciation of the American Hot was not the firmest of foundations for a friendship.'

'So how did Becca know that things were not going so well for you?'

'She didn't... not to begin with. You know we're close, but we can go for months without speaking to each other. She's busy, I'm busy, so it was a while before she suspected anything was wrong. Then of course she got on her charger and came to the rescue.'

While Kitti was in the bathroom, Phil made up the other bed. He lined up the boxy felt armchair and long footstool to make what the guest information pack described as "the day bed". He smoothed and tucked the flat sheet tightly under the cushions of the armchair and footstool to hold them securely together. By the time he'd shaken out the duvet and added the extra pillow and blanket from the wardrobe it looked like quite an inviting place to sleep.

He laid down to try it out; it was quite a squeeze, it wasn't designed for a man of his build. It was more suited to a child or a Munchkin and his feet hung out of the end. Since he wasn't sleeping much anyway he thought he'd be okay. He'd slept in far worse places, like slumped against the booming bass of a speaker in a night club in Malta until a thoughtful bouncer woke him and asked him to leave.

Kitti poked her head round the bathroom door and spoke to him with her toothbrush firmly in her cheek.'

'hang I horow a ee- urt?'

'You brought your toothbrush?'

Kitti removed the brush and gave him a rabid foamy grin.

'I was a girl guide you know… in truth not a very good one, I was never that well prepared. Like this…' She held up her toothbrush. 'I only remembered it at last minute, and I couldn't be bothered to unpack everything so I just bunged it in my handbag.'

Phil had arranged himself in what he thought was a seductive reclining position; knees bent so his legs weren't hanging out of the end of the bed, propped up on his side with his hands behind his head.

'So… have you got a tee shirt I can borrow?'

As he pulled himself up to a sitting position the two sections of the bed slid apart and Phil and the bedding sank into the crevasse leaving him lying on his back on the floor with his feet in the air.

After Kitti's giggling fit passed she managed to compose herself enough to help Phil to his feet. He was glad to hear her laughter even if it was at his expense.

'You can't sleep there… you'll do yourself an injury.'

'Well it's either that or the floor.'

'If you sleep on that thing you'll end up on the floor anyway.'

'I think it was designed for dainty ladies not great hulking blokes like me.'

'Listen, we'll share the bed, BUT - terms and conditions apply and you may lose an essential part of your anatomy if you try anything on – understood?'

'What, not even a cuddle?'

'I know where your cuddles lead Mr Drummond. Now, where's that tee shirt?'

Nine

The next morning he woke to the sound of the kettle boiling and could hear the shower running in the bathroom. Kitti emerged wearing the other robe.

'Sorry, did I wake you? I'm making some tea. Would you like one?'

While the tea brewed, she gathered up her clothes and stuffed them in her bag she'd had at the pool the day before.

'Your book's on the bedside, I have to confess I've been reading it.' Phil said, sitting up and throwing back the covers.

'What do you think?' Kitti asked, splashing milk into the cups.

'I'm reserving judgement.'

'So you're going to finish it then?'

'Becca told me she hasn't finished the last three book club books, I think I should show willing if I'm going to go.'

'You're just curious about why she sold more books than you.'

'There might be an element of that and so far I haven't a clue why she did.'

'The only reason her book sold more is because your readership is shrinking and her readership is growing. It's a male/female thing.'

'Is it as simple as that?'

'I think it probably is. Look, I'm going to leave you to it.'

'Okay. I'm going to jump in the shower. I'll see you down at breakfast in about half an hour.'

Kitti strolled back through the car park and took the back stairs up to her floor. As her door clicked shut behind her, she stopped dead in her tracks. Backlit through the curtains by the early morning sun she could see the silhouette of someone on her balcony.

Whoever it was, was trying to break in and was making a bit of a ham-fisted job of it. It was a bit impulsive, but feeling confident that the burglar was securely on the other side of the glass she quietly and slowly approached the doors. With the flourish of a magician, Kitti pulled the cord and drew back the curtains to reveal Fi standing on the balcony.

'Morning.' Fi mouthed at her sheepishly from the other side of the glass.

'What are you doing out there?' Kitti mouthed back before sliding open the door.

'We've been knocking and calling you and after last night... you know... we were worried when there was no answer. I climbed over from my balcony to make sure everything was okay.'

'Everything's fine Fi.'

'Where've you been?' Fi asked collapsing on to Kitti's bed exhausted by her failed cat burglar ordeal.

'After you left to escape the onset of piles, I went back to Phil's room to pick my stuff up. We got chatting and I fell asleep there.'

Fi leaned forward and left a pause in the conversation hoping Kitti would fill it with more details.

'Nothing happened, we were just talking...'

Kitti was saved from any further grilling by a knock on the door. Before she could answer it, the door burst open and Sam and Becca fell into the room with an anxious-looking hotel manager fussing behind them.

'Oh, here you are,' said Becca straightening up, smoothing back her hair and disentangling her cardigan from Sam's belt clasp.

'Everything okay madam?' called the obsequious hotel manager lurking behind Becca and Sam.

'Everything's fine thank you, or at least it was until Velma and Daphne turned up.' Kitti was a little miffed at their complete over-reaction.

'So does that make me Shaggy or Scooby?' Fi called from the bed.

The hotel manager awkwardly made his apologies and scuttled back to the security of his office.

'Sorry, we were worried when we couldn't rouse you,' said Sam, adopting a conciliatory tone.

'Sounds like Phil couldn't rouse her either,' sniggered Fi. Kitti gave her one of her well-practised withering looks.

'Has my brother been preying on vulnerable women?'

'No, I went to pick my bag up from his room last night and ended up staying there chatting most of the night.' Becca smiled and looked relieved.

'And here we were, worried you might have got yourself sandwiched in the trouser press, or had a hypoglycaemic attack brought on by the stingy quantities of shortbread fingers in the room. I might have guessed you were being led astray by my wayward brother.'

'Don't give him a hard time - he was being really sweet, he was looking after me.' Kitti turned to take some fresh clothes out of the wardrobe and to hide her rising colour.

'I'm amazed. He can't even look after himself at the moment...' Spotting the expression on Kitti's face, Becca trailed off.

Not really wanting to enter into a discussion about Phil's shortfalls, Kitti interrupted and changed the subject.

'Can you give me ten minutes and I'll see you downstairs? If they come to take our order could you get me a coffee?'

At breakfast Kitti headed off any talk about the previous evening. She didn't want to relive last night's emotional outburst. Not because she was embarrassed or felt any degree of shame, but because she didn't want it to overshadow their time left at the hotel. She did what she'd done for the last four years, folded up how she really felt until it was really, really small then wrapped it in a cheery persona, put on a smile and carried on like normal.

'So, who's having treatments this morning?' she asked.

'All of us except Phil I think,' answered Sam with a mouth full of croissant.

'Er well, that's not strictly true.' Becca replied, mischievously. 'I've managed to book him a session in the tanning salon.'

Sam coughed violently as some of her croissant went down the wrong way.

'He's going to love you,' she wheezed. 'How did you manage that? When I tried to book last night there were no slots left.'

'They're road testing this thing called "Biarritz Beauties" it's a new automated spray tanning booth and they were looking for guinea pigs – I mean willing volunteers.' Becca smiled wickedly.

'Does he know?' Kitti asked, struggling to push the plunger down on her coffee.

'Not yet, but he loves gadgets. If they'd had a "Biarritz Beauty" on the shopping channel, he'd have probably bought one by now. It'll be right up his street.'

'What's it like? Did you see it?' Kitti asked, finally pouring herself and Sam a coffee.

'It looks a bit like one of those automatic self-cleaning toilets. You know the kind of thing Fi?'

'I do but I've always been too frightened to use one. I always imagine the doors are going to slide open just as I'm majestically taking my place on the throne.'

Fi pushed back her chair and enacted the moment she'd described a little too loudly and graphically for the other genteel breakfast diners. To avoid the glares directed at her from over the top of numerous rustling newspapers, she made a swift exit and went to stake her claim on the freshly cut pineapple being delivered to the buffet.

Becca continued as she buttered her toast, 'One of the girls here was telling me that the company that makes "Biarritz Beauties" is planning on putting them in railway stations, shopping centres and airports. It's one thing for the doors to slide back and reveal you in full flow and quite another if it slides back and there you are a bright shade of orange, striking a pose in your paper pants. I don't think it'll catch on, do you?'

'No, but I'll be interested to hear how Phil gets on,' laughed Kitti, waving to Phil as he entered the dining room.

'What's funny?' Phil asked as he reached the table.

'Becca was just telling us about her pet guinea pig.' Kitti replied, trying hard to keep the laughter out of her voice.

None the wiser, Phil went and helped himself to some fruit. While he spooned a couple of green figs in syrup and dollop of thick natural yoghurt into a bowl he spotted Fi conspicuously loitering near the buffet. She was snaffling chocolate brownies and pastries and putting them in her handbag for snacking on after her colonic.

Ten

As Phil walked slowly along the corridor, he arched his shoulders and stretched his neck to try and relieve some of the aches and pains from falling off the bonsai sofa.

'I hope that wasn't my doing.'

Phil turned to see Julie grinning back at him.

'Oh no, the massage was great, but I think I undid all your good work by sleeping awkwardly.'

Julie glanced down at her appointment card

'Well I'm afraid you've got me again this morning.'

'Have I? I'm going for a sun bed, or at least I thought I was.'

'Yes and no. It's not a bed it's a booth, you stand up in it. It's the very latest in sunless tanning. There are only five in the UK. I went on a training session last week, so I'm the only one here that can do the demos at the moment.' Julie placed a reassuring hand on Phil's back as she ushered him through one of many double doors along the corridor.

'Don't look so worried; it's very straightforward. We all got to have a go and even though you're standing up it's still quite relaxing. I'm supposed to do five sessions a weekend and I've only done four so far so I'm really pleased you booked in, it means I won't lose my commission. It's only forty quid, but as they say "every little helps". Take a seat in the first room on the left, I'll be with you in two minutes.'

Phil opened the door to a smallish room with fierce air con. He stood and did a few more neck rolls and stretched his spine out before Julie poked her head through the door.

'All set? I'll talk you through how it works, what you need to do and then leave you to it.'

All that sales training was not wasted on Julie, again she went into her well-rehearsed spiel.

'We recommend you wear underwear in the booth. On the chair over there is a shower cap and a pair of paper pants to pop on. So all you need to do, is stand here in the centre of the booth on the footprint guides. When you're comfortable, push 'start' on the touch screen here and follow the simple instructions. This chrome hoop houses the spray nozzles, it glides vertically up and down, rotating as it goes. The spray comes out in a soft cloud ensuring you get a smooth even overall tan. The screen will show you poses to adopt to make sure areas like the under arms and other natural creases in the skin aren't missed.'

Julie made some balletic gestures to demonstrate the kind of thing.

'It usually takes around fifteen minutes and if you have any problems you can call me by pushing this intercom button here. Okay, any questions?'

'What colour will I be at the end and how long will it last?'

'There are plans to offer a whole range of shades but at the moment we are just offering "sun kissed"; it's a light tan. You'll have a warm natural holiday glow for about a week to ten days, and then you'll fade back to your natural skin tone. When you're in, this sensor here will measure your height and then you're all ready to go.'

Julie smiled encouragingly and returned to the solarium lounge. Again, Phil was thinking about cars. This was just like some glorified auto body shop.

Yesterday he'd had a light sand and his oil changed and today he was having a re-spray. Last year he'd lovingly booked his 1968 Citroën DS in for a paint job, it was worth every penny. He still felt swollen with pride every time he took her out. Thinking about it, he could virtually smell the sun warming the leather seats and feel the smooth ivory bodywork.

Did women feel the same buzz from their treatments or was the constant age offensive a huge pressure? He was glad he didn't have to keep this up for ever. He wondered if he could just sneak off to the pool. He opened the door a crack to check if the coast was clear. It wasn't. Hearing the door creak open Julie looked up from the reception desk.

'Everything okay? Do you need me to run through anything again?' He liked Julie. He couldn't let her down.

'No, no, I'm fine thanks, just making sure the door was closed properly.'

Phil slipped off his robe, rustled into the crinkly pants, put on the shower cap and stepped into the booth. He pushed the button on the screen and the door slid round to encase him, the fan whirred into life and he was ready for lift off. It was like that terrifying moment in the carwash. The calm before the storm as the green roller brushes moved into position. Would the aerial survive? Had he closed all the doors properly? Would the windows leak?

No, all was well. The spray hoop did a quick up and down to check for obstructions, before it puffed a fine digestive biscuit-smelling spray into the booth. Slowly it began its ascent from his toes to his nose. He'd imagined the spray would feel a little tickly on his feet but Julie was right, it was like standing in the mist of a warm steamy shower. He couldn't feel the spray at all. Looking down he suddenly saw why. He'd forgotten to take his socks off.

He'd drifted off a bit during the briefing. He remembered Julie recommending wearing underwear.

To him socks and pants were underwear. He hadn't given it too much thought. He tried to bend his knee up and reach down but the spraying hoop had reached his calves and there wasn't enough room and he wobbled around on one leg in an ungainly fashion bumping the side of the booth with an almighty crash.

He'd seen people who'd lost the use of their arms using their dextrous feet and toes for the most challenging tasks. Changing nappies, painting portraits. Using the toes on his right foot he tried to pull the top of his left sock down a bit, but was interrupted from this tricky manoeuvre by a pinging sound from the screen.

A pictogram of a woman bending her knees flashed on the screen and arrows showed her moving into a sitting position. Phil followed the instruction, which allowed the spray to reach the insides of his legs. Still bothered by his socks he stood the heel of one foot on the toe end of the other sock and wiggled his leg back, successfully managing to pull the sock down a bit. Again the screen pinged, showing arrows in an upward direction and the woman lifting her breasts.

What was he supposed to do now? Phil shimmied down through the hoop to finally pull his socks off. As he was at head level with the hoop it let out two more powerful puffs intended for the chest area but hitting him square in the face. He kicked his socks to one side as the hoop prepared for its final downward cycle. The screen pinged for the last time and he raised his arms above his head and crossed them at the wrists.

A short while later, the hoop came to a standstill in the recess around the central footplate. The fan blew warm air into the booth and, once dry, Phil pushed the release button and the door rotated open. He stood and admired himself in the full-length mirror. Dazzlingly white feet to the ankles, patchy brown body and face, with eyes framed panda-like by darker brown rings. Not a look popular in Biarritz, he felt sure.

While Julie was busy on the phone, Phil quietly snuck away. The corridors were empty, he was glad not to bump into anyone on the way back to his room. He quickly dressed his mottled, stripy body in a clean shirt and jeans and put on his sunglasses. With all the botched bits covered up, he actually looked quite good. Like he'd actually come from the beach, rather than Frankenstein's laboratory.

Eleven

Phil grabbed his things, stuffed them in his bag and went down to reception to check out. As he passed the library, Becca called him.

'Hello brown boy, look at you. How was it?'

'Unusual is probably the word I'd use. I don't think I'll bother with it again.'

'Why not? You look great.'

'I look great from a distance.' Phil came and stood in front of her, took his sunglasses off and pulled up his trouser leg.

'Is this some strange Masonic greeting?'

Phil told her what had happened. He laughed first, which Becca was grateful for, as she was struggling to hold it in.

'Can I have your keys?' Phil asked, heading for the door, 'I'll go and dump our bags in the car.'

'I was wondering if you'd mind travelling back with Fi and Sam. I think Kitti would like to have a bit of a heart to heart.'

'Yeah, no problem. I'll just sit in the back and have a sleep, I'm not big on conversation at the moment.'

'Did Kitti say any more to you about what happened?'

'No she was giving me helpful tips on how to sort my life out.'

'And, what's her life plan for you?'

'It was pretty good actually. The last thing I need is someone telling me to pull myself together. But Kitti doesn't make it sound like that, even if that's exactly what she's saying.'

'You know what I think? I think your problems are a welcome distraction for her. Someone else's demons are always easier to face than your own. It's often so easy to see the answer to someone else's questions and yet your own can remain unanswered for ever.'

'Well, the answer she gave me was writing.'

'Is writing really the answer? Isn't it losing your book deal that's tipped you over the edge?'

'Yes, but as Kitti rightly pointed out, writing and publishing are two separate things. Writing has always been my salvation; it's the whole publishing thing that's pulled the rug from under me. I think she's right making the distinction between the two. In my head they've always been inextricably linked, but now I think about it, when I was at the magazine it was only ever about the writing. The wonder of words - ordering my thoughts and reordering my life.'

'Are you going to go back to the magazine, is that what you're thinking?' Becca asked.

'No… I don't ever want to go back,' Phil said, seeing clearly for the first time in ages. 'I have to go forwards; besides it's all changed there now Jeffers has gone. It's new people writing about new wars. I'm old news.'

'I was hoping this weekend might give you a chance to get things clear in your head. It sounds like you have. If writing really is the way forward, you can start by signing your name in Fi's card.'

Becca passed the card. It had a picture of a fifties housewife, with the words "Domestic Goddess" on the front. Happy Fi-rty fifth birthday, love Phil x. It was hardly his literary renaissance, but over the weekend it really felt like something had clicked into place. Like crippling back pain gone in an instant as the spine's cracked back into alignment. He'd managed to create a small space in his brain, breathing space, space to think.

'Ah, very clever,' said Becca admiring his handiwork. 'The minute I have to write something witty and amusing my mind goes blank and I end up writing something completely mundane.'

Becca fished in her bag and pulled out an assortment of objects, some football cards, a Dr Who action figure and a handy-sized anti-bac cleanser. She piled them on the table and returned to her bag for a second trawl, successfully landing her keys at Phil's feet.

'I've settled our bill. I'll just finish my coffee and I'll meet you in reception.' Becca called after Phil as she returned to the celebrity wedding in her magazine – it'll never last, she thought.

Becca waved as Fi's Volvo scrunched out of the car park and down the drive, indicating left the whole way and then finally turning right.

'All set?' Becca asked a puzzled-looking Kitti as she wheeled her suitcase to where Becca was leaning against her car.

'One of the girls on the desk just gave me these. They're Phil's apparently.' Kitti held out a sanitary disposal bag. Becca opened the bag; it contained a pair of insanitary-looking socks.

'Hop in and I'll tell you all about it.'

They hadn't gone far when the sunshine was replaced by fine drizzle and then turned to a steady downpour slowing all the traffic, but making more time for chatting.

'I hope my little outburst didn't spoil Fi's birthday weekend,' Kitti asked with regret.

'You know Fi, it's really only men and machines that push her buttons. She's not worried about her weekend, she's more worried about you - we all are.' Becca said flicking the wipers into manic mode.

'I'm fine, or I will be... now it's all out in the open. It's hard keeping something like that a secret,' Kitti said, staring straight ahead, watching the rain run in rivulets down the edge of the windscreen. 'Didn't you ever wonder?'

'I did at the time,' Becca said. 'But you didn't mention it so I didn't like to ask. I assumed it was Slimy Simon.'

'No way... he'd had the snip and anyway I'd given him the chop long before then,' Kitti seemed slightly disgusted by the thought.

'I'm sorry I didn't tell you; I wanted to, but I knew you'd make me go the police and the one thing I was certain of was that I didn't want to do that.'

'You're probably right - I would have tried to talk you into going to the police,' Becca paused momentarily before asking. 'Am I a bully, Kitti?'

'No, not a bully... you just think you know what's best for people and often you're right... except maybe in this case.'

Kitti had been diplomatic, but Becca felt sad that she'd not been there for Kitti when she'd really needed her. Kitti hadn't been able to share her problems with her because she knew that Becca would push her in a direction she did not want to go. Her intentions were always good but she knew herself that sometimes she didn't know when to stop pushing.

'I'm Jachim's godmother and I've signed up to offer him spiritual guidance. I had always imagined that it would be more along the lines of which brand of vodka was best in a Bloody Mary. But if helping him understand who he is and what he's about is what he needs now, then you know I'll do anything I can to help.'

'Thanks, that really means a lot,' Kitti said, becoming a little teary.

'I suppose my biggest fear is the whole nature/nurture thing. I'm trying really hard but what if he's like his Dad and ends up...'

'You won't let that happen. The very fact you're worrying about it means you'll do everything in your power to keep him on the straight and narrow.'

'But that's what worries me. What if it's outside of my power?'

'I think you're underestimating yourself. Let's sort out what you're going to tell him.'

'I feel I've dealt with his current concerns, I want to be prepared for when he wants to know more than I can tell him.'

Becca successfully steered the conversation and her car through heavy rain, topics and traffic.

'I've got the Champagne and cake in the fridge at mine. Fi's going to drop Phil back, so, we can do the singing and give her, her present then. Did I tell you, I got her one of those Venetian mirrors she was admiring in the shop?'

'She'll be really pleased. It will look perfect in her new bathroom. Let me know what I owe you?'

'We'll sort it out later, I managed to do a bit of a deal. I exchanged it for those two stone cherubs I couldn't shift. A bit of a result all round.'

'Would you mind dropping me at mine, so I can let my Mum get off? She's going to a psychic thing with my Auntie Muriel. Bobbie came through for Auntie Muriel last time she went.'

'Was Bobbie her husband?'

'No, Uncle Vince is still with us. Although I sometimes think when I'm talking to him, that communicating with the other side might be easier. Bobbie was her Border Collie.'

'Was he able to tell her much about the after life?'

'No, not really, but now my Mum wants to go. They're going to see Penny Truman from that programme on TV.'

'She's amazing on that show, I've always been quite sceptical about that kind of thing, but when I saw her do that "Dead Men's Shoes" thing that she does, I started to think there was something in it.'

'She does that on stage. Mum's dug out a pair of Dad's golf shoes that she couldn't bring herself to throw out. You know what she's like, she said he'd only just bought them when he died and someone might be very glad of them one day. What she really means is, one day you might find yourself someone like your Dad. Someone solid and reliable, who likes a round of golf and takes an eight and a half shoe. She's a master of the unsaid my Mum.'

'How does it translate to the stage?'

'It's pretty much like the TV show. They line all the shoes up behind a barrier so that Penny can't see them. Penny comes on and she starts to talk about someone, describing their life, passing on any messages and then after she's done that for a bit they lower the barrier and Penny runs her hands along the shoes until she finds the ones that belong to the person she's connected with.'

'I'd be really scared if it was someone for me.'

'Me too, but I can see the morbid fascination. Part of me thinks it's a load of rubbish but I can't explain how she does it. The things she knows are just too specific. Sometimes it's things that people have never told anyone and Penny somehow knows. It's a bit freaky don't you think?'

'Yeah I do, I'm happy watching it from the safety of my house but I wouldn't want to go.'

There were no spaces in Kitti's road so Becca parked in the middle of the road.

'I'll walk round with Jachim when I've seen my Mum off if that's okay? He loves birthday cake, but he does always want to blow out everyone's candles.'

'No problem. I've got plenty of matches, just come whenever you're ready.'

'Okey dokey, I'll just see the ghost busters off and I'll be there.'

Kitti unloaded her bag from the boot then balanced it against her railings while she dug around in her handbag for the door key. Becca slid the car window down and called out her reassuring parting shot before Kitti disappeared inside her house.

124

'I wouldn't worry – there'll be hundreds of people there tonight - what's the chance they'll pick on your mum?'

Twelve

Becca put on her Mika CD. She danced across the kitchen and, as if carefully choreographed, opened cupboards in time to the music and closed drawers with a shake of her hips until she'd collected everything she needed. Champagne flutes, cake stand, dessert forks, napkins and plates. She arranged them on the island in the kitchen and carefully transferred the cake from the box to the stand. She was just sticking the last candle in place when the doorbell rang. Perfect timing.

Phil did the honours with the Champagne and Sam lit the candles with her lighter and relit them after Jachim had blown them out.

'Oh Becca, this is lovely. Wow! Not too much for me Phil, I'm driving.'

'Why don't you leave the car here and pick it up tomorrow?'

'Oh go on, then top it up, it's not every day you're thirty five. Although there'll be more cake and singing tomorrow, no doubt, when I pick my boys up.'

'Bring your drink through next door and we'll give you your present.'

Fi was clearly touched by their kindness, but not being the sentimental type she laughed it off with a few 'mirror mirror' on the wall quips. The party broke up when Jachim fell asleep. While they'd been busy chatting, he'd been dipping his fingers in all their glasses and licking the Champagne off.

Becca found a pashmina and Phil bundled him up in his arms and walked the few streets with Kitti back to her house. It was a starry night, the sky was clear and there was a chill in the air. They walked in an awkward silence for a while until Kitti finally broke it.

'I'm sorry for telling you what to do. It's none of my business. I should sort out my own life before I embark on major projects like yours.'

'It's fine. Don't worry. What you said made perfect sense. Things are starting to come together for me.'

They talked more easily as they walked down the hill and the conversation was only cut short by their arrival at Kitti's front door.

'This is me.' Kitti whispered. 'If I do the alarm, could you take him straight up?'

With the beeping alarm slowly fading Phil made his way up the narrow staircase, taking care not to bump his lightly snoring load. He picked his way across a floor scattered with Lego and Playmobil figures. He laid Jachim on his little bed, took off his shoes and socks and pulled the covers up and tucked Digger Dog in next to him. Jachim stirred a little and rolled over.

Phil stood and gazed at the little sleeping boy as he settled back to sleep. A floorboard creaked and Phil turned.

'Everything okay?' mouthed Kitti. Phil smiled and nodded 'Yeah, I was just thinking. If I'd known what pressures and struggles I was going to face in my adult life, maybe I'd have appreciated my carefree childhood more and not been in such a rush to grow up. We spend the early part of our life wanting it to speed up and the remaining part trying to slow it down.'

Avoiding the squeaky floorboard and toy-strewn carpet, Phil tiptoed back on to the landing. Kitti drew the curtains, turned down the light and pulled the bedroom door to behind her before continuing their conversation.

'I was in a rush to grow up, all kids are I think. Age is status, age is staying up late, age is more pocket money and more freedom. You know what my Dad was like, Phil. Family honour and duty and all that. I was desperate to have some independence.'

In a reflectful mood she paused and glanced back up the stairs to where Jachim was snoozing 'Maybe my Dad was right. Maybe having too much freedom ultimately meant I ended up with no freedom.'

'You wouldn't be without him now though, would you?'

'No. No of course not. I have no regrets about being a mum. Just about how it came about.'

Kitti did her strange little shrug shake and smiled, indicating an end to her musing on the past.

'Having your own kids gives you the chance to relive your childhood, to savour it. Don't get me wrong, I'm not living my life through Jachim, but some of his excitement rubs off on me, it's infectious. I feel like I'm experiencing life anew.'

'I'm really pleased for you Kitti. And if I'm honest, just the tiniest bit jealous.'

'You're joking. I never imagined anyone would envy my life. You're very good with him. You'll make a great Dad one day, you'll see.'

'I don't think so. Look at me; I can't even look after myself. I can't imagine how I'd cope with all that responsibility.'

Kitti touched him lightly on the arm. 'It could be the making of you.'

'Everything I've ever done I've imagined will be the making of me and so far it's all culminated in the breaking of me.'

'You're very tough on yourself, aren't you?'

'Being tough has always seen me right, driven me on…'

'Until now?'

'Yes. I guess so.'

'Time for some tlc perhaps?'

'Perhaps.'

The awkward silence returned.

'Well, thanks for bringing Jachim home for me.' Kitti blustered, changing the atmosphere in an instant. She'd opened up to Phil before and she was afraid of where the conversation was heading. 'He's so heavy now, I should have brought his buggy, but I didn't know he was going to get legless. He's inherited my Champagne taste, shame I've only got beer money.'

After a clumsy kiss on the cheek, Phil stepped out into the chilly night air and strolled home, spotting constellations as he walked back up the hill. Kitti slumped for a moment against the closed front door hugging herself before gaining the strength to climb the stairs to check on Jachim.

Becca was loading the dishwasher when Phil arrived back.

'I think that went well,' Becca called as she clattered the dirty dishes into the plate racks.

'Fi was really pleased with the mirror. You're a very good friend to your friends.'

'And sister to my brother?' Becca asked with a smirk, closing the dishwasher with a flick of her hips. Phil rolled his eyes, shook his head and did his best withering expression (who said men can't multi-task) 'Yes, you're a good sister to your brother.'

Becca counted four empties as she dropped them into the recycling bin.

'You were a bit too good with the topping up. I've had far too much. I was hoping to keep a clear head. I need to go to the shop and have a sort out before tomorrow. You'll be okay on your own here for a bit, won't you?'

'I could come and give you a hand if you like.' Phil offered half-heartedly, knowing how he'd really like to spend his time.

'Thanks, but it won't take long. I could really use your help tomorrow though.'

With the house to himself, Phil made a cup of tea and plumped the cushions - oh God now he was at it. He settled down on the sofa with 'handbags' as everyone affectionately referred to the book. He flicked through the pages until he found where he'd got up to.

This was not the kind of book he'd normally choose in a million years. Kitti was right, he'd been kidding himself that he was reading the book for the book group. The truth was, he was quite enjoying it. No, he was really enjoying it. It was his guilty pleasure.

It was so different from his own style of writing. This wasn't gritty or raw. No battles, no power-crazed dictators. It was light, quirky and witty. He'd found himself chuckling to himself as he turned page after page. He'd read several chapters when he heard Becca chatting on her mobile standing outside on the doorstep. He stuffed the book behind the cushions and went to open the front door.

Becca had the phone jammed tight to her ear. Her brow was furrowed in a deep frown. Phil lent out and touched her arm.

'Who is it?' He whispered. She paused, mouthed K-i-t-t-i to Phil, then continued her conversation. 'So, what did she say? What does that mean? Are you okay? Shall I come round? Tomorrow? Yes I'm in the shop, but I'm sure Phil can hold the fort for an hour.'

Becca looked at Phil, who nodded his agreement.

'I'll call round when we get back from the gym.' Phil grimaced at the thought. 'Okay, get a good night's sleep. Don't let this spook you. See you tomorrow.'

Becca let out a long sigh, dropped her phone in her bag and followed Phil into the house

'What's happened?'

'Kitti's had a message.'

'And?' Phil hated the cryptic conversations that Becca specialised in, 'I get them all the time. Usually from my bossy sister telling me what to do.'

'From the other side.'

Phil stared blankly.

Becca went on to explain about "Dead Men's Shoes" and Penny Truman.

'Penny did a whole load of stuff and right at the end she picked on Kitti's Dad's golf shoes. She said that the owner had died of a heart attack on the thirteenth hole.'

'And did he?'

'Yeah, thirteen really was unlucky for him. Kitti's Mum blamed it on all the ghee his Mum cooked with.'

'She said the owner was cross, as they were expensive shoes and he'd hardly had a chance to wear them.'

'Right again?'

'You got it. Everyone laughed when she said that the owner wanted the shoes given away, saying there was no point in keeping them as his daughter would never marry a golfer. I bet Kitti was relieved to hear her life would be free of diamond-patterned pastel knitwear.'

'All sounds pretty harmless so far. What's got her freaked?'

'Well, it's weird really. It sounds like it was a bit of a throw-away comment, mentioned in passing at the end. And I can't remember exactly what she said, but it was something about worries over a boy with bad blood.'

'I can't believe she's into all that mumbo jumbo?'

'I don't think she is really, but you have to admit, it's hard to dismiss it, when everything else she said was so on the button. She even mentioned Kitti's Mum letting the vegetable plot go to rack and ruin.'

'It's a bit vague though, what does worries about bad blood mean?'

'Well I know what Kitti thinks it means.'

'I didn't think these psychic people told you bad news.'

'Maybe Penny didn't see it as bad news.'

'That's a straw worth clutching at.'

Becca sat down uncomfortably on the sofa. She felt around under the cushions and pulled out her copy of 'Handbags at Dawn'.

'Are you reading this?'

'I've skim read it. I thought if I was coming along, I should make a bit of an effort.'

'If this is where you're up to...' Becca unfolded the corner of a page near the end of the book. '...you've made a bit more than a bit of an effort, looks like you've nearly finished it.'

'Have I? Yes, I suppose I have.'

'You like it, don't you? You don't want to, but you do. Come on, admit it.'

'Okay, I admit, in the absence of anything else to read, it's been good to have something not too challenging to pass the time.'

'Well I think it's brilliant. I'm up to where she goes to her granny's funeral and the hearse can't get into the cemetery because one of those eco cars is parked blocking the entrance and the pall bearers get out, lift it up and solemnly carry it out of the way, it's hilarious.'

'Yeah, that bit's quite funny.'

'What about the part where she goes to stay with her boyfriend's parents for the first time and their dog keeps stealing things out of her suitcase.'

'I don't remember that part.'

'The dog, Henry or whatever his name is, turns up while everyone is having breakfast with one of her panty liners stuck to his head, it's a classic.'

Becca's phone rang and she went and stood on the doorstep, the only place she got decent mobile reception.

'We're home. Call me on my home phone.'

'Was that Kitti again?'

'No, it was Mum. I forgot, I said I'd call her when we got back. She's probably calling to check up on you.'

'She could just call me and ask how I am.'

'She tried that before, remember? You kept telling her you were fine.'

'And I was – sort of.'

'She just wants a little reassurance, that's all. Don't worry, I won't mention your newly acquired criminal record...'

The phone rang. Phil put his palms together and tilted his head down on them in a bedtime gesture. Becca nodded, already recounting the week's events. While she was preoccupied, Phil slyly picked up her copy of 'Handbags' and headed for his room.

He flopped down on his bed and flicked through until he found his unfolded page marker. Half an hour later he heard Becca still on the phone, shutting the house up and then climbing the stairs to bed.

At 1am Phil closed the book – finished. He felt empty, hollow, flat. He felt a sense of loss. Not because he hadn't enjoyed the book. The exact opposite, he'd really enjoyed it. The ditsy humour, the quirky story, the pure escapism of it, but now there was no escape and it was that he was mourning. 'Handbags' had been a welcome distraction; slipping into someone else's world meant he didn't have to face trying to live in his – now he did. He realised that he couldn't look to others for a way out, only he could dig his way out of this one.

Sure Becca had tried and she'd done a good job, she'd pulled him out of his downward spiral, got him back on the rails. Now it was up to him. With that thought echoing around his head, he fell into a heavy, intoxicating sleep.

When he woke he felt fully revived and energised. In his dreams he'd been making plans, organising his life, getting his act together. The only problem was he couldn't remember any of the decisions he'd made or any of the conclusions he'd come to.

It would come back to him he was sure, or maybe his subconscious would guide him towards the decisions reached by the practical and dynamic Phil of his dreams. He pulled on his gym gear and bounded down the stairs to find Becca.

Thirteen

According to his own judgment criteria, the class had gone well. He hadn't injured anyone. He hadn't injured himself - success. Showered and refreshed he stood drinking coffee behind the counter in Becca's shop. It had a strong woody aroma from the white-painted dressers and armoires mixed with the large citronella-scented candles and the flowery perfume from pressed tablets of Savon de Marseille.

How did Becca do this? He'd been here two hours and only the postman had been in so far. To relieve the boredom he started to move a few things around. Wouldn't it make more sense to have the soap with the bathrobes? And the cushions would look better on the chaise and the greetings cards were randomly displayed. New baby was between engagement and wedding. Surely that wasn't right?

The door bell tinkled at the front of the shop and Phil was rescued from trying to solve the social dilemma. Standing with her back to him was the woman who had interrupted their lunch with Kitti. The unwelcome bookworm.

'Good morning, Aurore isn't it? Can I help?'

'Is Rebecca 'ere?'

'I'm afraid she's not at the moment, but she should be back soon.'

'Oh dear, zat's a pity.'

She strolled around, avoiding making eye contact, lightly running her hands over different pieces as she moved about the shop

'Rebecca tells me you 'ave an 'ouse in France.'

'Yes, I bought it after my second book was published. It was a bit of a wreck but it's lovely now.'

'My family have an 'ouse in a little village called Aubeterre-sur-Dronne in the Charente. It is beautiful - well wors a visit if you're ever passing trough.'Aurore stopped walking and turned to face him. 'I've come to pick up zat vase.'Aurore pointed to a tall etched-glass cylinder. 'It's a present for a friend and I'm on my way to meet 'er now. Becca said as a friend, she'd give me discount.'

'As I say, she's due back any minute.'

'She won't mind if I take it now.'

Before Phil could argue, Aurore lifted the vase from the window display.

'Don't worry about packing it up, I'll take it as it is and wrap it at 'ome. Tell Rebecca I'll give 'er ze money at ze book group.' She called as she was going out of the door.

Phil was still standing staring at the door when Becca came through it.

'Was that Aurore I just saw leaving?'

'Yes and she's taken the vase.'

'I don't suppose she actually paid for it? I thought not.' Becca said, seeing the apology written across Phil's face. 'It's not your fault. She does this all the time to the other girls, I'm sure she waits until I go out.'

'She said she'd pay you at book group.'

'Yeah right, I'll believe that when I see it. That's not for a few weeks and she'll have forgotten about it by then. It's a nightmare getting the money off her. She always complains how expensive everything is here and wants to pay what she thinks it would cost in France, forgetting what I have to spend to get it here.'

'Do you fancy a coffee?'

'No thanks, I feel a bit wired, too may espressos at Kitti's.'

'How is she?'

'She's OK. She's a bit paranoid about Jachim anyway, and the whole psychic thing hasn't helped. She seemed a bit more chilled when I left.'

Becca looked around the shop, spotting something was different but unable to put her finger on it.

'Have you moved things around?'

'A few things – sorry, I was bored.'

'Don't apologise, I think it looks great... the whole merchandising thing is not really my strong point, but it's obviously yours.'

'I've no idea what merchandising is. I was just approaching it from a logical perspective and grouping things together that I thought went together.'

'I love what you've done here.' Becca ran her hand along one of the decluttered dressers. 'I knew it needed doing but it was just too big a job for me and to be honest I didn't know where to start.'

'How about I come in tomorrow and do a bit more?'

'That would be fantastic. Are you sure you want to take this on?'

'Yeah, I need to keep busy, besides I'd feel like I was earning my keep.'

'You'd be doing me a really big favour, I need to sort this all out before I start to get any new stock in.'

Phil liked the idea of Becca being indebted to him for a change. One day helping out in the shop became two and before he knew it he was a regular behind the counter. Day after day they worked together side by side. Phil made suggestions and did the heavy shifting of furniture and Becca did all her trademark styling finishing touches; they made a good team.

On his third week in the shop Phil tackled the previously chaotic glory hole storeroom. Applying a commissariat approach he transformed it from an Aladdin's cave into an ordered and inventoried store that any army department would be proud of.

Phil thrived on their new routine. They started each day with a class at the gym, then cycled back to Becca's for a shower and a quick change. They'd pick up breakfast at the café and eat it at the counter of the shop while they planned out that day's jobs. If it wasn't too busy Phil would slip out for a run at lunchtime or join Becca if she was meeting up with one of the girls. As Becca kept telling him and anyone else who'd listen, It wasn't slave labour it was all part of "Rebecca's Rehab" and it was doing him good.

To be fair he felt fitter and he went to bed tired at the end of each day, but he wasn't sure if that was the days in the shop or Becca's almost unrelenting social calendar. Last week alone he'd been out for drinks twice, done a Thai cookery class, been to a shopping evening to help Becca choose a hat and shoes for a forthcoming christening and sat through a strange monologue at the arts centre about the menopause.

He was glad in more ways than one when Becca's boys had returned from Ireland. He'd offer his babysitting services as an excuse to sit out some of the social hurly burly. He wasn't sure that was going to work this evening though as Becca had a babysitter booked and she seemed very intent on him joining her for book group.

Becca called up the stairs to Phil and when there was no reply she went up and found him lying on his bed scribbling away in his Moleskine notebook, listening to his iPod.

'Are you going to change before we go?'

'Would you mind if I didn't come?' Phil did a theatrical stretch and yawn. 'I feel like an early night tonight.'

'Oh no, you've got to come. You're our star attraction, a real author. Maybe with you there we'll stay a little more focussed and talk more about the book and less about our kids, schools, men and house prices.'

'To be honest, I just don't know how I'll feel sitting there with everyone going on about how much they loved that book. I know rationally that it isn't responsible for what's happened to me, but I can't help feeling intense resentment. More so now I've read it. You see this as some kind of aversion therapy, kill or cure and all that. But I'm worried that it won't cure anything and it'll kill all the good things that are starting to happen. Kill the sense of calm and clarity I have at the moment.'

'I know you think I'm mad, but I think it will be good for you to understand what people like about the book. It'll depersonalise it. "Handbags" hasn't toppled you from your throne. Its success has just coincided with it. Your core readership has rejected reading as a whole, that's not a rejection of you - Phil Drummond the man. You're still a great writer.'

'I get what you're saying and it makes sense when you say it. Everything's so mixed up in my head, it's hard to know what's real.'

'I'll tell you what, why not come along for a while and if it all gets too much, we'll make an excuse and slip away early. Besides, you've got to come, you've actually read the book and everything.'

'Have you managed to finish any of the books so far?'

'One or two.' Becca replied a little defensively. 'What normally happens is I end up taking a backlog of book club books on holiday with me and catch up while I'm away from all the things that stop me reading at home.'

'What about Tess of the d'Urbevilles?'

'Yes… all right… okay - I couldn't face it so I got the video out instead. You mustn't mention that tonight though. Hardy's such hard work, it's all so grim and depressing with endless descriptions of brown, ploughed, furrowed fields.'

Becca had done her usual trick of lightening his mood and in less than half an hour he was shaved, showered and sitting on a sofa in Sam's lounge. An odd assortment of chairs from different parts of the house, were arranged around the edge of the room. It reminded him of the family get-togethers of his childhood, when even some of their rickety old flowery deckchairs were drafted in for active service. Phil and Becca were the only ones sitting down; everyone else was mingling in the centre of the room.

He hadn't really known what to expect but it was more like a drinks party than a book group. Plates of canapés were doing the rounds while Sam's eldest daughter worked the room pouring glasses of wine. Sam's arrival with a pile of books signalled the start. The conversation quietened and everyone took their seats.

Sam stood the books up on one of the bookcases.

One of the books, Phil noticed, was his. His first one.

'These are my suggestions for our next book. I'll pass them round later and we can talk about them more then. Is everyone here?'

Becca scanned the room and was relieved to see Aurore had not made it. Over the years, people had come and gone but the personality of the group hadn't changed. It didn't take itself too seriously, it was relaxed, friendly and there were no dominant characters. That was about to change - the doorbell rang and Sam went to answer it.

'Hi Aurore, glad you could make it. Here, let me take your coat. Go through, we're just about to start. Can I get you a drink?'

'Could I 'ave a glass of tap water?'

'Are you sure? We've got lots of non alcoholic drinks, juices elderflower lemonade...'

'Tap water will be fine.' Aurore replied in a clipped, abrupt manner.

'Oh, okay.'

There were a couple of empty chairs left, but Aurore squeezed herself on to the sofa next to Phil and Becca.

'Here you are, Aurore.' Sam placed her glass on a side table.

'Are you on the vodka already?' Joked Fi. Everyone laughed, with the exception of Aurore who smiled the smile of someone not in the least amused.

'Just before we start, some of you might know him already, but I'd like to introduce Phil, or as I've always known him Becca's big brother. Phil's written loads of books and he's kindly agreed to read an extract from his first book 'Soldiering on' for us tonight.'

Phil nearly choked on his mouthful of wine. He looked daggers at his sister but adopted Aurore's smiling technique, when what he actually wanted to do was throttle Becca.

Sam passed him his book. He stood up and held the book with trembling hands as he looked around at the expectant faces. The room was silent except for a ticking sound from the plumbing. Becca gave him a thumbs-up sign which he ignored. Once his books were published he never reread them, let alone out loud in public.

Phil flicked through the pages; Sam really had caught him on the hop, he didn't know where to begin or what to choose. The early chapters were the set up for the main story, Serbs, Croats and Muslims - a who's who of combat. It was important, vital to the overall story, but on its own it would be a bit out of context.

He thumbed through a bit further, he got to a bit about Muslim families having their houses torched; some while they were asleep in their beds, a bit brutal for this gathering he thought. But then again the book was about a very brutal war.

What about something from the end he wondered – Phil was soon reminded that very few of his books had a happy ending, particularly as a lot of it was based on his experience.

The last part of the book was the fallout from the war. The main character living with PTSD and coming to terms with life back home or in his case not coming to terms with it. How he'd mistake a window cleaner for a sniper and how a motorbike backfiring would leave him cowering behind a parked car. It was a bit close to the bone as it was lifted pretty much verbatim from his journal. No, that wasn't the right tone for the group.

He was about to apologise and give up when he came across a chapter about the Foča massacre. In no shape or form could it be described as an uplifting piece, but it was probably the closest he was likely to find in one of his books. It described Emaija one of his main characters, a 15-year-old Bosnian Muslim's escape from one of the many horrific detention centres, but at least she manages to escape. Phil cleared his throat and began to read.

As he turned the first page he was back there in the thick of it; all the old feelings of panic and despair were reawakened in the space of three paragraphs. How can it still be so vivid after all these years, he thought? No matter how deep he thought he'd buried those feelings, it was clear to see that it was and would always be painfully near the surface.

He was a soldier, he'd been trained for combat and all the stuff that goes with it, but keeping the peace was something new and Bosnia was something else. Nothing he'd seen anywhere had prepared him for the barbaric butchery inflicted by neighbour upon neighbour. The people who were hell bent on killing each other had once gone to school together, worked together and lived together on the same suburban streets – it was insane.

After eight pages Phil stopped reading and swallowed a couple of times – no good, his throat was still dry. The room was silent; even the plumbing had stopped ticking and was paying attention. He lowered his book a fraction to check that nobody had snuck out or fallen asleep. The room was still; everyone was wearing their concentrating face and listening raptly. Before anyone caught his eye, Phil swiftly raised his book and carried on.

He'd got to the pivotal bit where Emaija is planning her escape. She and several other women from her village are held prisoner in the leisure centre. At her leisure she notes every mundane detail of the everyday routine; every guard change, every cigarette break, every car in and out of the checkpoint. She bides her time until she knows the split second when time will be on her side. Phil continued his Jarhead Jackanory.

The papers had often said Bosnia was a living hell and it was, but two years on they'd buried their dead and were rebuilding their country. They'd been able to move on. Phil found himself home with the conflict over, but his own personal war was just beginning. His brain had still thought he was out there.

He'd never escape the sound of that grenade. Over and over again he'd hear it, see it and smell it. Campbell was the casualty that tipped him over the edge, the one that lifted the lid... opened the box. They'd talk in codes, they'd try and depersonalise it, but he wasn't just a man down, he wasn't just a T1 - he was Campbell, his mate... he'd died and at moments like this Phil felt he would always be the living casualty.

Phil was in full flow, when he was interrupted by a loud nose blow from Fi. The room was silent. Mascara ran and tissues were passed.

'I'm so sorry,' Phil stammered. 'I didn't mean to upset anyone...'

Sam blinked away her sadness and cleared her throat before speaking. 'Books are supposed to shake us from the everyday, they should involve and get a reaction...'

'So you're not upset?'

'No, not at all, this is us involved and reacting.' Sam looked around the group.

Everyone nodded their agreement and an impromptu Q and A session emerged from the silence. Bosnians, Serbs, Croats, who were the good guys? Where was Dubrovnik? Typical Fi, she'd been there on holiday once and wondered where it fitted in. He was on a real high now, he felt euphoric.

He glanced at Becca, who gestured towards the door. He shook his head, no he didn't want to leave while he was in his element, talking about what was important to him and being appreciated for what he'd done and what it had inspired him to write. He realised again just how much his writing had helped him to deal with his grief.

'What's your next book about?' Phil explained what had happened and how he came to be squatting in Becca's attic. He was heartened by their outrage at his treatment.

Sam took the floor once more. 'Please stop me if I'm reading the mood in this room wrong, but I think I speak on behalf of everyone here when I say we don't need to review the other books - our next choice is made.' There were a few "here here's" and muttered agreement. Phil was touched by their generosity of spirit, this was not the evening he had expected and he was enjoying it enormously.

'Will you come back when we discuss it?' Sam asked.

'I'd be honoured to, but you must be honest in your views. I don't want you saying you like it just because I'm here. That wouldn't be right.'

'You know me Phil, if it's a pile of crap I'll tell you straight.'

'Thanks Fi, I'm never left in any doubt on what your views are on any topic. You can always be relied upon for your honesty.'

'You mean she's got a tongue that would strip bark from a tree,' laughed Becca.

'Zis is all very nice but are we going to talk about ze 'andbag book or not?'

Her voice sliced through the self-congratulatory atmosphere. The whole group turned and looked, they'd forgotten about Aurore. She sat completely untouched by the high emotions of the group.

'Well yes… you're right. I suppose we should. Why don't you start us off Aurore?'

'Okay Sam, I 'ave some notes 'ere.'

Aurore put her glasses on and unfolded a large piece of a pink paper from her handbag. She proceeded to take them through chapter by chapter, her likes and dislikes in minute detail. They sat politely listening, but when she got to chapter 8, Fi interrupted her.

'It's great that you've looked at the book close up, but usually we summarise it in a simple "I loved it, I hated it" kind of way.'

'Oh I see. You're not interested in what I sought.'

'Yes of course we are, that's what a book group's all about. Sharing and discussing each others views and opinions, but what I think Fi was trying to say is…'

Fi opened her mouth to speak, but Sam silenced her with a sharp look. Fi never knew when to stop digging.

'…I suppose we're a bit more superficial. You're right, maybe we should dig a little deeper. We're lucky you've joined us. Having such an analytical mind in the group will make for some very thought-provoking discussions. If one of your friends asked whether you'd recommend the book, what would you say?'

'If zey were French I'd say no. Ze British humour is so – British. Fortunately I have lived 'ere long enough to understand, but it doesn't make me smile. If it were an English friend I'd say yes. I can see from ze TV zat zis is ze kind of sing zat zey like but it's not my kind of sing. It lacks sophistication.'

Sam paused for a moment before replying. 'You're right Aurore, it is a very British story but then again Lucy Stevens is a British author. It's every bit the story that the loose brushstroke illustration of the handbag-wielding women on the cover tells you it's going to be. No big surprises on that front.'

'Yeah, I agree.' Becca added. 'Although I was reading in the paper that it's been translated into ten languages including French and they're going to make a film of it, so they obviously think it's got worldwide appeal.'

Phil was in his own little world. He was so chuffed they'd chosen his book as their next read that he was oblivious to the debate batting back and forth around him. And then suddenly he was sucked back in, with no idea what they were talking about.

'Phil, do you agree with Kitti. Is it like baking a cake?'

'Sorry Sam?'

'Are there set ingredients… a recipe even, for writing a successful book.'

'Yeah I think there is. If you take my books, for example, the stories are all different, but if you dissect the story they're bound together in a similar way.'

'So it's the eggs that are important?'

'Maybe Fi, but to carry on the strange cake analogy it's not just the ingredients. It's no good having them if you can't cook.'

'Have you been talking to my kids?' Fi asked indignantly.

'No, what I'm saying is, you need to know what you're doing. You need to have the writing skills.'

'I can cook, it's that stupid bloody Aga.'

Phil lost Fi to a splinter debate with the woman sitting next to her on Aga v electric oven.

'Humour me, Phil,' said Sam, thinking out loud, 'Just say, I'm someone who has the skills, I understand the successful formula of a book like 'Handbags'. Could I write a blockbuster?'

'Yeah, I don't see why not. You could - anyone could.'

'Shame, because I can't write a shopping list let alone a book and I've no idea what 'Handbags' winning formula is. I guess I won't give up the day job just yet.'

'Just as well. What would Pharmic do without their top sales rep?'

'You're too kind Becca, but I think they'd survive.'

Sam opened another bottle and topped up the glasses. Without her at the helm, the conversation drifted away from books and on to the usual topics of property prices, schools and tutors.

Fourteen

Becca had clearly felt the frosty vibes he'd directed at her early in the evening. He could see from her face that she was not looking forward to the walk home. She was right to be wary, he'd been cross about her springing the reading on him. But then again if she'd told him, he wouldn't have come.

They walked in silence for a bit, but Becca had never been terribly good with silences, something her ex Dermot was always pointing out.

'I'm sorry Phil… I shouldn't have planned that without telling you…'

'Most sisters grow out of torturing their siblings but you…'

'I really am sorry. I wanted you to be the centre of attention tonight. I wanted everyone to see how amazing and talented my brother is and why I'm so proud of him…'

'It's okay Becca,' he cut in. 'I'm teasing you. I've had a great evening. You did good. You're right, I wouldn't have come if I'd known and then I'd have missed out.'

If that was true, why did he suddenly feel so flat. Making a connection with people through his writing had always been a real buzz; a feeling he loved and something he'd begun to wonder if he'd ever have again. The book group had reminded him why he wrote; what it meant to him and what it meant to his readers, dwindling though they may be.

It had been just like old times, chatting with likeminded people hanging on his every word. But now he began to appreciate that the evening had been just that, "like old times" it wasn't now – no matter how he might long for them, those days were gone - over. And pretending any different was not going to help him rebuild his life.

The evening, like his writing career, had been fun while it lasted. And just as a good book is an escape from everyday drudgery, you know that when you turn the last page, your life with all its baggage will still be there waiting for you.

The evening had been bittersweet. Sweet to bask in the warm glow of his previous accomplishments and bitter to be reminded that writing, something so important to him, was no longer part of his life. He was just harking back to the old days, a literary Norma Desmond, sans turban, although now he came to think about it, he'd always looked good in a hat. The bitter truth was, he had been a successful author but that was all in the past.

'So you're not mad with me?'

'How could I be?'

'It's just that you don't seem that happy. I'd hoped this evening would be a real boost for you.'

Phil stopped walking and turned to face Becca. None of that parallel positioning crap for him anymore – he could talk face to face and look his sister right in the eye.

'I know you've only been trying to get me back on the right track – and to begin with I was a complete arse; doing everything I could to derail all your efforts.'

'It's fine, I wouldn't want me telling me what to do either.'

'I guess tonight I woke up to myself; it's like I'm in mourning for something I've lost. It's also the realisation that I've burnt my bridges, I've missed the boat, the horse has bolted and I've spent too long sobbing over my spilt semi skimmed.'

'It's not too late… it's never too late.'

'Maybe, but if I hadn't gone into meltdown I could have made things a whole lot easier on myself.'

'What, and change the habit of a lifetime.' Becca linked her arm through Phil's and they continued their journey home.

'Why do I do it? Why do I always take the hard way?'

'You were trained to take the hard way, I guess it's a route you know well.'

Phil let out a long sigh.

'Mal tried to fix up all sorts of new deals and if I'd played ball none of this would have happened…'

'Yeah you're right, none of it would have done. You and I wouldn't have got to know each other again; to be friends not just family. No spa weekend, no shopping, no gym classes, no makeover, no nights out with the girls, no dodgy-named cocktails…'

'No being arrested for flashing.'

'Okay… so it hasn't all been good, but I'm a real believer in things happening for a reason. You only ever see the reasons looking back and I know that when I look back on this time I'll do so with great fondness.'

'Me too sis', me too.'

'So what now?'

He felt sure Becca would see it as impulsive, but in a sudden moment of clarity he knew what he must do.

'As they say on TV, I feel tonight has been a defining moment. Now I think it's time for me to get my act together, time to go out there and do something with my life – I've no idea what yet, but I feel in a slightly better place now, better placed to make some decisions.'

The next morning Phil woke early; he packed his things into his bag and carried it downstairs.

'Are you sure you're ready to go? Why don't you stay for a bit longer? I feel my book club plan backfired; rather than building you up, it's knocked you down. It's caused you to make hasty decisions and that was never the plan.'

'That's just it, I need to make my own plans now.'

'Everything I've done has been to help get you back into the real world. Now I think I've pushed you too far.'

'And I'm very grateful. The very fact I can appreciate what you've done shows me how far I've come. I have stopped wallowing in my pit of despair and have realised that things need to change and only I can change them. Living your life has been fun but I need to live my own. And now I'm ready to do just that.'

He didn't know if that was strictly true, but what he did know was, five weeks of "Rebecca's rehab" had taken him as far as it could. He had to get away to find his own path. His big fear was that rather than taking control of his life and making a fresh start he was just doing his usual thing; slipping back into his old ways and running away when things got a bit tricky.

'So what are you going to do?'

'I'm going to go home. Check everything's okay, pick up my passport and then do what I do every summer. Fly to the house in France and enjoy the summer. I may even do some writing; something different, a new start.'

'Do you need to go home? Couldn't you sort things out over the phone? You're in London. Wouldn't it make more sense just to take a plane from Heathrow?'

Becca was doing her level best to dissuade him from returning home. 'Hang on a minute. Why don't you want me to go home? Do you think I'll just slide back into my old ways? Don't you trust me?'

'No. I mean yes. It's not about trust… '

Becca was flustered and looked very guilty. Phil felt some satisfaction in catching her out but he wasn't entirely sure what it was he'd caught her doing.

'Okay I confess. Mrs Emerson called me. She's been away looking after her sister and couldn't believe the state of your house when she got home. She was worried about you and called me.'

'I didn't know she had your number.'

'She didn't. I dropped it off with your keys before we left. Anyway, she's arranged for a cleaning company to do the house from top to bottom and a couple of the rooms are being decorated. A gentleman friend of hers, she says you've met him. Mike the cab driver?'

'Yeah, he's driven me around the bend a few times.'

'Well, he's bringing his lawnmower collection over. Says it's a big job. He's going to sort your garden out and shift all those boxes in the study. You see, you don't need to go back and sort things out. Things are or will be sorted out pretty soon.'

'Just one flaw in the master plan – my passport.'

Becca opened the long drawer under the island in the kitchen and from under a pile of napkins, pulled out a passport.

'Is that mine?'

'Yes. I picked it up when we were at yours. I thought if things worked out okay it would be useful and if they didn't, it was safer that I looked after it.'

'Did you think I'd flee the country?'

'I didn't know what you'd do but there's no need for me to hang on to it.'

Becca handed the passport over and began the non-essential job of tidying the napkins in the drawer. 'I can see you've got a bit of your old spark about you. I'll be sad to see you go.'

The napkins were now all in neat piles arranged by colour. It had provided a small distraction but Phil could tell from the tremble in her voice that she was upset.

'I've loved having you here. I can't remember when we last spent so much time together. I'll really miss you.'

She walked over to the window and stared into the garden with her back to him, hiding her teary eyes. Phil went and stood behind her and wrapped his big ungainly arms around her.

'I'll miss you too. I don't know how to thank you for what you've done. You know I've never been very good at the whole emotional thing but I just want to say I love you big sis'.'

They stood rooted to the spot for a little while watching the rain run down the glass pane and then Becca sprang into action.

'You can thank me by not putting me through this again. Don't rush into anything, have a break in France and think over your options.'

Becca booted up her laptop and checked the flight times. 'There's one at half past three. I could drop you off if you like.'

'I'll get a cab, it'll be easier. Besides, shouldn't you be in the shop?' Phil hated goodbyes and he'd rather not drag it out any longer.

'Yes, I suppose I should. I could reschedule all my appointments for my postponed buying trip.'

'When are you going to do that?'

'It depends on when I can sort it out. If I leave it too long all the factories will have closed for the summer.'

'Are you planning on coming south?'

'I was thinking about going to a ceramics studio near Arles.'

'Why don't you take a little detour? The house is not too far away.'

'What, and check up on you?'

'I was thinking more of a long weekend, oysters and fine wine.'

'Yuk! You know I hate oysters.'

'All right, mussels in that little restaurant out on the sand bar'

'Now you're talking.'

'After all, I think it's my turn to look after you.'

Feeling in a thoroughly French holiday mood, Becca prepared the breakfast. She put a pot of coffee on to brew and took some croissants from the freezer to warm in the oven while Phil booked his ticket online.

'All done?' she asked, spooning strawberry jam into a small glass pot.

'Yeah, I'm booked and I've sent a text to Didier to let him know I'm coming. I've had a few cryptic texts from him.'

'Are there any other kind?'

'You're right I'm sure the petit problem he mentions is just that, you know what they're like.'

'Indeed I do.'

'Hopefully he'll open up the house, switch the gas and electricity on and put the car battery on to charge. You know… I'm really looking forward to it.'

'And so you should, it's such a different pace of life there, it's just what you need.'

'It's ages since I've been on holiday. I mean a proper holiday not a few days tagged on to a book tour. Hopefully, I'll be able to get a real tan while this blotchy one fades. Would you mind booking me a cab for midday?'

'Your flight's not 'til three thirty you know?'

'I want to go to the airport early so I can do some shopping. I'm going to treat myself to some new shirts and a pair of shades.'

'You've definitely been here too long. You're actually looking forward to a shopping spree. What have I turned you into?'

'I thought it would complete my slightly dodgy makeover.'

'I know the tan's not great, but I have to say, I think you look the best you've looked in years.'

'Thanks, but I think you're a little biased. I'm sure Trinny and Susannah always think they've done a fantastic job too.'

'It's not just me; you got a big thumbs-up from the girls. I won't be the only one sorry to see you go. They've loved having you around. In fact I'll get a whole load of earache if I let you go without saying goodbye. Before I ring for a cab, I'll see if anyone's around to meet for a quick farewell coffee.'

Becca made her calls while Phil cleared the table, loaded the dishwasher and gathered the rest of his things together.

'Sam and Kitti will meet us there at eleven. Fi's got a chiropodist appointment and said to give you a big goodbye kiss from her.'

'I think I had a lucky escape there. A big kiss from Fi is a frightening thought.'

'Fi in full flight has caused many a man to quake in their boots.'

'That I can well believe.'

Becca held the phone to her ear with her shoulder while she scribbled the booking reference on the back of an old envelope from the recycling bin.

'I've ordered your cab to pick you up from the café, so we'll take your stuff with us when we go and you won't have to rush back here.'

'Are we booked in for a class this morning?'

'Yeah, but we can skip it if you like.'

'No I'd like to go. I don't want you thinking I'm wimping out on my last day of Rebecca's rehab.'

'Fine. I'll just touch up my makeup, grab my stuff and then we're good to go. '

Phil was on a real high. Was it because, for the first time in a long time, he felt in charge or was it the endorphins racing around his body? Either way, he felt great. The class had been fun. It was typical, he'd just got the hang of it and now it was time to go. At the end

154

of the class everyone called their goodbyes and see you tomorrows as they left. They seemed really disappointed when he told them that actually they wouldn't. He was disappointed too, but he knew the life he was living wasn't his and it was time to give it back.

Phil sat drinking his latte at a table in the window, while he waited for the others. Becca had gone to check all was well at the shop and Kitti had sent a text to say they were running a little late and would be there soon.

'Yes please and one of those strawberry tarts.' Becca called to the girl behind the counter, who by way of a question was holding up a teapot with raised quizzical eyebrows. Becca pulled up a chair from another table. 'I've made few calls and despite my terrible French I've fixed up some meetings or at least that's what I think I've arranged. So, I'll see you mid August, if that's okay.'

'Perfect. I'm not planning on going anywhere, so just give me a call and let me know nearer the time.'

Kitti and Sam edged their way past the window and into the café, trying to hide something behind their back.

'So what's with the great escape then?' Kitti asked. She was smiling, but there was a touch of disappointment in her voice.

'It just seems like now's a good time to go. Last night reminded me of how I'd come to terms with much greater sadness than someone not wanting to publish my book. It put it in perspective, made me feel a bit pathetic, I need to do some of the things we talked about at Radleigh Hall.'

Sam and Becca exchanged knowing looks when they thought he wasn't looking. Phil would miss the girls and Kitti in particular, their paths kept crossing but they never seemed to converge.

'I'm really sorry if I put you on the spot last night,' Sam said, giving him her customary hug and peck on the cheek. 'I sensed that Becca hadn't asked you about doing a reading.'

'Your senses are finely tuned.' Phil shrugged it off. 'Loath as I am to keep saying it - she was right; there's no way I would have come if she'd told me, but it did me the world of good.'

The waitress came and took more drinks orders, and Kitti ordered a plate of pastel-coloured macaroons - a very sophisticated and distant relative of the coconut variety favoured by Mrs Overall in Acorn Antiques.

'It was completely genuine... the response I mean,' Sam broke his thoughts. 'You're a great writer. Everyone's looking forward to reading your book.' Sam broke the pale pink meringue in half and continued as she nibbled on the soft chewy centre. 'It's quite different from the usual group choices, it's powerful stuff.'

'I'm sure I've got a few copies of that book somewhere at home, I could ask my neighbour to send them up... save you forking out, it could be like a little thank you.'

'Well actually, that's one of the things that delayed us.' Sam held up a carrier bag from the bookshop at the bottom of the hill.

'After all that's happened, it seems only right that we should add a few more sales.' Sam finished the remaining half of the macaroon. 'I know twelve more books isn't going to make your publisher change their mind, but it just feels like the right thing to do - show them people still value you... want to hear what you have to say.'

'You are a lovely woman Sam Richards and my sister is very lucky to have a friend like you.'

'I can't take all the credit - It was Kitti's idea, she suggested it; she's been carrying that book around for days.'

Sam rummaged in the bag and brought out the copy he'd read from at book club.

'I keep hoping there'll be the right moment to ask... a bit embarrassing really.' Kitti blushed. 'And now that you're going there won't be another right moment; this is it.'

'It's not embarrassing. I'd be happy to sign it for you.' Kitti handed him a pen and the book.

Phil turned to a blank page opposite the opening chapter and wrote.

Thanks for reminding me that words aren't just marks on a page, they tell the story of who we are and how we'd like the world to be. I still have a few more blank pages to fill thanks to you.

'You say everyone's looking forward to reading it – What, even Aurore?' Phil asked.

'I think we put her off and she won't come again. Wouldn't you say Sam?' Becca asked hopefully.

'I'm sorry to say she paid me for the book and I said I'd drop it off when they come in.'

'No... I'm amazed,' Becca groaned. 'Firstly that she wants to come again and secondly that you managed to get some money out of her. You know she didn't pay me for that vase. She said her friend spotted a chip on the rim and she's going to bring it back.'

'Yeah right, she's done that before hasn't she? That's the last you'll see of that,' said Kitti with a mouth full of pistachio macaroon.

They drank, ate and chatted for a while longer. Completely stuffed, Kitti sat back in her chair and then having squashed it she remembered the bag that was tucked away there.

'We couldn't let you go without a little parting gift,' she said, passing the bag to Phil. He took out the neat tissue paper bundle and unwrapped it carefully on the table. He untucked the ends and there, nestled in the centre, was a pair of pale blue Vilbrequin swimming trunks with a repeat pattern of bright green frogs on them.

'Kitti chose them,' Sam added with a knowing smile. 'Strangely, she seemed to know your size.'

Kitti blushed deeply. 'I couldn't help noticing the state of your trunks when we were at Radleigh Hall. And the frogs seemed rather appropriate...'

'I love them. I shall wear them every day when I have my early-morning dip.'

As Phil tucked them in the top of his bag and zipped it up, he heard the throaty chug of a diesel engine; he looked up to see a black cab pull up outside and knew it was time to say his au revoirs. Kitti and Sam decided to do French-style cheek kissing.

'They do four in the some parts of France.' Phil bent forward, offering his cheek to them again.

'When you two have quite finished. Do I get a chance to say goodbye?'

Phil gave Becca a huge bear hug, swept her off the ground and spun her around.

'Thank you, thank you, thank you,' he whispered.

'You're welcome, welcome, welcome.'

Putting her back on the ground, Phil stood back and opened his mouth to speak, 'I'm not very good at goodbyes - to be honest I'm not that good at hello either, but I just want to say...' Becca gestured with her hand and waved away his words.

'I know - it's okay you don't need to say those things to me. Look the meter's running, off you go.'

As the taxi pulled away, they ran alongside for a bit waving until the cab finally turned the corner and was gone. They were suddenly aware of the waitress running and waving along with them.

'I didn't know she knew Phil.' Kitti said with surprise.

'She doesn't - we haven't paid our bill.' Becca laughed.

Fifteen

Friday July 2nd 2010

The seatbelt sign pinged on, the plane dropped through the clouds and the familiar line of the coast came into view. As they passed above the houses in the hills, Phil could see the small jewel-like blue rectangles of swimming pools below, and then the sandy stonework of the aqueduct in the old city.

His ears popped and the plane dropped further; banking gently to the left, as they made their final descent across the salt marshes and down into Montpellier airport. The engines roared in reverse thrust and the interior fittings rattled as the wheels bumped down on the runway.

The plane slowed to a gentle speed and the engines died away as it taxied to the stand. Over the intercom the purser welcomed them to France and thanked them for flying British Airways; the door slid back and the chilled, recycled air was sucked from the plane by the intense dry heat of the Midi.

Phil was glad he only had hand luggage; he bypassed the scrum at the carousel and was first in line at the taxi rank. He gave the driver the address; Phil wasn't thinking in French yet; he usually found a couple of glasses of wine helped with his fluency, but it was a bit early in the day for that.

Barely had he strapped himself in and they were off. The stark new roads around the airport soon gave way to long avenues of plane trees with neat clipped verges punctuated every so often by roundabouts surrounded by light industrial and retail units selling sofas, speedboats and swimming pools.

They skirted one of the popular seaside towns; above the harbour buildings Phil glimpsed the pulsating lights and rotating hydraulic arms of one of the rides at Lunar Parc. He recalled taking his nephews there a couple of summers back – he must do that again soon, once he was back on an even keel.

A slip road took them away from the fairground and on to a wide stretch of dual carriageway he'd nicknamed "Hairdryer Boulevard". It had lampposts sporting bonnet-like shades that were reminiscent of the hairdryers that as a boy he remembered his mum had sat under for what seemed like hours; happily reading Woman's Own in her hairnet and rollers with wads of cotton wool protecting her ears from the heat and din.

Unlike the lush green of the wet British summer he'd left behind, here the grass was yellow, crisp and dry. With the exception of the roundabouts which were little oases, complete with trickling fountains and modern sculptures; floral displays bursting with colour and municipal pride.

They turned off Hairdryer Boulevard and the road hugged the edge of the eggy-smelling étang - the salt marshes where motionless flamingos balanced on one leg. And opposite at the riding school a few lone horses were chewing on the coarse, unappetising-looking brown tufts growing through the dusty soil.

Before long they were on the home straight. They came round the final bend past the ostrich farm and La Cave where you could buy wine by the litre out of something not dissimilar to a petrol pump. Straight ahead stood the village. It looked slightly fortified, standing as it did on a small hill. The bell tower of the church towered like a keep above the jostling tiled roofs of the adjacent houses. It really was beautiful.

The only blot on the landscape was the ugly concrete water tower on the edge of the village; with its wide conical top and short stocky stem, it looked like an oversized birdbath. Phil was glad that his house faced out over the vineyards and that he couldn't see it from his windows.

The taxi drove slowly through the village; the bar was doing a roaring trade. All the tables outside were occupied. A waiter was delivering a long, cold Pastis, and as he walked near the passing taxi he lowered the tray close enough for Phil to have leant out of the window and taken it. He didn't, but it was tempting. He was looking forward to strolling into the village later and sitting in that very spot and enjoying one of his own.

Outside the Mairie, old women sat chatting on benches in the shade, watching their men play Pétanque. The car pulled up opposite by a high stone wall, in which were set ornate, double wrought-iron gates. They were rusty and in the process of being repainted. He wondered if Didier had hurriedly started this when he received his text. Phil handed over a wad of euros and, avoiding the wet paint, pushed open the gate and walked along the curving path towards the house.

As he neared the house Phil could hear shouting coming from the side passage; he stopped on the path when suddenly a goat shot around the corner of the house with Karel in hot pursuit using her mop ineffectually as a crook to herd it. Karel was Didier's wife, she was Dutch and not easily fazed – the goat was the possible exception.

Didier looked after the garden and pool while Karel cleaned and did the laundry and kept the house in order. They were a great team - every home should have one, he thought. The goat dodged Phil and headed for the garden. Out of breath, Karel sauntered over to greet Phil.

'Oh Monsieur Phil, thank heavens you're here.'

Karel was in her fifties, but acted and dressed much younger. Her sister-in-law ran the local hairdressers, so Karel's hairstyle changed on a regular basis. Usually when her sister-in-law wanted to try out something new. Today it was a dark-brown feather cut with a small red streak in the fringe; it matched the angular glossy red glasses that framed her dark eyes.

'Some welcome party huh? Welcome home, Monsieur Phil.' Karel leant her mop against a gnarled olive tree, planted four cheek-skimming kisses on him as the goat doubled back the way it had come.

'Did you get Didier's message?'

'Which one?'

He'd had loads from Didier, but they were just the usual about Phil's summer arrangements – when he'd be arriving and how long he was staying.

'About the goats… Oh Monsieur Phil it's dreadful, your poor garden. All the plants and flowers…'

Phil had no idea what she was talking about and sensing that it might be easier to show him than try and put it into words, Karel took his hand and led him away under the trees towards the garden.

'We've tried to stop them but they just keep finding new ways to get in. Our dedication to keep them out is only matched by their dedication to break in. And they just chew and chew and chew until there's nothing left to chew; they destroy everything in their path.'

'I don't understand… where are they coming from?'

'They're from the farm at the back of you. You know, Madame Durand's…'

'Well she's a lovely old lady, when I bought that land off her to extend the garden and put the pool in she couldn't have been more helpful. I'll just pop over and have a word, I'm sure we can sort this out. What's the problem - a broken fence panel?'

'I wish it was that simple.'

Karel's ever-present mask of jovial capability dropped momentarily.

'If it was Didier could easily have fixed it – this is a bit more complicated – we've tried to fix it but we've failed…' She took great pride in her work and keeping everything on an even keel, this problem happening on her watch had really upset her.

'Colette Durand was a lovely woman… sadly she passed a few months ago and her nephew Gérard's inherited the farm. It's a pity he's not inherited her manners and easy-going charm too.'

'So what's his beef?'

'No… no beef just goats but I think there used to be a couple of old hoses…'

'No, sorry – I mean what's his problem – why's he doing this?'

'He's a nationalist… how do you say – nutter? You know that foreigners buying up all the houses round here aren't that popular – people like Gérard say it pushes up the property prices and then families that have lived here for generations can't afford to live here any more. People like him say "keep France for the French" that we need to take action to preserve our way of life.'

Karel snorted derisively. 'Things change you can't make the world stand still or even this little patch of France. We should welcome new people. We need new people, young people bringing their skills, spending their money. Otherwise we'll end up like a retirement village. I've lived here twenty-one years and still some of the elders treat me like Jean the foreigner.'

'Johnny Foreigner.' Phil corrected.

'Exactly…'

Karel then went off at a tangent explaining how unwelcoming she'd found the village when she first arrived and how hard she'd worked and how it had taken years to be accepted; to become a part of the community.

'Sorry to interrupt... I'm still a bit confused, slow down... can you start from the beginning and tell me what's happened?'

'Okay.' Karel took a deep breath and pushed her glasses back up onto the bridge of her nose. 'It all started after Colette died; Gérard went through the whole house and sold off everything he could. While he was clearing out he found some old deeds to the farm that show an easement... I don't know what the word is in English... a servitude?'

Phil shook his head. 'What does that mean?'

'It means there's a right of way over your property. It's old, been there for years. Madame Durand should have got the notaire to make a new route, maybe she didn't know it was there, we'll never know, but now there's trouble. Gérard's goats can trot back and forth through your garden just as they please and as you'll see they please quite a lot and there's nothing we can do about it.'

'But there are loads of other paths linking the top and bottom field, why would they choose the one route that takes them through my garden?'

'There are no other routes, Gérard's blocked them and taken down sections of fence on your border forcing the goats to use the only other available path through here.'

Karel waved her hand towards the garden as another goat appeared from behind the mock orange bushes on their left. Karel clapped her hands and the goat skittered off back in the direction it had come.

'What does he want? What's in it for him?'

'Like I'm saying, he's a nationalist it may be a moral objection - he may want to drive you out so he can buy up this place cheaply or more likely he's after some easy money.'

Karel dabbed her brow with a tissue.

'It was hard work, but Colette Durand always seemed to make a decent living from the farm - from what I've heard and seen he's a lazy sit around, a good for something'

'Lay about - good for nothing.' Phil corrected.

Karel ignored him and carried on. 'He can't be bothered to make a go of the farm, it's too much like hard labour – and then along comes an opportunity to make some money with very little effort and bob's your...' Karel racked her brains trying to remember the expression.

'Uncle,' Phil laughed, finishing her sentence.

Karel loved all these little sayings she'd picked up from Phil, Becca and her boys over the years; she scattered them liberally into conversations with Phil regardless of whether they actually illustrated the point she was making or not.

When he was in England and thought about France he pictured himself in his garden; beer bottle in hand strolling along the gravel paths, butterflies and bees buzzing around. He could almost smell the heady mix of scents from the jasmine and citrus geraniums.

The garden was always at its best at this time of year; the white-themed borders would be brimming with roses, peonies hydrangeas and poppies. The white tufted lavender would be reaching its peak and as for the succulents they had a reproduction rate rivalled only by the rabbits in Madame Durand's fields.

When he was planning the garden Becca had lent him some books for inspiration. He thought what he and Didier had created (mainly Didier) would not have looked out of place on the pages of any of Becca's books.

Before they rounded the corner of the house, Karel pulled Phil to a halt.

'Are you ready for this? They've made a real muck up of everything.'

Phil nodded and turned the corner.

Karel was sometimes prone to drama queen tendencies, but on this occasion she wasn't exaggerating. Today the garden looked more like it did in the Autumn when everything was severely cut back for overwintering. There was little evidence of his and Didier's careful landscaping plan; there were big gaps where some of the plants and shrubs had disappeared completely.

The lavender hedge edging the path was chewed back beyond recognition to short woody stumps and the trellis on the fence was bare. The herb garden was a trampled mud patch and the goats had performed their own savage style of topiary on the box, rosemary and bay.

The fruit trees he'd planted last year were stripped of their bark and new shoots, the one saving grace was that the heavily laden branches of the mature peach tree was beyond the reach of the goats massacring molars.

In an attempt to contain the goats Didier had made a makeshift barrier across the bottom of the garden using a couple of old doors, some chicken wire and assorted bits of wood from the garage.

'We thought if we could make a sort of barricade it would contain them and they could pass through to the bottom field without causing too much damage. The trouble is they jump. They're like little acrobats, they climb up on to each other's backs and then they leap over. In a circus it would be funny, but here no one's laughing.'

This was not what Phil was expecting – France had always been a sanctuary, somewhere he came to escape; somewhere he could write in peace without the distractions of his life at home.

'Didier's gone to Leroy Merlin to get some stronger wire fencing.'

'I really appreciate all you've done. I can see you've worked very hard to try and fix this problem, you mustn't feel bad about what's happened - this is not your fault. What I need to do now is to get this whole right of access thing changed. When Didier's back we'll go around and see Gérard and have it out with him. I'm not standing for his bullying behaviour.'

'Don't think Didier hasn't tried - Gérard wouldn't talk to him, he let his dogs out and they chased Didier off his property. It's been a long time since I saw him move as fast.' Karel smiled as she relived her husband's misadventure. 'Besides I think Gérard must be away, I haven't seen his car there for a few days.'

'Are you sure? No… he can't be away… he's running a farm. Who's feeding the goats?' He knew the answer before the words were out of his mouth. 'Oh of course… I am.'

'Yes I'm afraid so.'

'So what do I do? I can't carry on with a mad petting zoo at the bottom of my garden.'

'Don't worry. Didier's got a plan, he's appealed to the Maire and asked for him to intervene.'

'What, like the United Nations?'

'Men like Gérard respect the Maire - it's part of the old ways of doing things, if the Maire talks to him I think he'll listen.'

'I really hope so.'

'Gérard's telling people you took advantage of his aunt. He says you paid less than the market value for the land and that you knew about the servitude, but kept quiet about it to avoid paying more legal fees.'

'That's utter garbage – we had the land valued and I paid more than the valuation price as I was so grateful to Madame Durand for selling it to me.'

Phil was trying to keep his cool; to keep his holiday head on and take this all in his stride, but the accusation that he'd swindled an old lady was the last straw.

'I know this.' Karel said soothingly. 'But the truth doesn't always make for such an interesting story. I wouldn't worry too much, I'm not sure anyone is actually listening to him.'

'So what's the mayor going to do?'

'He's going to vouch for your good character and put some pressure on Gérard to get this in the tin can.'

Phil rubbed his temples while Karel continued the story.

'This has been going on for a couple of months now – as you know nothing moves very quickly down here, but there's a meeting tomorrow night and apparently after a bit of jiggy pokey you're on the agenda.'

Phil gave up correcting Karel. 'So I just have to hope the mayor comes up trumps.'

'Trumps?' Karel asked confused.

'It's a different kind of trump.' It was a favourite expression of Becca's boys and clearly Karel couldn't see how the mayor's flatulence was going to help this situation.

'Oh I see.' She said, her expression clearly showed that she didn't.

'What I mean is – I hope he can help.'

'With election time coming up soon he needs to be seen to be doing, rather than just talking. If he can sort this out, you might make him a few good headlines and he could certainly use some of those right now.'

'He'll get in though, won't he? I thought he was really popular.'

'I don't know about the UK, but here once they're in power people bore quickly of politicians. His clean-up campaign has backfired amid rumours of back-handers over planning permission for some holiday apartments. He really needs to be seen as lighter than white. You'd be like a celebrity endorsement.'

'I don't know about that, but if he's going to help get rid of the critters then I'll happily shake his hand and have my photo taken.'

'Since the whole pool thing you're a bit of a local hero; they've even got your books on the library bus.'

'It just seemed like such a waste. The children being bussed out miles to the nearest pool and here I was, next door to the school with a pool barely being used. It's worked out rather well I think.'

Phil's arrangement with the village school meant that they could use the pool for free during term time. In return Didier, who was also the school caretaker, kept an eye on his house and maintained the pool.

'Well, it's Didier they should thank, he does all the hard work. It never would have occurred to me, if he hadn't mentioned it. It was a few years back now. I can't remember the exact conversation, it was one drunken night after the fête.'

'There's been quite a lot of those since then.'

'And I'm looking forward to many more to come.'

Phil was glad to focus on something else. He and Karel walked back towards the front of the house.

'Have I missed all the festivities?'

'The bull run is next week and there's the dance with a band on Sunday.'

'Sounds good.'

'You might not fancy it with all the mess, but just so you know Didier's changed the chemicals in the pool. You can't use it today, but he says it should be fine by the morning.' Karel smiled and held the front door open for Phil.

'At least everything is tip top in here.' Phil said glancing around at the tidy, ordered reassuring sameness of the inside of his house.

'Tip top.' Karel rolled the phrase around in her mouth. 'Tip top I like that.'

'Well it's you that keeps it all that way.'

'That's what I'm here for.' She said tying up a bin sack and putting it outside the front door.

Phil was still scanning the living room when his eyes came to rest on a motley assortment of jars on the draining board.

'Ah yes, I was hoping to get those all out of the way before you arrived.' Karel went over and started to tidy them away.

'Don't worry about them now… they can wait, leave them.' Phil said, keen to reclaim his house.

'Well don't throw them out, I'm going to clean them and use them for the tapenade and confiture de peche.'

Karel was in no hurry to leave. 'Before I forget, Madame Becca called earlier to see if you'd arrived.'

'I bet she did...' He'd only been gone a few hours and she was already checking up on him.

'She said she was coming to visit so I've made all the rooms up. I wasn't sure if she was bringing her boys. How are they? All grown up big boys I'm sure.'

Guiltily, Phil admitted he hadn't had too much to do with them while he'd been at Becca's.

He explained they were away with their Dad for a couple of weeks and then he'd been a bit too wrapped up in his own affairs.

'You go and unpack and I'll finish off and be out of your way. I bought a few things at the market for you this morning and there's beer and wine in the fridge.'

'Thanks, I'm sorry it was such short notice.'

'Don't worry... we wondered where you were, you're usually here much earlier. We guessed you were busy.'

'Yes, something like that.'

Phil didn't want to go into all that now; he'd come to France to escape the events of the last few months. He let the conversation hang, closing it down so he could take his leave.

'Right, I'll let you get on with your unpacking and I'll see you later.'

Phil hung his new shirts in the wardrobe and opened the shutters, letting the sun stream into his room. He folded them back and stood surveying the carnage in the garden below. The vine on the pergola under his window was heavy with grapes. Beyond it he could see the pool, the hose was writhing on the surface like a large water snake.

Phil spotted the cause of the moving hosepipe; nearby another goat was chewing on the end of the hosepipe as it dragged it across the garden.

Phil took off his trainer and threw it out of the window. It was a fine shot but landed short of the goat. Spying something new and tasty to feast on the goat swapped its attention to Phil's trainer and sucked in the laces like a strands of spaghetti.

'Oi, shoo – get out of here!' Phil threw his other trainer, but in his haste bowled less accurately and it landed with a gentle splash in the pool.

By the time he'd got the net from the garage and reached the pool both the goat and his trainer had vanished. Irritably he fished his remaining trainer out of the pool before returning to his unpacking.

His garden and any hope of a relaxing break were trashed. Clutching at straws for anything to redeem the situation he noticed the olive and peach trees had weathered the goats and winter well and looked as if they'd yield another bumper crop. He could look forward to a good supply of Karel's homemade conserve and tapenade.

They were a staple part of breakfast and lunch during his summer sojourn. Karel called out au revoir from the floor below. He heard the front door slam; he was alone - peace at last. There was a bleat from the garden below, a sharp reminder that he wasn't alone and that he wouldn't get any peace until the squatters at the bottom of his garden were evicted.

After showering, he sat on the terrace sipping a cold beer. Idly he peeled the label off the bottle while nibbling on a packet of cheesy croutons he'd found in the cupboard. They were past their best but he needed something savoury with his beer and they were the best he could do.

He glanced down at the damp sticky label wrapped around his fingers and there between the woodcut illustration of hops and barley as if taunting him was a beardy, cross-eyed goat – was there no escape from these bloody caprine curs? Normally he'd sit so he had a good view of the garden, but today he turned his seat so that the devastation was behind him – if only it was.

Phil opened his laptop; the curser blinked impatiently at the top of the empty page. He took a deep breath and began to type. He stopped, read what he'd typed, then highlighted the whole lot and deleted it. Blink, blink, blink. It was no good. He couldn't do it. What was he thinking?

He'd always written about a world he'd been fully immersed in. Had he really believed, reading one book would give him enough insight? He was a one-trick pony; there was only one kind of story he could write and it was more about killing than killer heels.

He closed his laptop, put it back in the bag and headed into the village for something a little more tasty than the rock-hard chemical croutons. He decided on the crêperie and stepped from the warmth of the evening sun into the cool of the high-sided alleys that led to and from the church.

The tables outside were not laid so he ducked down the stone steps and into the vaulted stone basement. It was quiet - a few people were eating, but most preferred to dine later. He ordered a carafe of rosé, which he'd practically finished by the time his spinach and ricotta crêpe arrived. After his coffee Phil moved and sat at the bar.

David, the proprietor chatted with Phil in between serving customers. They talked about business, the village, Phil's goat infestation and the new French president and what changes were in store. After reading about the British press's take on the man, his policies, and the fashion sense of his wife, he was always interested to hear what the local perspective was. He'd pick up a Midi Libre tomorrow; it would put him in the picture pretty quickly.

As he was going home at the end of his evening, the rest of the village were just beginning theirs. Children played le loup or what he'd have called tag in the main street and couples walked arm in arm heading for the bar and restaurants.

He'd adjust to local time over the length of his stay but now he needed his bed. The evening was hot and still. Phil switched on the ceiling fan, pulled back the duvet and lay under a thin sheet drifting off to sleep, listening to the percussive chirruping of the cigales.

The sun rose early and was revving up for another scorcher. Phil rolled over to hide his face from the sun and screwed his eyes tightly shut. He wanted to lie in, he wanted to be asleep but it was hard to sleep in the heat of his spotlit room. At seven he gave in and got up. He must remember to close the shutters tonight.

The jars were still on the counter in the kitchen; lined up like lab specimens. Phil turned the jars inspecting them more closely; without the labels he'd have had no clue to their contents. He carefully shook a large jar and from the depths of its murky, pond-like contents, a lone cornichon appeared against the glass. They were like a macabre collection of snow globes that would not have looked out of place on a shelf in the Addams' family home.

Holding his breath and the jar at arm's length, he unscrewed the corroded lid and emptied the slimy liquid down the sink. Not wanting to overload his delicate French plumbing he tipped the lumpy sludgy dregs into the bin. The remaining seven jars; flageolet beans, artichoke hearts, petits pois, bottled pears, capers and mustard all went the same way.

He stacked the smelly jars in the dishwasher and set it on the hottest wash. How long had those jars been here? One of them looked like the remnants of some pickled onions his dad had brought out with him from home, that must have been at least eighteen months ago. He was glad Karel was having a clear out or they could well have been here when he visited next year.

He'd splashed some of the goo up his arms, but it was nothing that a quick dip in the pool wouldn't sort. His new trunks were a good fit, and thanks to Rebecca's rehab there was less of him hanging over the top than there had been. He ran his foot along the water's edge. It was cold, very cold. He could either suffer the slow torture of the steps or the short sharp shock of a dive.

He opted for the latter and swam quickly to warm up, conscious that his external organs were fast retreating to become internal organs. After twenty lengths front crawl he rolled over and tootled up and down on his back. As he reached the end of the pool for the fifth time he became aware that he wasn't alone; he turned his head sharply and came face to face with a goat eyeballing him curiously with its head on one side. There were two of them happily bobbing about in the shallows.

'Maaaaaaa,' said goat one.'Mehhhhhh,' replied goat two, as if discussing the pool temperature.

'Get out, go… go on shoo!' Phil splashed water at the goats, but they showed no interest in hurrying their ablutions. 'Okay, so you want to play it the hard way.'

Phil rolled his shoulders, linked his fingers and stretched his arms above his head limbering up for battle. He attacked with a water cannon splash barrage. He scooped, he slammed - backhand, forehand, drop shots in a manic racket and ball-less one-sided watery tennis rally that lasted five minutes.

When the air cleared and the last of the drops rained back down on the pool, the goats were gone. Victory. Phil punched the air, waded to the shallow end and climbed the tiled steps out of the pool. He stood warming himself on the sun-baked slabs as water ran off him and pooled around his feet.

He roughly towelled himself dry and then lay on a wooden lounger to dry off. Barely two minutes passed when there was a crash from the house; Phil looked up and caught sight of goat one helping itself to the contents of the upturned kitchen bin. He threw down the towel; throwing in the towel might have been more appropriate.

He dashed across the terrace at speed and through the open patio doors. The tiled floor was wet with mud from the garden and water from the aquarobic goats. Phil skidded, slipped and then fell in the fetid soupy veg sludge leaking from the upturned bin.

As Phil reached out a slimy hand to grab the tail of goat one it escaped by jumping up on the sofa, covering the off-white upholstery with muddy, gunky hoof prints in the process.

It was now so off-white it was off the off-white scale. Goat two was pulling on the end of the linen runner on the refectory table. As it pulled, the runner moved like a conveyor belt of doom; the contents of the table were brought to the edge before smashing on the ceramic tiled floor below.

On the kamikaze conveyor belt tonight we have two crystal candlesticks - smash, an original artisan glass platter with four ornamental ostrich eggs - smash, a faux orchid in a glass planter - smash, six Norwegian hand blown shot glasses - smash.

There was no cuddly toy, but the way things were going Phil would like to have the goats stuffed and mounted on the wall as hunting trophies.

Phil clapped and shouted, but this just confused the goats and made them more skittish; they crashed into the large bookcase that divided the dining and living area before heading for the front door. Phil ran forward and caught the bookcase as it toppled forward sending books, a driftwood sculpture and photo frames showering down on him.

Karel opened the door as the two goats shot through it, practically mowing her down in the process.

'I just popped over to sort those… jars out…' Karel tailed off as she quickly took in the state of the house.

'Don't worry about the jars. They were one of the few things the goats didn't smash,' Phil called out from behind the bookcase.

'So what happened… you invite them in for tea?' Karel picked up some of the fallen books and a couple of larger shards of a broken glass decanter.

'No, they goatcrashed.'

'This is no good, those goats are making you a prisoner in your own house. You can't spend the next month here locked up in your house.'

Karel took the broom from the cupboard and began sweeping all the broken glass and china into a pile.

She was right, even with its thick old walls the house did get very hot. The terracotta roof tiles acted like some great storage heater; soaking up the sun's rays throughout the day and then slowly releasing all the heat into the house. If he couldn't have the doors and windows open for fear of another goat invasion, he'd absolutely cook.

'Hopefully it will only be one more day of pain and then the mayor can say what a jolly nice chap I am and then everything will be sorted.'

Phil was pinning all his hopes on the mayor. If this carried on any longer he'd have to make alternative plans. He couldn't stay here, much less find a space where he could write something new and fresh or at least new and fresh for him.

Maybe he could move to the hotel for a while. No, that wasn't going to work. When he wrote, it was the flow of ideas that dictated the timetable not the rigid structure of hotel mealtimes. It would mean he either didn't eat or he'd have to keep breaking off to sit on his own in the soulless dining room when he really wanted to be sitting at his laptop.

Renting another house in the village or one of the holiday apartments down on the coast might be a better idea. But this was peak season and he'd be very lucky to find anything half decent at this late stage.

No, all his money was on the mayor. He wasn't asking for much, just for the mayor to say he was decent and honest; not someone who diddled old ladies and that he was happy to pay for the notaire to draw up a new boundary.

He and Karel made light work of sorting the bookcase; Karel wiped the veg slime off the books with a damp cloth and Phil stacked them back on the shelves. Anything that was still intact or could be mended went on the table; everything else Karel swept into her growing pile of broken china. It looked like the fallout from a good night in a Greek restaurant.

Karel had said she'd finish off while Phil took a stroll into the village. The bakery was busy but he was in no hurry to return home, so he joined the queue on the pavement. He bought his gros pain and Madame Broussard slipped him an extra Tielle, a local mussel pie and a millefeuille. Last summer her son had fallen in the millpond, but thanks to swimming lessons in Phil's pool he'd swum to safety.

He pulled a lump off the loaf and chewed it while he read the headlines of the English newspapers outside the tabac. The weather back home was grim, he wasn't missing anything. He paid for his Midi Libre and sauntered home. The housework fairy had worked her magic and everything was returned to a state of ordered calm.

He cut two generous slices from the loaf and spread them with a thin layer of rich, salty butter followed by a big dollop of Karel's peach and almond conserve. He took a big slurp of coffee and carried his plate and cup out to the terrace.

His French was more than a little rusty but he'd always found it easier to read French than to speak it. There were only so many times you could ask someone to repeat themselves, but with the newspaper he could go over it again and again, looking bits up in the dictionary if he wasn't sure.

Some local politician was up on corruption charges, the threat of strikes over pension scheme reforms and the largest oyster ever found. It took him over an hour but he liked to try and read it from front to back. The personal column was something else.

He knew when you were paying by the word that you needed to keep it brief but he had a sense that some of the abbreviations were codes for some very unusual offerings. When he'd first been house-sharing he was puzzled for a while by GSOH. But this was more like the enigma code.

He was jotting a few down to ask David about when he was suddenly aware of Karel reading over his shoulder.

'If you're looking for a little company, Didier's niece is a very nice girl.'

'Oh, hi Karel. No I wasn't looking for me...'

'For a friend of yours, perhaps?'

'Yes... er no, I was going to ask David what some of it meant.'

'Which one?'

'Well, what's this?' Other than the goats, no one was eavesdropping, but Karel glanced around and then whispered in his ear.

'No way,' Phil blushed. 'In the Midi Libre? No wonder they write it in code.'

Karel shrugged. He loved the Dutch, nothing shocked them, they really had been there, done that and worn the wet tee shirt.

'So what do you think? Shall I arrange something with Didier's niece? A drinks party or dinner?'

'Thanks, but once this is all sorted I just want to have a nice, quiet uncomplicated stay.'

'No problem. I just popped in to say come and have drinks with us tonight if you're free.'

'I'd love to. What time?'

'Eight thirty.'

'And no matchmaking.'

'Of course Monsieur Phil.'

'Okay I'll see you later.'

Phil sat staring at his laptop. His success had been based upon writing about what he knew. He had heard of other writers who'd spent years and years researching their book. Getting to know their subject like the back of their hand. He'd never had to do that, his whole career was his research.

It was a simple enough question. Could he write a story like 'Handbags?' He'd said himself you needed a talent for writing; he had that. You had to understand what makes for a successful story. With him it was instinctive, he couldn't really put it into words, but it was woven into all his books. And you had to know your readership. That was the tricky bit. Even when he thought he did, he clearly didn't, otherwise he'd have seen that his readership was about to evaporate.

The rules were the same: strong characters and a good plot. He could do that; it was just that he was writing about a world he'd been a guest in for a very short time. Could he write it like he lived it everyday? Could he answer the six million dollar question? What would interest Becca and her friends? What would they want to read about? The seed of an idea began germinating.

This was very different. Were the last five weeks intensive induction into his sister's life and those of her friends, enough? Could he really do it? There was only one way he'd find out. Phil began to get some of his ideas down.

He wrote a quick synopsis; it was a character-based story about a close-knit but slightly eccentric group of friends. Becca is the backbone, the lynchpin that holds the group together, constantly there for each character as they take a tumble on the potholed road of life. But when Becca their glorious leader takes a tumble it really tests the strength of the group's friendship, teamwork and organisation skills.

On return from a buying trip in France drugs are discovered hidden in some furniture in Becca's van. She gets arrested for smuggling and banged up in a women's prison pending trial. Becca's friends follow the example she's set them over the years and in her absence step in to run her life; look after her children, run her shop and mount a campaign to free her.

But without Becca at the helm, the group of friends make a series of ill-judged, disastrous decisions... often with hilarious outcomes.

Yes that could work, and what else? Every good story needs a baddie and he could think of no one better to base her on than Aurore. He'd need to flesh that out a bit more to work out what Aurore's motive is. Maybe she mounts a smear campaign against the drug-trafficking Becca. Aurore encourages people to boycott the shop with a view to running the business into the ground so she can snap it up at a fraction of its value. Not bad for a first draft he thought.

And what about Becca? After the stark reality of prison life sinks in, Becca carves out a niche as an interior designer for the incarcerated and is in great demand to bring a little Kelly Hoppen style to the Holloway cells. The story's climax is the trial and it's often hard to see if the friends involvement is a help or a hindrance.

Happy with the rough structure of the story Phil began to type.

Becca's Friends
Chapter 1

He was on a roll, the opening few pages came to him easily. After a couple of hours he decided he'd done enough. He'd quit while he was ahead; it was time for a break. He didn't read what he'd typed; he'd come back to it later when he could look at it afresh.

Sixteen

Much as he loved the market and the local epicerie, there were things he could only get at the supermarché, like real milk. Tea and coffee tasted disgusting with UHT. He'd pick up a few other things while he was there, so that he could return the favour and host his own soirée one evening.

He took the car key off the hook and walked around to the garage. The garage had originally been one of the outhouses, with thick, stone, windowless walls and a steeply sloping slate roof. It was the first part of the building that Phil had renovated.

It was perfect for storing the building materials and after installing a floor in the high eaves it had become Phil's lodgings and base for overseeing the renovation - a cool retreat from the 500-year-old brick dust floating around the main house during the building work. Now, as well as being home to his car, it was also his wine cellar and wood store.

The battery was still charging on the bench. The charger was a French one Didier had bought and Phil couldn't make head nor tail of the dials, but surely it would be done by now. His Citroën looked amazing; driving it was one of the things he most looked forward to when he came to France. Phil turned the key; it started after a couple of tries.

Slowly he drove out through the large barn doors and out of the village past the water tower. He opted for the dual carriageway rather than the winding back roads; he bypassed the villages he'd come through in his taxi, now he could get up a bit of speed. The road was quiet; just one truck in the distance on its way back to the quarry. Phil hadn't gone far when he spotted a little vegetable stall by the side of the road and decided to stop.

He'd bought stuff there before; the tomatoes tasted amazing. Was it because they were organic or was it that they were regularly dusted with petrol fumes? Either way, they were delicious. The stall was unmanned, so he chose what he needed and dropped the money in the honesty box. It was very trusting of the owner, but the stall was opposite the austere concrete monolithic prison, an ever-present reminder that crime doesn't pay.

Phil slid back into the warm leather seat and turned the key in the ignition – nothing. He tried again and again. He waited a little while then had another go - still nothing. He got out and sat under the trees and ate some of his cherries. Stupidly, he'd left his mobile on charge back at the house; he couldn't call anyone.

When all that remained was a bag of cherry stones, he got back in the car. It was no good, it still wouldn't start; that was it: the car was not going anywhere. He was on a deserted part of the road; there were no houses, only the prison, and he didn't fancy knocking on their door. He'd seen Midnight Express.

Parked in an open space by the side of the prison was the white camper van belonging to the local madam. She was here every year and seemed to do a decent trade. Sometimes when the guards came off shift there were a few sitting in deckchairs waiting patiently as if they were going to see their GP. There was no traffic; no one to flag down for assistance. Phil crossed the road and knocked gingerly on the door of the van.

Now this really would be a test of his French. Sitting on the bed was a woman in her late thirties. She wore a sheer silky robe and was smoking and reading a magazine. She smiled and stood up to remove her robe.

'Non! Non! C'est ma voiture. Elle ne fonctionne plus.'

She looked quite relieved as she retied her robe and sat down with her magazine; it must have been a good article.

'Est-ce que je peux utiliser votre téléphone?' Phil asked trying hard to remember the correct grammar.

'Oui, il est sur la table.'

She pointed to a table with a desk diary, a stack of business cards and a mobile phone. Phil called Didier and explained what had happened. Didier apologised, he'd forgotten to switch the charger on at the socket and Karel had flicked the switch when she called in earlier in the morning. He'd asked her to mention it, but she'd obviously got distracted.

The battery had been on charge for less than half an hour. Phil pushed the little red button to hang up then placed the phone back on the table.

'Il arrive dans vingt minutes.' Phil said making a move to return to his car.

'Café?' The woman asked gesturing towards a bench sofa.

'Merci oui,' Phil said shuffling in behind the table and taking a seat.

'Je suis Sophie.' The woman said as she got cups out of an overhead cupboard.

'Phil, je suis ravi de vous rencontrer.'

They shook hands politely and Sophie gave him one of her cards. He was glad of the coffee as he'd nearly exhausted all his schoolboy French. He'd been taught what to say when visiting the bank and how to buy stamps at the post office. He was sure that the boys in his class would have paid more attention if the correct dialogue for this situation had been included in the curriculum. It gave a whole new meaning to French oral.

As Phil slipped the card in his wallet the shopping list fell out. Sophie picked it up.

'Merci, c'est ma liste d'achats.'

Sophie turned the list over and raised her eyebrows in surprise. On the back were the codes he'd copied down from The Midi Libre personal column.

'Non, non de l'autre côté.' Phil said, feeling the colour rising in his cheeks.

It took some explaining, but he did well and Sophie got the gist of why Phil had written the codes down in the end. She told him what some of them meant, but his French did not extend to that level. So what followed was the strangest and funniest game of charades he had ever played. They'd done most of the codes when he heard a car on the road outside.

Phil stood on the steps to the van and handed some money to Sophie to cover the cost of the call and to thank her for the coffee; the whole experience had been quite an education.

The car was not Didier's. It slowed down as it passed and staring out, slack-jawed in complete amazement, was the mayor and his wife. Fortunately there were no other cars on the road as they swerved across two lanes. There went his character witness and there went his chance of sending the billy goats gruff back to the troll on the farm.

Sophie would not take his money and Phil was still trying to press it on her when Didier pulled up. The jump leads did the trick. Phil decided he'd had enough excitement for one day; he'd leave the shopping for tomorrow and head home with Didier following behind in case he had any further problems.

Phil was glad to be back in the cool comfort of his home. He checked his email, looked at the weather forecast and compared the Euro to Sterling exchange rate. In fact, anything, but look at what he'd written earlier. When he'd exhausted all other distractions, he clicked on the file he'd been working on that morning. He read it through, made a couple of changes but overall was pleasantly surprised.

Phil sat in the still, dry heat of the afternoon and wrote solidly for the remainder of the day. He was getting such a buzz from it that when it was time to get ready to go to the drinks party he had trouble tearing himself away. It was a feeling he loved and yet hadn't had in a very long time. He could do it. He would do it.

With a chilled bottle in his hand and his hair still wet, he pushed open the side gate, behind which he could hear laughter and gentle conversation. It wasn't really French etiquette to take wine but they were used to him. Most of the guests he already knew.

Much as he'd wanted to stay home and write he was glad to have come out. Everyone made him feel so welcome, there was much kissing, hand shaking and back patting. Karel guided him around the group and introduced him to the few unfamiliar faces. One of which was Didier's niece.

Karel excused herself to get some food out of the oven. Phil chatted politely, but as soon as an opportunity arose he slipped away to find Karel.

'I thought I said no matchmaking.' Phil admonished her.

'Moi?' Karel said innocently, then whispered 'It's okay, she was already coming. I haven't mentioned anything about you.'

Phil helped carry out some of the dishes and passed around the small spicy sausages, olives and whole king prawns in garlic butter. Didier made a toast and while he had everyone's attention, he nudged Phil.

'Phil 'az 'ad...' Didier struggled to find the words as he fought the rising laughter.

'An exciting day out today.' Karel chipped in to help him out.

Phil told the story and Karel translated while Didier acted some of it out, particularly the part with Sophie.

The gentle laughter became raucous. They laughed 'til they cried. Phil had already been labelled a flasher in his home country, he really could do without that reputation following him here.

While everyone returned to their drinks Didier took Phil to one side and reassured him that he'd go and see the mayor the next morning to explain any misunderstanding and smooth everything out. He was sure it would all be fine.

Encouraged, Phil rejoined the guests and asked about the upcoming festivities, the bull run, village dance and the joust. They made arrangements to meet in the bar on Tuesday and all go to the bull run together.

Phil looked at all the empties. They were lined up waiting to go in the recycling. He did a quick calculation, number of empties divided by the number of guests = a bottle and a half each. It was definitely time to go; he checked his watch, it was late. The guests bid their hosts good night and ambled as a group back into the village. Couples peeled off at different points, as they wended their way home. By the time he reached his gates, Phil was on his own.

He remembered to close his shutters and was asleep soon after he lay down. He dreamed about his story. It was set in France but Becca was there and Sophie was dancing with the mayor and then some bulls came along and chased them all away.

Despite his strange dream, he slept well. He wasn't sure whether the wine had anything to do with it or not but he hadn't woken in the early hours for days. Maybe that was because he was still sitting on Didier's terrace in the early hours. No, this definitely felt different; there had been a positive shift.

Phil swam, went to the bakery then sat typing in the shade of the pergola, while he ate his breakfast. His fingers were sticky with peach conserve and he was dropping crumbs on the keyboard. He didn't want to wait until after breakfast, he was impatient to get going on his story. Now he knew what it was he needed to do, he just wanted to spend all his time doing it. The ideas came quicker than he could get them down. He couldn't type properly, but could manage a reasonable speed with two fingers.

Lunchtime came; he stopped to make something to eat. He opened his cupboards - there were plenty of things for preparing or serving food but as he hadn't made it to the supermarket there were limited ingredients.

With the remainder of the breakfast bread and the tomatoes he'd bought from the roadside he pulled together a fine bruschetta. He drizzled over a mixture of olive oil and balsamic and garnished it with a few torn basil leaves rescued from the garden.

The sun had moved round and the terrace was now bathed in sunlight. It made the screen difficult to see, but he persevered and typed as he munched and crunched his way through the next twist in the plot. The shadows rotated slowly around the garden, growing longer and longer.

Phil sat and tapped away. The story flowed easily; it was as if someone in his head was dictating and he was merely typing it up. The sky was splashed with red and orange, the sunset heralded another day of perfect weather tomorrow.

Didier popped round with an update following his smoothing-out chat with the mayor. The upshot was everything was as far from smooth as it was possible to be. The mayor was unconvinced by the broken down car story, he'd said he didn't feel he could confidently vouch for Phil's character having witnessed him leaving Sophie's camper van. He said that he couldn't afford to be associated with the remotest hint of sleaze at this very delicate stage of his election campaign.

Taking on board what Didier had just told him, Phil sat heavily on a garden chair causing it to creak loudly in protest.

'So where does that leave us?'

'I've been sinking and I 'ave a plan you might like.'

'At this stage I'm willing to give anything a try.'

'Well, up until zis point I 'ave been trying to…'

Didieir gestured with his finger to his newly installed wire fencing.

'Coral? Contain?' Phil guessed.

'Yes, I 'ave been trying to contain ze goats, to limit zeir… accéder?'

'Access?'

'Yes, to stop zeir access to ze garden – zis 'az not worked - for every barrier I've put in place zey've found anozer way over under or around. But zen I sought zey 'aven't found a way to break out of your garden and so all ze damage zey've caused has been caused to just you. My plan is, if we were to leave ze gates open ze goats could escape into ze village. Zey've pretty much eaten all ze plants you 'ave to offer, but in ze village zere are many more gardens zey can be problems in.'

'It seems a bit mean to just pass my problem on to someone else…'

'Yes ze servitude is in your garden, but ze goats do not 'ave to be. You wait and see, once ze goats start being a difficulty to more different people, pressure will get bigger and bigger for Gérard to mend zis problem. And if zey…' Didier did a nibbling goat impression, '…les planteurs outside ze Mairie zat will be a bonus.'

He laughed and seemed very pleased with the ingenuity of his plan. Phil had to admit it was a good plan, but it would have been even better if Didier had thought of it earlier and at least some of his garden could have been saved.

'So I sink we should give it a try – no?'

'Yes I think it's worth a try. I feel bad about inflicting my problems on my neighbours, but you're right: maybe a little collateral damage is a small price to pay if we can get this fixed once and for all.'

'We are in agreement zen. I will put down ze grillage.' Didier said pointing to his neat new wire fence running across the width of the garden. 'And from now on all ze gates are open – yes?'

'Yes, let's see if that does the trick.'

Phil returned to his writing while Didier busied himself undoing his recent handiwork; pulling out the tall metal stakes that secured the fencing.

As the sun fell, the lights along the paths in the garden flickered into life. Moths and midges came out to play and flitted around the now illuminated stunted trunks and stalks shaped by the curly-horned pruners. Some insects were drawn to the glow of the laptop screen and then fled as the words advanced at speed down the screen towards them.

Phil poured himself and Didier a glass of rosé and drank it as he helped pack the rolled-up wire fencing and stakes into the garage. Alone again he strolled around the garden; he imagined inhaling the garden's evening scents instead of the actual musky animal stench that assaulted his nostrils.

His bum was a bit numb after sitting on the wooden garden chair for hours. He cleared the table and moved inside; nestling back in the cushions on the sofa, he carried on where he'd left off. He'd forgotten to put his watch on that morning, so other than the fact it was dark outside he had no idea what time it was.

He remembered reading an article by an author who'd said that no one could write anything of any note for longer than three hours a day. That wasn't a view he subscribed to; he wrote in an avaricious kind of way. The intensity of his focus was exhausting. It was an insatiable need, he wanted to do more and more and didn't want to stop until he physically had to.

As he was now struggling to keep his eyes open, that time was fast approaching. Phil distractedly brushed his teeth. His brain was still buzzing, but the muscles in his eyelids and various other parts of his body had called it a day. Reluctantly, he climbed into bed and was out like a light.

The next few days followed the same routine. During a rare break, Phil reflected on the last few months. They had been dominated by an overwhelming feeling of emptiness. His life had had no sense of purpose. He'd been unable to do anything; he didn't want to see or talk to anyone.

Ironically, he now had a strong sense of purpose but still would rather not see or talk to anyone or do anything that would take him away from his writing. His mental state had changed and yet so much had stayed the same.

It was a subtle shift, but the difference was it was a temporary state. He knew that once he'd finished his story, he'd want to go to the beach or drive up to the mountains. He was in control, he was choosing to spend his days like this. It made him happy. In fact, some of the things he'd written had made him laugh out loud.

Karel had called in at one such moment to find him alone chuckling to himself. She had always seen him as the eccentric Englishman and ignored his strange behaviour and added it to the list of other odd things she'd seen him do. Like the scary hedge-cutting technique he'd copied from his dad, which involved him launching himself from the top of the ladder with the hedge trimmer and cutting the hedge while lying on top of it. She was glad Didier had persuaded Phil to let him take over this job in future. She was sure he'd end up trimming himself as well as the hedge. It would be hard to type without his fingers.

Karel could sense he was not in a chatty mood so she kept it brief. She reminded him about the bull run the following day and, seeing the empty fridge, offered to pick him up the things on his list. He didn't want to appear rude, but things were going well and he didn't want to break the spell. Karel unclipped the list from the fridge door. She took some money from the housekeeping pot in the cupboard and closed the door quietly on her way out.

When she returned he was exactly where she'd left him. Phil stopped typing and came to help unload the bags.

'Thanks so much, I'm sorry about earlier. The writing is using up all my energy. I don't have any left for anything else.'

'Like shaving?' Karel smiled, as she ran a finger across his stubbly chin.

'I promise I'll smarten myself up before we go out tomorrow.'

'It's not just the shaving,' Karel said in mother hen mode. 'You need to make sure you're eating properly. I could make you a nice salad.'

'That's very good of you but I've decided I'm going to try and be a bit more disciplined about taking regular breaks.'

Phil's thoughts drifted back to writing. He was writing a story, a different kind of story to see if he could do it. It was just a challenge he'd set himself. When he'd had his last major bout of depression, writing had saved him. He wanted to see if it could again. He was trying to get it finished by the time Becca arrived and give it to her as a thank you.

Just like all the stories he'd written for her when they were young. They were such memorable pieces of literary genius, that he could only remember two. 'Princess Becky and the Dragon' and 'Rebecca's racehorse'. He wondered if she'd kept them. This was a dry run; just a silly short story. If he could pull it off then maybe he'd branch out and write something new.

Karel was still talking and he wasn't listening. He quickly tuned back in. She was taking him through an inventory of the groceries as she unpacked and stored them away. What went with what and what he should eat and by when.

'I know you're busy so I've got you things that don't need too much doing to them. There's lots of salad, a cooked chicken, pâté and cheeses.'

'You're too kind. That's really helpful. I'm writing the story for Becca and it's not long before she arrives so I'm pretty up against it.'

'Up against it?' Karel repeated with a frown.

'I don't have much time.' Phil explained.

'How romantic. Someone writing a story for you.'

'I'm not sure romantic is the right word. She is my sister...'

'I think it's beautiful.'

'Oh… well… good.' Phil said, returning to his laptop.

'You know you can come and eat with us any time you like. I don't mean our usual French lunches that go on and on. I mean come, eat and then get back to your work. I could send food over if you like?'

'You've done plenty already. I think I'll be fine with all this stuff. There's enough here to last me until next week. I'm so grateful to you.'

'Well, you do pay us to look after you. It's our job.'

'I know I do, but you do so much more.'

'You're not just the boss, you're our friend and friends do that for one another.'

'Thank you, I just want you to know I appreciate it.'

'Okay, you need to get on. Remember, eat the ham today and we'll all meet in the bar tomorrow. It will be fun, you need a break - all hard work makes Jacques not an interesting person.'

'Yeah… close enough.' Phil thought. Karel was right; he needed a break and what harm would one day off do.

Seventeen

Metal crash barriers had been arranged along the sides of the main road. Vendors walked the edge of the barriers calling out their wares. Feeling a bit peckish after skipping breakfast, Phil bought a bag of chichi - caramelised peanuts. But, as always, the taste was a disappointment after the enticing burnt sugar smell that wafted from the large copper pan where they were being prepared.

The bulls were safely corralled in the car park. Blue, white and green flags fluttered from the tridents of the gardians. They had a kind of 'military-meets-agriculture' look. In their smart black jackets and black hats they stood sentry-like, guarding over their wards. Phil thought they were the French equivalent of the Masai warriors, except they looked after bulls, not rhino.

These bulls were a unique wild herd of the Camargue; bred for their distinctive-flavoured meat and for bull running. Scrub that thought, they were nothing like the Masai warriors. No one was trying to poach them and there was no market for ground bull's horn, although maybe it would be worth giving it a try. If anything they were more like cowboys. Riding around the herd on horseback and living in thatched cabanes on the land they farmed.

On a temporary stage draped with cheap nylon bunting, an over-excited man was speaking loudly through a crackly PA system. His disjointed address to the crowd was punctuated regularly by tinny trashy Europop. The road outside the bar was crowded. Phil found himself caught in the crush. The creeping flow of the throng carried him further away from the bar and nearer to the stage.

The man on the stage was getting very excited, whipping the crowd up into a frenzy. The crowd sang along to the crappy tune and the compère clowned about on stage with volunteers from the audience.

Phil managed to edge himself round in the direction of the bar and saw Didier standing in the doorway looking out, trying to spot Phil in the crowd. With his back to the stage Phil waved, hoping to catch Didier's attention. Didier didn't see him, so Phil tried again, this time climbing up onto one of the municipal planters and standing on his tiptoes, to elevate himself above the crowd and give himself more chance of being seen.

It worked. He had been seen. But, sadly, not by Didier. Still with his hand firmly in the air, the crowd around him parted making a clear path from where Phil was standing to the stage. Phil climbed down from the planter, but climbing down from his inadvertent volunteering to take part in the bull run would be more tricky.

He tried to explain there was some mistake; his words were lost amongst the cheering and chart-topping trash. The crowd closed behind him, gently nudging him forward. Everyone was clapping and the man with the mic's maniacal grin was beckoning him towards the steps leading to the stage. He had no choice but to join the other stupid fools or as they preferred to be called brave razeteurs.

He'd been to a few auctions when he was furnishing the house. His golden rule was to keep his hands firmly in his pockets. He was someone who tended to wave his arms around when he spoke and could easily find himself inadvertently bidding for a whole load of stuff he neither wanted nor needed. If only he'd been as careful here.

Didier had spotted him; he called Karel and the others out from the bar and was pointing at the stage. Even at that distance Phil could see the look of extreme concern on their faces.

What could he do? He couldn't bow out now and be labelled the lily-livered Englishman. No, he had to do this and try and get through it with his dignity and the rest of him intact. Besides, he'd seen the run in previous years. All he needed to do was keep to the side and let the bulls run through the middle. Easy.

That didn't take into account that these bulls were mad, vicious beasts who'd like nothing more than to skewer him. The crowd dispersed behind the barriers and the razeteurs lined up on the start line. The man from the stage was explaining about removing the cockade from the bull's horns.

Was he out of his mind? He had no intention of getting anywhere near any of the bulls, his priority was to get through it in one piece, without losing face or control of his bladder.

A bell rang out and once the route was clear the gardians released the bulls from their pen. When they were contained the bulls had been still and placid, a picture of idyllic pastoral calm. But the minute the gates were opened, they went berserk, colliding with each other in their eagerness to escape.

They went mental. And he was mental too. What was he doing? The air horn sounded and they were off. The men of the village ran past the bar towards the main road. The crowd were cheering and banging on the metal railings. So far, so good. Everything was going to plan, if he kept to the side he'd be okay.

As he passed the bar, Karel and Didier shouted across to him. They'd disconnected one of the barriers creating a gap that in his younger days he'd have easily fitted through. They were trying to open it wider when a bull slid on the wet cobbles, aquaplaned, veered to one side, and then, regaining control, headed straight for Phil.

He saw it in the nick of time, picked up his pace and ran at top speed, following the other runners. All those body-sculpting classes he'd done with Becca were paying off. Now all he had to ensure was that one of these brutes didn't try their own kind of body sculpting on him.

Didier had pushed his way through the spectators and was level with him on the other side of the barrier. He was shouting something to Phil but was drowned out by the clatter of hooves, the baying crowd and the crowd's incessant tapping of coins on the metal barriers.

'Zey can smell your nuts. Drop your nuts.' Didier cried, straining to be heard.

'W-h-a-t?' Phil shouted back in the rough direction from which he'd heard Didier's voice; he didn't want to take his eyes off the fast approaching bulls not even for a second.

'Y-o-u-r n-u-t-s.' Didier screamed back.

In the split second when the crowd paused for breath, Phil heard Didier's words at long last and muttered to himself under his breath – 'yeah great, very helpful, just what I need a comment on my mental health at this particular moment in time. Like I don't know I'm nuts…'

'Drop your nuts,' Didier called again.

Phil looked down to see he was still carrying the bag of chichi. The penny finally dropped and he finally dropped the nuts, or rather threw them. Big mistake. Caught by the wind the chichi guided missile sailed in a smooth arc and struck the flank of a nasty-looking spotty bull up ahead. The bag burst on impact, sending nuts flying in all directions.

The spotty bull stopped dead in its tracks, turned and eyed Phil for a few menacing seconds before lowering its horns and charging at top speed straight for him. Phil turned to run in the opposite direction but found he was caught in a pincer movement between Mad Spotty advancing at speed on the left and the last of the bulls from the corral on the right.

With only one escape route open to him, he tried to clamber over the crash barrier. It was easier than he'd imagined. Phil managed to get both legs over and was sitting atop the heavy iron fencing with Mad Spotty a good two metres away. But as he jumped to the ground he caught the belt loop of his jeans in the process.

He was frantically trying to release himself when the bull saved him the bother. Mad Spotty crashed into the barrier with such force that it threw Phil to the floor, trapping him face down underneath the barrier, Mad Spotty trampling him in his bid for freedom.

Phil was winded with a sharp pain down his left side. He lay still for a little while and listened to the remaining bulls pass by. It was not long before he heard concerned voices and as he turned his head saw faces staring down at him through the bars in the barrier.

He wasn't sure why, but the pain seemed to increase as the heavy metal weight of the barrier was lifted off him. Didier and Karel were at his side. Didier shouted for someone to fetch Doctor Chenard. Where was the field hospital when he needed them? Phil mused. He had a few war wounds. His old granddad had always comforted his grazed knees by saying "scars make you more interesting." Phil thought he may have taken this idea to the extreme during his career, potentially making him one of the most interesting people on the planet – not a view shared by most of his girlfriends.

His hands and face were shredded from the gravel on the road. He had a cut above his right eye and a fine selection of bumps and bruises were ripening all over his body. He tried to sit up, but as he pulled on his stomach muscles, pain exploded around his ribs.

'I'll never eat another nut again.' Phil spluttered through a mouthful of blood and grit.

'Il est en délire,' offered a concerned bystander.

Another member of the village people (no, not those ones) folded his jacket and placed it as a cushion under Phil's head while Karel carefully picked gravel from Phil's wounds. Doctor Chenard arrived and pushed through the crowd, shouting for everyone to move back.

With brisk efficiency he pulled up Phil's shirt and examined his chest, which seemed to involve being poked and prodded in all the most painful places.

After some more tapping and pressing, Doctor Chenard pronounced his diagnosis. 'Une rupture.'

Carefully, Phil was helped to his feet, with David from the crêperie and Didier taking much of his weight and holding him up.

Phil cradled his right arm and held it as still as he could manage. If he tried to lift or extend his arm the pain was excruciating. With his two props Phil shuffled slowly, following Doctor Chenard to his surgery.

Carefully he lay down on the couch. While his cuts were cleaned and dressed, Doctor Chenard had another feel of his ribs and examined his arm. He talked and Karel translated. A rib was fractured but he didn't think there were any internal injuries.

He thought Phil's arm was broken, but he'd arrange an X-ray to confirm it. He would give him something for the pain and he needed to rest. No lifting and no strenuous exercise and definitely no typing.

Before strapping his arm up he showed him some deep breathing exercises and showed him how to hold a cushion to his chest for support while coughing, sneezing or laughing. It would be useful for the first two but he hadn't had much cause for laughter on this trip so far. Except maybe for the odd outburst while writing.

It was a shame about the swimming. It really woke him up in the morning. Maybe he could still potter up and down on his back?

Doctor Chenard rang a nearby Polyclinic and booked him in for an X-ray later that day. Phil returned home from the pharmacy with a big pick-and-mix bag of goodies. Antiseptic cream for his cuts and another for the bruises, dressings in different sizes and some anti-inflammatories, which he was relieved were not suppositories.

At five o'clock Karel ran him to the Polyclinic and went in with him to act as interpreter and make sure he understood what was happening. The doctor/nurse/radiologist type person or whatever she was explained step by step what she was doing and Karel dutifully translated for Phil.

In addition to his fractured rib he also had a broken radial head in his right elbow. That explained the shooting pain when he tried to lift, turn or twist his forearm. The outcome was he'd have one week in heavy cast and then five possibly six weeks in a padded sling.

She gave him a sheet of exercises to do every day and explained that he'd need to return to the Polyclinic for a weekly physio appointment to measure the angle of his joint to see how it was mending. She asked what he did for a living and when Karel answered for him, the doctor shook her head solemnly.

So, goats, bulls, a fractured rib, arm in cast and not allowed to type – this trip just got better and better.

He declined Karel and Didier's kind offer to stay with them, so instead each day Karel came over with his meals. In the morning she arranged a stack of cushions behind him on the sofa and placed everything he needed close at hand: laptop, phone, remotes for the TV and CD player and all his pills and potions and that's where he spent his days.

Phil tried to get comfortable but it seemed that whichever position he sat in he was resting upon a bruised, grazed or broken bit of his body. Just moving was a challenge, he hadn't realised how much he used his stomach muscles until he'd had a painful reminder each time he tried to reach, stand, sit or in fact do any of the things he wanted to do.

Phil flicked on the TV. Just a month ago, he'd have happily lost a whole day grazing on daytime fodder. He did a couple of loops but he couldn't settle on anything; nothing interested him. He'd come here to write and now that he'd actually made a start and had a rough plot planned out in his head, all he really wanted to do was get it down on paper.

He made a mental list of the top ten things he'd discovered he couldn't do with his injuries.

And just in at number ten it's cutting up food – he either had to do it with his left hand which usually resulted in him shooting food off his plate in all directions or in a medieval banquet style just picking the whole thing up and biting bits off.

At number nine and down two places from yesterday it's putting on deodorant – he couldn't lift his arm high enough and judging from the smell his attempt to spray some left-handedly in the narrow gap under his arm had been unsuccessful. Maybe that explained why Karel was always in such a hurry to leave.

Unchanged at number eight is tying shoe laces – that was okay, he could wear flip flops

A new entry at number seven it's going to the loo – enough said.

Still at number six it's getting dressed – doable but involving escapologist-style wriggles to feed his right arm through the sleeve first and then pull the tee shirt over his head before his left arm was released. The first few attempts had resulted in him wearing tee shirts back to front, but he wasn't going anywhere and what did it matter if the Abercrombie & Fitch logo appeared across his right shoulder blade rather than his chest.

Down two to number five it's cleaning his teeth – these were automatic tasks that he did every day, but now he had to stop and consciously think about where he wanted the brush to go and what angle to tilt it. It felt weird relearning to do all the things he took for granted and did subconsciously.

Straight in at number four it's opening things – Nothing so grand as a garden fête or a new hospital wing. Although he could probably just about manage to pull the cord and slide the mini velvet curtains back to reveal the commemorative plaque. There wasn't much call for that kind of thing in his corner of France and certainly not by him.

No this was the mundane everyday kind of opening: milk cartons, crisp bags, jam jars and bottles and usually had an explosive outcome with the contents being sprayed across the kitchen. His single-handed attempts at clearing up resulted in him smearing the spills over an even larger area - particularly the jam, which had created some kind of wasp convention centre and caused all the local pests to swarm to his kitchen.

Another new entry at number three it's swatting – not for an exam, although if there were exams in the frustrations caused by goats, bulls and broken limbs he was certain he'd get an A star. This was the swatting required as a result of all the tempting insect magnet-type spills he'd liberally spread across the work surfaces.

At number two it's driving – it was one of his stupidest ideas; he had to admit there was some stiff competition for that particular accolade. It had been painful and exhausting folding himself in behind the wheel. But once he'd gone to all the bother of getting into the car he felt he had to have a go at reversing it into the garage.

To get the old Citroen's heavy steering on full lock had pulled hard on his abs, sending them into a throbbing spasm; he abandoned the car only a couple of metres from its original position.

And still top of the chart for the third day running was... typing – he'd had a go with his left hand, but it was painfully slow and the results were riddled with mistakes. Using the shift key involved his fingers doing stretches of contortionist proportions.

The far right of the keyboard was a no-go area; any sentence requiring a capital P, L or speech marks were out of the question. If he used the shift lock he invariably forgot to turn it off and the dialogue looked as if it was shouting from the page.

He used the mouse like a complete novice with the cursor frequently moving in the opposite direction to that which he wanted. Typing was more bother than it was worth and would end up with him spending more time fixing his mistakes than writing the story.

Phil woke with a start when he heard the door. He had no recollection of dozing off; maybe his drugs were making him drowsy. The TV was still on. Karel called out from the kitchen competing to be heard over the panel show host. Using his foot, he slid his untouched lunch under the sofa.

The remote had fallen on the floor, so Phil bent forward and reached for it, 'owww!'

'What are you doing? Here, let me...' Karel was carrying a large pile of glossy magazines that she dropped on to the sofa before helping Phil back into his seat.

Phil picked up a magazine.

'They're not for you... they were throwing them out at the salon and I thought Madame Becca might like to have a look through them,' she said, moving the remote on to the arm of the sofa.

'Now... you need to rest. Rest and eat. I know you said you didn't have much of an appetite, but you should try and eat something. I've left you a few things in the fridge.'

Karel returned to the kitchen and cleared up Phil's attempt at clearing up the breakfast things.

'Thanks,' he called, glad of the company. In the absence of anyone else, he'd been talking to himself earlier.

'Would you like a drink of something?' Phil shuffled forward to the edge of the sofa. There was a bottle of Listel open in the fridge; he and Karel could share a glass and catch up on the village gossip.

'No thank you.' She shouted over the watery gurgling of the dishwasher. I'm only popping in on my way out… now don't forget to eat something… I'll see you tomorrow.' The door slammed and she was gone.

He was alone again; even the goats had stopped calling in on their way through to plunder the rest of the village for food. Phil watched the clock - eight o'clock. What was he going to do for the rest of the evening? What was he going to do for the rest of his trip?

The last couple of days had been bad enough. He couldn't spend the next few weeks just sitting on the sofa bored out of his brain. If he'd been well enough to fly he'd have given up on France and gone home. Phil woke in the early hours still on the sofa. He switched off the TV and headed for bed.

Karel called in with bread around nine before hurrying off; one of the girls was off sick at the salon so Karel was helping out there whenever she could. When he was busy and had no time she always wanted to chat, but now he had all the time in the world to chew the fat, Karel had turned into Jack Sprat albeit with a fine haircut.

He felt marooned, cut adrift. He didn't really feel well enough to go out and yet there was nothing to occupy him at home. It was the fifth empty day after his accident; he'd been through every copy of Marie France, Elle, Cosmopolitan, Marie Claire, Avantages and Madame Figaro and knew every inch of them.

If there'd been a test on which perfume ad appeared in which title and on which page he was pretty confident he'd get a top score.

He made himself a drink (and a big sticky mess). While on his shopping spree at the airport he'd bought another book by Lucy Stevens in WH Smith. After all, it was reading "Handbags at Dawn" that had sparked the whole idea of writing some chick lit. While he was laid up he'd do a bit more research. If he couldn't write, he'd read; study the language, dialogue and characterisation it would help take his mind off all the things he couldn't do and hopefully it would help with his story.

While he drank the menthe cordial he read the first five chapters; enough to get into the plot and become hooked. He stuck in stickies, scrawled left-handedly in the page margins and highlighted passages of text. It was an exercise that in truth only served to make him more frustrated. He was right, it was inspiring, it gave him some great ideas. But then he couldn't do anything with them. He couldn't get them down on paper or only as illegible footnotes. It was no good; in the end he gave up and returned to the sofa.

He flicked on the TV, it was HTLGN (How to Look Good Naked) weekender on the Lifestyle Channel. Phil kidded himself it was more research, but after three episodes back to back he switched over to a news channel. The bloodiest month in Afghanistan so far and a woman banned from wearing a burkha on a London bus. After a couple more news stories he started to feel his eyelids getting heavy, when something pulled him up short.

The story that had caught his attention was a press conference; an earnest journalist was doing a piece to camera. The man was talking about the latest extract from Stephen Hawking's forthcoming book that argues that God did not create the universe. A live link up with a church leader was cut short amidst a barrage of flash photography followed by a close up of Stephen taking to the stage.

In addition to the - who could take the credit for the earth thing, he was saying that he believed that extraterrestrial life almost certainly exists, except of course he wasn't saying it – he was using his computer to voice his thoughts. Phil was suddenly wide-awake, would that work in reverse? Was there a wizzy program that could turn his spoken word into typed text?

As fascinated as he was by Stephen's theories, he had other, more important things on his mind. He muted the TV and slowly with his left hand tapped in his password and logged in. He wasn't quite sure what to type, he tried speech activated program – the search revealed a stack of voice recognition software.

One program in particular cropped up again and again. Phil clicked on the link and within half an hour was trying out his free thirty-day trial.

Phil had endured the enforced recuperation of Rebecca's rehab and now he found himself in Karel's convalescence home. Some might see it as out of the frying pan into the fire, but now he had the voice recognition software he thought it was perfect. If perfection could ever be described as being trampled by a mad bull and suffering a broken arm and rib.

Now he could concentrate all his energy on his story. No one had any expectations of him, other than to take it easy and that's exactly what he planned to do. Now, where was he?

The weeks passed and a fresh routine moulded itself around his new-found writing tool. He started each day with a cup of coffee and his pills. Propped up in bed, he tried to recall and order the thoughts that had been running through his brain overnight.

He then re-read and made the necessary nips and tucks to his previous day's writing. A little after eight,

Karel would arrive bringing fresh bread and a few extras from Madame Broussard.

It was like a gourmet meals on wheels. Whatever Karel was cooking for Didier and herself, she made a bit extra and delivered it, plated up, to his table. After he'd done his physio, he'd take up position by the pool on his sun lounger. He'd carry on writing or voicing as he called it until the sun was high in the sky overhead. Then he'd retreat to the cool tranquillity of the house and recline on the sofa.

Karel dropped in with lunch around twelve and then in the late afternoon he'd return to the sun lounger with a beer and voice some more. Dinner arrived promptly at eight and then he'd watch a bit of TV before bed.

It was eight fifteen, Karel had been in early with her bakery delivery and he was breakfasting in bed. He dipped his croissant in his coffee while he checked his mail. His laptop and his bed were covered in crumbs. But that was one of the joys of being on your own. There was nobody to apologise to and nobody to complain.

As well as breakfast, Karel also delivered some good news: under considerable pressure, Gérard had agreed to implement some long-overdue goat border controls. He'd open up the blocked access routes to the bottom field and replace the fence panel preventing the goats from trotting into Phil's garden, as Karel put it, nilly-willy. Phil would have to stump up some cash for the notaire to draw up the new boundary paperwork, but all in all it was a good result.

There were a couple of contradictory stories doing the rounds as to what had prompted Gérard's miraculous change of heart. Gérard was telling people it was all his own doing – his undoing more like. He said he could see now that he'd misjudged Phil.

He'd thought of him as a typical Rosbif wanting to have a little bit of England in France, an expat unwilling to embrace the French way of life. And then when he'd seen Phil at the bull run he saw he was wrong, that Phil was someone throwing himself wholeheartedly into the French community. He'd said if his Aunt had trusted him, then he should too.

Karel said she thought the other story was probably the most likely source of Gérard's recently discovered conscience. Once Madame Broussard heard about goat gate as Phil was now referring to it, she went around and gave Gérard a piece of her mind. She, it turned out, was old lady Durand's cousin. She really gave him a tongue lashing - drew quite a crowd by all accounts.

This was another reminder that in the village, you had to be very careful what you said to who about whom as in all likelihood they'd turn out to be related. He didn't care which story was true, he was just glad that it was over and that his garden was his own again. Didier's open gate plan had worked, but he hadn't been able to replant or repair the damage – now he could, not that he was in any state to.

Since he'd told Becca about his accident she had been mailing him every day to check he was okay. She was going to change her plans and come and see him at the beginning of her buying trip rather than at the end. Until he'd managed to reassure her that he really was on the road to recovery. He'd told her about his physio and follow-up appointment with Doctor Chenard, all his bruising and swelling was going down and with the painkillers he felt fine.

Actually he felt a bit of a fraud. When he had mentioned to Karel that maybe he was well enough to go to the shops and cook for himself, she would not hear of it. She had looked slightly crestfallen at the suggestion.

She'd said that carrying heavy bags of shopping was not good for mending his ribs. Phil had suggested that he could shop for light things, rice cakes and lettuce. Karel had dismissed his remark with a roll of the eyes.

They'd agreed to carry on as they were until Becca arrived. Karel said she'd feel a whole lot happier handing him over to Becca, knowing she'd keep a close eye on him. How right she was: he'd spent his whole life with his sister keeping a close eye on him.

In under ten days he was out of the heavy cast and now had a padded sling to wear for the next few weeks. The physio was pleased with how things were healing and Phil thought he'd risk giving two-handed typing another go.

The weeks had passed in a blur, in less than two days Becca's Pantechnicon would roll into town. The story wasn't finished, but if he kept at it, with a few late nights he was hopeful he'd get it done.

The voicing had worked really well but there were a few bits of tidying up to do on the formatting. When he'd first started he hadn't quite got the hang of the 'quote that', 'italicise that', 'new para' instructions. Also, Karel had an annoying habit of shouting her chitter-chatter from one room to another; before he knew it a whole load of her nonsense was recorded and included in the narrative - 'delete that'.

Phil had returned to taking his morning swim. Doctor Chenard had said it should be okay as long as he didn't do any arm strokes. It was like saying walking is fine as long as you don't use your legs. Lying on his back with his bad arm resting across his chest, he gently kicked his legs and tootled up and down.

As he swam, he went over the last part of the story. It was all falling into place; there were just a few loose ends he needed to tie up. It was always the same while he was writing: whether he was awake or asleep he couldn't get it out of his head. He'd be glad when it was complete.

He didn't regret doing it; he'd enjoyed it, it had kept him out of trouble. Well, not out of trouble, it had kept him busy. And now he knew he could do it. He hadn't had a final read through, but the parts he had read were pretty good, even by his standards.

The downside was that he didn't feel he'd had much of a holiday so far. He was determined that over the course of Becca's stay he'd have some time off from thinking about writing and his future. He'd have a holiday from all that and have some fun.

Eighteen

Becca's van was a monster; a gleaming white Mercedes box truck with double tailgate and side-sliding doors. It beeped loudly as she reversed through the school gates. She parked it like a pro, away from the school buildings on the left side of the playground.

'Thanks Didier. Is it okay here?' Becca asked as the tinted window slid down.

'It's better here I sink. It will be out of ze way,' Didier replied.

Becca killed the engine and jumped down from the cab. She'd have looked quite at home further along the coast at the more chi-chi resorts – she'd have to swap her truck for a yacht though. The sun had awakened her freckles and scattered them liberally across her nose and cheeks. He remembered she'd always hated them as a child but maybe now she was grateful for the fresh, youthful look they gave her.

Becca was the most glamorous trucker he'd ever seen and not a tattoo in sight. Picture a heyday Jackie O behind the wheel of one of the Stobart fleet. Sporting large shades, a snug aquamarine vest top with a sheer white open-neck shirt tied at the waist, teamed with a pair of tailored three-quarter-length white linen trousers and vertigo-inducing heels – how could she drive in them, let alone walk?

Accessories... yes, very important he mustn't forget to mention them; matching bracelet and necklace with what looked like sterling silver links joining large, flat, irregular-shaped glass beads in the blue-green palette. Bag... often a statement piece, important as it can be shorthand for the reader telling them in an instant all they need to know.

At a glance he'd say a Fendi white glazed raffia tote bag with rope effect chain straps – a simple weekend look for signature chic. Gok had taught him all he knew and in his head they were high fiving and doing a celebratory dance.

Becca gave Didier a big hug; she was much more careful with Phil.

'Which side is it?' she asked, eying him carefully and scanning him for other signs of injury.

'It's here,' Phil pointed gingerly with his good arm. 'So no bear hugs.'

Becca pecked him on the cheek and then with a loud clunk, she unlocked the rear doors of the truck and they creaked slowly open.

'It's a good job your trip is nearly over, you haven't got room for much more,' Phil said, surveying the interior of the truck, which was chock-a-block with furniture and boxes.

'I've one more port of call; I want to go to a place in Sète that makes wine cabinets. I'm hoping I might squeeze a couple in and then that's it.'

'When you said you were hiring a van I was expecting a Transit...' Phil said, full of admiration at his sister's hitherto unknown trucking skills.

'I'd thought so to, but when I used the little gizmo on the van hire website to calculate how much space I needed it recommended this. I'm covered on my licence – so I thought why not? To be honest, it's not so different from driving the school mini bus. I was such a chicken the first time I did that, but you soon get used to the size and being high up gives you much better visibility,' Becca said, lifting her case and bags out of the cab.

Didier took them all and pulled up the handle of the case and loaded it up with luggage, then effortlessly pushed it to the gate. Feeling a bit useless, Phil helped secure the van.

'Karel and I are going to ze wedding of mon neveu tomorrow; for ze gate I'll get you a spare key - zen you can go and come as it pleases you.'

'Thanks Didier... for this and for looking after Phil.'

'C'est un grand plaisir.' He smiled a broad Gauloises-stained toothy grin. Didier put the bags down when they reached Phil's door.

'When are you back?' Becca asked.

'Dimanche in ze morning some time.'

'By way of a thank you, why don't you come over for lunch,' Becca said, looking at Phil for approval.

She'd only just arrived and already she was taking over. Chill out Becca, you're on holiday, Phil said in his head. Maybe he'd be brave enough to say it out loud later; he cut his sister a bit of slack as she'd only just arrived.

'I'd like zat. Sunday roast?' Didier asked hopefully.

Becca laughed, she was clearly thinking of something more summery – barbecue perhaps. Phil associated roasts with cold winter days at home, but if that's what he wanted it was the least they could do.

'If you like,' Becca replied, lifting her case. 'I'll check with Karel and make the arrangements.'

Didier checked his watch. 'Let me help you upstairs wiz ze bags and zen I have to be off. Karel will be back from ze coiffeur any minute and if I'm not ready, it will be me zat gets ze roasting.'

Phil made some lunch while Becca had a shower, unpacked and settled in. He laid the table on the terrace, sliced the bread and unwrapped the cheeses. There were two local peppered goat's cheeses and a large slab of salty Roquefort. He uncorked the wine and poured two glasses and sat drinking it while he waited for Becca to join him.

Becca had changed into a pair of slate grey cotton shorts, with cream halterneck top and matching cream beaded flip flops. Her long, damp hair was clipped up with a few loose corkscrew curls framing her face.

'Wow, this looks lovely.'

'I assume you're talking about lunch and not the garden.'

'When you described it, I did think how much damage can a few goats cause? And here's my answer...' Becca shook her head as she surveyed the wreckage. '...Complete devastation. But garden aside, it's great to be here.'

'It's great to have you here. Karel has been brilliant. But the last week has felt a bit claustrophobic cooped up here. I've been counting the days to you coming.'

'I thought the idea was you were going to look after me.'

'And so I shall. I'll show you my lumps and bumps once you've eaten. Actually there's not much to see now. It did look bad. Towards the end it looked a lot worse than it felt, but now I feel pretty much back to my old self.'

'Which old self is that?' Becca teased. 'Is it the buying crap off the shopping channel old self or the post Rebecca's rehab old self?'

'Post rehab definitely... I'm great, everything's great. Best I've felt in ages.'

Becca tucked the loose strands of hair behind her ears and chinked glasses with her brother.

'Here's to new beginnings.'

'And happy endings too,' Phil added, taking a large swig of the chilled Picpoul. They chatted as they ate and Becca told him about her boys and all that had happened since he'd left, which in truth was not a lot. It was very quiet and everyone seemed to be away for the holidays.

'Aurore not been in for a spot of light shoplifting then?'

'Fortunately not, I've not seen her since book club and talking of books... what's happening with the writing?'

'I'll show you later. I've got a few tweaks to make then you can have a read if you like.'

'I would like, I'd like that very much. Is it a book?'

'Wait and see.'

'Okay, man of mystery, I'll be patient. Who was on the phone?' Becca asked, finishing the last of the goat's cheese.

'Karel, she was returning your call. She said they'd love to come on Sunday, and in response to your question about cuts she said she'd sort it with the butcher in the village and you can pick the joint up tomorrow.'

'That's brilliant, when it comes to French beef I'm never quite sure what I'm buying.'

'Or any meat for that matter. Do you remember the andouillette incident?'

'How could I forget it? That's why I asked for Karel's advice. They looked like big, tasty, juicy sausages. It was the smell I remember most. They smelt like those loos on that French campsite we used to go to as kids. The ones without the u-bend, just a sheer drop. How was I to know the sausages were made from a pig's rectum.'

'The smell might have been a bit of a clue. Surprisingly, they tasted quite good if you could get past the smell.' Phil said, taking a swig of wine.

'I couldn't... I kept gagging every time the fork came anywhere near my mouth.'

'You'd never survive in the army.' Phil laughed

'I could drive a tank after my last few days' experience...' Becca replied in her defence.

'We're not talking driving tanks. More eating something that smells as if it's come out of the septic tank...'

'Really? I never knew an army marched on andouillette.'

'You know what I mean. And even though not a morsel passed your lips I bet you've dined out many a time on that story.'

'Yeah, in that respect I got my money's worth.' Becca smiled, cutting another wedge of cheese.

When they'd eaten and lunch was cleared away, they made some plans for the next few days. Becca wanted to do her trip to Sète, visit Aigues Mortes and spend some time chilling on the beach.

'I think I'll go and look at the wine cabinets tomorrow and get that out of the way. You can come if you like, but I'm planning on leaving early so I can get back in time to sort lunch out,' Becca said, while searching on her phone for the address details.

'Why don't I stay here and do the veg and get things under way?' Phil offered, lying back on the sofa.

'Sounds like a plan,' Becca replied, making a note of the postcode on her phone to put in the sat nav for her excursion the following day. 'Mum's sent a text wishing us a happy holiday and to say Alice has died.'

'Alice who?'

'Alice... you know, three doors down from them. Alice with the caravan.'

'Yeah vaguely. Do you fancy going for a cycle later?' Phil asked, yawning, as he enjoyed the effect of his lunchtime glass of wine. 'Will you be okay on a bike?' Becca tapped a quick reply before popping her phone back in her bag.

'It's lifting and strenuous upper body exercise I have to lay off. Provided I don't fall off, I should be fine.'

The still oppressive heat of the afternoon had given way to a welcome breeze. It was funnelled through the regimented rows of vines that ran perpendicular to the cycle path, waking the cigales in the crisp long grass who began tuning up for their evening performance.

Riding two abreast, Phil and Becca followed the cycle path up the steep incline of the bridge crossing the Canal du Midi. Their exertions silenced their chat until they were freewheeling down the other side.

As they turned on to the coast road Phil asked after his literary muses; much as he liked Sam and Fi, it was Kitti he was most keen to hear about. But singling her out would attract awkward questions that he hadn't worked out the answers to yet.

So he listened distractedly as Becca regaled him with Fi's Italian holiday escapades. He managed to laugh in all the right places despite his mind being elsewhere.

Since he'd been in France he'd been thinking about Kitti a lot. Initially he'd dismissed it; attributed it to writing about her and really trying to capture her on the page. But it was more than that, writing about her made him realise how much he liked her.

She really got him; she didn't push, pry or pressurise him. He could be himself and unlike all his girlfriends she didn't want him to be somebody else, but then again why would she, what was he to her?

'And Sam?' Phil asked, drifting back into the conversation. 'What's she up to?'

'She's on good form. She dropped me at the van hire place before I set off and is keeping an eye on the girls in the shop while I'm away.'

'What about her job?'

'She said the summer's notoriously quiet; she's got a stack of admin to do and appointments to set up and she says she can do that as easily from the shop as she can from home. I couldn't have done this trip without her. I've got her a little dresser, it's similar to one she had a liking for in the shop.'

'It's a wonder you make any money, you're always giving away your stock.'

'It's not really giving it away. Sam won't take any money for helping out in the shop, so it's wages.'

'And Aurore ?'

'Well that's not so much me giving it away as her helping herself to whatever she fancies.'

'And you just let her get away with it.'

'I do my best. I'm terrier-like in my efforts. I dropped all the book club books off for Sam and I put an invoice for the vase in hers. But she'll probably just ignore it. From what Fi's told me, she doesn't care. When things aren't as she'd like them to be, she tells herself over and over what she wants to believe until she eventually convinces herself that it's the truth.'

'So she probably thinks I gave her the vase.'

'Probably. Who knows what's going on under that finely coiffed bob?'

'How's Kitti?' he asked casually while they parked their bikes outside one of the beach cafés.

'She's good; she's taken Jachim to Portugal with her Mum.'

'Oh I love it there; the Vinho Verde, the sardines cooked on driftwood and sold by beach vendors on the praias….' While Phil reminisced about some of his previous golfing holidays, Becca dropped a bombshell.

'They're staying in a villa that belongs to one of her old boyfriends.'

Phil was suddenly hoiked back from the manicured turf of the Algarve.

'Sorry… I was still on the fairway in Vale do Lobo, did you say boyfriend?'

'Yes Phil, try to pay attention… or at least pretend to be interested in my friends.' Becca chided as she struggled to remove the key from her lock.

If only you knew, he thought. 'Sorry, it's just that no one's mentioned him before… I'm just a bit surprised that's all.'

'Well I'm not surprised, she's gorgeous, funny and clever and it was only a matter of time before someone snapped her up.' Becca said in a very "you had your chance and blew it" kind of way.

'Old boyfriend you said…' Clutching at straws, Phil was hoping that was all he was or would ever be.

'They met when she was in her first year at uni'; it was all over by the time I got to know Kitti.'

'So you've not met him then?'

'Apparently I met him at a couple of parties, but I can't even remember the parties let alone anyone at them...'

'The sign of a good party by my reckoning.'

'Yeah... happy times.'

'I'm surprised you lot have not checked him out yet.'

'You're joking, can you imagine unleashing Fi on some poor unsuspecting potential suitor. It would be the kiss of death. She'd be straight in there interrogating him about his intentions and future prospects; she's very protective of Kitti and Jachim – we all are I guess.'

'So it's a recent thing?' He asked, leading the way through to the rear of the café where the deck snaked down to the beach.

'Yes, he contacted her through one of those "see what people you didn't like at school are up to now" websites.'

They chose a table and sat under the flapping orange parasol emblazoned with the Miko logo. They paused the chat and studied the laminated pictorial menu.

'So has he gone with them... the boyfriend?'

'No Marcus is away filming in Spain, that's why he offered his place. It's going to be empty for the whole summer. After all the building work she's had done on her place Kitti's a bit strapped for cash at the mo'. She was planning a staycation so when the villa was mentioned she jumped at the chance.'

Why had he never thought to offer his place in France to Kitti? Oblivious to the fact that she'd lost Phil again, Becca continued 'We'll get to meet him when she's good and ready. But I have to admit I was very curious; I didn't like to ask too many questions so I Googled him. He's got his own film production company, it was only a small pic on the website but he's very good-looking and Kitti says Jachim just adores him.'

"You idiot," Phil kicked himself. In fact, he had a one-man, two-round bout of Taekwondo but it didn't make him loathe himself any less.

Becca was right. He'd had so many opportunities with Kitti; so many lost opportunities. But like the serial commitment phobe he was, he always scurried away rather than stay and try and make something of it. Just like his time in 'Rebecca's Rehab', it was the longest he and Kitti had ever spent together; they'd really got close, but again he'd run away to France rather than take it further.

That was unfair, he'd had to get away. He needed space to think, he needed to get his head straight; sort out one bit of his life first before he could even begin to contemplate whether he and Kitti had any kind of future.

Well that was one less thing he needed to concern himself with – the question he'd been struggling to answer had been answered by the gorgeous and talented Marcus. Phil and Kitti didn't have a future – end of.

What was it that always held him back? He'd always been scared off by women with kids in tow. For a start, he struggled with the whole long-term relationship thing and maybe the idea of taking on someone else's kid was a commitment too far. He'd always referred to it as the Pot Noodle family - made in an instant. No, it was way too complicated too quickly.

Almost as if sensing this, some girlfriends wouldn't mention the fact they had kids for ages and he found himself in too deep to back off. They'd casually drop it into a conversation: 'I think it's about time I introduced you to Billy'. 'Who the hell's Billy?' he'd want to ask, but instead would mutter 'That would be nice.'

They'd have some horrible weekend with his girlfriend trying too hard to play happy families and little Billy resenting him for not being his dad and throwing him death stares behind his mum's back at every opportunity. That was usually the death knell and the relationship would slowly slip into a coma beyond resuscitation.

The waiter came and took their order for two huge Café Liégeois.

'Any more messages from the other side?' Phil asked, not wanting to hear anything further about wonder boy Marcus.

'She hasn't mentioned it, it's all died down - pardon the pun.'

'Talking of relationships, has Karel tried any matchmaking on this trip?' Becca asked, spooning coffee ice cream and Chantilly out of the tall sundae glass.

Phil was glad of the change of subject and Becca managed to squeeze a few laughs out of him as she reminded him about some of the appalling mismatches Karel had contrived to fix him up with over the years.

'Who was the woman with the dogs?'

'Estelle.'

'Estelle - yes that's right. Didn't she like to have the dogs in bed with her all the time?'

'Yeah, when it got to the crucial moment they joined in the howling, it used to put me off my stroke.'

'I'm not surprised.'

'And then there was Colette. Didn't she like to dress up?'

'No, she wanted me to dress up. She had a thing about men in uniforms and got really cross when I didn't take my role play seriously.'

'So you've escaped this trip?'

'Sort of. She was trying to fix me up with Didier's niece. She seems really nice, but then I had my run-in with the bulls and Karel's efforts were required elsewhere.'

'The lengths you'll go to, to escape her playing Cupid.'

The beach was emptying and they decided to make a move too. As they passed the bars, they were arranging the tables and chairs, preparing for their evening trade. The wind surfers on the étang were dismantling their boards and packing up for the day. The traffic was backed up over the bridge and as they bypassed it all they were glad they'd left the car at home.

Phil showered and changed. Becca had said that having spent the last few weeks in shorts and tee shirts it would do him good to dress up and go out for dinner. He was not so sure; he wondered if their idea of dressing up was the same.

He put on one of his new shirts and a pair of freshly laundered jeans; at last minute he changed out of his trainers and slipped his tanned, sockless feet into a pair of black suede loafers. Was this dressed up, he thought, as he glanced in the mirror? It would have to do.

He could hear Becca using the hairdryer; while she was busy, he took the opportunity to print out the final draft of his story. He loaded up the paper cassette and clicked on print. The printer whirred into life and the final page rolled out into the print tray, followed by the next and next. He left it to run and went to find something to put it in.

He pulled the loose staples from an old padded envelope and then slid the still warm stack of paper into it.

They drove out of the village and on to the main road; past the prison and past Sophie's van. Phil smiled to himself, but he couldn't get anything past his sister.

'I'd like to think it's my presence that's responsible for your good humour, but I know you better than that..' Becca said, gently teasing him to share his thoughts.

Phil retold the story of his car breaking down and his lesson in advanced French vocab.

'I really can't leave you alone for five minutes, can I? You should put that in whatever you're writing.'

They talked about how it would fit in with Phil's genre of writing; maybe it could happen to one of the guys while he was on leave.

'It'd make a bit of light relief from all the battles and bombing.'

'Too late for this one. Maybe I'll save it for the next one.' He replied distractedly, following the signs to the beach and then turning on to a narrower road running parallel to the salt marshes.

In the half-light, a small spec of blue neon shone in the distance. It gave the illusion of being out to sea. It was, in fact, at the end of a narrow track that dissected the étang leading to a narrow sand bar.

As they went further down the track, the blue dot became recognisable as the familiar signage of their favourite seafood restaurant. The beaming maître d' welcomed them and showed them to a table overlooking the sea. Looking at the menu was a formality; they knew what they wanted. There was only one thing to have and that was the Moules Provençal served on a bed of garlic beans.

With all the ordering out of the way, Phil lifted the weighty envelope and passed it to Becca.

'So this is what's been keeping you busy, is it?'

'It's just something I did for me - a little test; actually it's something I wrote for you. It's my way of saying thank you.'

'You've said thank you already...'

'I know, but I say thank you when someone holds a door open for me or in a shop when they give me my change. It somehow undervalues it. I guess I wanted to show what it meant to me. What you mean to me.'

Becca opened the envelope, pulled out the manuscript and placed it on the table. She read the title out loud.

'Oh my god. Is it an exposé?'

'I prefer to see it as a portrait of you and your life. And what a wonderful life it is. I should know, I've been living it with you.'

'Wow.' Becca thumbed through the pages. 'A whole story all about me; let's skip the mussels, I want to go back and read it now.'

'It will keep; there are some other familiar faces in there too. I've used a little artistic licence, embellished stories for dramatic effect and some bits I've made up just for the fun of it.'

'So have you made me a slightly built, voluptuous temptress with gorgeous hair?'

'I don't need to make that up. You're very much you. The reason I wrote it was to say that I'm glad you're who you are. And yes you're a pain in the arse sometimes… all the time, but I wouldn't change that.'

'You were doing quite well up until that point.'

Becca skim read the first page.

'Don't you know? It's rude to read at the table.'

'Oh go on. Let me just read the first chapter? It's like giving a child a toy and then not letting them play with it.'

'I'm kidding, it's yours. I want you to read it. Maybe not all now, but I want to know what you think. If it wasn't about you, would you be interested in it? Is it a style of book I could write and that other people might want to read?'

'Give me a chance, I'm only on the first page.'

'Sorry. It's just that I've put so much into it. And while it is predominantly a quirky present for you, I'm wondering if it's also a lifeboat for me. Do you know what I mean?'

'I know exactly what you mean.'

Their two-person book group was suspended temporarily by the arrival of their food. It tasted as good as it did in his memories. The mussels were plump and succulent, the tomato sauce fresh and zingy, and the beans unbelievably garlicky.

Becca pushed her empty plate to one side and reopened the manuscript.

'You made light work of that.'

'Sorry, I was really hungry. With the cycle and the sea air I'd worked up quite an appetite.'

'An appetite for food or reading?'

'Both.'

'I only finished the last page yesterday. I know I should have waited and given it to you at the end of the meal, but I was really excited and now I've given you indigestion.'

'You sound like Mum, you'll be passing the Rennies round next.'

A waiter took their coffee orders and they moved to a table on the veranda. Becca read and Phil sat back and listened to the sea.

'Apart from my Sindy riding stables, this is the very best present I've ever had,' Becca said, thumbing through the pages.

'I'll take that as a compliment.' Phil kicked off his shoes and put his feet up; he wiggled his brown toes in the warm sea breeze.

'Oh my god... Aurore's in it too, this just gets better and better.'

Nineteen

Becca had left by the time Phil got up the next morning. On the fridge were two lists, one of instructions and the other a shopping list. After a quick dip, he showered and went into the village to fulfil his hunter-gatherer role.

He chose the vegetables. Proper mutant vegetables, all different shapes and sizes with the honest earth they had grown in still stuck to them. Not like the cosmetically enhanced flavourless pretenders of the supermarkets back home. France was in the EU, so how did they get away with curly cucumbers, he wondered.

Last stop, the boucherie. Karel obviously thought they were feeding the five thousand. The joint she'd reserved was massive. It was also incredibly heavy and just as she'd said, the weighty bags pulled on his chest as he carried them home.

He checked his list for further instructions. Pre-heat the oven. Peel the potatoes. Lay the long table on the terrace. He'd just placed the last knife on the table when he heard the familiar beep of the van as it reversed into the playground.

Phil returned to the pool to cool off. He did a few gentle lengths on his back and then busied himself hosing the goat poo from the terrace.

Despite the heat, Becca calmly brought the meal together. The roast potatoes were crisped to perfection.

The Yorkshires had had an uprising that the Hungarians would have been proud of and the vegetables were bubbling away gently on the hob. The smell of cooking permeated the whole house and transported him back to his childhood.

Karel and Didier arrived on the dot of two. Karel, the coiffeur chameleon, was sporting a fuller dark brown bob that had a slight purple sheen when the light caught it. This was perfectly accessorised with glasses, belt, bag and shoes. Phil was tuned in to notice all these things now; all things that would have previously passed him by.

Didier was struggling under the weight of a large plastic bakery crate full of plants.

'What's all this?' Phil asked, taking one side of the crate with his good arm.

'They're from your number one fan,' Karel said, holding open the doors, so they could take the crate straight through to the terrace.

Phil shrugged, none the wiser. Even after all these years he still hadn't quite perfected the French shrug, but he was working on it.

'Madame Broussard, of course,' Karel said, a little exasperated at his reluctance to take part in her guessing game. 'She's had a poster up in the bakery explaining what happened to your garden and asking for donations of plants. There's six more crates out there,' she added, ushering Didier out to fetch the next one.

'Here Didier, let me get one of those handles,' Phil offered as a walking Kew Gardens appeared in the doorway.

'That's so generous…' Becca said, tasting the gravy.

'I sink the village people…'

Childish he knew, but Phil couldn't help his reflex response to sing a little burst of YMCA in his head.

'Zey would like to… montrer?'

'To show…' Karel called from the garden.

'Yes, zey would like to you show you zat not everyone sinks like Gérard.'

'I didn't imagine for one minute that they did, but this is a wonderful way to have my assumption confirmed.'

'You might need to move the crates into the shade; some of the Cosmos are starting to wilt.' Becca said filling a large jug with water and passing it out to Karel.

'If it won't disturb you and Madame Becca, Didier can plant them out for you next week.'

'That would be great.' Phil said, wiping his earthy hands on his trousers. 'I don't think I was a huge help last time we did it but if it's possible, I'll be even less help this time.'

'Well, maybe Phil and I could help with the plant plan.' Becca said returning to the hob. 'We could lay out the plants and Didier could put them in.'

'Zat sounds like a good plan.'

Phil served the drinks and they chatted about the wedding in the kitchen while Becca poured, strained and carved. Between them they carried the serving dishes, plates and the large rack of beef to the table. With everyone seated and served, they clinked glasses. Karel and Didier exchanged glances, each trying to encourage the other to say something. Reluctantly, Didier caved in to the pressure.

'Oh all right,' he said with a shrug. Becca and Phil looked at him with bemusement. 'Do you know what zis is?'

'Er, roast dinner?' ventured Phil.

'Beef?' tried Becca.

'Yes, but more zan zat – it is… taureau.'

'Bull.' Karel explained excitedly before taking over the story.

'I suppose Didier should have asked not what is it, but who is it?'

'No way… you're kidding me… it's not… What, poor old Mad Spotty?' Phil asked incredulously.

Karel nodded. 'He chewed up your rib and now we'll chew up his - karma.'

'It was an idea of Karel's,' Didier continued.

'I ordered it a while back. It sounds like retribution, but it wasn't really. He'd already been earmarked for a trip to the boucherie.'

'It's a circle of life thing.' Becca laughed.

'I was going to cook it for you,' Karel explained. 'But then when you invited us to lunch and asked me about the meat, it seemed like too good an opportunity to miss.'

'Come on then, dig in, let's have a taste,' Phil said, loading his fork. 'Mmmm, delicious! Well, he may have trampled my body but now he's tantalising my tongue.'

Phil raised his glass in a toast to Mad Spotty. They ate and talked and talked and ate. Didier had a soft spot for the Yorkies and ate three. He would have had four, but as he was helping himself, Karel gave him 'the look' over the top of her glasses and he put it back.

The lunch may have been British but the length was very French and it was early evening before their guests left. Becca yawned long and loudly.

'I'm knackered.'

'Me too, that's what drinking at lunchtime does; it wipes you out for the rest of the day,' Phil said, stacking the plates on the drainer.

'I think it has more to do with my late night and early morning.'

'We weren't too late last night,' Phil added, drying the last of the wine glasses.

'We weren't, but then I stayed up half the night reading.'

Phil apologised before drying his hands and joining Becca for the last of the sun on the terrace.

'It's not your fault,' Becca chided him, 'You know what I'm like when I'm reading a book that I'm really enjoying. I just want to spend my whole time reading.'

'So you like it then?' Phil asked animatedly.

'It's fantastic. To be honest when I read the title I was unsure. I live my life, it's hardly worthy of a biography.'

'It isn't a biography.' Phil corrected.

'I know and that's what I love. The characters are real and they're unmistakably me, Kitti, Fi and Sam. You've got us down to a tee. The location is real, even some of the things that happen are based on fact. I'm thinking of how you handle the whole Kitti, Jachim thing. It's really sensitively done. I guess what I'm trying to say in a longwinded roundabout way is, it's not a long list of random events. You've woven them all together into a story. You're a great storyteller. I just love the bits about Aurore – and they say girls are bitchy.'

'I couldn't resist it. It was a way of dealing with her scandalous behaviour. Bringing her to book, so to speak,'

'It made me laugh; the girls will love it. Can I show them?'

'It's yours, you can do whatever you like with it. To save you printing out more copies, I'll bung it on a memory stick and you can mail it to them.'

'I know this isn't for publication and in many ways I'm glad, but you have a real talent and you mustn't waste it.'

'I don't intend to. I've got my direction back. When I get home, I'm going to start my next book. I'm already planning it out.'

'I have to admit I didn't think writing was the answer, but you've proved me wrong,' Becca said, looking him straight in the eye.

'Now that's something worth having in writing.' Phil replied, nudging his sister with his elbow.

'Which rib was it again?' Becca asked, playfully raising her fist.

Becca's visit was nearly over; Phil had worried that having only recently spent so much time together they'd run out of things to talk about. He needn't have worried. They were relaxed in each other's company and liked doing the same sorts of things. Maybe living Becca's life for five weeks had homogenised their interests and his outlook.

They'd managed to fit most things in. Although, once he'd given Becca the story, she didn't seem to care where she was; she was happy just to sit and read. Whether it was a bar in the square at Aigues Mortes, the beaches of the Gulf de Lion or on a lounge chair by his pool glancing up occasionally to offer advice on the planting plan.

Didier had arrived each morning with more crates. Remembering how they'd approached the task last time, he unpacked the plants, carefully grouping them into shade or sun lovers and then clustering the plants by shape, size, colour and seasonality. It was a complete hotchpotch; entirely different from the controlled and restrained planting of the previous scheme.

Becca looked at the plants and colours in a way that suggested that they might not have been what she'd have chosen. But the fact that other people had been kind enough to make cuttings, dig up plants from their own gardens or in some cases buy new trays and pots from Jardiland , was what made it special to him.

In three days the makeover was complete; Phil, Didier and Becca had created a garden that Ground Force would have been proud of. It lacked the obligatory water feature, but Becca (their answer to Charlie Dimmock) said the pool would have to suffice.

'I think we should have a grand opening and invite everyone who donated plants,' Phil announced, admiring their handiwork.

'We can ask ze maire to a… couper le ruban,' Didier laughed, making a scissor-cutting gesture with his fingers.

'That's not such a bad idea.' Phil thought that building a few bridges and showing that there were no hard feelings would put goat gate well and truly behind them.

'You know you can stay longer if you like,' Phil said as they sat finishing their drinks in the village bar. 'It's a real shame you won't be here for the garden party.'

'I know and I'd love to, but I can't impose on Sam for too long and besides the boys are back on Friday. I'm desperate to see them. I know after a couple of days I'll be complaining about how much they eat, the state they leave the bathroom in and how loud they are, but I've really missed them.'

'So have I. Tell them I want to fix up a boys' day out when I get back.'

'I will. You're their favourite uncle.'

'I'm their only uncle.'

'That's why you're their favourite.'

Phil tucked a ten euro note under his cup and they wandered arm in arm back through the village.

'Are you packed?' he asked as they reached his gates.

'I think so. I didn't bring too much, I wanted to leave as much space in the van as I could for stuff for the shop.'

'I'm coming back in a couple of weeks or so,' Phil said, turning the key in the lock. 'If you've left anything I can bring it back with me.'

'Great… right, I need to get this loaded up,' Becca replied, gathering her stuff she'd left in the hall. 'If I carry the bags, can you pull the case?'

Becca cautiously drove through the school gates and lowered her window for a final au revoir. Didier and Karel came to wave her off.

'Will we see you next year?' Karel called over the revving of the engine.

'I hope so. If I manage to get this lot through customs without getting arrested I'm going to make regular trips. So far it's been a lot easier than dealing with the shipping companies. Maybe I'll bring the boys to help with the lifting and carrying next time. We can have a road trip holiday.'

'Or they can fly down with me. I'll take them to the water and theme parks. We'll do all the things you hate, before you arrive,' Phil called, moving out of Becca's way.

'I think the answer to your question is yes, I'll be back. And don't worry Phil; I did a thorough search of the van and there's no huge stash of hash secreted in a false-bottomed drawer.'

'That's good to hear. You're not really cut out for a life in Prisoner Cell Block H.'

Becca tooted her horn and waved as she negotiated her way along the narrow village street. Phil felt deflated. He often felt like that after he'd finished a book. Becca's company had softened the blow but now she had gone too.

The completion left a vacuum. He knew that it would eventually be filled by the return of the rest of his life, the life he suspended during the intense period of writing. But for now he felt flat. The house seemed big and empty; he wandered from room to room not knowing what to do with himself. He enjoyed sharing the house. His mum and dad were regular visitors and even Mal had spent a week there with his family.

What he needed was a little project to keep him busy and maybe organising the garden party was just such a project. How could he tell everyone about his idea and check suitable dates? He knew just the person to help with that – he checked his watch; the bakery should just be finishing the morning rush, he grabbed his wallet and keys and headed into the village.

It was all set for the Sunday before Phil was due to head home. Posters were up in the bakery. The mayor had agreed to perform the ceremonial duties and in return his office had asked if a journalist and photographer could attend – the more the merrier was

Phil's philosophy. A friend of David's was in a jazz band and they were going to come and play as a warm-up before they headed off to the Montpellier Jazz Festival – it was all coming together nicely.

Karel was right, most things in the village went at a snail's pace like the bureaucracy and paperwork involved in drawing up the new boundary. But when it came to partying and having fun well, that was quite a different matter and things galloped along at a cracking pace.

Over the next ten days Phil busied himself bringing all his plans to life. He ran his pen down his checklist to see what still needed doing. Wine? Tick… he'd been to the Cav and filled three catering-size plastic casks with the local red, rosé, and white. Glass hire? Tick… actually they were plastic, not so nice, but he didn't want to take a chance with the likelihood of so many children coming.

Soft drinks? Tick… with limited space in the fridge the garage was the next coolest place he could think of to store the cartons of juice, Orangina and water. Beer? Tick… he'd got quite a taste for the Goat Beer and it somehow seemed appropriate so he'd bought several crates. The old stone water trough that they hadn't replanted would be great for the beers once it was filled with ice. Ice… he needed to pick up the ice or was David doing that? He'd call in and check with him later.

Before he knew it, the day of the party had arrived. Phil stood at the doors to the terrace and stared out into the garden, everything was as it should be. The plants had settled in well; a fair few were in bloom and it was all looking pristine. Didier had borrowed some tables and chairs from the school and set them up around the garden. Karel had entwined patriotic blue, white and red ribbons and strung them across between two trees at the entrance to the garden.

It all looked perfect, with the possible exception of the hedge; it badly needed a trim. Didier had said he'd do it, but then had got tied up with some maintenance work at the school.

Where the goats had repeatedly forced their way through the hedge they'd created large gaping holes. They'd munched all the new shoots at ground level, so the hedge was completely bald at the bottom with the only new growth out of their reach at the top.

It looked a real mess, and with everything else in the garden now rosy it was really letting the side down. It probably wasn't the best thing for his rib, but he'd have to get back to doing some of these jobs once he got home. So why not start now?

Phil walked round to the garage and slid the heavy door open. Carefully, he lifted the stepladder off the rack on the wall; it wasn't too heavy, he should be able to carry it. Normally he'd struggle round with a big pile of stuff but he was sensible and made more trips than usual to gather all the things he needed.

In a token gesture to protecting his rib, he unhooked an orange life vest from the wall. It was one he used when he went sea fishing. He put it on and zipped it up. It was just the padding he needed.

Time for some hedge surfing.

Twenty

After her mammoth seventeen-hour journey, Becca was relieved to be on the home straight. It was 1am and the South Circular was still clogged. Where were all these people going? She'd got a little bit of sleep on the ferry but was longing to climb into her own bed. At least with a lot of people still away, she had no problem parking.

She'd made it. Home sweet home. Except, it didn't smell very sweet, the bin needed emptying. There was a stack of post on the kitchen table, she'd look at that in the morning. It was the morning - well, later on.

There was a note from Sam. Saying everything was fine. It had been quite busy at the shop and she'd take Becca through it all later. She had to go to head office for a meeting, so she wouldn't be able to take Becca to the van hire place. But Fi had offered to take her instead.

With her eyes barely open, she sent two texts, one to take Fi up on her offer and the other to let Phil know she was home in one piece. Becca pulled back the duvet, her heavy, weary body sank gratefully into the mattress.

She was woken by the phone; she mumbled into the receiver and was greeted by Fi's cheery, wide-awake voice.

'Hello lovely… sorry, did I wake you?'

'It's okay,' Becca sleepily muttered with her eyes still shut. 'I probably should be up.'

'I got your text and was wondering, what time you need to have the van back?'

'Before twelve. What time is it now?'

'Just after ten. 'Fi heard a long groan and then some swearing.

'Hello. Are you still there?'

'Yes, I'm still here and I wish I could stay here, but there's no chance of that.'

'Shall I pop over now? I can give you a hand unloading if you like.'

'That would be great if you don't mind. I'll put the kettle on.'

With no time for a shower, Becca tied her hair up and whacked on some mascara; she was ready to face the world. She parked up near the shop and unloaded on to the pavement. Fi scurried to and fro. They stacked all the boxes up by the stairs to the storeroom; Becca would sort it out over the weekend.

Nigel stopped for a chat on his way to get a coffee. Becca nabbed him and requisitioned his services to help carry the heavier pieces of furniture from the van to the shop.

When the van was returned, Becca invited Fi back to hers for a well-earned tea break. Becca was bursting to tell her about Phil's book. And after politely listening to further tales from the Amalfi coast, she got her chance.

'So, how was your time with Phil? What's he been up to? Has he been behaving himself?' Fi asked.

'On the whole yes. He's been writing and you'll never guess what about.' Becca looked at Fi hopefully. 'Well aren't you even going to try?'

'You said I'd never guess so what's the point.'

'You could just humour me.' Exasperated, Becca left the kitchen and returned holding the manuscript. She plonked it down on the table.

Fi read the title. 'You're right. I'd have never guessed that.'

Fi flicked through the pages, she came across a bit about her and read with amusement.

'The cheeky bugger.'

'Do you mind? Do you think it's offensive?'

'You're joking, I love it. It's superb, he's got my number all right.'

'Mine too. Look what he's written about me here.' Becca turned a couple of pages and pointed to a paragraph halfway down the page.

'That's not true, is it?'

'No, but I wish it was.'

'Can I borrow it?' Fi asked eagerly.

'Yeah, when I've made some copies.'

Fi looked disappointed. Becca was reminded why her kids hated the 'we'll see' expression so much. She didn't want to wait.

'But, Phil's given me the file.' Becca unzipped her purse and took out the memory stick. 'I could mail it to you.'

'You know me, and my stupid, bloody email. It filters out everything that I actually want to read and lets through messages from the Prince of Congo who wants to deposit one million dollars into my bank account and others about where to get the best penis enlargement. I've already got one big dick in the house; I don't need another. Can't I just borrow the memory stick?'

'Yeah, all right, but let me have it back when you've taken it off. I want to send it to Sam and Kitti.'

'I could probably manage that. Sending is fine; it's receiving mail my computer objects to. I'll give it a go when I get back.'

Fi dropped the memory stick in her bag and got up to go.

'I need to dash I'm afraid. The tree surgeon is finally coming to lop that overhanging branch off next door's tree.'

'Well, that's a result.'

'Not exactly, it's taken nearly two years and we're footing the bill.'

'Thanks for your help today.'

'No problem.' Fi picked up her car keys.

'See you later in the week.' The door slammed, shaking the entire house and she was gone.

Becca listened to her phone messages as she waded through her post, sorting it into three piles: interesting, boring bank stuff and the 'so dull it's not worth opening'. Most of it ended up in the recycling bin. She turned on her laptop and while that was starting up, made herself a coffee.

She tapped in her password and felt her heart sink. She had seventy three unread emails. There was one from Fi entitled 'here come the girls'. Becca opened it.

Fi had written a funny note and attached the story. She'd suggested a mini book group discussion for later in the week. As she was logging out and closing the window, Becca noticed loads of names in the recipient box. Stupid cow, Becca thought. Fi had replied all to a mail Sam had sent and inadvertently circulated the story to the entire book group.

Becca grabbed her phone and scrolled through the address book to the f's. It went straight through to voicemail.

'Hi Fi, it's Becca. Just calling to say I got your email but unfortunately so did the entire book group – all twelve of them, including Aurore. Call me back when you have a minute. Speak to you soon.'

Becca took a deep breath. She didn't care if Aurore read what Phil had written about her, but Kitti was a different matter. Becca was annoyed with Phil; he knew how sensitive Kitti was at the moment. Why did he put that stuff in the story? That was unfair, she couldn't really blame him. He'd intended the story for their closed circle. It was supposed to amuse and entertain them. He didn't know it was going to cause her all this grief.

Was she over-reacting? So what, a few more people than she'd intended had got their hands on the story. It was only her book group for god's sake. She liked them, they were nice people. If she asked them to keep it to themselves, she knew they would.

Sure there were things in the story that she may not have necessarily wanted to share with the group, but they were so mixed up with other extreme flights of fancy that it would make it difficult to separate fact from fiction. As for Aurore, maybe Fi had done them a favour. Maybe she'd stop coming to book group and boycott her shop altogether.

Was it her fault? She knew that the combination of Fi and technology was not a good one. She should have listened to that voice in her head screaming 'noooo' as she handed the stick over to Fi. She never imagined that Fi would slap a certificate U on the story and send it to the world and his wife!

Becca didn't know what to do for the best. She could send a follow-up email to the book group, asking them to keep it to themselves. Or would that simply draw more attention to something that most of them would probably ignore anyway? One thing she knew for certain was that Fi should not be the one to break the news to Kitti. She was not known for her diplomacy skills.

Becca picked up the present for Jachim and decided to pop it round. Strike while the iron's hot; that was the advice she always gave everyone else.

Becca pushed the bell and waited. No answer. She was relieved, she didn't really want to break the news to Kitti, but she just felt she ought to. Just as she was turning to leave, she heard footsteps in the hallway on the other side of the door.

'Hiya, come in. I didn't know you were back. Sorry, have you been standing there long? We're in the garden, Jachim's in his paddling pool.' Kitti closed the door and led the way through to the kitchen. 'Tea?'

'I'd love one.'

Kitti asked about her trip and Becca told all - well almost all. She tap-danced her way around her reason for calling in, for as long as she could. But then Kitti asked if Phil had done any writing while he was away. There was nowhere to hide, she had to 'fess up.

Becca didn't go into too many details about the revelations in the story. She didn't want to prejudice her reaction, she wanted her to read it and judge for herself.

'I'm glad he's been writing,' Kitti said, cradling her mug. 'I'm just not so delighted it's personal stuff about me. It's not that I've done anything I'm ashamed of, it's just having things written down in black and white can have a habit of coming back and biting you on the bum.'

'I know exactly what you mean. The number of times I've written things in emails only to regret them the moment I've clicked the send button – now I give anything remotely controversial the overnight test.'

'You wouldn't like to pass that bit of wisdom on to Fi would you?'

Kitti flashed her well-practised calm, carefree smile, but the rest of her face betrayed her true feelings.

'All I'd say is read it and if you're still worried we'll track down all the copies and destroy them.'

'You're right, I guess... my worry is that in a few years' time Jachim might stumble upon it and read it; will he be able to separate fact from fiction? How will he feel about Phil's take on how he came into the world...'

'Like you, I don't want the whole world to know my business, but we are only talking about our book group...'

'You're right... I count most of them as my friends and they probably know pretty much all there is to know anyway.'

'So you're not mad?' Becca asked with more than a hint of relief.

'Like I say, if it's what I think it is,' Kitti said, glancing out to Jachim. 'I wouldn't want to shout it from the rooftops, but book group's no big deal. But promise me one thing…'

'Of course what is it…'

'Don't ever entrust anything involving computers or technology to Fi; she's lovely but you know what a liability she is.'

'I know. I'm sorry, the minute I handed it over I knew it was a mistake – never again I promise.'

Kitti topped up their mugs and the conversation moved on to safer ground.

'So how was your holiday?' Becca asked dunking a Hobnob.

'We had a great time, the villa's gorgeous, the sun shone every day, we ate out most evenings and Jachim played happily in the pool with mum while I caught up on my reading list. What more could a girl ask for?'

'A holiday romance?'

'No, there was no chance of romance.'

'What about Marcus?'

'He was filming in Seville the whole time we were there. We spoke a couple of times on the phone. He just wanted to check all was well at the villa, but it's not really like… you know…'

'No I don't know…'

Becca had more questions but they'd have to wait;

Jachim padded into the kitchen, dripping water and leaving a trail of grass clippings and muddy footprints in his wake.

'Hello, there. I've got something for you.' Becca gave him a big hug and then handed over his present.

While Becca brushed the wet grass and leaves from her jeans Jachim made light work of the wrapping paper and pulled out the large yellow box.

'Un sous-marin' Kitti read aloud the type splashed across the front of the box. 'Wow Jachim, it's a submarine and look it's got little toy sailors you can take out.' And lose, was her unspoken thought.

Becca was good at choosing presents; though she said it herself, she had a talent for shops and shopping.

'Now what do you say to Becca?'

Not taking his eyes from the pictures on the box outlining the submarines many features, Jachim offered a distracted thank you.

'And what about a kiss for Becca too?' Reluctantly he handed the box to his mum.

After a struggle, Kitti managed to release the colourful plastic vessel from the vice-like grip of several twisted plastic ties. The toy was more securely fixed to the backboard than most shelves to the walls in her house. She broke a nail in the process and finally had to resort to using a large kitchen knife.

'Hold it up and give me a big smile,' Becca said, snapping a few shots with her iPhone.

Before she'd managed to put her phone back in her pocket, Jachim had run back into the garden to launch the submarine in his paddling pool.

'I thought you said Phil's story is fictional.' Kitti used the soggy wrapping paper to clear away Jachim's garden debris trail.

'It is… sort of. We're obviously not fictional and there are a few bits in the story that are based on real events. But mostly it's pure fantasy.'

'After you've gone I'm going to get it up on my computer. If I'm lucky I might get half an hour to myself while he's happy out there playing sea admirals.'

Becca took this as her cue to leave. 'Thanks for the tea. I'm going to head off. I've got all my dreaded unpacking to do in the shop.'

'Jachim's going to a party this afternoon so I might pop in and see you later.'

'You'll be very welcome, but you could well end up with a job to do.'

'I don't mind. I'm keen to have a sneak preview of what you've bought.'

When Becca got home, there was a long rambling message from Fi on the answerphone. In fact, there were two. The first had been so long and rambling that she'd been cut off mid-apology and she'd had to call back to leave the rest of her waffly missive.

Becca returned her call and told her that all was well. That Kitti was still speaking to her and that it was an innocent mistake. Now completely paranoid about having the memory stick, Fi arranged to drop it off at the shop. She said it worried her having it around in case she mistakenly sent it to anyone else or inadvertently sold the film rights.

The house was a tip. Becca put a load of washing on and carried her case upstairs to pack away in the eaves cupboard. She wanted to stuff it in and close the door. But there was no room; before she could put it in she had to take a load of stuff out. She had to reorganise it and make some space.

At the back of the cupboard next to her sewing machine was her treasures box. She lifted it out, it was heavy and the lid was broken on one corner. It had been a while since she'd been through it. Mostly she lifted the lid and dropped things in. Carefully she sifted through drawings from her art A level and her certificates for gymnastics.

Underneath her eighteenth birthday cards was a bundle of Phil's original hand-written stories. Even though there were a hundred and one other jobs she should be doing, she continued her stroll down memory lane. Becca sat and read the thin stapled books. Even as a ten year old he wrote a good story. The spelling was very creative and the illustrations really funny.

Becca placed his new story in the box with the others. It would be safe here and would neither cause nor come to any harm. As she was about to put the lid back, she noticed some old photos, a beach holiday - Isle of Wight, maybe. Phil would have been around four and was holding a toy sailing boat.

Becca put the lid back on her treasures box and carefully stacked everything back in the cupboard to make space for her suitcase. She wasn't sure why, but she kept hold of the photo and when she went back downstairs she tucked it in her handbag.

For the rest of the day she shifted boxes to the storeroom and made a note of things that were going to be marked down in the sale to make space for the new stock. Fi dropped the memory stick off and while she was there, Kitti arrived. There was an awkward silence, which was soon filled by them both talking at the same time.

'Sorry, you go first.'

'I was just going to say I'm really sorry. I had no idea I'd sent it to everyone. I....'

'It's fine, Fi. It wasn't everyone. It's only our book group. I must admit I was a bit freaked to begin with, but then I thought, most of them don't read the book we've actually agreed to, let alone an extra-curricular one sent by email. It's a storm in a tea cup, I'm sure.'

Rather shiftily, Becca asked how she knew people didn't read the books.

'Most people come for the wine and the chat, don't they?' Kitti picked at the corner of a strip of packing tape. 'Sam admitted to me that she'd only skim read one of the books.'

Fi joined in. 'You can usually tell who hasn't read the book because they don't say much or they'll only talk about what happened in chapter three.'

'I've never noticed that,' Becca replied, fearing her guilt was written large on her face; she moved herself out of the danger zone for fear of being uncovered and returned to the safety of her boxes. 'I'll be watching out next time.'

Phil will be very disappointed if anyone's bluffing it at our next group.'

'Everyone will read this month's book. They'll all want to impress Phil. Actually, I've already finished it,' Kitti said as the packing tape finally surrendered and she peeled back the long strip.

'You're very keen,' Becca called, rummaging in the drawer under the till for the scissors.

Kitti blushed. 'I took it to Portugal, Jachim was happy playing with Mum so I had loads of time. It was like my old life. Do you remember when we used to take half a dozen books away with us? Those were the days.'

Becca was in two minds whether to raise it, but it was out of her mouth before she could weigh up the pros and cons.

'Did you get a chance to read any of the other book club story Fi kindly mailed you?'

'Oh, don't Becca. You know how terrible I feel,' Fi said, embarking on another long apology.

'I read a bit, not as much as I'd have liked or been used to over the last couple of weeks,' Kitti replied, lifting a large weighty bubble-wrapped package out of the box. 'When Becca told me what he'd been writing about... I'll be honest, I was none too pleased. I couldn't imagine how Phil's raw, gritty writing style would adapt to telling my story.'

Kitti stripped away the last of the packaging to reveal a rough stone urn lamp base. 'His usual writing style is very raw and brutal, he doesn't wrap anything up, it's just "here it is". But then I guess his usual subject matter doesn't call for sentimentality – that's what gives it its power.'

'And..? What do you think now you'd read it?'

'I couldn't have been more wrong... I needn't have worried, this is completely different. It's like it's written by another author. I found the bit about Jachim asking where his Daddy was. It made me cry.'

'Oh sweetheart.' Becca left her unpacking and put her arms around Kitti.

'Ignore me, I'm being stupid,' she sniffed. 'It didn't upset me, it was just strange seeing it through someone else's eyes. It was lovely, beautifully observed - almost as if he'd been a fly on the wall.'

'Yeah, for someone who's lobbed their fair share of grenades in their time, he's a sensitive soul, your brother,' Fi added, inspecting closely and then passing Kitti a cleanish bit of loo roll she had tucked up her sleeve.

'Yeah, he's full of surprises, that's for sure,' Becca said, returning to her boxes.

'So you think it'll all be okay?' Fi asked.

'Yeah,' Becca replied, attacking a particularly stubborn strip of packing tape with a pair of scissors. 'As good as the story is, who else is going to be bothered to read it other than us three?'

Twenty-One

It was eight o'clock by the time the last of the guests left. Phil cleared the tables and gathered up the beer bottles, plates and glasses. The party had been a triumph; a fitting end to his sojourn. The mayor rambled on and on and then after some heckling he finally declared Le jardin de l'Amitié open. The children had played in the pool and the band had played under the pergola. The wine and conversation flowed easily.

Admittedly it hadn't quite got off to the start he'd hoped for, but it had all turned out well in the end. His hedge surfing had been a disaster; it looked like Edward Scissorhands had been blindfolded and let loose on it. Phil had nearly finished the job when he got his foot tangled in the cable. He'd slipped, the ladder had wobbled and dropped from under him.

As Phil fell, the belt on his life vest got caught on a branch, leaving him dangling a couple of metres off the ground. He wriggled, trying to unzip it, but the more he wriggled the more the vest rode up until eventually it obscured his face completely, giving the impression of a headless spectre. He had no other choice than to dangle motionless like a fairy on a Christmas tree and call for help.

Rather unfortunately, the mayor's party were the first on the scene. His wife gasped and covered her eyes when she first saw the limp lifeless body still gripping the hedge trimmer. It must have looked like they'd stumbled upon a tragic domestic accident. As it turned out, it was rather tragic for Phil as his hedge high jinks upstaged the party and became the focus of the journalist's news story.

An unflattering photo of him strung up like a marionette ran in the Midi Libre under the headline 'Mayor saves man from hedge trimming terror'. It may not have necessarily been the publicity the mayor was after, but Phil thought he came out of it a lot better than he did; a hapless Englishman and incompetent handyman.

It had now been two weeks since Becca had left and now it was his turn. Phil had organised his departure into a series of piles and they were laid out on the long dining table. He added his passport to the airport pile and looked out on his handiwork in the garden.

Rather than take a taxi he was going to drive to the airport. His car was due for a service. To kill two birds with one stone he had booked to take it in to the Citroën garage by the airport and they would deliver it back to the house once it was done. Phil checked through all his piles as he loaded each of them into their correct place.

Passport, money, medicine and mobile in his laptop bag. Presents, books, and clean clothes in one side of his suitcase and laundry and shoes in the other. There was a pile of stuff to throw out and a pile to leave at the house - all done.

Karel and Didier were out of town. He left a note saying he'd see them in October and a case of Picpoul de Pinet by their door. This trip had gone so fast, it only seemed like a few days ago he had arrived. But that's how holidays were; over before you'd really had a chance to unwind. He locked the gates, slammed the boot and steered the car out of the drive.

It was quiet as he drove out through the village; only the market traders were up and about setting out their wares for the day's trade. At home, he associated markets with knock-off tat; somewhere to get things on the cheap, it was far from a pleasurable shopping experience.

The overpriced farmers' markets that had cropped up at home were the norm here – all French markets were farmers' markets. In France, it was about fresh local produce; none of the nonsensical size and colour ratio supermarket rules applied. No air miles; just real veg grown on the farm down the road.

The stripy canopies fluttered gently in the early-morning breeze; an entire stall was devoted to plump, purple-veined strings of garlic and rolls of yolky yellow fabric with traditional repeat patterns of olive sprigs and lavender were being unloaded from an aged Renault van.

On another stall the gas was lit under a vast shallow pan in which an army-sized portion of Paella would be cooked. Phil could get pretty much everything he needed from the market and even a few things he could well and truly live without.

The music stall yet to be unpacked was always well stocked with CDs of people he'd never heard of. Despite usually giving it a wide berth, it was hard to escape the unmistakable melody of Una Paloma Blanca played on an accordion or Amazing Grace on the bagpipes as it drifted obtrusively across the idyllic market place.

Phil had allowed loads of time; with the windows wound down, he drove leisurely through the narrow back roads, across country to the airport. Once he got near the airport it became more complicated. He'd never managed to come the same route twice.

New roads and road layouts were introduced each year to test his orienteering skills. Today was easier. He dropped the car at the garage and walked the short distance to international departures, bypassing all the various junctions on the confusing perimeter road.

The airport was surprisingly busy. The departure board was showing loads of flight cancellations. The queue for check-in was massive and snaked back and forth across the twenty check-in desks, the atmosphere was tense.

Phil joined the line and waited patiently. He wasn't in a hurry; unlike some of the other agitated passengers, he didn't have any connecting flights to race for – he would stay calm.

Every ten minutes, the queue edged slowly forward. At the front of the queue there was much waving of arms and raised voices. Despite the long queue, there was no apparent sense of urgency from the check-in staff. Of the twenty desks, only two were open. There were more staff, but they were busy chatting and filling out paperwork.

The man in front was getting cross, and was talking loudly and very slowly.'I – n-e-e-d t-o g-e-t b-a-c-k f-o-r a m-e-e-t-i-n-g.' He turned to Phil and shook his head. 'Only trouble with France is, it's full of French.'

'I am very sorry sir.' The man behind the desk said as he called over another member of staff. 'My colleague 'ere will try and 'elp, if you go wiz 'im.'

Phil was finally at the front of the queue and the man behind the desk waved him forward. Phil was embarrassed about the behaviour of his fellow Englishman and went on a charm offensive to try and try and patch up any damage done to Anglo-French relations.

'Bonjour,' Phil said, handing over his passport with his e ticket printout tucked inside. The man at check-in looked carefully at Phil and then the ticket before handing it back.

'Non.'

'I'm sorry?' Phil asked, Cheshire cat grin fading fast.

'Non.'

'What do you mean non?'

'I mean non, you are not flying.'

The man looked through Phil and beckoned the next customer.

'Hang on a minute. What are you saying? I'm booked on the next flight to London.'

'Yes zat is correct, but zat is not today.'

'But look it says here on my ticket. Look that's today's date, isn't it?'

'Yes, but zere are no flights to London today.'

'Well, why have I queued up for an hour then?'

'I don't know.' The man behind the desk then did a masterclass in the French shrug with the complete ensemble of hand gestures and facial expression. 'I suppose you sought zere were flights.'

Phil was trying hard to stay calm. He'd been embarrassed by the attitude of the man in front of him who had been rude and obnoxious. But try as he might to keep a lid on his temper, this man was testing his patience.

'So you're telling me there are no flights today.'

'Zat's right.'

'Why?'

'Ze French air traffic controllers are on strike so zere are no planes 'ere and zose zat are cannot leave.'

'So why is everyone queuing up?'

'To check-in of course.'

'But there are no planes.'

'Zat is correct.'

'So why aren't you telling anyone?'

The man looked most affronted. 'I am. I just told you, didn't I?'

'Only after I'd queued up for an hour. There should be announcements or signs…'

'Zere have been announcements. Listen… zere's one now.'

'It's in French.'

'Yes zat is right, you are in France and we speak French.'

'Shit, shit, shit! Excuse my French.'

Completely exasperated, Phil turned around and called out to the anxious-looking family in the line behind him. 'It's a waste of time. There are no planes, no one's going anywhere today.'

His message buzzed along the queue and as it passed from one person to another, loud groans and sighs and the odd expletive erupted from the weary travellers behind him.

'Will there be any flights tomorrow?' Phil asked as some of the queue gave up and headed for customer services while others moved forward to hear what was happening.

The man behind the desk shrugged nonchalantly.

'If it's not too much trouble, could you find out?'

The man picked up the phone, turned away from the crowd clustered around the check-in desk. Phil couldn't follow the conversation, but it seemed to have a friendly, chatty tone, like he was calling his mother to enquire after her health.

He chatted on for a while, laughing and joking with his phone friend. Beaming from ear to ear, he put the phone down and turned back to the hopeful faces staring at him. His smile evaporated instantly.

'Non.'

'The next day?'

'Maybe, but we do not know for sure.'

Phil eased himself out of the now ramshackle queue and away from the desk. He went and bought a paper and sat in the café while he made up his mind what to do. He drank his coffee and flicked through the Midi Libre. There it was on page two. A big strike over working hours and pensions, with no end in sight.

So what were his options? He could take the train. He then read that the railway workers were expected to come out in support of their disgruntled brothers at the airport. He could go back to the house and wait it out or he could drive. He liked the idea of giving the car a good run. He could do a couple of stopovers and extend his holiday by a few days. After the last couple of hours in the airport he felt like he needed a holiday.

He checked the ferries online, which, not surprisingly, were pretty busy. Caen looked like his best bet. A few hours on the ferry to Portsmouth and then an hour back to Dorset. With his new travel arrangements unfolding in his head, Phil walked over to the garage and explained his change of plan.

In the workshop they were just finishing his car and, with the exception of replacing a wiper blade, it was in good shape. And so it should be given the amount of money he'd lavished on it recently. Phil pulled in at the side of the perimeter road; he unfolded and pored over his Michelin map.

He could opt for what looked like the quickest route and just hammer up the Autoroute, but if this was going to be an extension to his holiday he fancied overnighting somewhere interesting - on the coast perhaps or a vineyard where he could do a bit of sampling. This should be a bit of an adventure. He'd turn this stumbling block into a stepping stone.

With a rough idea of the direction he wanted to go, he followed signs to Bordeaux. He liked the idea of having the car at home and it didn't really matter how long it took; there was nothing he urgently needed to get back for. What difference would a couple of days make?

Twenty-Two

By the time the young waiter came to clear the table where Phil had been sitting, he was zipping merrily up the A61 to Carcassonne. The waiter slid the coins from the silver dish into his apron pocket and stacked the debris on to a tray. As he did so, the discarded Midi Libre vibrated and buzzed in his hand. It made him jump and he dropped the paper on to the table.

Tentatively, holding the paper at arm's length, he unfolded it. There, tucked in the middle, was Phil's mobile. The phone stopped. Relieved there had been no explosion, but not wanting to take any chances, the waiter called over one of the scary gun-toting security guards who took the phone away.

'He's not answering, I've been ringing him all day,' Becca said, putting her mobile back on the table. 'If he's been to the airport he'll already know about the problems and if I know Phil, he'll use this as an excuse to stay for a bit longer and come back when it's all blown over.'

'Top up?' Sam emptied the teapot into Becca's cup without waiting for an answer. Becca's phone rang.

'Ah that'll be him. Hello big boy. Oh hello Fi. No I'm not, why? Okay, okay keep your hair on.'

Becca hunted for the remote, which she eventually located with some trading cards and a Kit-Kat wrapper tucked down the back of the sofa cushions. She switched the TV on. 'Yes I've put it on… it's the golf. Well, I don't know - what channel are you on?' Becca hated playing this kind of telephone charades with Fi, she just wished she'd get to the point.

Sam was sitting across the room, but even at that distance she could hear the unmistakable tone of a Fi rant. Flustered and impatient, Becca tried to follow Fi's instructions as she barked them into the receiver.

'Hold your horses, I'm flipping through them… yes here we go.'

Becca had stopped on an early-evening magazine programme and the husband and wife presenters were talking about some competition they were running.'

'I'm sorry Fi, I'm still not getting it. All right, all right, I am listening.'

On the TV, the couple were talking about shortlisted entries in their new writers' competition.

'Now Fi, if you're thinking about Phil that's very sweet of you, but you know he doesn't want to publish his new story… Now Fi, there's no need for that kind of language.'

Becca held the phone away from her ear, stopped talking and listened as Michael, the tanned, white-toothed, smooth presenter read out the synopsis of the final shortlisted story. For a moment there was silence, and then they were all talking at once.

'Oh my god, I can't believe it, that's Phil's story. How the hell did it get there?' Becca watched with open-mouthed incredulity as Michael continued.

'So that's the final story selected by our panel of experts, and remember you can vote for the story you'd most like to read by visiting our website. We'll be announcing the winner live on Friday's show, so get voting. Don't go away, we'll be back after the break when we'll be discussing fibroids. See you in a couple of minutes.'

Becca dropped the phone and scrambled for her laptop. Fi was left talking to herself until Sam rescued her from her telephonic solitary confinement.

'What's the web address?' Becca called, not taking her eyes off the computer screen. Fi read it out to Sam down the phone, who in turn shouted it out to Becca. They stood and stared at the spinning ball waiting for the page to load. 'Right, here we go. Recipes, bladder problems, weight loss. Where is it?' Becca scrolled down until she found what she was looking for. 'Book club. Do you think that's it?'

The page loaded and there were the titles of the five short-listed stories. Becca scanned the list and then pointed dumbfounded at the screen. Becca's Friends By Aurore St John

'No! She's gone too far this time.' Becca crumpled back against the worktop. 'It's my fault. I should have stood up to her. I've let her get away with things for too long. It's one thing helping herself to the odd thing from my shop, but stealing Phil's book and passing it off as her own is, is...'

'Underhand? Dishonest? Corrupt? Immoral? Downright sneaky?' offered Sam.

'Yes, yes, all of those things,' replied Becca, pacing the length of the kitchen. 'She won't get away with it, not this time. She'll be sorry she ever crossed the threshold of my shop.'

'What are you going to do?' Sam asked.

Becca stopped pacing. 'I'm going round there right now to have it out with her. This conversation is way overdue.' Becca was in battle mode. She grabbed her handbag and headed stridently for the door.

'Do you even know where she lives?' Sam asked, taking the wind out of her sails.

Becca stopped in her tracks. 'Good point, actually no.'

'I know someone who does,' Sam said, picking up the phone from the worktop where she'd left it. 'Are you still there? Good, can you look on your class list and see where Aurore lives.'

While she waited for Fi to find it, Sam got her shoes and coat. 'If you think I'm going to miss this, you're wrong, I'm coming with you.'

Fi was waiting outside when Sam and Becca arrived.

'Is this it?' Becca rang the bell. Behind the stained glass of the front door, she could see movement. 'It's no wonder she's ashamed to show her face.' Becca rang the bell again and this time she heard someone come to the door. Becca raised her hand, poised for finger wagging, but it wasn't the door that opened. And the face peeping through the letterbox was not Aurore's.

Becca, Sam and Fi bent to meet the curious eyes spying on them. They blinked a lot and peculiarly were devoid of eyebrows, which instead had been tattooed on and were a dark shade of green. 'Is Aurore here?' Becca asked.

'No, she not here,' replied green eyebrows.

The flap on the letterbox flapped shut. Becca rang the bell again and slowly the letterbox opened again. Still bent forward like a strange Japanese greeting, the three of them continued their conversation with the woman with green eyebrows.

'Will she be back later?'

'They all in France for the summer. She don't tell me nothing. I just cleaner.'

'I need to speak to her urgently,' Becca called. 'Do you have a number for her?'

The letterbox snapped shut loudly; they heard the vacuum cleaner go on, their little chat was over.

'Is there a mobile number on that class list?' Sam asked. Fi read it aloud and Becca tried the number. After a while, it rang the long strange tone of an international call, but went straight to voicemail.

'Zis is Aurore, sorry I can not take your call...' mimicked Becca. 'You've no idea how sorry you're going to be.'

'Here, have this list.' Fi handed Becca the crumpled piece of paper. 'Save that number on your phone and keep trying it. She's bound to answer at some point.'

'I can't believe that. I was all fired up to cut her down to size. What do we do now?' Becca sat down resignedly next to Sam on the low garden wall.

'Are you okay Sam?'

'I'm just thinking. I'm trying to put myself in the twisted mind of Aurore. I've heard lots of the playground stories about her, but I don't really know her, so it's not easy. Why would she do this? What does she have to gain?'

'Have you read what Phil wrote about her? It was a complete character assassination. Does that help your theory Miss Marple?' laughed Becca.

Thinking out loud, Sam continued. 'Maybe it's some kind of revenge then. If it gets out that Phil actually wrote the story, she can say he put her up to it to try and rescue his flagging career. His credibility will be shot to pieces.'

'Hers will too, won't it?'

'Maybe, but she behaves appallingly all the time. She doesn't seem bothered about her reputation; she's oblivious.'

'And if it doesn't get out?' Becca asked, still not really seeing Aurore's motivation for passing Phil's story off as hers.

'If it doesn't get out and "Becca's Friends" wins she gets the glory, her moment in the limelight and the satisfaction that she's got one over on us again.'

The three of them sat in a row on the wall. Fi was the first to respond to Sam's theory and she spoke slowly, talking off the top of her head.

'If you're right… about the glory hunter bit… that will mean… she'll want to be there… on the show… to pick up her prize.'

The other two turned to face her, each planting a kiss on her cheek.

'Fi, I love you. You're a genius.' Becca cried.

'I am? Yes, yes I am,' mused Fi, unsure of the significance of what she'd said.

Becca joined up Fi's thinking. 'With these kinds of competitions, they don't know until the last minute who the winner is...'

Sam finished Becca's sentence.'...So, all the short-listed winners will be in the studio on standby until the votes are counted and the winner is announced.'

Becca stood up, her fire had returned.

'We need to be there on Friday. Phil needs to be there. Let's go back to mine and make a battle plan.'

Becca tried Phil's mobile, but it was dead. She rang the house in France. On her third attempt, Karel answered. She told her Phil had left. She said they'd assumed he'd managed to get a flight somehow, but when the car wasn't returned Didier called the garage and that's when they discovered he was driving back.

That was good news. At least he was on his way. But would he be back by Friday? Sam had called up a friend of hers who worked for ITV and discovered that "Teatime" was filmed at West Bank Studios in Hammersmith.

Fi called the production company and, using her slightly rusty journalist credentials, had blagged them some press passes. She had warmed to the deception and said they were planning on doing a spread: a story in pictures and a little write-up on the winner. She didn't mention that the publication she wrote for was Pet Lover monthly.

Twenty-Three

With no planes flying anywhere, he'd imagined the roads would be packed; not so, people were obviously taking advantage of the situation and extending their holiday until the dispute was resolved. If it turned out to be like the miners' strike they were in for a very long vacance.

Phil zoomed along through the beautiful Van Gogh landscapes; blighted only by the repetition of electricity pylons that to him looked strangely like a goat's head made out of Meccano, bloody goats, they were haunting him everywhere he went. Pylons aside, this was the way to travel; windows down and volume up.

He'd had an early start and he'd skipped breakfast and lunch. Even with Coldplay blaring out, he could hear the growling plea of his stomach. He'd pull off soon and get something to eat; as he approached the next junction, a large brown sign showed a graphic illustration depicting a church surrounded by rolling countryside with the name Aubeterre-sur-Dronne underneath. The name was familiar and yet he couldn't think why.

The road curled round and up; set high above a bend in the River Dronne, was the amphitheatre-shaped village. It was like a film set; a little less rustic than his village and a lot more chic. Cascading, colourful window boxes adorned the shuttered windows overlooking the main square. There were boutiques, antiques and bric a brac shops, artisan studios and galleries.

The restaurant's clientele were smartly dressed; out to see and be seen. Phil felt too scruffy even for the brasseries. He decided to pick up some food and eat it on one of the benches in the shade of the gnarled lime trees. As he was crossing the old village square, he was reminded of how he knew the name of the village.

Out of the boulangerie stepped Aurore. Phil stopped in his tracks; he was in her direct line of vision. Cars tooted Phil as they swerved to avoid him; he stood immobilised in the road. Suddenly, Aurore darted behind a car and disappeared.

Phil crossed the road towards the bakery. There was no sign of her. He walked along the line of parked cars and there she was, crouched down in the gap between two parking spaces.

'Aurore?' Phil called to the back of the squatting figure. She looked up and smiled. 'It's Phil. Becca's brother.'

'Ah yes, of course. What a lovely surprise!'

'Are you all right down there?'

Slowly Aurore stood up, dusting down her linen skirt. She seemed less proud and self-assured than in their last encounter.

'I dropped some money. I sink it went under ze car…' Aurore said, unconvincingly.

'Allow me, I'll get it out for you.' Phil stepped forward gallantly. Aurore moved sideways, blocking the area where she'd been hiding.

'Don't worry it's only a few cents I am sure. So what brings you 'ere?' she asked, changing the subject.

'Well, I was supposed to fly back…' Phil started to explain.

'Ah yes of course, ze strike…'

'I needed to stop and get something to eat and I discovered I was nearby so I followed your advice and came to see your beautiful village.'

'So… 'ave you eaten?' Aurore asked, regaining her confidence.

'No I was just going to get something.' Phil gestured towards the bakery.

'I live just a short walk away. Why don't you come and 'ave somesing wiz me? I can give you a bit of a tour on ze way.'

This was a different Aurore from the one he'd met in London. Maybe she felt more relaxed on her home turf. She was trying hard and Phil thought it would be rude to refuse her hospitality.

'I'd like that very much,' he said.

'Excellent. Come, follow me, it's zis way.'

Aurore led him through the narrow, cobbled streets that wound up through the village. Around each corner, gaps in the buildings revealed dramatic vistas of the patchwork countryside below. As they walked, Aurore pointed out things of interest.

'Up zere is the church of Saint Jacques. It was rebuilt in ze seventeenz century after the religious wars. It's a magnificent example of Moorish architecture. If you 'ave time you must visit ze underground church of Saint-Jean, it's very impressive. Zey're 'olding a season of night-time concerts, which 'ave 'ad very good reviews.'

Aurore's house was on the upper edge of the village; Phil followed her up the stone steps and through the heavy front door. From the exterior, the house was like all the others in the village. But the interior was quite unexpected.

Aurore folded back the shutters and from the shadows revealed a massive open-plan, loft-style living space. It was very simply decorated which emphasised the spectacular view from the four floor-to-ceiling windows.

She chatted about the history of the house, how long it had been in her family. How her father had inherited it from his parents. How he had been an architect in Paris and had done much of the work himself. She talked of years of family holidays where she was one of the many family labourers roped in to help make her father's plan come to life. For many years, the house had got worse before it had got better.

Aurore emptied the contents of the fridge into bowls and laid them out on the table. Phil helped himself to fresh figs, prosciutto and mozzarella.

'I'd planned to stay somewhere in the Cognac region, a château perhaps; I thought I'd do a bit of tasting, but now I'm thinking I'd like to see some of the things here that you talked about. Is there somewhere you'd recommend that I could stay?'

'Yes, I can sink of somewhere very nearby zat would be perfect.'

'Great, is it far from here?'

'It is 'ere.' Aurore giggled girlishly.

'Oh, I couldn't impose, but it's very kind of you.'

The meal was one thing, but Phil was still wary of Aurore, she had a fearsome reputation.

'It wouldn't be an imposition. Actually, it would 'elp me out.'

This was more like it, more like the Aurore he knew. She didn't do anything for anyone unless there was something in it for her.

'I 'ave to go back to London zis evening for an important meeting tomorrow and you could 'ouse-sit for me. David 'as taken ze children down to my mozer's and won't be back until Saturday. I don't want to 'ave to shut ze 'ole 'ouse up and turn everysing off for ze sake of a couple of days.'

Phil thought it over. This was so peculiar, Aurore was the last person he would have chosen to spend time with, but here she was being kind, considerate and generous. He'd always said it; Becca was a bad judge of character, always writing people off at their first transgression and never giving them a chance to redeem themselves. Perhaps he'd been wrong about Aurore too.

'You should bring Rebecca 'ere, she'd love ze antique shops and ze artist studios. It would be ze perfect place to pick up sings for 'er shop.'

'You're right, she would, I'll tell her to add it on to her next buying trip. Talking of Becca, you don't have her number do you? I've lost my mobile. It's weird, I can still remember our home phone number from when I was six but since the days of having them all programmed into your phone I don't know any off by heart any more.'

Aurore made a show of looking in her phone contacts. She scrolled down through all the missed calls from Becca and deleted them.

'I'm sorry, I sought I did but I don't. Don't worry zough, I'll pop round zere when I get back tomorrow and give her ze number 'ere, so she can call you.'

'If it's not too much trouble, I'd really appreciate that.'

'It's really no bozer.'

And it really would be no bother. She had no intention of going anywhere near Becca. She'd thought for a brief moment during her farcical game of hide-and-seek in the square that Phil had discovered what she was up to and had come for a showdown. She soon realised that he was, as she'd first thought, completely clueless. He was blissfully unaware that she'd read all the vile things he'd written about her. He'd choke on those words, she'd see to that.

The audacity of the man; he'd insulted her and then sat at her table, eaten her food without the remotest hint of remorse. Well if he wasn't sorry now, he soon would be. There were any number of ways she could play this and in all of them it was bad news for Phil Drummond. She could not have planned this better; with him safely detained, there was nothing that could get in her way.

Aurore gave Phil a set of door keys and a guidebook and sent him off to explore the village. While he was gone she worked quickly, shredding her copy of "Becca's Friends" and unplugging the router from her media hub. She needed to ensure that he remained incommunicado for the duration of his stay.

She put a few essentials in her overnight bag, wrote a note telling Phil to help himself to anything he needed, including any bottle of wine from the bottom rung of the wine rack. These were a bit rough, she used them mainly for cooking, but she didn't want to waste any of the decent stuff on him.

Twenty-Four

Becca had called Aurore's phone several more times and had been round to her house. The curtains were drawn, there was no answer or signs of life. She kept checking the voting and "Becca's Friends" was currently in third place. If it stayed there, all might be okay. She voted a couple more times for the number one choice just to be on the safe side.

While she was online, she sent Phil another email explaining what was going on while he was lost in France.

Phil slipped effortlessly back into holiday mode and spent the rest of the day strolling around the ancient churches and art galleries. He decided to move his car and although it was only a short walk to the house he discovered it was a circuitous route by car. One-way streets and pedestrian walkways barred his way at almost every turn, sending him off in the opposite direction to that which he wanted to go.

Aurore had already left when he finally returned to the house. He read her note, but didn't feel like cooking and besides there was a great choice of places to eat in the village. After freshening up, with his laptop tucked under his arm, he returned to the main square on foot. He sat in the brasserie, drank a cold beer and watched the world go by.

While he waited for his third beer, he tapped out a few words about his visit to the underground church and his morbid fascination with the cults thought to have operated there. The baptisms in bulls' blood sounded particular macabre, although after his run-in with Mad Spotty he could see the appeal.

Initially he'd been really stressed out about the loss of his phone but to his surprise he discovered that it was actually quite liberating; these days there were so few occasions when he was completely uncontactable. Like everyone else, he was on call 24/7, constantly at the whim of whoever wanted to barge into his consciousness and demand his attention... often for things he had little or no interest in.

No, he didn't want to:

switch energy supplier,

get a comparison quote for car insurance,

see if he'd been mis-sold an endowment policy,

or transfer a credit card balance.

The assumption that he was completely incapable of deciding for himself whether or not he wanted any of those things without a prompting telephone call drove him mad. If he did, he'd pick up the phone and organise it.

He'd always been a bit crap with his mobile and when he'd been living with Gillian she'd constantly chastise him whenever he left it at home. The way she behaved you'd think he'd gone out and forgotten to take one of his essential organs with him. "What if I needed to get hold of you in an emergency?" she'd say, but her idea of an emergency was running out of risotto rice. In reality he hadn't ever had an emergency call – in his previous line of work it had been more likely that he would be the emergency.

Yes, it had been lovely to get a text in the early hours announcing the arrival of each of his nephews, but for him hearing the good news a few hours or even days later wouldn't have diminished its pleasure in the least.

In his experience there were very few messages that couldn't wait and as he smugly watched his fellow diners held hostage by their shiny black rectangles; constantly checking, swiping and typing, he savoured the peace of isolation.

But as he sat enjoying his beer and his smugness, an irritating niggly thought was barging its way forward from the back of his mind. "Excuse me, annoying thought coming through, excuse me can I just squeeze through... hello... excuse me..." The annoying thought had pushed its way to the front of his conscious thoughts and was goading him.

What was he playing at? He should be checking his mail for confirmation of his ferry booking or at least looking to see what was happening with the strike.

The annoying thought had a point... a quick sneaky peek wouldn't do any harm. If you can't beat them... he thought as he logged on and checked the news headlines. The industrial unrest continued and more and more unions were becoming involved. Something would have to give soon or the whole of France would grind to a halt.

He checked his email and saw that most of his visible inbox was taken up with mail from Becca. He took a long swig of beer and scrolled down through the messages to start from the beginning of the mail thread.

He opened the first.

Lovely Bruv'
Thanks for wonderful time... blah blah blah... left shoes in wardrobe ...blah blah blah... could you bring them back...?

Oops, he'd drop Karel a line and see if she could post them. If the strike carried on at its current pace they could well beat him back. Becca would probably class the loss of her pink suede wedges as an emergency, but it was as he suspected, so far there was nothing that couldn't wait.

Next one from Becca

Hi
You probably already know but there's an air traffic control strike…blah blah blah

Yep I know and there's not much I can do about it, he thought, I'm just going with the flow and I'm following my nose home.

Next

Hi Phil
It's nothing urgent but I just wanted to…

Nothing urgent, then it can wait, Phil scrolled down to the next message.

Next

Hi Phil
Can you call me, when you get a chance…

Yep, I'll call you when I'm home in a couple of days.

Next

Hi Phil
I know I said it was nothing urgent. Well I lied, I didn't want to worry you, and now I guess reading this I am worrying you and I was trying so hard not to – hurry home as soon as you can.

Everyone's fine, nobody's died or anything like that, well they probably have you know what it's like in Mum and Dad's road – more deaths than Midsomer.

Anyway, something's happened that needs sorting out urgently.

Lol (lots of love, there's no laughing out loud here at the moment)

Becca xx

Maybe he was wrong, this sounded like it could be an emergency. He took another long sip of beer and clicked on the next message entitled "Horror Story".

Hi Phil
You're still AWOL so here's the thing, the sort of urgent thing I mentioned. Aurore has upped her game from snaffling small trinkets for free from my shop and wherever else she can and she's entered – my story – well, your story really – Becca's Friends, your story about me – it doesn't really matter who's story it is... except of course it does sort of because Aurore has entered it into a TV competition in her name and while I might be a bit confused about whether the story is yours or mine there's one thing I know with all certainty, it's definitely not Aurore's.

So I need you here, I need you to call me – it's an emergency!!

Lol (as before but more so)

Becca xx

Phil started to type a reply but then with Gillian's words echoing in his head he realised in an emergency only a phone call would do. He hastily bunged some money in the dish with the receipt and ran across the square to a payphone. He perched his laptop on the shelf and scrolled down the email to find Becca's phone number.

270

'Come on, come on, answer… Hello, it's me – I've lost my mobile and I'm on a pay phone so we need to talk fast. I've just read your email. I can't believe it, how has that happened?'

Worried that they might get cut off at any moment, Becca spoke quickly and gave him a potted history of events.

'My first reaction was to get on the phone and tell the production company that Aurore is a plagiarist and a fake. But Sam, ever the voice of reason, said I should speak to you first, before I waded in.'

'Sam's right, this isn't something you can sort out over the phone – I need to do this face to face.'

'Where are you?'

'Well, you're not going to believe this – I'm at Aurore's house.'

'But I went round there this evening. I rang the bell for ages. Why didn't you answer?' Becca asked with concern. 'She's got you tied up hasn't she, is she holding you prisoner?'

'Not exactly, I'm at Aurore's house in France.' There was a long silence.

'Becca, are you still there?'

'I am, but I'm speechless… I can't believe it, we're all busting our butts here trying to sort this mess out and there you are en vacances with the hell bitch herself. You're unbelievable, do you know that? So what did you do, swap addresses and arrange a cosy meet-up over the summer?'

'It wasn't like that… it's a coincidence, sort of… she duped me, I fell for the smiles and charm – I should have known, I should have listened to you…'

'Too right you should, I'm glad to hear you talking sense at last. Is she there, is she still with you?'

'No she's long gone, she said she had an important meeting she needed to get back for…'

'Well, guess what? Her important meeting is actually your important meeting...'

The phone beeped and Phil fed a few more Euros into the slot.

'Listen, we can talk more once I'm back – what we need to do now is make a plan for how we're going to stop Aurore.'

To the right of Phil, a group of young girls were crowding around some youths on motorbikes. They revved their engines loudly and wheelied past, drowning Becca out. Phil fed the last of his coins into the slot.

'Are you still there?' he asked as the phone continued to beep.

'I am, but worst of all you're still there and where you need to be is back here sorting this out.'

'I know, I know. I'd jump in the car right now if I could, but I've had a few drinks so I can't. Don't worry, at the crack of dawn tomorrow I'll zip up to Calais and get on the first ferry. All being well I should be with you by lunchtime.'

'Okay, I suppose that's the best we can do. The programme goes out live tomorrow, and if we're going to head Aurore off, we need you to be at the TV studios by 4.00pm - earlier if we can.'

Phil had run out of coins and the line went dead as Becca was cut off mid sentence. They'd said all they needed to, Becca had made the plan quite plain; what he needed to do was get his brain in gear and his arse back to London tout suite.

He was kicking himself for falling for Aurore's little act. He didn't know what she was up to, but what he did know was, it spelt trouble.

He didn't sleep well; different scenarios kept popping into his head. Just as he'd rationalised one, mentally talked it through and decided how he'd deal with it, another worse thought would rise to the surface.

He saw every hour pass on the clock. He couldn't believe he'd been swanning around, wasting time when he could have been trying to stop whatever it was that was about to happen. At 4am he gave up the pretence of sleep, got in his car and drove to the port.

The plus side of being on the road while most people were snug in their beds was that most people were snug in their beds and not on the road. He tagged along with the nocturnal commuter community of distribution and freight lorries, most heading in the same direction as him.

He made good time and it only got sticky as the rush hour traffic kicked in. He followed signs to the docks through the oppressive, grey, industrial landscape of pylons, gas towers and containers stacked like toy bricks.

The ferry was in and had disembarked. At 9am he drove through the customs checkpoint and joined one of the many long lines of cars and caravans and waited. Half an hour passed; other passengers had left their cars and were walking down towards the front of the line.

Phil got out and followed them to find out what was happening. When he reached the dock a group of passengers had gathered around one of the orange, high-vis-vested ferry staff.

Phil got as close as he could and listened in. It seemed, that like the planes the ferries were not going anywhere either. The man in the high-vis vest pointed out to sea where a line of fishing boats were lining up to form a blockade. As he strained to hear over the wind and the defiant horns of the fishing boats, he heard the word solidarity and he then knew that the strike action had spread further.

High-vis man suggested trying the tunnel or one of the other ports. It was beginning to look like he wouldn't be joining Aurore for her important meeting after all.

Twenty-Five

Sam and Fi sat in Becca's kitchen each on their laptop clicking away at the online vote. Fi had been there since 7am. She felt wholly responsible for Aurore getting her hands on Phil's book and wanted to play her part in resolving matters.

'What time will he be here?' she asked.

'He was trying to get booked on a train. He thought he'd be here around two,' Becca said, not looking up from her laptop.

'Has anyone spoken to Kitti? Does she know what's going on?' Sam asked casually, trying not to make Fi feel any worse than she already did.

'Yeah, I told her, I couldn't not.' Becca looked apologetically at Fi.

'Does she want to kill me?'

'No... well maybe, but she wants to come with us. She's dropping Jachim at her Mum's and then she's coming here.'

'Oh no!' Fi cried.

'What? I had to ask her...' Becca said defensively.

'Not Kitti, look.' Sam pointed at her screen. The others lent over and saw that "Becca's Friends" had opened up a narrow lead. The others were puzzled.

'It's not in the lead on mine,' said a puzzled Becca before refreshing her screen. 'Oh now it is, but not by much. Quick, let's get back to voting.'

By 2pm "Becca's Friends" had slipped back into second place. Becca paced up and down the kitchen.

'Where is he and why hasn't he called?'

Sam finished ironing Phil's shirt and hung it on the doorframe with a suit and tie borrowed from her husband. 'I think we've done all we can with the voting, but we're not out of the woods yet. If we don't leave soon we won't make it to the studios in time. Does Phil know where he's going?' Sam asked, buttoning up the shirt.

'No. I didn't tell him where it was, because I thought we'd all go to the studios together,' Becca said, still pacing. 'You're right, we need to go. We'll have to meet him there.'

Becca typed in the postcode and printed out a map. She left it on the table with a cab card, her mobile and some money.

The traffic into London had been atrocious – it was a Bank Holiday weekend; he'd thought everyone would have been leaving London; he was wrong. The sunshine had brought everyone out. Even the traffic couldn't dampen his spirits, Phil was overjoyed to be back on home ground. Admittedly, he was an hour and a half later than he'd said, but he'd made it.

He rummaged through his bag and found Becca's house keys. She had, as he expected, already left. He couldn't face any more driving so he rang the cab company and put it on hands free while he quickly changed into the clothes Becca had left hanging in the kitchen doorway.

By the time he'd knotted his tie, buttoned his cuffs and shrugged on his jacket, he'd been reassured that he was a valued customer six times and was on the eighth verse of Greensleeves. As he tied his last shoelace, Greensleeves was cut short. Would that make it a green tee shirt, he wondered. Not a very inspiring title for Henry's 16th-century seduction fest.

Following his nonsensical thought process, Phil was oblivious to the voice of the taxi controller on the line.

'Hello… hello. What's the postcode of your destination please?' After a brief conversation with the controller, Phil discovered the wait time for a taxi wouldn't get him to the studios in time; He rang Kitti to break the bad news.

'I've made it. I'm back,' Phil shouted. 'Where are you?' Kitti relayed the conversation to Becca, who was driving.

'He says there's a forty-minute wait for a cab and the traffic's crap.'

'Tell me about it. I'm sitting in it. Tell him he'll have to take James's bike, it'll need some more air in the tyres but it'll be quicker than driving.'

'She says take James's bike…'

Cycling was a great idea and after nine hours behind the wheel it might even stretch out his aching calf muscles. One thing was for sure: it would be quicker than by car and he might even catch them up. The bikes were locked up out at the front of the house and he had no idea where the keys were. He called Kitti but it went straight through to voicemail.

Fortunately, Becca's bike was not locked. Unfortunately, it was still dressed for Mardi Gras. No need to lock it up – who'd be seen dead on it? Phil banished that thought from his head; maybe it was tempting fate. He tried to pull the pink Union Flag off its bendy flagpole, but it was not budging and he ended up tearing the seam of the fabric, leaving a large gaping hole in the double-thickness fabric.

He wondered if he could use it for carrying some of his stuff in but on second thoughts it was probably safer in his pockets. To minimise his embarrassment, he wrapped the flag tightly around the flagpole and tucked the end in to hold it in place.

Clutching the print-out of the map with Kitti's scribbled directions in one hand and the handlebars with the other, he set off down the hill, gathering speed as he went. He'd had to read maps in some very challenging situations and now he could add uncontrollably hurtling downhill with dodgy, squealing brakes to the list.

He was going way too fast. The bike forcibly shook; he now fully understood the term 'bone shaker'. The front forks acted like a lightning conductor except in this case they conducted every bump in the road up through the frame, along the crossbar and up through him. It felt like his teeth were being rattled out of his jaws, but just as it seemed he'd completely lost control, his own airbrakes kicked in.

The flag unfurled, billowing out behind him like a drag parachute on a land speed record; it slowed him to a more manageable speed, allowing him to corner smoothly into the Northcote Road like a Lycra-clad velodrome pro.

The road was packed with frustrated, impatient motorists. The pavements were packed with carefree, latte-swilling locals watching the static traffic being overtaken by an assortment of buggies and prams flanked by their micro-scooter sibling outriders cutting a swathe (and many an ankle too) through the promenading folk of SW11.

Phil swerved right to avoid shoppers as they stepped out into the road from the market stalls. He carefully scooted through the narrow gap between a huge supermarket delivery lorry and the backed-up cars. He was glad to emerge from the warm diesel fug of an increasingly close squash sandwiched between a bus and the low-slung clanking chains of a skip lorry.

Dodging potholes and broken glass (this was no time for a puncture), he turned off as directed by the church and up the hill past the old bingo hall and into the relative quiet calm of the back roads towards Wandsworth Town. As he passed The Union, the bike drew a gale of wolf whistles from a group of lads using the pub's smoking facilities: a sand bucket and a bench on the pavement. Phil turned and whistled back.

He felt a strange kind of connection with everyone he passed, almost as if they were cheering him on in his crusade to put right a wrong. The herringbone brick surface of the road gave a satisfying rattle as he rode over it. Phil didn't feel tired or apprehensive about how things might play out. He was surfing on a frothy white wave of endorphins and adrenalin – he was unstoppable.

Even the traffic lights were with him; he slowed to the pace of the pedestrians and mingled in the middle of the crowd as they crossed the South Circular. Then he nipped off to the right, ahead of the traffic and down the slip road past the DIY store where large lorries were offloading bloom-filled rack after rack of pink, red, and white cyclamen in advance of a busy Bank Holiday gardening weekend.

His stomach rumbled as he caught a tantalising whiff of onions caramelising on a hotplate coming from the burger van where a crevice of builders from the nearby builders' yard were sitting in deckchairs on the pavement enjoying afternoon tea. At the turning circle, he escaped the stand-off between a cement mixer and a dustcart and quickly pedalled away over the little estuary bridge. Here he caught his first glimpse of the Thames at the mouth of the Wandle.

Cycling through the industrial estate, he felt like a human pinball as he dodged mechanics reversing cars out of their workshop on his right and a forklift truck laden with wooden pallets lurching out from behind a parked lorry on the left. With the odd white van thrown in for good measure, it was with some relief that Phil passed through the shiny chrome bollards into the wide, paved walkways of the Riverside Quarter.

Prime waterfront real estate with every balconied apartment craning for a good view of the river. He followed the cycle path and knew for a while at least he wasn't going to be mown down. He glanced down at the map; still a fair way to go and following the bend in the river didn't make it a very direct route.

278

Here before him was the Thames proper. A couple were sitting on the deck of one of the houseboats moored to the Venetian-style stripy poles. Relaxing in the shade of a fluttering parasol, they were drinking wine and playing cards while motor boats large and small chugged idly past. Phil cycled along the embankment through the little park. He scrunched over a few early autumn leaves that were scattered across the path.

There was the unmistakable thwack of leather on willow and Phil watched the frenzied excitement of the young fielder's fumbled attempts to see off the batsman. Phil passed joggers, dog walkers and children playing a paperchase game; drawing a succession of chalk arrows on the pathway before scurrying away.

Phil returned the friendly wave of an elderly gentleman standing barefoot on the grass. It suddenly dawned on him that the man wasn't waving but practising T'ai Chi; embarrassed, Phil pretended to be swatting away a swarm of gnats and cycled on a little quicker than before.

To his right, sitting in a row on the railings of the embankment wall, were about a dozen crows. As he passed, one by one the crows took flight; it was a beautifully choreographed example of nature's ballet, the avian equivalent of a gun salute. As the last took to the air, Phil turned into a shady, cobbled courtyard of a riverside townhouse development. The cobbles clinked together as his tyres ran over them.

Back on the road again, Phil passed under the wrought-iron latticework of a Victorian railway bridge as an Underground train rumbled loudly overhead. Phil followed the blue cycle signs that directed him back to the riverside. The sign pointed to a narrow alley; it bent sharply to the right and then opened on to a busy paved area with bars and restaurants, which the sunshine had turned inside out.

As he crossed the square, he was engulfed by a culinary cloud of aromas, it reminded him of the rare occasions when he'd been on the hunt for a present for Gillian or Becca. He'd step through the doors of one of the large department stores to find himself in a full-on olfactory assault by the cosmetic counters.

This was a bit different; there was no mass histamine release. Here the smells were a wonderful blend of sweet strawberry ice cream, freshly ground coffee and herby garlic flatbreads. With those tempting smells still lingering in his nostrils, Phil pushed on, wishing he could stop for a pint and a bite to eat.

Mole-like, blinking cinema goers spilled out of the side exit on to the square; the crowd breaking around a modest grey stone war memorial acting as a pedestrian roundabout. Phil waited for the crowd to disperse - peeling off from the roundabout heading home on the Tube or by bus or towards the bars and restaurants on Putney High Street.

As the crowd thinned, he saw the tattered cluster of weather-beaten poppy wreaths wired to the war memorial. They sat forlornly under the worn inscription "We will remember them". Phil remembered, he could never forget; his slow salute drew a few strange looks from the straggling cinema goers, but he didn't care.

He scooted across the square and back towards the main road. The cycle lights were green and he flowed around the busy junction by Putney Bridge and then back down to the quiet safety of the embankment.

The river was low and exposed a large strip of shingly beach along each bank of the Thames. Amongst the Frisbee throwers and duck feeders, he spotted a group of four young children on a scavenger hunt. They were picking through the stones searching out gem-like pieces of glass; combing through the mud and slime in search of something precious.

Their perseverance was rewarded by an oval of smooth, frosted turquoise. The tumbling Thames had knocked off all the sharp rough edges, leaving no trace of its previous form. Phil mused that the army had done a pretty similar job on him.

He was distracted by this thought as he steered his front tyre along a wavy line of damp, mashed twigs, leaves, knotted orange nylon rope and the brightly coloured mosaic of tiny plastic fragments washed up on to the road by the last high tide.

There were lots of people milling about outside the boat houses. Phil rang his bike bell and cautiously slalomed into the throng. In the centre of the crowd was an elderly bearded man who could easily have been a relative of Captain Birdseye. With ease, he wheezed his accordion into life and played the opening bars of the sea shanty. As he did, the ambling crowd around him suddenly took their places and, oblivious to a cyclist on the dance floor, began their nautical morris dance.

Phil tried to escape, but his exit was blocked on all sides as the dancers swung their partners out. A little way into the routine, Phil saw his chance. When the dancers formed an arched tunnel with their arms, quickly he made his move and to the cheers of the crowd he cycled through the arch and out the other side, ringing his bell in time to the music.

He'd barely changed gear when he was delayed again by a four-oared boat; it was being carried pallbearer style above the heads of its crew, across the road and down the slipway. While the crew in their wellies and flip flops waded into the Thames, he was on his way again past the tennis courts and playground.

Phil slowed again to let two police horses amble over the small bridge by the weir; the officers tipped their hats as they passed. In the boatyard to his left the wires restlessly tink-tinked against the masts of the sailing dinghies, like the drumming of fingers impatient for the wind to be filling their main sails and send them tacking across the Thames.

If Phil closed his right eye so he couldn't see the towering floodlights of Fulham football ground across the river, it was like being in the country; just trees and open common to his left. Long grass, wild flowers and the dry skeletons of cow parsley edged the bumpy and uneven path. As he veered and wobbled a little too close to the river, he realised that cycling with one eye closed was not such a great idea.

As he approached the sign for the Wetland Centre, three green parrots swooped down just above him and for a few seconds tracked his progress along the path and then, in formation, disappeared up through the canopy of the trees. Phil was zipping along; there was the gratifying scrunch of gravel under the tyres and the snap of twigs as he rode over them.

Suddenly there was a far from satisfying snap, followed by the fingernail-on-blackboard, spine-tingling grinding of metal on metal as the bike slowly ground to a halt. Phil couldn't see what the problem was until he got off the bike. The bracket holding the derailleur had snapped off and the chain and entire rear mechanism had become jammed in the spokes of the back wheel. The wheel was stuck fast; it couldn't move backward or forward.

Phil tried to release it, but it had broken some of the spokes and the wheel was well and truly stuck. All he'd got for his trouble was bike grease on his hands and up the sleeve of his jacket – well, actually not his jacket. So that was that. He wouldn't make it. He'd lost.

He could walk back to Putney, but then what? The traffic was still abominable. He looked at the map. The studios were across the river by Hammersmith Bridge. Phil looked through the trees up river and he couldn't even see the bridge.

He dragged the bike and parked it against the railings surrounding a stone monument. Phil read the inscription. It was a memorial to Steve Fairbairn, champion rower and founder of The Head of the River Race. It proudly marked a mile from the Boat Race start in Putney.

Looking at the map again, Phil's finish line was over a mile further down the river – it may as well be five hundred miles; there was no way he could get to the studios in time. Phil slumped down on a bench. He'd come so close. He'd outwitted the best efforts of the French unions, the air traffic controllers, the fishermen and Aurore, only to be beaten at the last hurdle by Barbie's bloody bike.

Phil kicked the bike out of frustration. The heavy, steel-framed lump barely moved; taking his anger out on an inanimate object hadn't make him feel any better, just the big toe on his right foot a little sore.

Phil was sitting silently with his head in his hands when he heard a faint but commanding voice; the acoustics on the river were strange and he couldn't make out where it was coming from. Was it talking to him? Slowly he looked around; not a soul was in sight. Now I can add schizophrenia to my long list of woes, he thought. 'Sit up straight,' said the disembodied voice.

Phil felt a little self-conscious, but did as the voice asked. He was uncertain of how exactly sitting up straight was going to help, but at this particular point in time he was willing to give anything a go.

'You can do it,' said the voice echoing around him.

'How, exactly?' Phil tentatively whispered in reply.

'Easy,' called the voice.

'Well, it might be easy for you...' Phil said impatiently. 'But I haven't got a clue...'

'Keep going,' called the voice, cutting him off.

'My bike's broken... how do I keep going?' Phil replied.

'Only the spoon, not the loom,' called the voice.'

Now you're making no sense at all...' Phil said loudly, losing patience and standing up suddenly, glancing around trying to find the offerer of useless advice.

A lady walking her dog emerged through the bushes; on seeing Phil talking to himself she eyed him suspiciously and hurriedly edged past him, defensively holding her Westie's dog lead. Phil sat despairingly staring ahead at the river; slowly into his line of vision and heading up river came an octo of rowers.

In a small flat-bottomed motorboat chugging along beside them was their coach - the disembodied voice; shouting instructions and encouragement through his megaphone.

'That's nice – take a stroke,' called the coach as, in perfect unison, the rowers pulled on the oars and the pale yellow boat glided effortlessly forward.

Not really thinking it through, Phil scrambled down the bank, tearing his trousers in the process. Gingerly, he stepped across the pebbly beach to the river's edge. He took his jacket off, waved it above his head and tried to flag them down. Slowly his feet began to sink into the thick, gloopy mud of the riverbed. The boat drew level and the coach turned his attention to Phil and boomed through his megaphone.

'What do you want?'

Phil called out, but the coach couldn't hear him. When he tried to move nearer, his left shoe was sucked under the dark silty mud.

'What is it this time? Lost your dog? Surely not another jogger had a heart attack?'

'No... nothing like that, but I need your help though.' Phil shouted - the crew stared back irritably at this interruption to their precious training time.

'Hold her hard,' the coach called into the megaphone and the eight oarsmen stopped rowing and the boat came to a halt. The motorboat broke away from the rowers and came towards Phil.

'Are you okay?' The coach's amplified voice asked, full of concern.

'I need a lift.' Phil shouted back. 'I have to get to the Westbank Studios...'

The coach shook his head in disbelief.

'I've driven all the way from southern France to be there and now my bike is knackered and I'm going to miss something really important...'

'We're not running a bloody taxi service you know,' shouted the coach irritably. 'You can't just hitch a lift... I only stopped because I thought it might be an emergency...' The coach began to turn the boat back towards the rowers.

'It is an emergency... well kind of,' Phil shouted, seeing his last chance of putting everything right slipping away. 'Please, I'm desperate,' Phil pleaded. 'Someone's trying to steal something that belongs to me and I need to be at the studios to clear my name.'

'Oh all right...' uttered the disgruntled coach with a shrug. It was clearly against his better judgment, but he turned the tiller and Fate swung in Phil's favour. 'Wait a minute, I'll need to bring her round.'

The boat was about a metre from the shore; if it came any nearer it would ground.

'You'll have to wade out, I'm afraid,' the coach shouted, steering the boat slowly towards Phil. The engine popped as it ticked over gently; it was as if a food mixer had been attached to the rear of the boat.

Phil removed his remaining muddy shoe and socks and rolled up his trousers; the water was cold and splashed up his bare legs. As he clambered aboard, the boat tipped, but he managed to keep his balance until the coach pushed the throttle hard. The boat surged forward across the current and out into the river, causing Phil to crash backwards in a heap on to the damp bench seat.

The rowers left in limbo were drifting with the tide. Shouting over the noise of the outboard motor, Phil told the coach what was going on, who in turn relayed the story through the megaphone to the bemused rowers following behind.

Like a stone, the boat bounced as it skimmed across the water. As they rounded the bend in the river the coach pointed to a whitewashed blocky building on the starboard side of the boat. There was a sheer three-metre wall from the river's edge up to the embankment.

The coach looked at Phil over his shoulder and, as if reading his mind, he nodded towards a jetty not far to the right of the studios with steps leading up to the embankment. The coach expertly moored and wound his rope around the cleat and secured the boat while Phil clumsily disembarked. Phil thanked the coach and crew and squelched up the steps and along the embankment. Okay, Aurore, your nemesis has just arrived.

Twenty-Six

When he reached the doors to the studios, not surprisingly, the security guards were not keen to admit him. Dripping wet and smelling like a wet dog, Phil sat on the kerb and rang Kitti, Becca answered. While he was still talking to her on the phone, she appeared at the entrance and smoothed things over with the guys on the door.

'Look at the state of you. What happened?' Becca led the way and Phil filled her in. 'Boy, am I pleased to see you, even if you do smell faintly of sewage. Now listen, no one's going to take you seriously looking or smelling like that, so we need to get you cleaned up.'

Becca pointed him in the direction of the gents' loos while she sprinted off to look for something else for him to put on. Phil rinsed the worst of the mud off his shoe and dried himself off with paper towels. Five minutes later, Becca returned.

'Get this on. I don't know if it's your size but it's the best I could find.'

'You're amazing, where did you get this from?'

'I borrowed it from a dressing room.'

'As in stole?'

'Just get it on.'

Sam had saved them seats on the end of a row near the front, and Phil and Becca slid into them moments before the studio doors were shut. The warm-up guy was finishing off with some applause practice for the audience. A clock on a monitor above them counted down to transmission time. Thirty seconds to go.

The hosts, Michael and Millie, were in place on the sofa and the sound engineer was checking their radio mics, while the make-up lady applied a final dusting of powder. The familiar "Teatime" theme music reverberated around the studio and from the dimly lit gallery the director cued the presenters.

'Is she here?' Phil whispered to Becca.

'We haven't seen her so far. We've left Fi and Kitti on lookout upstairs in the green room. It's where the press will interview the winner later.'

'I don't know why they call it the green room,' Kitti said looking at the beige walls and trying hard to distract Fi from thinking about her bladder.

'It's no good, Kitti,' Fi said, getting up from the sofa. 'I've got to go; all I've done since we arrived is drink tea, which is a shame given there's all this free booze.'

'You can have a glass of wine once this is all over. In fact, I think we might need a few,' Kitti said as she watched the "Teatime" opening sequence on a large plasma screen mounted on the wall to her right. 'What if Aurore comes while you're gone?'

'I'll be as quick as I can.' Fi called over her shoulder as she bounded towards the door.

Fi hurried along the corridor. A ladies' loo with no queue? There was a god, she thought. The loo was empty; she nipped into the first cubicle. Afterwards, while she stood washing her hands and tidying her hair in the mirror, the door to one of the other cubicles behind her opened. Bold as brass, out stepped Aurore.

'So, this is where you're hiding is it?' Fi said, rounding on Aurore.

'Iding? Why would I be 'iding?' Aurore replied casually, pushing past Fi to the basins.

'Don't play the innocent with me.' Fi stabbed an accusing finger in Aurore's direction. 'I know what you're up to, I'm not stupid.'

'Sending zat book to me was spectacularly stupid I would say.' Aurore's lip curled with disdain as she reapplied her lipstick in the mirror.

Her colour rising, Fi lunged towards Aurore. But before Fi could reach her, Aurore sidestepped Fi, sending her crashing into the hand dryer. Aurore made a dash for the door and scuttled through it and down the corridor as fast as she could, which wasn't very fast; her high, spiked heels were no match for her spiked running shoes. Fi meant business: she kicked off her Birkenstocks and sprinted after her; this was one mum's race she intended to win.

'There's no point running, Phil's here, he's already caught up with your twisted little plan,' Fi shouted in hot pursuit as she sprinted past the green room. Pausing briefly, Fi stuck her head around the door and called for back-up. Kitti and Fi were close on her heels and Aurore it seemed had no idea how to find her way back to the main entrance.

Desperate to find an escape route, Aurore tried every door handle along the corridor; they were all locked. She turned left and came to a dead-end, there was nowhere else to go. Aurore was backed into a corner. When they caught up with her, Fi and Kitti had run out of breath and patience.

'Come back with us,' Fi wheezed, holding out her hand in an olive branch-like gesture. 'Come clean about the book and it'll all be forgotten about in a few days.'

As Fi and Kitti slowly approached Aurore, she backed further away, until there was nowhere else to go; cornered at last.

'You can't run from this Aurore. You went a step too far this time and it's finally caught up with you.'

As she spoke, Fi stretched forward. Aurore was within spitting distance, but as she was frequently telling her boys spitting was very bad manners indeed, besides which she didn't want to spit at Aurore, tempting though it was. What she really wanted to do was grab hold of Aurore tightly and take her back to the studio to face the Teatime theme music.

'It's all right for you in your cosy little group.' Aurore spat out the words like a master sommelier faced with a corked Merlot. 'Do you have any idea what it is like as an outsider?'

'Sorry Aurore...' Fi butted in. 'I'm not buying that, there's loads of French families here, the locals jokingly call it the Givenchy Ghetto.'

'Fi's right.' Kitti chipped in. 'There are five families in my road alone - SW11 has become the new Petty France. You're hardly an outsider.'

'It's easier to buy a millefeuille than a pork pie in the shops around us.' Fi was a connoisseur of both.

'Yes there are lots of French - but mainly from the nors or sout. As a Parisienne even amongst my own countrymen I'm an outsider. For me I don't mind, I'm used to it, but I want somesing different for Amity.'

'Amity has friends – she's included. I've seen her in the playground, she looks very happy.' Fi countered. 'The school is very inclusive. They're good at that sort of thing.'

'I make sure she's included.' Aurore spoke softly. She had a vulnerability about her like a wounded animal cornered by its prey. 'I make sure sings are different for her. I don't leave sings to chance. I don't want her going trough what I went trough at school...'

Fi and Kitti were momentarily stumped by Aurore's unexpected little outburst; Aurore was a master of manipulating seemingly underdog situations to her advantage and coming out as top dog. It soon became apparent to Fi and Kitti that the sole purpose of Aurore's little speech was to buy her time while she worked out her next move.

And while she was in full flow, the answer presented itself. She was backed right up against the fire escape door. As she leant back against the bar, to her surprise it clicked open and she fell backwards through the door.

'It's been nice chatting but I have to dash now. I have a prize to pick up – au revoir ladies.' Grabbing the door frame to steady herself, Aurore seized her chance; she stepped back on to the fire escape and skittered along the gantry that ran across the back of the building.

She clattered down the narrow iron steps at the end; her heels battering out a rhythm like the hammers on a piano. Faster and faster she went. Unfortunately, a bit too fast; her body carried on moving at speed, but her spiked heel on her right foot had got wedged in the elaborate punched metalwork of the stairs.

She was anchored to the spot and the force that had been carrying her forward was now working with gravity to bring her crashing down; her ankle twisted as she fell and her foot slipped free of her strappy Louboutin. She tried to right herself but lost her balance; Aurore crashed to the ground tumbling over and over as she fell.

It was the kind of scene you might see a stunt double perform expertly and convincingly and then walk away from without a scratch. Although Fi and Kitti watched the last few seconds unfold in slow motion, they knew that this wasn't a film but a real-life drama and now they had to play their parts. Aurore finally came to rest on the half landing below - how the mighty had fallen.

Fi and Kitti flew down the steps after her. Fi knelt down by Aurore and gently smoothed her hair away from the gash on her forehead. She was conscious and groaning. Her leg was grazed and splayed out at an awkward angle and her cheek was bleeding. In an instant Fi was in full-on Girl Guide mode; she called an ambulance then sent Kitti around to the front of the studios to alert security.

She rummaged in her handbag, remembering Phil telling a story about how a tampon had been used to staunch the bleeding of an injured soldier's wound. Without a second thought she tore the wrapper off the TENA Lady pad and held it over the gash. It was a free sample with Good Housekeeping; she knew it would come in useful even if it wasn't for its designed purpose.

'You've still got it girl...' Fi muttered to herself as she secured the pad to Aurore's forehead with a couple of Compeed blister plasters. She wouldn't win any prizes for style, but her improvised dressings were testament to her hard-earned first aid badge.

'Is my dress torn?' Aurore uttered in a defeated whisper. 'It's Chanel... last season.'

Pride comes before a fall, Fi thought; she sat holding Aurore's hand and comforting her as she listened to the distant siren drawing closer.

The camera panned across the clapping audience and then as cued from the gallery, cut to camera one. Michael smiled his warm friendly 'thank you for letting me into your home' smile and wrapped up the last item before linking into the next.

'Thank you Moira, for that wonderful insight into bat boxes.'

It was slick and smooth - he could do this standing on his head - now there was an idea. In fact after ten years of the same format Michael was always looking for ways of livening things up a bit if only to relieve some of the monotony for himself, if not for the audience.

He'd often go off piste, deviating from the autocue and throwing in a few of his own personal observations – "keeping it real". It drove the gallery mad and despite the gentle knuckle rap in the wrap meeting he couldn't help himself. Besides, the "Michael's funny little asides" were always mentioned in the focus groups as a reason to watch.

It was his and Millie's natural rapport in front of the camera that had made and kept them the king and queen of teatime TV. The clock on the monitor was counting down the last ten seconds of the VT on the writers' competition - three - two - one - he was back on cue.

'So now it comes to the moment of truth. For the last few weeks, our panel of esteemed literary judges have been poring over all your entries. We locked them in a room until they'd sifted through the hundreds of entries and narrowed them down to a shortlist of just five. Then it was over to you. And we've received an amazing number of votes; it's been incredibly close, it really seems to have captured your imagination - and that's what it's all about folks – imagination. Where would we be without it...'

'Stick to the script please, Michael.' We're running over – I'll speak to batgirl later, she needs to sharpen up, three minutes to the ad break.

A consummate pro; Michael continued without any flicker on his face of the other voice calling the shots from the gallery. It was a skill he'd learnt at an early age. His mum and dad had had the habit of running two completely different conversations simultaneously and in parallel; sometimes shouted from different rooms in the house.

Being able to join in and make sensible contributions to both his mum and dad had made him a natural in front of the cameras. He could read the script, take his cues and appear as if all his attention was devoted to his guest on the sofa.

'As you'll remember our "Write Time" competition is aimed at showcasing new writing talent; and while we knew Teatime had some very talented viewers, we were completely bowled over by the quality of the entries making the shortlist no easy task for our panel. And if you need reminding, here's what our would-be authors are all vying for.'

The camera homed in on the trophy and oversized cheque.

'The winner will receive a cheque for five thousand pounds and their story will be published and on the shelves in time for Christmas. It'll be an ideal stocking filler and 10p from each book sold will go to "Tap You Up", our charity bringing clean drinking water to outlying African villages. See our website for more details or if you missed it, you can see the video from Millie's trip to Mali earlier this year. Also on our site there's a synopsis of the shortlisted five stories and full terms and conditions of the competition.'

'Twenty seconds to the break...'

'If you haven't made your mind up yet, don't worry. Get on our website now – that's www dot teatime forward slash write time. There's just five minutes left before the vote closes so get clicking. We'll be back with you after the break to announce the winner - but until then pop the kettle on... it's Teatime... see you in five.'

'Nicely done, Michael,' said the disembodied voice in Michael's ear. 'Could we get Millie touched up and her radio mic checked please, we're picking up a bit of a crackle...'

As the music faded and the applause petered out, Phil watched the scruffy crew members as they invaded the set. It was designed to look like the interior of a modern, open-plan riverside apartment. To the left of the famous red sofas was a kitchen area where Trevor the resident Teatime chef demoed his cook-along 'Turbo Teas' and to the right was a circular dais used for bands and fashion features.

The windows behind the sofas seemed more obviously fake and the view through them, a romanticised painted backdrop of the city skyline, a lot cruder and riddled with geographic inaccuracies. All in all, the set was smaller and scruffier than it appeared on TV; cables taped down with elephant tape snaked across the floor, which was scratched and bumpy, clearly visible under a thin cosmetic lick of paint.

Seeing all the rough edges usually cropped out on his plasma TV made it all seem a bit less magical. A bit like the time where a young Phil had peeked into the back of the Punch and Judy tent and seen the lifeless puppets hanging from hooks.

The make-up lady had leapt into action. Slung low around her waist was the equivalent of a builder's tool belt; in place of chisels and torque wrenches, she was armed with mascara, lip gloss a large selection of brushes and a compact. She wielded her brush with the swift efficiency of an experienced archaeologist tending to a recently discovered treasure.

While she dusted Millie's nose and chin, a thin, wiry man in skinny jeans and an asymmetric haircut teased and smoothed out a few stray hairs on Millie's glossy helmet of hair. Mille smiled and gave her trademark wink by way of a thank you. Like insects scuttling away from the bright light, the crew returned to the shadowy world of behind the camera.

'Okay people, we're back in 5, 4, 3, 2, 1 – cue Millie.'

'Welcome back, if you've just joined us – where've you been? You're missing a real gem of a show today. If you've tuned in to cook along to Trevor's 'Turbo Teas', I'm sorry to disappoint you – he'll be back with us on Monday when he'll be cooking moussaka, you'll find the shopping list on our website. But if you've tuned in to find out who has won our 'Write Time' competition you won't be at all disappointed…'

Phil wiped his sweaty palms on his trousers and yawned – recap after recap, why can't they just get on with it?

'It gives us great pleasure to announce the winner of our new writers' competition. So, without further ado, Millie will you do the honours?'

'Thank you Michael. The winner of this year's "Teatime" audience vote is…'

There was a tacky drum roll while Millie opened the sealed card.'…for best new writer is… "Becca's Friends" by Aurore St John.' The intro music played and the cameras turned toward the archway, through which some very famous guests had entered over the years. The music played on and on, both Millie and Michael craned their necks waiting for the winner to appear through the archway.

Becca, Sam and Phil held their breath, waiting in anticipation for Aurore's smug, beaming face to appear on the screen mounted above them, but the archway remained empty.

'Looks like it's mission accomplished by Fi and Kitti,' Sam called along the row.

Becca nudged Phil. 'You're on.'

'What shall I say?'

'You'll think of something – the truth's not a bad place to start.'

Phil stood up and made his way down the steps towards the set. The boom operator swung the furry mic around towards Phil.

'Aurore will be so disappointed as she really wanted to be here today. She really wanted to be here to pick up this award and take the credit for a book I wrote. A private book, a book I wrote as a tribute to my sister and her friends...'

In the gallery the producer was apoplectic, shouting at the director and production assistant.

'Keep the cameras off him. Go to a break, no - move on to the next item.'

Michael pulled his earpiece out to silence the chaotic rant from the gallery. Oblivious to the fact, the producer continued.

'Ofcom will have a field day with this one, if we get fined again for another dodgy competition we'll be taken off air – end of. Make it clear we didn't know anything about it...'

They cut to an ad break and everyone with possible exception of the producer relaxed.

'Who the hell are you?' asked a stocky guy with a clipboard barring Phil's way. Another girl wearing large headphones was using a walkie-talkie to summon security. A short while later, the undynamic duo Becca had charmed at the front entrance crashed through the double swing doors at the back of the studio.

'I said we shouldn't 'ave let 'im in – I could tell 'e was gunna be trouble,' shouted one of the henchmen double act to the other.

So that was that. He'd come all this way for nothing; he'd made a prize fool of himself on live TV without a chance to explain he wasn't a fraud. At the moment it looked as if he was trying to pass himself off as a new writer using Aurore as a pseudonym. Poison pen pal more like. Far from bringing Aurore to book, he'd booked himself a steerage ticket to Loser Street.

Just as Phil was being bundled out of the studios, Michael called out into the semi-gloom beyond the cameras.

'Hang on a minute… don't I know you?'

The guards stopped briefly and Phil called out over his shoulder.

'I'm Phil Drummond, I think we met once at a charity lunch…'

'Put him down boys.' Michael pushed his way through the production team ring of steel and went over to where Phil was dusting himself down and rearranging his collar and tie.

'I'm so sorry about that, you'll be glad to hear we didn't treat J K Rowling like that when she joined us last month…'

Phil smiled and extended his hand, showing there were no hard feelings.

'Listen, Phil. I've no idea what's going on here, but here's the thing – we've got fifteen minutes of show to fill and no winner – I'll need to check it out but how would you feel about being our Philler?'

At last things were starting to go his way.

'So what do you think, do you fancy a cosy little chat with four million viewers?'

'I had no idea how it would pan out today, but I guess my one hope was that I'd get a chance to explain how my book ended up winning and to put the record straight.'

'Good man.'

After a swift conflab in the gallery, it was agreed that for damage limitation purposes Michael should go ahead and interview Phil.

'Welcome back. And for those of you who have just joined us, we anticipated that there'd be great deal of excitement surrounding our new writer competition. What we couldn't have imagined was that well-known action hero writer, Phil Drummond would be here picking up the award.'

Michael welcomed Phil on to the set, handed him the etched-glass book and offered him a seat on the opposite sofa.

'I'm quite surprised to be here myself. But I'm not here to pick up any prizes.' Phil placed the trophy on the table between them. 'This award isn't Aurore's and it isn't mine either. It belongs to the genuine new talent that entered your competition. I'm truly sorry to have robbed them of their moment of glory, but I know you'll make sure that the prize money and publishing deal is awarded to the rightful winner.'

Phil had done a few radio interviews in his time. It was part of the dreaded book launch publicity machine and they weren't his favourite. The minute the light came on showing they were on air his heart quickened, his body shook and he stumbled over his words. Gunfire was no problem but the quick fire of an interviewer's questions made Phil go to pieces. No matter how well rehearsed he was, he couldn't remember what he'd planned to say.

He thought TV would be the same and that he'd feel self-conscious in front of the cameras. But he'd been through so much over the last few months; it was like water off a duck's back. Besides, this wasn't like an interview; it was more like a chat with an old mate. More like therapy, more like a session with Mark.

'So Phil, what brings you here? And how did you, an established writer and your book "Becca's Friends" end up winning our new writer competition?'

'Well Michael, they say the truth is stranger than fiction and after what's happened to me over the last six months I'd have to agree.'

Phil started with Lysistra and losing his publishing deal, through to Rebecca's rehab and how that sparked the idea for the book. The goats and Mad Spotty raised a few laughs and Phil began to enjoy himself playing to the audience.

'I see. But what I don't understand is, what was Aurore doing with your book?'

'I gave the book to my sister as a thank you, I'm a high-maintenance big brother – war wounds, failing career, whatever the trauma she's always there picking up the pieces.'

'Is she here with you?'

'Of course, I don't know where I'd be without her - actually yes I do, I'd be stranded in France.'

'Becca?' Michael called out. 'Can you stand up for us darling?'

The camera and spotlight scanned the rows of the audience before resting on a flushed and flustered-looking Becca who quickly pulled Sam to her feet for moral support.

'Oh and that's Sam, she's also in the story...'

'Ladies and gentlemen I give you Phil Drummond's literary muses.'

The audience whooped and cheered. This was turning into Surprise Surprise; bring on Cilla, he thought.

'Going back to your question about what Aurore was doing with the story... it's simple. The story is a work of fiction but it's about Becca and her friends. So, understandably, Becca wanted to share the story with her close friends. Aurore is one of my sister's closest and dearest friends; they share everything, they're like sisters...'

The microphones didn't pick it up but from the darkness Phil heard Becca's distinctive gasp from the audience.

'No offence Phil and I love your books by the way, but you're hardly new talent. Why would Aurore enter your story into our competition?'

Phil had been racking his brains all the way back from France about how he'd answer that question. He felt no sense of loyalty to Aurore but equally if he made too big a deal of it, it might all blow up into a huge nightmare. What he wanted more than anything was for it all to go away, so he could go back to concentrating on his writing.

As his old granddad used to say "if you're going to start throwing mud around, sooner or later some of it will stick to you".

'I'm not entirely sure, you'd have to ask her, but I think Aurore's intentions were good. The thing I love about Aurore and it's one of her most endearing characteristics, is that she has a tremendous sense of fair play. She knew what had happened to me and she felt I'd been mistreated. I think she misguidedly believed that by entering my book, it would draw attention to me and help relaunch my career.'

Phil caught sight of Becca in the audience, shaking her head in disbelief.

'You say misguidedly,' Michael smiled down the barrel of the camera 'but I have a sneaky suspicion she might be right. I can see this whole episode reawakening a huge interest in you as a writer.'

'Who knows? I've certainly enjoyed writing about other stuff. It's taught me so much about myself...'

'Have you been on a journey Phil?'

'I most certainly have and now I'm pausing to enjoy the view.'

'What have you leant?'

'Well for starters, I understand women more; I'd have made a much better boyfriend to my girlfriends, if I'd known then what I know now.' The mainly female audience clapped in admiration.

Before the interview drew to a close, they talked about France, the bull run and Phil's future plans.

'When I discovered that I could write about things other than war it was a moment of fantastic enlightenment – "Becca's Friends" isn't for publication but watch this space I'm going to put this whole experience to good use and I'm already planning out my next book.'

'Is there a handsome and charismatic chat show host in it?'

'You betcha.'

'Phil Drummond everyone…' Michael held out his hands and the audience replied with warm applause, 'thanks for joining us, now over to Millie in the kitchen.'

Phil unclipped his mic and quietly thanked Michael.

'Nice suit, by the way, Millie's bought me one just like it.'

Phil, Becca and Sam slipped out of the studio and back to the green room. On the scent of a story they were followed by a couple of journalists and photographers.

'You didn't tell me you'd nicked the suit from Michael's dressing room.'

'Would it have made any difference?' Becca laughed, but he could tell he was in her bad books again. Still that was nothing new, he felt sure his entries in her bad books ran to several volumes and would give the Encyclopedia Britannica a run for its money.

'I'll pop it back in a minute and he'll be none the wiser. Anyway, if we're dishing out accusations, I can't believe that after everything that woman's done, you let her off the hook.'

'I thought about hanging Aurore out to dry, but then I thought what would be the point in that? I just want to draw a line under this and move on.'

When they arrived at the green room, Kitti and Fi were already taking full advantage of the hospitality. Phil retold his story of the last few months to the journalists and then Becca, Sam, Fi, Kitti and Phil posed for a few photos, while questions were fired at the speed of the camera shutter. He'd kept going and going, but now Phil needed to sleep.

'I'm really sorry guys, I've got to go now. I'm absolutely knackered. I've been up since four this morning and I've been running on adrenalin and coffee. Now I need to go and recharge. Call me tomorrow and I promise, I'll answer any questions you like.'

'Excuse me, could I have a word?'

'I'm really sorry, but like I said to the other reporters…'

'I'm not a journalist…' The man handed Phil his card. Seeing no sign of recognition the man went on to explain. 'I was here to present the cheque and sign the deal with the winner.'

The colour drained from Phil's face, he'd well and truly cocked up this guy's plans. No new author. No publicity shots of him presenting the cheque. No news story.

'Oh - I'm sorry. I'm probably not top of your list of favourite people. I've messed everything up…'

'Please, don't apologise. In a strange kind of way you've done us a big favour, the competition will get more coverage now than we could have dreamt of. But that's really not important, what I wanted to say is, we would be very interested in publishing your book.'

'It's good of you to be so understanding about this whole mess, but I'm sorry, as I said earlier "Becca's Friends" isn't for publication. It's caused quite enough trouble as an unpublished missive; I'd hate to think what damage it could do out in the big bad world.'

'I liked "Becca's Friends" enormously, but actually, I was thinking of the story you just told the journalists. The story behind the story so to speak – the hero to zero to hero - it's a great story.'

'Do you want a beer Phil?' Fi called from the bar. 'I'll get it as a take out...'

'Anyway, I know you need to get off, so I won't delay you any further. Have a think about what I said and I'll give you a call in a couple of days.'

Phil tucked the card in his wallet. Maybe Michael was right; things were looking up. Stranger still, it was all thanks to Aurore.

Twenty-Seven

The girls were all hyped up and buzzing. Each telling their part of the story and reliving the excitement of the afternoon.

'Michael's a lot taller in real life.' Fi swooned.

'I got his autograph for my Mum.' Sam held up a branded Post-it note with an illegible scrawl on it.

As Becca pulled out into the traffic, Kitti's phone rang.

'Hi Mum.'

The look on Kitti's face silenced the buoyant chatter.

'Hospital? Why what's happened? Is he okay? Where are they taking him? I'm on my way. I'll be there as soon as I can.'

Then they were all talking at once again.

'What's going on? Is everything okay?'

'Jachim's had an accident. He slipped away from my Mum and ran ahead chasing a pigeon. The pigeon flew across the road and Jachim followed it. He's been knocked down by a car. My Mum's with him in the ambulance. They're on their way to Chelsea and Westminster.'

Brakes screeched and horns blasted as Becca U-turned, swinging her car round in a loop. Fortunately, the traffic had cleared a bit while they'd been at the studios.

'I can get a cab, just drop me here.' Maybe Kitti feared Becca's driving would put her in casualty too.

'Nonsense… no way, we're coming with you,' Becca called, pushing out into three lanes of traffic, narrowly missing an oncoming van on the Hammersmith roundabout.

Phil was not a great passenger and found Becca's driving scary at the best of times, but now she was on a mission; skipping amber lights and undertaking in the bus lane. After a couple of other sticky patches they soon found themselves on the Fulham Road. Becca pulled up at the hospital drop-off and let Kitti out before challenging her car's suspension, trying vertical take-off over the speed bumps leading to the underground car park.

They waited what seemed like an age for the lift to take them up to the main reception. Following the instructions from the man on the front desk, they ran out of the hospital and around the corner to A&E. Puffing and panting, they managed to explain who they were there to see and they then followed the red paw prints to paediatric A&E. There was no sign of Kitti so they sat and watched Dora the Explorer while they waited.

'Are you all together?' a smiley young woman in blue scrubs asked.

Becca stood up. 'Yes, we're here with our friend Kitti. Her son Jachim, Jachim Chaudhry, is he here?'

'Let me just go and check for you.' In less than two minutes she was back. 'Yes he's here. I spoke to his Mum and let her know you're anxious for some news. She'll pop through in a minute. Shall I turn that off?' She saw the look of disappointment on Phil's face. 'Oh – okay, I'll leave it on. It's a good one.'

Two episodes of Dora later, Kitti appeared. She'd been crying and looked drawn and fragile. 'He's conscious, but he's lost a lot of blood.'

'So they'll give him some, right?' Becca asked.

'It's not that straightforward. Nothing in my life ever is. He's got Bombay blood…'

Fi was struggling to make the connection. 'Was he hit by a rickshaw?'

'No, it's got nothing to do with the accident. He's always had it, it's genetic. I can't really remember, they did explain it when he was born. It's very rare, something to do with antigens, I'm Hh and his Dad must have been too.'

'Sorry if I'm asking stupid questions,' Fi paused while she gathered her thoughts. 'Can't they just give him some of the Bombay mix?'

'They could if they had some – it's like hen's teeth. They've taken some of mine but what if he needs more?'

'Is mine any good?' Fi asked.

'That's so sweet of you but they said it has to be from a relative, the Mum or Dad. If they give him anything else it can trigger a severe reaction.'

'How severe?' Becca asked.

'I was bit too scared to ask, but it sounded pretty serious.'

They were swapping notes on their different blood types, when Phil piped up.

'I'm AB Hh.' They all turned open-mouthed in astonishment and looked at him. 'What?' Phil asked defensively not entirely understanding the implications of his revelation. 'I didn't know for ages. In previous tests, I'd always shown up as O, I only discovered it when I was being tested for something else. A pedantic lab technician picked it up – I'm one in a million apparently.'

'Well I could have told you that,' Becca smiled, taking his hand.

'It was a major nightmare for the field hospital, as they always had to bank some of my blood to keep in stock. Fortunately I never needed it.'

Becca suddenly clicked. The photo of Phil as a young boy in her treasures box and Jachim. That was the likeness she recognised. Becca, Sam and Fi made themselves scarce and the smiley registrar held the double doors open for Kitti and Phil.

Becca carried the tray across the atrium café and put it down in front of Sam and Fi.

'I don't get it. Was it him that, you know - in the park while Kitti was out of it?'

'Fi. How could you think that?' Sam interjected.

'Sorry Becca, I know he's your brother and all that, but that's when Kitti said it happened.'

'And I'm not disputing what Kitti said,' Becca bristled slightly, 'I believe her, but just suppose…'

'…she was already pregnant.' Sam finished her sentence.

'Oh right, I see. I didn't know they were – you know…'

'Neither did I Fi, I'm only his sister - he doesn't tell me anything.'

They sat quietly wrapped in their own thoughts while Fi wrestled to unwrap the chocolate muffin; eventually opting to burst the pack. She cut the slightly squashed and lopsided cake in half. Who was she trying to kid? She didn't plan to share it.

Sam popped off the plastic lids on the corrugated paper cups containing the unpromising-looking tea. She peeled back the lids on the small plastic pots holding the equally plastic-looking UHT. She poured and stirred until the tea looked just about drinkable; five pots for each cup.

'Well Penny Truman got it right, didn't she?' Sam mused as she stirred the last cup.

'Yeah, except it wasn't worries over boy with bad blood but bad blood worries over for boy. And I really hope they are over. I was worried I might lose my godson today, but instead I've found a nephew and I don't want to lose him either.'

'Come on, drink up. Let's go ask if we can see him.'

Becca slid their snack debris off the tray into the bin before they hurried back to A&E.

The smiley registrar was looking down the throat of a young boy when they returned to the reception. 'Hi guys, they've just taken Jachim up to the ward. Take the lift at the end of the corridor up to the third floor.'

The nurse directed them to a room off the main ward. Jachim was sleeping. He had a canula in one hand and a drip in the other, which Kitti was clutching in hers. Above his oxygen mask, his forehead was dressed and taped.

'Can we come in?' Becca whispered, peeping round the door.'Of course. Grab a chair.' Kitti pointed to a stack of plastic NHS utility chairs in the corner of the room. Phil applied a little of his natural brute force to separate them and then placed them at the foot of the bed for Sam, Fi and Becca.

'Thanks Phil, but if it's all the same I'd rather stand,' Becca smiled weakly.

'Stupid question I know, but how is he?' Sam asked, brushing Jachim's hair back out of his eyes.

'He's got a nasty cut on his leg, but miraculously no broken bones. They're worried about head injuries. He landed with quite a smack, according to my Mum. He might need a CAT scan but it's a case of watching and waiting for the next forty-eight hours.'

'Can we do anything useful or get you anything?' Becca asked.

'Would you mind taking my Mum home? Auntie Muriel's coming over to keep her company. She's in a terrible state. I've told her I don't blame her. It's really hard to hold on to him sometimes, he just runs off. He's got no sense of danger.'

'Like his Dad,' Becca replied. For a second the lines of worry melted and Kitti's natural sparkle returned; despite the awful circumstances she looked up and smiled at Phil. He rubbed her cheek with the back of his hand; the moment passed and they both returned their attention to Jachim.

Becca shepherded Kitti's red-eyed Mum back to her car and after dropping Sam and Fi off she sat in Kitti's lounge with her Mum and waited for Muriel to arrive.

'It's been quite an eventful day, all in all.'

'Yes,' Becca answered. 'It never rains, but it pours.'

'It's very kind of you to stay, you don't have to you know, I'll be fine.'

'You've always treated me like one of your family, and now I discover I am. Family looks after itself. I'll stay till Muriel gets here then I'm going to bed so I can go back to the hospital early tomorrow. I'll take you if you like. I'll give Kitti a call in the morning and see if she needs any clean clothes or anything.'

'Thanks love, I think Muriel and I might go up on the bus a bit later. You know, give Phil and Kitti some time on their own.'

'Okay, well the offer's there. Call me if you change your mind.'

'Phil's a lovely man, I've always had a soft spot for him. Kitti's Dad would have liked him too. What size shoe does he take?'

'Eight and a half I think.'

'Does he play golf?'

Saved by the bell. Auntie Muriel arrived with a large overnight bag and a bottle wrapped in pink tissue.

'I got Vince to stop at the off licence. I got you a bottle of Bailey's for the shock.'

'I thought you were supposed to have brandy for shock.'

'Well I'm a St Bernard with a very sophisticated taste,' Muriel laughed. At this point, Becca left them to it.

The front door closed behind her and Becca reflected on a most extraordinary day as she drove the short distance home.

Kitti and Phil sat holding hands perched on the edge of the fold-up bed that an orderly had set up next to Jachim's.

'Well it's good to have...' Kitti said thinking out loud, '...but I don't imagine I'm going to sleep tonight...'

There was a long pause before Phil finally spoke.

'So what does this mean... for us?'

'Well I guess we could take it in turns, do shifts to keep an eye on him...'

'I don't mean about getting some sleep, I'm talking about you know – us. You and me... do we have a future?'

Kitti ran her fingers through her hair. 'I don't know Phil, this is all happening too fast...'

'Becca told me about Marcus. Does he know what's happened? Have you told him?'

'Yes, I sent him a text earlier.'

'So he's on his way is he?'

'Yeah he was on his way to the airport.'

'Well I'll stay until he gets here... then I'll make myself scarce... I don't want to be in the way...'

'What are you talking about? He's not coming here... he's on his way to Chicago for a job.'

Phil was more confused than ever. There was another long, awkward silence before Phil filled it.

'Hear me out, okay?' I'm not very good at this stuff.'

Kitti nodded but stared ahead at their silent, sleeping son; a small mound in a large bed, his reassuring and familiar much-loved furry friends replaced instead by beeping monitors, wires and tubes.

'I'm stupid, don't say "most men are" but I'd just realised that you were the one... you know the one for me. You make me laugh, you never judge, you're a great listener and you're fun. I'm a bit backward in coming forward and I know I'm too late and everything, but I just wanted to tell you... what I mean is, it's just my luck that some other bloke had the same idea.'

He could tell from her face that she didn't follow.

'Are you talking about Marcus?'

'Yes, of course I'm talking about Marcus. How many other old boyfriends are going to come out of the woodwork?'

Kitti laughed softly and shook her head.

'This isn't a joke or it's not to me at least.' Phil turned to Kitti, cupping her face in his hands. 'I love you.'

'And I love you too, but…'

'Yes I know, I'm too late, there's someone else – blah blah blah.'

Kitti took her eyes off Jachim for a minute and turned her full attention to Phil.

'I don't know what Becca's been filling your head with. I think she's been reading a bit too much between the lines and jumping to conclusions.'

'That's her speciality.'

'Well, she's half right, I have been seeing someone. It's early days, I've known him for years and yet only recently have I got to know him properly. If I'm honest I think I've always loved him, now I know I do and he says he loves me, so…' Kitti tailed off.

'Well he's a very lucky man…'

Kitti's laugh filled the silence. 'It's you, you idiot. I'm talking about you.' She turned and kissed him on the forehead. 'There isn't anyone else.'

Phil didn't want to be the first to break away from their hug and besides he was enjoying inhaling the vanilla scent of Kitti's hair.

'I just assumed what with the holiday…'

'It was only a holiday, Marcus wasn't even there. Just because I stayed in his villa, it doesn't mean I want to spend the rest of my life with him.'

'Doesn't it?'

'No it doesn't.'

'That's a shame'

'What do you mean?'

311

'Well, I was rather hoping that's exactly what it meant because I was going to ask you to come and stay at my place in France.'

Phil turned and kissed Kitti lightly on the cheek.

'There's always an exception to every rule.' She smiled, holding his gaze. 'But before we make too many plans, let's get our little boy out of here first.'

'You're right, one step at a time.'

Phil arranged the steamrollered and lifeless NHS pillows against the wall and they snuggled under the blanket on the squeaky camp bed. He and Kitti chatted as the hour hand turned on the clock above their heads; their conversation punctuated only by the night staff popping in to check up on Jachim.

'That night you talked about while we were at Radleigh Hall... '

'When my drink got spiked...'

'Yeah.'

'What about it?'

'I'm just a bit confused...'

'You're confused. How do you think I feel?'

'Well, this is good news... isn't it? If I'm Jachim's dad it means...' Phil tailed off not knowing how to finish the sentence.

'Yeah, it's good news. I guess I'll never really know what happened that night. I'd buried all those feelings – I'd faced the things I could and hidden the rest away.' Kitti nestled back into Phil's shoulder. 'It was only when Jachim started asking about his dad that I realised it wasn't just about me; I couldn't hide those thoughts away any more. I thought what happened that night would haunt us for ever.'

Phil kissed the top of Kitti's head. 'Well, the next time he asks, you can answer without fear or worry.'

'I'm not waiting for the next time. When we're home, when this is all over we'll tell him – not everything...'

'But enough for him to know he's got a mum and dad who love him.' Phil's arm had gone to sleep with Kitti resting against it, but he didn't want to move for fear of breaking the spell. The room was quiet apart from the occasional beep from the monitor.

'Promise me one thing.' Kitti said suddenly in a very serious tone.

'What?'

'You have to promise.'

'Tell me what it is and I will.'

'Promise me you won't go filling his head with brave soldiering stories.'

'I promise, but I can't promise that he won't want to read my books.'

'Yes you can, no other boys do,' Kitti teased.

'Ouch! That was a bit below the belt.' Phil did his best at a mock wounded expression.

'Okay then, we'll buy him a PlayStation. That should sort it.'

'I didn't think mums were supposed to approve of those sorts of things.'

'I don't, not really. I'll have him playing Animal Crossing until he's nineteen.'

'Do you think my mum and dad wanted me to go into the army? You can't tell your kids what to do, not when they're older at least.'

'Yeah I suppose you're right.'

'If you try and stop them from doing something, you end up making it all the more attractive. Teenagers love that kind of thing. You'll remember torturing your dad, doing all the things he expressly told you not to do.'

'Oh yeah, don't remind me.'

'I think the most important thing is not to glamourise war – I always tried to tell it as it was in my books. I don't want to hide that part of my life away, but I want him to know, he doesn't need to follow my path to make me proud of him.'

'And that's why you'll make a great dad.'

'It's strange isn't it?' He shifted slightly, the bed creaking under his weight. 'The thing that scared me the most... having kids, the whole family thing, is what's brought us together.'

'It's not strange – it's predestined.'

The following morning, while Becca was sitting at the traffic lights, she saw a lone, incongruous figure on the common, trundling along on a mobility scooter. Her broken leg strapped up, resting on the footplate and her Hermès handbag tucked securely in the basket on the front. Becca waved but Aurore didn't, or chose not to see her.

Twenty-Eight

13 June 2011

Phil sat on the terrace in the shade of the pergola as Jachim splashed about in the shallow end of the pool. Kitti placed a coffee on the table next to him.

'I love it here.'

'I love, that you love it here.' She put her arms around his neck and looked at the cursor blinking impatiently on the blank page.

'Sorry, am I distracting you?'

'It's the distraction I've been waiting a lifetime for.'

'It's weird isn't it, how sometimes what you're looking for is right under your nose and you can't see it for looking.' Kitti shaded her eyes with her hand as she watched their son run and jump into the deep end, creating dark Pollock-esque splashes on the paving stones before the heat of the day returned them to a blank canvas.

'That may have something to do with the size of my nose.' Phil self-consciously gave it a rub.

'You could be right.' She said. 'I have a feeling Jachim might have inherited the fine, Drummond family nose.'

'Dad. Dad. Look, look at me.'

'I don't think I'll ever tire of hearing that.' Phil said taking a sip of coffee.

'That's good, because very soon you'll be hearing it in stereo.' Kitti said rubbing her swollen-belly.

'Bring – it - on.'

'I always said you'd make a great dad.' Kitti ruffled his hair.

'You always said I made a great soldier.'

'Great soldier, great writer, great brother, great dad…'

'Great husband?' He asked with a wry smile.

'Is that a proposal?'

'It might be…'

'It's taken us thirteen years to get to this point, I don't think we should rush it. Do you?' Kitti laughed and returned to the kitchen.

Phil typed

Soldiers And Sisterhood (SAS)

By Phil Drummond.

Acknowledgements

A few thank yous:

To my family for their unstinting patience throughout my time writing SAS. There were often a hundred and one other jobs they'd have liked me to be doing instead, including tightening guy ropes and banging in more tent pegs during 55 mph storm force winds in Cornwall.

Apologies to my friends and family for my magpie-like tendencies with anecdotes.

Mum and Dad, you're an inspiration in so many ways. Thank you for all those happy holidays in the Languedoc. Dad you'll always be the Midi Libre inquisitor and hedge-surfing pioneer.

To our lovely French neighbours who are nothing like Aurore.

To the real book group who inspired my descriptions - I hope I've captured your highbrow literary gatherings.

To Jo Lamiri for dotting all my i's and crossing all my t's.

To Elspeth Sinclair for her enthusiasm, sound advice and encouragement.

To Sisterhood – I know you're out there.